"A wildly original and magical twist on the Robin Hood narrative, Kendra Merritt's *By Wingéd Chair* is packed to the spokes with complex characters, wry humor, and flawless world building."

-Darby Karchut, best-selling author of DEL TORO MOON and FINN FINNEGAN

"With a wonderfully crafted blend of swords and sorcery and characters based on Robin Hood, Merritt tops this story off with the lead character readers need nowadays; a strong, independent, powerful female mage who also happens to be in a wheelchair. Readers will be constantly turning pages to see what happens next to this fun group of characters through the twists and turns they won't see coming."

-The Booklife Prize

"Kendra Merritt's prose is fresh, with one-line descriptions that crack like a whip, and she doesn't miss an opportunity to surprise the reader. From the first line to the last, I was enchanted with *By Winged Chair*."

-Todd Fahnestock, best-selling author of FAIRMIST and THE WISHING WORLD

A Matter of Blood

A Mark of the Least Novel

KENDRA MERRITT

BLUE FYRE PRESS

This one's for Arielle, who manages to be both sister and best friend.

I'm sure she's forgiven me for all the scars I gave her when we were kids. Thank you for the unconditional love that inspired both Eira and Karina.

PART ONE

CHAPTER ONE

Nothing terrified the people of Ballaslav more than the sight of a crimson cloak. The day's brightness faded and colors muted until the only thing visible was the splash of red moving down the sidewalk. Crowds parted around the woman in red, some of the shoppers leaping into the slush to avoid her. Even the mud seemed to slide back as the edge of her cloak swept over the ruts in the street.

I stared as the woman moved away from the caravansary in a world of isolation, her only human contact the widened eyes and curled lips of those who judged her.

One day, that would be me. I couldn't keep my secrets forever, and the red cloak waited for me at the end of my uncertain freedom. *O'in*, I prayed. *Let Mabushka be long past caring by then. Let Eira's sharp tongue be dulled by the time she finds out.* I'd keep the truth from my grandmother and sister as long as I could, but that meant I couldn't get caught here in a city, miles from home.

I pulled my plain brown cloak closer as I turned away

from the gray sky and stepped into the dark caravansary. If I didn't find a job by the end of the workday, I would spend the night in the freezing street. I'd already been turned away from five different caravans too poor to warrant a place in the massive caravansary.

Several stalls stood across the wide central space, barring the way to the actual caravans. If you wanted a job with one of the traveling villages, you needed to go through the gate-keepers first. I stood in line, hands bunched in my skirt as the man at the counter filled out paperwork and sent the hope-fuls in front of me either further into the building or back into the cold.

When it was finally my turn, I stepped up to the stall and raised my chin. The man straightened his papers and glanced up at me.

"Name?"

"Reyna Daryadoch."

"Trader or traveler?" he said.

I swallowed. "Trader."

"Goods or services?"

"Services, I'm a healer."

The man raised his eyebrows. "There's always a place or three for a good healer. Are you looking for a temporary or a permanent contract, *lubonitsva?*"

I hid my flinch when he gave me the honorific I hadn't earned. *Lubonitsva* and *maktep* belonged to those who had actually finished their training. Not to those who'd fled their mistakes. But this was not the place to argue that difference.

"Temporary," I said instead.

He rubbed his bulbous nose. "Ah. Where are you trying to get to?"

Apparently, I wasn't the only one looking for a job that would take me home. "As close to Darayevo as I can manage."

He chewed his lip and nodded. "Shouldn't be a problem."

My shoulders relaxed, and I allowed myself a breath of relief. "Great. Do you need me to sign anything?"

"Right here." He pulled a sheet of paper from his stack and slid it across the counter. But he didn't let go when I reached for it. "I'll need to see your wrists, *lubonitsva*."

I'd heard the same words too many times that day. I pulled myself up and tried to look down my nose at him. Mabushka had always managed that look well, so why did I feel like I was going cross-eyed? "Surely that isn't necessary."

He shrugged. "It's a condition of the contract."

My fingers gripped the ragged ends of my long sleeves as if he would leap across and rip the fabric from my arms to reveal my shame. I needed words to guard me. Words to convince him to give me the job anyway. I put my hand down on the counter. "I don't need to stand here and take such insults."

He raised a skeptical eyebrow and pulled the paper back so it brushed my fingertips. "No?" he said. "Then I suggest you go elsewhere for employment. May I suggest the laundries? Or the dung merchants? They're less picky about hiring blood mages."

Da'ermo, he'd actually said it out loud. "Wait," I whispered, leaning closer. "Please, I'm not...Can't you make an exception?"

He sat back as far as he could, avoiding the air I breathed. I jerked back as his lips pulled tight in disgust.

"Blagoy," a voice called behind him. A young woman stepped out of the shadows between the great columns. The handle of a weapon rose over her shoulder, but in the dark, I couldn't tell what she wielded. "Are you sending us a healer sometime this century or what?"

She was young—only a year or two older than me at eighteen—and she wore her blonde hair braided and out of her way. She stopped beside the caravan director and crossed her arms. Two ax hafts rose over her shoulders.

The director, Blagoy, tried to glare at her and at me at the same time. The result made him look like he'd been mulekicked in the head.

"What was wrong with the last three I sent you?" he said.

The girl shrugged. "I'm not the boss," she said. "But we've been stuck here three days past our leave date. We'll take anything at this point." For one brief moment, her eyes met mine.

"Maybe I could find you someone if you left me alone long enough to do my job." He gestured at the line wending away behind me.

She huffed and turned on her heel.

He spun back to me, muttering. "I'll find you someone. I'll find you someone with a stick as big as yours up their—"

He caught my interested gaze as my eyes followed the girl's back. "Not you, *ublyduk,*" he said, cutting off that train of thought. "There's no place in Elisaveta for mages who won't bare their arms."

I'd gone from honored healer to dirty mongrel in three minutes flat. A new personal best.

He snapped and a couple of big men detached themselves from the shadows and stalked toward me. They wore dull red uniforms, trimmed with black, and they carried clubs and hammers. Weapons designed to hurt and kill without drawing blood. *Viona krovaya.* Blood swords, trained to hunt and capture blood mages.

I staggered back, holding up my hands, careful not to let my sleeves fall down my forearms. My heart thudded in my chest. Could they hear it?

I ducked around the carved post beside the wide doorway and waited, mouth dry, to see if they followed. Stupid. I could have blown everything by refusing to show my arms.

My fingers dug into the elongated stag carved into the woodwork.

I had to get home to Mabushka and Eira. I'd made it from Valeria and across the mountains, but I'd only be able to get across Ballaslav if no one succeeded in rolling up my sleeves. My homeland had always struggled with blood magic—we had the ancient Rites to prove it—but I'd had no idea it had gotten this bad. No one was hired without being checked for the two telltale scars of an initiate because no one trusted all blood mages to declare themselves with the red cloak.

Shame swept through me, leaving me hot, then cold. They wouldn't find the two scars under my sleeves, but who knew what they'd make of the mess on my arms. At this point, I'd settle for a caravan heading in any direction, so long as it was away from here.

I glanced over my shoulder. The *viona krovaya* whispered to each other, casting looks my way.

Far behind the director's stall, the blonde, ax-wielding woman spoke with a farrier in a leather apron. How desperate was her caravan?

How desperate was I?

The *viona krovaya* straightened, their faces set in hard, unforgiving lines, and they stepped toward me.

A group of drivers, complete with dusty knee boots and whips at their belts, passed me and headed toward the back of the caravansary.

I held my breath and trusted my instincts. Then I slipped in around them as they passed my hiding spot. I moved with them, keeping one of the drivers between me and the *viona krovaya*.

The blood swords kept moving down the steps toward the street.

As soon as the dark closed around us and my eyes adjusted, I blew out my breath and slipped away from the group. The blonde girl with the axes had finished her conversation with the farrier and moved deeper into the caravansary.

I followed.

The building resembled a massive, well-built stable. Caravans pulled up to the outside walls, where big double doors allowed them access to the farriers and blacksmiths and horse doctors that plied their trade inside. Pillars the size of trees rose into the rafters where carved hammer beams held up the roof. Expensive mage globes illuminated everything because no one would risk an open flame.

The young woman strode to the back corner. Halfway there, she glanced over her shoulder, and I ducked behind a pillar. She didn't need to guess that I was following her.

Waist-high walls divided each caravan's space from the next, and she disappeared behind the last partition on the left. An older man and woman stood talking. Behind them, a wide doorway let out on the gray day where a wagon was pulled in close to the building.

I clenched my fists and strode up to them before I could lose my nerve. "*Ser. Sudinya,*" I said as my grandmother had taught me. "I hear you're looking for a healer."

The woman surveyed me, her sharp blue eyes a strange contrast with the fading hair just visible under the edge of her kerchief. Once she might have been blonde but now the color blended seamlessly with the gray.

"We are," she said. "Did Blagoy send you?"

I made a noncommittal noise as the man turned to look me up and down. I flushed. There was no way to hide my threadbare skirt and bodice, but I wished I'd stopped to pin up the straggling ends of my dark hair.

"You from the university?" he asked. He had no hair to tell his age, but the lines around his eyes indicated many years of laughing.

"I, uh, did a couple semesters," I said.

The man frowned, but the woman gave me a sympathetic smile. "That's more training than our last healer had," she said to the man.

I returned her smile. "My grandmother taught me everything she knew before I went to Valeria."

The man tilted his head. "Do you speak the language at all?"

That seemed a little random, but it was an easy question to answer. "My father was Valerian," I said. "I'm fluent."

The man nodded. "Might be useful on this trip. We have a traveler from down there. Karina has enough Valerian to ask for the outhouse, but Eva and I can't tell his words from his farts."

The woman shoved him. "Watch your language." Her tone was sharp but the corner of her mouth lifted. "Besides that, we're looking for a healer with any kind of training. Broken bones, sniffles, we get them all on the road."

"Doesn't sound like anything I can't handle," I said.

She nodded. "We'd like someone permanent, but we're late and we can't be picky. Our route usually takes us through Darayevo and all the way up to Post da Konstantin."

"That sounds perfect," I said, a little too quickly. "I'm trying to get home. Just a little outside Darayevo."

The man nodded and reached to shake my hand. "I'm Pyotr and that's Evgenia."

"Reyna Daryadoch."

He cocked his head at the woman. "You want to draw up the contract?"

Evgenia winked at me and disappeared out the opening toward the nearest wagon. Its roof glinted with fresh paint.

Pyotr turned back to me, and my blood went cold when he glanced down at my sleeves. *No, no, please let him forget.*

"I just need to see—"

"Pyotr," a familiar voice called. The blonde girl I'd

followed stood in the broad doorway. "Boris cracked an axle. He wants you to look at it."

Pyotr rolled his eyes and made an exasperated noise in the back of his throat. "How could he crack an axle? We haven't budged in over a week."

She shrugged. "Says he just noticed it. Swears it wasn't there before."

"*Pohomzhet da ma Baud*, the man could sink his wagon in a mud puddle." He strode away, waving at me over his shoulder. "Sorry, Reyna. Eva will get you settled."

The girl gave me a strange look and a nod before following Pyotr.

My heart gave one last thump before resuming its normal beat behind my ribs. Maybe O'in was looking out for me. They'd already sent the blonde girl as an angel to guide and guard my steps.

"We travel with four personal wagons and the rest are all cargo," Evgenia told me as we walked between two wagons.

"What do you usually carry?" I said, stepping over a puddle.

"Grain mostly. It's boring, but it always sells well. And we keep one of the wagons free for travelers. It'll be two weeks before we get to Darayevo with a couple of stops along the way."

Two weeks more. That wasn't that bad. If Eira was going to get into trouble without me—and let's face it, she would— then she would have done it in the two years I'd already been gone. But for some reason, the logic didn't make me feel any better. It didn't make two weeks feel any shorter or the longing for my sister's laugh and Mabushka's sarcasm any less.

The wagons circled a row of rough-hewn benches and a stone fire-pit just outside the caravansary. The flicker of fire-light between the wagons turned other caravans along the wall into gray humps in the rising darkness. Several people dressed in fur-lined cloaks and boots came and went around the circle.

"You'll meet everyone in stages, I'm afraid," Evgenia said. "People come and go while we're in town. It's their last chance before we head out."

"How many people do you normally travel with?"

"There are ten drivers, one for each wagon. Five *viona uchenye* to take care of any bandits. Isov and Nico take care of the animals. And Pyotr and I run things. Or pretend to. Oh, and our son should be traveling with us." A shadow crossed her face and I almost asked where he was, but she bustled toward the crackling fire and the four people sitting around it.

Two of the men she introduced as drivers. She stumbled over the third man's name, Corwin Blythe, the traveler from Valeria. The fourth woman was my angel.

Evgenia introduced her as Karina. One of the *viona uchenye*. Sword poets. A slightly different breed of warrior than the ones who hunted blood mages. That explained the axes.

"On the road, everyone sleeps under the wagons with a partner to stay warm. I'll pair you up with someone who can show you where the blankets are kept."

"I'm free," Karina said.

Evgenia's brow drew down. "Aren't you with Ivana?"

Karina shrugged and drew one of her axes to examine the cutting edge. "She said I'm too quiet. Drives her nuts."

Evgenia raised her gaze to the sky. "If I didn't know any better, I'd suspect you of deliberately driving your fellow *viona* crazy."

"Me?" Karina said, gesturing to herself. "Do I look like a trouble-maker to you?"

Evgenia narrowed her eyes as Karina grinned over her ax. "The worst kind. Just show Reyna around and try not to drive her off before she's even had a chance to get settled."

"Yes, Mamat," Karina said.

Evgenia rolled her eyes, but secretly she looked pleased to be called "mama" as she turned to me. "You're free to roam while we're still here. Collect your things from whatever hostel you stashed them in last night. But the armies of O'in won't keep us from leaving at first light tomorrow, so be sure you're back by then." She gave me a warm smile. "And I'd better go give the stock a final check if I'm to keep that promise. Take care of her, Karina?"

"The armies of O'in won't stop me," Karina said with a strangely intent look.

Evgenia snorted and bustled off, moving surprisingly quick for a woman her size.

Karina looked me over, slipped her ax back into the leather harness on her back, and stood up. "Well, you want to get the rest of your stuff?"

"I—" Heat flared in my cheeks, and I fidgeted with the strap of my small satchel.

Over a year ago, I'd left Ballaslav with an entire trunk packed lovingly by my sister and grandmother to tide me over during my time at the University. But things changed. I'd made mistakes. Burned some bridges. And when I'd decided to scurry home with my singed tail between my legs, I'd had to abandon the trunk and its contents in Valeria. Nothing could have convinced me to go back and face down Luka in order to retrieve it. So, most of my meager savings had dwindled in the weeks it had taken to get through the mountains.

I'd fought for this job with exactly three silver reyevs in my satchel and the clothes on my back.

"This is it," I told her, raising my chin.

Karina's lips tightened, and her light eyes burned with fierce light.

I stepped back, flustered, but she blinked and the look was gone.

"Well," she said, voice rough. She gestured to the benches. "Make yourself at home, then. There's plenty of stew left. If you're hungry."

I sat on one of the benches opposite the fire. "Thank you." Maybe she'd heard my stomach rumble. Or maybe she could tell I hadn't eaten yet that day from the way my shoulders sagged.

She nodded. "I'll find you a bowl."

I could have fetched it myself, but she was on her feet before I could protest. She cast one more look at me before she disappeared around the end of a wagon.

I rubbed the back of my neck, which tingled. I had the

strangest feeling there was something deep and different about Karina. Like she was telling me something when she looked at me, but I kept missing it. Like trying to find the next rung of a ladder in the dark.

"Your name is Reyna?" The question, spoken in Valerian, caught me off guard. I hadn't heard the language spoken in weeks, but I would never grow rusty in my father's tongue.

The Valerian traveler—Corwin, I reminded myself—sat forward on his bench, his dark eyes intent on my face.

"Yes," I said in his language.

He drew his hands through his dark brown curls and laughed. The two drivers sitting around the fire looked at him askance.

"You have no idea how good it is to hear even that one word," Corwin said. "I can't begin to wrap my tongue around the version of Ballaslavian the locals speak. And the names. Does everyone need a name as long as the coastline?"

I shrugged.

"Where are you going? Where are you coming from?"

"I, uh, came up from the University in Benevere. And I guess I'm going wherever the caravan is going for now."

"Right, this is definitely an interesting way to see the country. I'd have hired a personal carriage, but they're so expensive up here. But then I guess I'd miss out on the whole experience if I didn't at least try to embrace the local customs. However unsophisticated they might be."

I choked on a snort. My Valerian accent must be better than I thought. Maybe I should tell him I grew up with polar bears and icebergs.

"I'm trying to get to Post da Konstantin. The Valerian

ambassador agreed to host me, but I've only just started my journey, and I feel like I've been in this benighted country forever. Does the sun never shine here?"

"There can be beauty in gray." I glanced up at the various shades that rolled and seeped above us.

"Sure there is," he said. "But how much beauty are these people missing by never seeing anything green or blue or yellow?"

I was saved from answering by Karina's return. She handed me a full bowl of stew and gave Corwin an exasperated look over her shoulder. Water slicked the outside of the bowl as if she'd washed it just for me.

"I'm sure it's a lovely country...once you get used to it," he said. "And it will be much better when I can share at least some of the journey with another Valerian."

I bit my lip to hide a smile. "Before you get too excited—"

"Too late," Karina muttered in Ballaslavian before settling on the bench next to me.

I shot her a look. "I should tell you my full name is Reyna Sofya Daryadoch."

His mouth had opened for another flood of words, and now he stared like a club-struck hare.

"Maybe if we set him outside camp, he'll ward off evil spirits," Karina whispered.

I choked on a bite of stew and coughed to cover my laugh.

"You're Ballaslavian," Corwin said.

"Half and half, actually. But my father moved north when he married my mother, so I was raised Ballaslavian." I shrugged. "Sorry."

He waved his hands in the air. "Why are you apologizing? This is perfect. You must have so many insights into the Ballaslavian mindset and you'll be able to communicate them to me. Karina here has been trying—"

"But my accent is terrible," Karina said in barely passable Valerian. "And I can't understand him when he goes fast."

Corwin smiled sheepishly. "I speed up when I get excited. So, what do the names mean? They can't be long just to confuse foreigners."

"They are our lineage," Karina said. "A way to honor those who came before us."

"My mother's name was Darya," I said. "So I'm Daryadoch. Darya's daughter."

"Pyotr is Grigorsyn," Karina said.

"Grigor's son," I said.

Corwin looked like he wished he was writing this down. "So, women are named for their mothers, and men are named for their fathers."

"Usually," I said. "Though sometimes children are given the name of a grandparent or a great ancestor."

"And what's the middle name for?"

Karina glanced at me out of the corner of her eye. "That's more uncommon. In case there are more people to honor in your lineage."

I shuffled my feet. "My mother insisted on naming me for her mother as well. Though I don't know why; she never spoke of her side of the family."

Corwin nodded thoughtfully. "Is that why your Grand Duchess has so many names?"

The fire popped, sending a shower of sparks toward the

clouds. Karina followed them with her eyes as she answered. "There are many to honor in the ruling lineage."

"Can one of you say it for me? Slowly?"

"Yesofya Borislava Yekaterin Konstantinadoch," Karina said, voice hushed and reverent.

Corwin tilted his head. "My people just call her Grand Duchess Sophie."

Karina drew an outraged breath, and I reached out a hand to touch her arm before yanking it back when I thought better of it.

"That's probably easier," I said, giving Karina a quelling look.

As she settled back, grumbling, her gaze shifted over my shoulder. I turned to look for what had caught her eye and stifled a gasp. A boy stood at the edge of our circle, eyes wide, the firelight flickering off his blood-red cloak.

Corwin's eyes crinkled, but the two drivers stood with mutters of, "*ispor'chennai*," and stalked away so there would be less chance of the blood mage soiling them.

I ground my teeth. None of them could have had any experience with a mage in Blood Lust or they would have looked at his eyes, not his cloak or the single perfect scar on each of his wrists. The Blood Lust ring was especially visible in the sun, but that didn't mean you couldn't see it at night if you knew what you were looking for.

"What is it, *malvo o'in*?" Karina said, her words gentle.

I glanced at her in shock. Little misguided one?

The boy dropped a cloth bundle on the nearest bench, his expression pinched. "Parts from my master." He twitched the cloth out of the way so we could pick up the metal fittings within without having to touch what he had touched.

Karina stood and plucked the objects from the bench. The boy flipped the cloth into the fire.

He started to turn and Corwin reached out.

"Wait, I've been wanting to ask someone what the red means."

The boy lurched away from Corwin's touch, stumbling around another bench. The edge of his cloak barely brushed Corwin's boot, and Karina stopped the Valerian with a hand on his arm.

"Leave him," she said as the boy escaped between the circled wagons.

"Why?" Corwin said. "Why is everyone so afraid of them?"

"He's a blood mage," I said, speaking the truth to remind myself as much as to inform him. "Unclean. Everything he touches must be burned. Everyone he touches has to go through special Rites." An ache started in my belly and reached for my heart.

"Right. Unclean. You people have a lot of rules about being clean, I remember."

Karina and I stiffened at the same time.

"If you're unclean when you die, you're forever separated from O'in," Karina said, her eyes flicking to me. "The Rites allow us into Their presence again. But a blood mage can't be cleansed. The magic ingrains the evil too deep. Someone who is touched by a blood mage must go through special Rites. But a blood mage himself is damned, forever apart from Them."

I shivered and pulled my ragged sleeves down my wrists.

It was too easy to sit here by the fire and forget what I was. Forget that I was damning everyone around me.

I drew into myself, keeping my elbows from brushing Karina. I couldn't afford to forget. I couldn't afford to get comfortable and chatty. The *viona krovaya* would hunt me down eventually, and when they did, none of these people would want to admit they'd sat beside me. They'd fed me. They'd touched me.

There was only one man who'd known of my crimes and hadn't cared. And in the end, his acceptance had hurt me more than all the dirty looks and murmurs of *"ispor'chennai."* I just had to remember that and it became a lot easier to keep myself apart.

CHAPTER TWO

I knew better than to sleep on the cold ground, but I desperately needed this job and I wasn't going to lose it by complaining. Which just meant that the next morning I woke with an ache in my joints that reminded me how fragile my life was. Fire burned through my feet and knees, the joints tender and swollen like Mabushka's in the winter. Karina bounced up to start her day, and I crawled out after her, forcing my stiff limbs to respond.

Da'ermo, of all the days for my illness to show up, it would strike when I needed to prove myself strong and useful.

I gritted my teeth and pushed through the pain in order to stand and fold my blanket and join the line for breakfast. The sun had barely crested the horizon, casting weak light across the crouching shape of the caravansary. Pyotr ruled the giant stockpot balanced on the edge of the fire-pit, doling out servings of *memka.* He'd liberally dosed the boiled grain with cinnamon and nuts, and I wished I could look forward to it.

But all my concentration went to a small healing spell that would reduce the swelling in my joints and maybe keep the rest of the pain at bay.

The line passed the pump in the middle of the caravan's site and each employee pumped the handle for the next in line as they murmured the words of the Rites. All except the foreigners.

Ahead of me, Corwin took his bowl with a dubious look and went to sit with the other travelers paying for passage.

Most of the drivers stayed away from them. The foreigners didn't follow our Law, and no one wanted to go through the longer, more expensive Rites just because an unclean Valerian asked you to pass the salt.

My hands shook as I held them under the stream of freezing water. All I wanted was to curl back up under one of the wagons and start again tomorrow. Exhaustion threaded my limbs, and I hadn't even eaten breakfast yet.

When I got to the front of the line, Pyotr smiled and ladled *memka* into a bowl for me, but I fumbled the dish and lunged too late to catch it. I stared at the precious grain spattered in the dirt.

"I'm sorry," I mumbled, mortified.

Pyotr shook his head. "Don't worry, *mushka*," he said. "We all have those days." He ladled me another bowl and held it out.

True, but I had more of those days than most. I took the second bowl gingerly, holding it close and letting the warmth seep into my hands.

"What's wrong?" Karina asked behind me, reaching for my shoulder.

I stifled a gasp and stepped away from her touch. I was breaking the Law just by being here. But I would protect as many people as possible along the way. "Nothing," I said.

She looked at me askance as I moved away and found an empty space on one of the benches away from everyone else. I stared down at my chapped hands clenched around my breakfast. Why couldn't this have waited until I was home? I'd have been able to get the rest I needed, and Mabushka would have been there to take care of me.

Moisture leaked from the corners of my eyes, and I clenched them shut before I could embarrass myself by crying. How many times had I wished I could go back in time and not leave home for Valeria? Everything that had gone wrong had stemmed from that moment.

"I'll ask again. What's wrong?" Karina straddled the bench beside me, kicking up some half-frozen mud. "And don't say nothing. You look like a corpse," she snapped.

"Seen a lot of those?" I huffed a laugh.

"Plenty. Or did you forget what I do for a living?"

I sobered. *Viona uchenye* were more deadly than a bear with a stick up its rump, and I'd do well to remember that. Every *viona krovaya* who hunted a blood mage had been *viona uchenye* first.

"There's nothing you can do," I said. "This isn't something anyone can fix." My trip to Valeria could be labeled many things, but it had proved that beyond a doubt.

Her brow furrowed. "What is it?"

"I'm...sick," I said. "I've had this illness for most of my life now."

She drew back, and I fought to keep my face still.

"I promise it's not contagious," I mumbled. Not that it would matter. The Law dictated that those who were visibly ill were to be quarantined until the sickness passed and the Rites had been performed. "I just get really tired and achy for days at a time."

She settled back and poked at her breakfast. "I'm sorry, I didn't know."

I glanced up from under my lashes. "How could you? It doesn't always show on the outside." I fiddled with my bowl. Since I looked fine, no one understood the way I would need more rest or quiet. Eira had always complained about doing my chores when I was in bed with the aches.

"What do you need?"

Karina leveled her intense gaze at me, and I swallowed. "What?"

"You're sick. What do you need? Medicine? Healing? I can talk to Eva."

"No, don't," I said. "I mean, rest is the most important thing, but I can't right now. I need this job. If they know, they'll leave me behind."

"They're not going to—"

"Please."

"All right," she said, her eyes narrowed. They were a strange mix of green and brown. One of her parents must have come north over the mountains.

Movement caught my eye, and I turned to see one of Blagoy's *viona krovaya* striding through the caravan, a short man trotting at his heels.

He stepped up to Pyotr. "Got your healer, Grigorsyn," the *viona* said.

Oh...oh, muck. This was bad, this was really, really bad.

Pyotr blinked at the big man with the club and the smaller one next to him. "There must be a mistake. We hired the healer he sent yesterday."

The man's eyes narrowed, and he glanced around the caravan. "What healer?"

I ducked behind the wide driver in front of me and glanced at Karina. Maybe she could distract them while I slipped away. But the bench next to me was empty. *Da'ermo.* So much for being my guardian angel.

"Tell Blagoy to check his records," Pyotr said, stooping to lift the empty stockpot. "He sent us a healer yesterday and we hired her. We're on our way out of town. Finally." He waved his free hand and turned his back on the duo.

Thank O'in for tight schedules. The *viona* and the healer grumbled and left, but not before the big man took one last look around the caravan. I kept myself down, but I couldn't be sure he hadn't seen me. My thoughts raced across all my options. Could I convince Pyotr and Evgenia to get the caravan moving before Blagoy put the pieces together and came running?

I raced to stack my sticky bowl with the others. When I turned, I had to stumble back to avoid running into Evgenia and Karina.

The older woman narrowed her eyes at me. "You're right," she said. "You can see something in the eyes."

Cold shot through me and my hands clenched on the ends of my sleeves. There shouldn't be anything about my eyes. I was clean. As clean as I could ever be.

"Come along, *mushka.*" Evgenia turned.

I didn't have much choice but to follow her. I could try to run, but I'd only make the aches and the exhaustion worse. I'd never outrun the *viona krovaya*, and I'd end up dying in the street, mortifying Eira and Mabushka both.

She led Karina and me to one of the personal wagons. There were four. Two for the paying travelers, one for Pyotr and Evgenia, and one extra.

My hand clutched my bodice over my heart. Was this where they would keep me until the authorities came to drag me away and force me into a red cloak?

"You can rest here, *mushka*. You should have told us you were having trouble. There are bags the size of grain sacks under your eyes."

Relief washed through me in a wave of shivers before consternation replaced it. I turned on Karina.

"You told her?"

Karina's jaw hardened. "It turned out all right."

"That's not the point." I turned to Evgenia. "I don't want to slow you down." I didn't want her to fire me.

"As long as you don't mind a moving wagon, you won't be altering our schedule at all," she said. She smiled and reached to pat my arm.

I shifted out of range.

Her smile fell, and she gestured me up the steps of the wagon. "You just rest until you feel better."

How horrible was I to make her feel bad for trying to help me? I gave her an apologetic grin. "I thought I was the healer."

Her smile returned. "Believe me, if someone breaks a leg,

we'll come rouse you. Now go get settled. We raise dirt in five minutes."

Karina offered me a hand, but I grabbed the doorframe and hauled myself up without her help.

"Do you need anything?" she said.

I didn't meet her eyes. I wasn't in the market for this sort of attention. Her care only made me think of Luka. "I'm fine."

I ducked through the little door and closed it behind me.

Little red painted flowers climbed the inside walls, curling around the door and two windows. I recognized them as heart's blood, a spring flower that bloomed early enough to withstand the snow. Often, my sister and I had stopped on the path to the house to find the little scarlet blooms poking through a fresh sheet of snow.

Two narrow box beds took up most of the small interior. Blue and yellow hand-sewn quilts made them inviting and I sagged onto the left one. Finally, I drew up my knees and curled into a ball against the wall. Once I laid down, I wouldn't want to get up again until the swelling and the pain had passed entirely, but Evgenia had been so understanding. She'd told me to rest.

I reached out and pulled the edge of the quilt over my shoulders. A tear leaked out of the corner of my eye and ran down my temple, and I brushed it away with an impatient hand.

I was done feeling sorry for myself. Mabushka always said, "Why worry about the things you can't change?" And my trip to Valeria had proved I couldn't change anything about my illness.

Almost a year ago, bright sunlight had poured through an open window, sending tracks of yellow and gold across the hardwood floor and the neatly made beds. At least here, in Valeria, a sickroom could have fresh air. At home, there were only two months out of the year when you could open the windows without killing your patient.

I never got tired of the green either. I took a deep breath and imagined I could smell the color. It wasn't hard to believe that I had finally found the help I needed in this green-gold garden. The sunlight glared against the red swelling around my toes and ankles, but surely something they had here, some tonic, some spell would make my illness disappear forever.

A footstep rang across the ward, and I looked up to see my favorite teacher walking toward me.

"Professor Benson?"

She didn't answer me and the deep lines around her mouth made my chest tighten.

"You don't know what it is," I guessed when she stopped in front of me.

"We know," she said quietly.

I drew a breath. *Pohomzhet da ma Baud*, I was dying. I would expire here, miles away from home with only Valerian strangers to sing my Rites.

She knelt before me and clasped my hand. I clung to it. "It's not as bad as you're imagining," she said. "It's a type of rheumatism. The pain and fatigue come from the swelling in your joints."

"The cure?" I asked, though I knew what she was going to say from the set of her lips.

"There isn't one."

At least she was honest about it.

She squeezed my fingers and tilted my chin up with her other hand when I wanted to look away. "It doesn't mean that you're dying. With care and rest, we can manage your symptoms. And you're not dangerous to anyone, whatever those Laws of yours say."

I squeezed my eyes shut. Try telling that to an entire country of stubborn believers.

"There aren't any spells?" I said, forcing myself to face her sympathy.

"As you learned in my class last week," she said with a slight smile. "There are many spells for pain relief and energy, the energy ones being more dangerous. I will teach these to you, and you can use them to combat the aches and the exhaustion when they come. They won't have the power to make you feel completely well. But they will make you feel better. You'll have a new normal."

I turned my face away, toward the fresh air and light.

"There's nothing that says you can't be a healer. You can still graduate. You can still help people."

Sitting in the sunlight, I could imagine she was right. The spells would be enough. I could live with the left-over pain and fatigue. But I couldn't help the niggling thought that if I was always trying to heal myself, I would never be strong enough to heal anyone else.

I hadn't been strong enough to save my parents.

There was a shadow in Professor Benson's eyes, and I'm not sure she believed her own words.

I spoke the words of another spell and twisted my fingers so the magic spread over me where I lay in the bunk. One spell to fight the fatigue, one to fight the pain. That's all I allowed myself now. I didn't trust myself to handle more.

Even now as the energy flowed through me, barely putting a dent in the ache, I longed for something more. An itch in my gut urged me to draw more power, to fill myself with the energy called *vytl*, until the pain and the exhaustion receded, and I could do what I was called to do without reservation.

Raised voices penetrated the fog in my head, and I opened my eyes to find my fingers stretched halfway to my belt knife.

I snatched them back, breathing heavily. *Da'ermo*, would the hunger never leave?

Someone banged on the side of my wagon, making me jump, then groan with pain. I raised myself up on my elbow to peer out the little window. One of the drivers, Ivan, leaned back with a boyish grin. "All tucked up tight in there, *mushka?*"

I gave him a weak smile through the crack in the shutters. "Yes."

He waved a hand and leaped to the driver's seat.

Shouts and creaking made a confused cacophony as the drivers urged their animals forward and the wagons sorted themselves out. Pyotr and Evgenia's wagon broke free of the circle and bounced the wrong way across old ruts until it rumbled onto the road.

A shout made me turn, and I caught my breath. Blagoy raced along behind the last wagon, waving his arms. Two *viona krovaya* followed him, hands on their clubs.

Blagoy ran to a driver. "Stop!" he shouted as he peered up into his face.

The driver's brow scrunched, but he didn't have time to answer as the caravansary director ran to the next wagon and repeated himself. He paid special attention to the two wagons where the paying travelers stared down at him through their windows.

The drivers swung between him and Pytor's wagon, wondering who to obey.

Karina clung to the back of one of the passenger wagons, the only one close enough to hear Blagoy and close enough to call out to Pytor.

She glanced back at the irate director. She set her jaw, and then she turned her back on Blagoy and gestured the drivers on.

My wagon shuddered and lurched forward, joining the line.

Blagoy stopped racing after the caravan and glared at the rest of us. I ducked down as my wagon bounced past him.

In moments, we'd passed through the gate and left the director behind.

CHAPTER THREE

I might have been the healer but Evgenia's orders had been spot on. With rest and the chance to set my healing spells, I was able to rejoin the rest of the caravan within a day.

By the time I emerged from the heart's blood wagon, we had left Blagoy and Elisaveta far behind. An ancient forest marched on our right while rolling hills covered in yellowed grass sprawled on the left. The caravaners had circled the wagons in a well-trampled clearing beside the road, and Pyotr had set up his cookpot over the central fire.

He got some good-natured gruff from the drivers, who teased him for doing women's work, but they wolfed down his stew and tore into his bread fast enough.

I dipped my hands in the water bucket, shook them off, and sang the words of the Rites under my breath, cringing at my own hypocrisy. *O'in forgive me. O'in wash me. O'in work in me and make me new.* Then I took my dinner and joined the others in the circle of wagons, settling myself in a relatively dry spot on the grass.

Across the fire, Karina sat cross-legged with two of the other *viona uchenye*. She studied me as if to check that I was all there after my absence while her fellow *viona* chattered at her. It was too bad she wasn't born with four legs; she'd have made a great guard dog.

As if summoned by the thought, a tall mutt with wiry gray hair slunk across the clearing to me. He lay down and put his head on his forepaws, his eyebrows twitching a mournful suggestion. When I didn't immediately extend my dinner in enthusiastic offering, he whined and scooted closer.

"Don't let him fool you," Evgenia said, passing close by. "Victor is the best-fed worker among us. Go on, you greedy thing. How can you be sniffing for trouble when you're begging from Reyna here?"

The dog gave me a hurt look and slunk off around the line of shaggy horses picketed at the edge of the forest.

"Do you feel better, *mushka*?" Evgenia asked.

I wanted to curl up in a ball and hide or bristle. Instead I tried to smile. "Much better. Thank you. You didn't have to let me stay in the wagon."

Evgenia beamed. "Of course I did. I don't get to fuss over my own little one right now, so I'm going to fuss over you. I hope you don't mind. Just don't tell anyone else." She whispered the last part and gave me a broad wink before heading over to chastise one of the drivers, who sat with his feet up on a bench.

Beside me, Corwin balanced his bowl on one knee while he tried to sort through a sheaf of ragged papers. He ducked to dip his pen in the ink-pot beside his foot, and with extraordinary grace and poise, he managed to dump everything at once. He cried out as ink poured into the dirt and his papers scattered in all directions.

I sighed and gathered the ones that drifted closest to me.

"What are you writing?" I said, handing them back.

He blinked, the firelight flickering across the pages he held. "My notes on Ballaslav."

I chuckled. "Are you studying us?"

His brow furrowed. "That's why I'm here. I'm a Disciple of Wonderment."

I nodded. That explained a lot.

"Disciple?" Karina had joined us.

"A follower," I said. "Of one of their Saints. Wonderment is the saint of scholarship."

Karina frowned. "Sacrilege."

Corwin sputtered, and I shook my head before he could say anything. "They don't worship the saints," I explained. "They pledge their service to O'in through them."

She crossed her arms. "It dilutes faith, to go through an intermediary."

I shrugged. I didn't disagree, but I'd lived in the south long enough to know what a useless argument it was.

Corwin drew himself up. "The Saints are not intermediaries," he said. "They are examples for us to follow. Don't you have heroes, people in history you revere and model your behavior on?"

Karina tossed her braid over her shoulder. "Sure, we have the *Izavitals*. But that's different. They're picked out by O'in to guide us in times of strife."

"That is exactly what our saints are," Corwin said, but

Karina wasn't listening anymore. She stared over our shoulders.

"Hush," she said.

"That's no way to win an argument—"

Karina lunged forward and pressed her hand against his mouth.

A moment later, Victor started barking.

Karina signaled the other *viona uchenye,* and they faded quickly into the forest beside the road, their movements silent and efficient.

Pyotr rounded the rest of us up by the fire, hushing questions and forming everyone into a circle. The drivers stood around the outside with whips and clubs at the ready while the travelers, the boys who tended the animals, and I stood in the middle.

We waited, tense and expectant in the silence, until a cry broke the night air. The clang of metal made us jump and shiver, and we huddled closer together. Who were they fighting? Bandits? Blood mages? I wrapped my arms around myself and let my eyes flick over the gray trees, searching for movement.

Pohomzhet da ma Baud, were five *viona uchenye* enough against whatever was out there? The cries of pain and anger, the sound of weapons gave us no clue as to the adversary or to the winning side. Once, I thought I heard Karina's voice raised in triumph, but it was cut off with frightening abruptness.

A minute or a lifetime later, silence fell, and we waited in the clearing to see who would come out of the dark.

Metal gleamed between the trees, and Karina stepped

into the firelight. The four other *viona uchenye* coalesced behind her. They stood in a row, a motley collection of leather armor and weapons, unified only by the fierce looks on their faces. I sucked in a breath when I realized the dark splotches on their skin and clothes weren't shadows.

I pushed against the drivers in front of me. A couple of them frowned and closed ranks around me. I shoved again. "I'm needed out there. Let me through."

"Let her go," Pyotr said and followed me to the edge of the clearing.

Karina held up a bloody hand to keep me from coming any closer. "We're all fine," she said. "None of it's ours."

"Are you sure?" The way she held her shoulders caught my eye, like her posture masked pain. I took a step.

Karina ducked out of reach. "I'm sure."

"I should really go with you to check."

"It's not needed."

I shook my head, hard enough to make it ache. "It's what I'm here for. The caravan travels with a healer for a reason. Let me do my job."

"No, Reyna." Her voice barked across the space between us.

I drew back, arms across my chest. Pain that had nothing to do with my illness sliced through me.

Karina didn't meet my eyes as she spoke to Pyotr. "We've cleared the area. You should be safe until we return."

"What was it?" Pyotr asked quietly.

"Raiders. Probably after the grain with winter coming."

Little grew in the bare, rocky soil of my homeland. Our cities depended on trade from other countries, especially our lush neighbor, Valeria. Trade routes sprang from the passes through the mountains and spread north through Ballaslav.

But raiders knew the caravan routes as well as the honest traders did.

The *viona uchenye* each turned away with a lazy salute and left to make their own camp separately, protecting us as they were called and trained to do.

I stood at the edge of the firelight, watching Karina's back as she disappeared into the dark.

I had a calling, too. Did Karina even realize she was keeping me from it? Or did she think she was protecting me?

"You can check the others when they get back," Pyotr said, making me jump. "Make sure they really are all right. Karina, though, you'll have to convince separately. She takes her job very seriously."

My lips pulled in a frown. All right. I could be subversive if my patients needed me to be.

I spun on my heel to return to the fire and nearly ran into Corwin.

"Why wouldn't she let you help?"

I was not in the mood to answer his questions. I glanced around the clearing, where the firelight flickered on relieved faces and lit up the painted sides of the wagons. But there was no one else who spoke his language, and I didn't have the heart to leave him friendless.

I jerked my head at one of the benches beside the fire and spoke when he followed. "I think...I think it's because she's *viona*. She's used to protecting people."

"Valerians have guards, too, you know. And they know the value of a good healer, especially after a fight."

I flopped down on the bench and propped my chin in my hand. "They're not just guards. They protect us physically, yes, but more importantly, they protect us spiritually."

Corwin tilted his head, then reached behind him slowly and pulled his notes into view, his gaze never leaving my face. "How so?"

I chewed my lip. Maybe if I started from the beginning. "We have the Law," I said.

He rolled his eyes. "I know that."

I continued as if he hadn't spoken. "The Law protects us from spiritual death. If we follow the Law and perform the Rites, then we will be clean when we die, and O'in can welcome us."

"That's why you're always washing your hands and singing that prayer of yours."

I nodded slowly. "Yes, it's one of the Rites. There are others for death and sickness and blood."

He scribbled on his page. "And what does that have to do with the *viona uchenye*?"

"They protect us from the last. They are sword poets, in your tongue. Scholars of the Law and the blade. The Law states that blood is unclean. So, anyone who draws blood is unclean before they go through the Rites. The *viona uchenye* do this so the rest of us don't have to."

"So, they actually think they're protecting you by not coming back to the camp?"

"They'll stay out there until they've made themselves clean again," I said, ignoring the skepticism in his words.

"And Karina is protecting you by not letting you treat her wounds."

I pressed my lips together. If you believed the priests, my soul was already forfeit. Nothing Karina did would protect me from myself.

But as damned as I was, I was a healer. It was the one thing that had gotten me into the mess with Luka. And it was the one thing that had gotten me out.

Karina might have been serious about her job, but so was I. She was just going to have to learn that, whether she liked it or not.

"How bad is it?" the *viona* asked craning his head around to see. "It didn't seem like much after the fight. Didn't even notice it till I slept on it."

I suppressed a smile. The *viona* was almost as old as Mabushka but he fretted like a girl with a ripped hemline.

"It isn't even bleeding anymore. Your shirt took more damage than you. Just keep it clean and if it pains you at night come to me, and I'll give you some willow to help you sleep."

"Thank you, *lubonitsva.*"

"Just Reyna, please."

The *viona* flashed me a smile missing several teeth. He shrugged back into his jacket and hopped off the back of the wagon.

I checked to be sure Karina hadn't seen me treating the man, but she was checking the perimeter as the drivers unhitched their teams. After the *viona*, I only had one more patient.

Ivan, one of the drivers, hoisted himself onto the back of the grain wagon and held out his hand.

It was just a wrenched finger, and I finished bandaging it before the sun had completely set. Luckily, there'd been no blood for either of them and therefore no need for any of the more extensive Rites. I'd have had a harder time hiding those from Karina.

Ivan moved away to finish his chores, and I gathered up the borrowed healer's kit. My fingers brushed the cool handle of the sharp little knife and I shivered.

Best to be careful with that. I flipped the leather edge of the kit closed on the bandages, salves, and knife and tied it with a vicious knot. I would not think about the feel of a blade in my hand. I would not remember what it was like to slice through skin.

It was the whole reason I'd left my personal kit in Valeria.

The sunset streaked the sky blue-gray and gold as I headed back toward the heart's blood wagon. I didn't sleep there. I was an employee, not a passenger, and after that first awful night, Karina always bundled in extra blankets and huddled close enough that I slept all right under the wagons. But Evgenia and Pyotr allowed me to keep my small satchel in the heart's blood wagon. And the few healing supplies they had collected over the years were stored under one of the bunks.

Voices floated around the partially open door of the wagon as I approached.

"—not like he's never seen the place before, Eva," Pyotr said.

"I just want everything to be perfect. He deserves that at least."

I poked my head around the door, and Evgenia jumped.

"Sorry," I said. "I didn't mean to interrupt. I just wanted to put some things away."

"Come on in, Reyna," Pyotr said. "We're just straightening the place up."

I cocked my thumb over my shoulder. "Would you like me to store these somewhere else, then?"

"No, no," Evgenia said. "Aleksei won't mind."

"Aleksei?" I asked.

"Our son." She beamed around to the wagon. "He's been staying with some friends of ours while we travel, but he'll be joining us finally when we get to Darayevo."

I smiled at her happiness. "That's wonderful. And he'll be using the wagon?"

"As long as he needs it to feel comfortable on the road."

So, Aleksei would be joining them as a passenger while his parents traveled the Ballaslavian trade routes. It would seem like such an adventure to a little boy.

There'd been a time when I'd dreamed of my own adventures. I'd never been the daredevil Eira was. I was always the one standing on the floor of the barn while Eira swung from the rope Papa hung in the rafters. But there had still been dreams. Quiet heroics in my own head.

Evgenia fingered the fraying edge of one of the quilts and frowned. "The whole wagon needs a good scrubbing. And these need repairs."

"I could help," I said, then bit my lip when they both raised their eyebrows at me. "I mean, if you need any." I'd be on my way home by the time they reached Darayevo, so I would never meet little Aleksei, see his shining eyes as he set off on his first adventure. But I could do something to make that adventure more special.

Evgenia's surprise turned calculating. "Can you sew?"

My mouth crooked. "I have the straightest seam in Ballaslav, according to my grandmother."

She gathered up the quilt she'd been eying. "Well, if you like sewing..."

I laughed. "I didn't say I liked it. I said I was good at it." I took the quilt from her and peered at the loose seams. "My sister was never patient enough for sewing, so I was the one who sat with Mabushka to do the mending while Eira cooked or swept. I always hated her for it. Funny how it doesn't seem that important now."

Evgenia gave me a gentle look. "How long has it been since you've seen them?"

Too long. I swallowed. "Almost two years. Who knows what she's gotten up to while I've been gone?" It had seemed like such a good idea to leave. For my education. For my future. That's what I'd told myself anyway. Now I wondered if I hadn't been a little tired of looking after my sister. Was it stupid to miss something I'd been so ready to escape?

She clicked her tongue. "And to think I was feeling sorry for myself for missing Aleksei the past six months."

I nodded, not trusting myself to speak again.

"Here." Evgenia stooped and rummaged under the other bunk. "My sewing kit. I imagine you left yours at home, maybe hoping that sister of yours would pick it up."

I laughed. She'd fly first.

Outside, the drivers all sat around the fire, some with little bits of work in their hands. Bridles, harnesses, things that needed mending but weren't important enough to halt the caravan for during the day. The *viona uchenye* sat amongst them, their weapons out, their eyes watchful.

One of the drivers had an old battered fiddle up to his chin, and his bow pulled a slow, sad folk song out of the instrument.

Karina returned from walking the perimeter and met my eyes as I searched for a place to sit. She jerked her head, inviting me over with the other *viona*.

I pressed my lips together and shook my head. Then I sat as close to the fire as I dared with the quilt, using its light to illuminate my work. Victor passed me on his rounds, and I spared one hand from my task to scratch him under his chin. He groaned softly, but when I stopped, he moved on without complaint. There were so many hands to pet him he'd never want for a rub.

Karina settled beside me with a creak of leather, folding her long legs easily.

I narrowed my eyes at her.

She shrugged. "You're alone too much. You can use the company."

I almost laughed. She wasn't wrong. But too many things lurked under my surface, and the closer anyone got, the more danger they were in.

"Maybe I like being alone," I said to my hands.

I caught her stiffen out of the corner of my eye and waited for her to give up and walk away. But after a second, her knees relaxed again and she leaned back on her hands.

"Then I'll just shut up and we can sit here alone together."

That...wasn't what I'd intended. Or expected. But when I tried to meet her eyes, she had tilted her head back to survey the stars, keeping her word.

It wasn't bad. I could make this work. And it was nicer than I wanted to admit, sitting beside someone who didn't need any input from me. I leaned further into the light.

The quilt was easily mended with a couple of stitches and a patch or two, and I settled into a comfortable rhythm. The fiddle player's tune reached deep and pulled out a memory of Mabushka braiding my hair while humming the song. I couldn't help humming along now.

When he'd finished, he started another, and I smiled. He must be from around Darayevo, too. He knew all the best songs.

I sang the chorus along with his bow, quietly at first, then my voice gained strength as no one laughed or rolled their eyes. Karina stretched her legs out, closing her eyes. By the last word, the others around the fire had stopped what they were doing to listen.

"Pretty," the fiddler said.

I flushed. "*Spaasebo.*"

Singing was the opposite of sewing for me. I loved it, but I wasn't very good at it. The only practice I'd had was the rare occasion I'd been alone in the house and I'd felt brave enough to sing out with no one listening. Eira always said my problem was confidence. If I just sang like I didn't care what people thought, that would take care of those little wobbles and sour notes.

Easy for her to say. She never cared what people thought.

"Do you know this one?" The fiddler set his bow to his strings again and struck up an old hymn.

Everyone knew that one, but I considered staying quiet. I'd opened my mouth the first time because no one had really been paying attention and the homesickness had overwhelmed me.

But two of the men came in strong, their deep voices confident if not entirely perfect, and it felt only natural to take the upper line, balancing the song between us.

When it was done, someone called out, "I'll bet she'd make a wonderful Svetanka."

I knew the ballad he was talking about—my parents had sung it together, and it had been one of our favorites growing up—but the fiddler shook his head. "No, we don't have an Anastasy. Not until—" He glanced at Pytor, who listened quietly from the shadows, before striking up another livelier tune than the suggested ballad.

I shrugged and lowered my head to my work. The quilt was done, but I wanted to do something else for Aleksei. Worn scraps of discarded clothes and blankets filled Evgenia's sewing kit, and a particularly soft grey material caught my eye. I fingered it while I sang, running it between my fingers and imagining the possibilities.

Victor sat beside me with a huff, giving me the best idea. Every little boy needed a fierce companion. Someone to share his adventures.

I dug in Evgenia's kit to see if there were any buttons.

CHAPTER FOUR

While Elisaveta rose among the foothills, rivaling the mountains on its doorstep, Zhivko sprawled across the plains, rambling east and north along the river.

At the edge of the city's caravansary, I stopped and stared, letting the stink of damp streets and the rumble of thousands of people and horses and vehicles wash over me. It wouldn't be too hard to find an apothecary with so much of the city to explore, but I would have to be careful to stick to the main roads or I'd be lost in seconds.

"A real live Ballaslavian city," an excited voice said behind me.

I snorted and turned to give Corwin a smile. "This isn't your first. You saw Elisaveta."

"That hardly counts. It's too Valerian. Zhivko is far enough from the border not to be tainted."

I hid my face so he couldn't see my pained expression. When I'd told Evgenia I wanted to replace the healing supplies I'd already used, she'd enthusiastically pressed money into my palm, insisting on paying for whatever I thought they needed. But she'd also suggested I bring Corwin along to carry things. From the harried look in her eye, I figured I'd be doing her a favor by taking him off her hands.

I tried to think of him like an exuberant puppy as I led him down the street or a child still learning about the world. It helped me keep my sense of humor when he asked endless questions.

"What's that?"

"An *yshkiniva*. It's like a chapel in Valeria."

"What smells so good?"

"*Chapoc* pies. You can try one if you'd like. They're very sweet."

"What's that?"

"Corwin, that's a house."

"But why is it all red and blue like that?"

"I imagine the man who lived there was a member of the underground movement fifty years ago to usurp Ballaslav's throne and swear fealty to Valeria. He painted his house as a secret code so other members would know it was safe to lodge there during dangerous times."

"Wow, really?"

"No, I'm totally making that up."

All right, so mostly I kept my humor. And sometimes I had to make up some humor.

I found most of what I needed only ten minutes from the caravansary. The apothecary was out of any numbing creams, but he suggested another shop just two streets down.

Outside in the wan sunlight, I juggled the little wrapped packages of herbs and bandages and started piling them in Corwin's arms. A cart passed in the street, splattering mud while the clatter of wheels bounced off the upper stories of the buildings around us. I turned my hip expertly so the mud only splashed the bottom edge of my brown cloak.

But Corwin got the brunt of it.

He laughed good-naturedly while I brushed feebly at his green jacket.

"It's all right. Maybe I'll blend in more this way. Why don't you people ever wear bright colors?"

I shrugged, letting the "you people" slide right off. "Lots of people wear bright colors. Just not while traveling. And some colors are reserved for special things. Just like the royalty in Valeria are the only ones allowed to wear indigo."

"Like red here. That one belongs to the blood mages."

My hands stilled. "Yes."

"And to whoever those fellows are."

I spun to follow his pointing finger.

Across the street, two *viona krovaya* stalked among the pedestrians, rust-red jackets hard to miss and clubs hanging from their wide black belts.

I gasped and hauled his hand down so he wouldn't draw their attention. "Yes, yes, the blood swords. Er, loosely translated." I kept hold of his hand as I searched the storefronts on our side of the street, then I hauled him toward an alley.

"I thought we still had to go to that other apothecary," he said.

"We do." There really wasn't any reason to run. It's not like the *viona krovaya* could tell just by looking at me...unless Blagoy had sent them my description from Elisaveta. "I think we can save time going this way." The words came out thick, my tongue heavy in my dry mouth.

I didn't let go of his hand until we reached the end of the building. I expected the alley to lead eventually to the next street over, but we came up against the back of another brick building, narrow passageways stretching on either side of us.

"Um." I plunged left on a whim and raced down the skinny path. My breath hissed through my teeth even though I knew the *viona krovaya* couldn't have seen where we'd gone. It just made my skin crawl to think of walking down the same street as them, having their gaze slide over me, a thin layer of fabric between me and all my crimes being registered.

"Do you think we should have turned right back there instead of left?" Corwin asked, eying the darkening buildings around us. Piles of trash lined the alley and a couple of them looked like they might get up and scuttle away if we got too close.

My pace slowed. A stack of crates and a broken cart blocked the space ahead, forcing us down a corridor between another two buildings. A block down, the alley opened up but not into a park or another street. A building had been torn down and packed in its place was a squalid little city.

Battered crates and boxes connected by boards formed drafty walls and ragged burlap hung overhead, keeping out some of the chill and most of the light. Men with hollow cheeks and women with chapped lips and fingers turned to watch our slowing approach. I couldn't be sure in the dim light and from this distance, but I could guess that some had a thin, rust-colored ring around their irises.

The sharp panic in my chest receded, replaced by the heavier ache of dread. I knew these faces. Not personally, but despair and hopelessness looked the same whether they belonged to Valeria or Ballaslav.

"Definitely should have turned right," Corwin whispered, his body pressed against my arm. For once, I didn't mind the physical contact.

"*Isavit*," I said, my feet reversing on the slick cobbles.

"What?"

"It means 'correct' or 'you've got that right' or 'hell yes.' Pick whichever one you like best."

"As long as it's followed by 'let's get out of here,' I don't care."

My gaze caught on one pitiful figure among the dozen, and I gulped against the knot in my throat. "Wait."

He hissed in impatience as I stepped forward, but I ignored him.

A girl huddled against one of the makeshift walls just in front of us, her lank brown hair straggling across her damp face. She had wrapped bloody rags around each of her arms. The others in the alley all still had enough strength and pride to draw back when we'd stumbled in here. But this one just stared blankly.

I knelt beside her. She flinched away, and I held up my empty hands.

"It's all right," I murmured. "I'm not going to hurt you."

From the shivering, the clammy skin, and the glazed eyes, she was clearly feverish. She didn't smell like vomit, so hopefully, it wasn't one of the fatal bowel-rending diseases so feared in the city.

But the wounds under her makeshift bandages looked all too familiar.

"Reyna," Corwin said, voice rising. "I was serious about the leaving thing."

"I have to do something for her," I said. The racing, rushing drive that had chased me in here had died in the face of her need, and my hands were steady as I reached for her arm.

She shuddered but let me extend her elbow and unwrap the sodden cloth. The wounds weren't new but they still bled freely. How much blood had she lost already? That could explain the fever.

"The package we bought at the apothecary. Can you open it and leave it within arm's reach? Then step back. Unless you want to go through the Blood Rites for your research."

He didn't answer. He just did as I asked, sliding the open paper package across the muddy cobbles.

Bandages, a mixture of mint and yarrow to clean the wounds, and a spell to close them until her body did the rest.

If it ever would. Depending on how many times she'd been used already, her body might not know how to close itself anymore, and she'd be dead by nightfall no matter what I did here.

I shook away the fatalistic thought and gently cleaned her cuts. The *vytl* released from the spilling of blood should have hung in the air, taunting and tempting me, but it had all been used already.

I wrapped her arms in clean bandages and sent another

spell through her body to burn out the sickness. At least without that to fight, she had a chance to survive.

"Who did this to you?" I whispered as I wiped my hands and gathered up the open packages. "Someone here?"

Her eyes widened. "It—it was an accident."

I snorted. The lie wasn't even original.

"Cuts that won't heal, reoccurring illness, fever. I've seen a blood mage's goat before. It's hard to forget the signs."

Especially when my own wounds took longer to heal than usual. Any longer on the path I'd been on and I'd have looked a lot like this girl.

"You don't have to tell me if it will put you in danger," I said. "But you should leave this place. There are people who can help you get away." I'd take her myself if she gave me the slightest sign she wanted to leave.

She stared down at her clenched fingers and shook her head.

"You want him to do this again?" I took her arm and made her look at the fresh white bandages. "Isn't going through the Rites better than being his goat?"

Corwin coughed and hacked as if he were trying to get rid of a lung, and I looked up to see a man settle himself against the makeshift wall above us.

Mud and other things I didn't want to name stained his ragged breeches, and his neckcloth hadn't been white in a very long time. Washing his neck probably would have helped, but this guy looked like he'd sooner kiss a pig than take a bath. If the pig didn't run away first. He'd tied his filthy hair back with a length of string, and he grinned down at me with crooked yellow teeth.

Though his smile wasn't what made me shiver. It was the bright red ring surrounding his irises that did that. Sunlight revealing the worst of his soul.

"You trying to scare off my goat?" he said, voice quiet and pleasant.

The girl shrank into herself, folding her arms against her chest.

I raised my chin. I could rail against him for how wrong it was to bleed someone for *vytl*. I could tell him it was illegal; it was damaging him as well as her. But anyone who bore the ring of Blood Lust knew exactly what they were doing. You couldn't look in the mirror and ignore the physical sign of your actions.

"She's going to die if you keep using her," I said. The only argument that might mean something to him. "And people will ask questions."

He crouched beside the girl and leaned toward me. "You want to replace her?" he said, leering at me.

"I would make a poor goat," I said, refusing to let him see how I shook inside.

"Aw, you sell yourself short, *blenni*."

I flinched. No one had called me that since Luka and the endearment held too many memories.

His fingers reached out to caress my hand where it rested on the open package, and I jerked back before he could make contact. He smiled and looked down. Then fell still.

"Or maybe you don't," he said, quiet voice filled with glee. "Because you're not like her, are you? You're like me."

I glanced down to see my sleeve ruched up, revealing the first thin scar.

I yanked my sleeve down, heart pounding. "I'm nothing like you," I said, forcing the words between my clenched teeth. I hauled my supplies toward me and surged to my feet.

"I won't tell," he said, standing as well. He held out his hands soothingly. Like we were friends. "There's safety in numbers, *blenni*. As well as comfort and provision." He gestured down at the girl. "My mamat taught me to share my toys."

I gagged. "You're disgusting."

I went to push past him, but he planted his feet to block my way. If I wanted to force the issue, I would have to touch him, and I already had goosebumps from his proximity.

Corwin's eyes were wide as they darted between the two of us and the girl. I could only be glad he didn't speak a word of Ballaslavian.

"You won't have to hide for long," the blood mage said. "We're going to be on top soon. You can join us and be part of the greatest thing to happen in Ballaslav since the Bloody Epoch."

Considering the blood mages had nearly killed everyone in Ballaslav during that particularly gruesome era, I wanted no part of it.

"Let me pass," I said. Every spell I knew was for healing, not self-defense. And the amount of power I could draw wouldn't impress him. Not with his eyes brimming with the *vytl* he'd stolen from the girl.

"Or what?" His teeth creaked as his smile widened.

A familiar voice spoke amiably from the other side of the makeshift wall. "Or I send to meet O'in with several missing body parts. I'll let you decide which I lop off first."

Karina stepped around the wall, an ax in each hand, clearly *viona uchenye*. Trained to make her threat a reality.

The blood mage backed away, his hands raised. "Easy," he said. "I was just talking with the lady. Thought she might like another option."

"I think you made a mistake."

He shrugged and backed away another step. "Maybe. But how was I supposed to know she didn't belong here?"

"How about when she told you 'no.'" Karina jerked her head at Corwin and me, and we scuttled toward the alley we'd come down in the first place. Karina followed, slowly, her eyes never leaving the man's face.

When we got to the end of the alley, I turned to check Karina, but she shook her head and grated out, "Go."

She didn't let us slow down until we reached the street where we could disappear amidst the carts and carriages and pedestrians.

"How did you find us?" I asked, speaking Valerian as a courtesy to Corwin.

"I followed," she said, her eyes surveying everything from the passing carts to the second-story windows of the shops.

I stopped in surprise. "You followed us from the caravansary?"

Karina glared and I hurried on. "I protect the caravan and it's people. That doesn't just mean on the road."

I tugged the edges of my cloak tighter around me. If she'd been with us the whole time, what had she heard in that alley?

"You could have said something. Let us know you were there."

She shrugged without meeting my eyes. "Sometimes it's better if the one you want to protect doesn't know you're there. Then they can't give you away to the enemy."

I opened my mouth to protest, then glanced at Corwin, who wore every fleeting emotion as a banner across his face. I hid a wince.

"Thank you for the rescue," Corwin said, beaming at the *viona*.

"You're welcome," Karina said. "Though the *ublyduk* had a point. How was he supposed to know you didn't belong if you just waltzed right in?"

"We didn't waltz," Corwin said. "We took a wrong turn."

"And why didn't you turn and get out the moment you realized your mistake?" Karina said.

I clenched my fists in my skirt, lifting the hem out of the muck in the street. "I had to help," I said, quietly. "She needed what I could give her."

"Even if it was wasted on a goat?" Karina said under her breath.

I inhaled through my nose, lips pressed thin as cold spread through me. "She was a victim. You think she's worthless just because she's been used by a blood mage?" How worthless would she think I was then?

I'd stopped again and a woman carrying a loaded basket glared as she swerved around me.

Karina flushed. "I did not mean she was worthless. Only that your healing was wasted. She will probably die the next time she's bled."

"Her death would have been certain if I hadn't helped."

"And now you have to go through the Blood Rites. Was it worth it?"

"Is it worth it to you?" I snapped. "When you have to go through the Rites after every fight?"

"Of course." She stared back at me.

"Exactly." I threw up my hands and spun to step into the street between a passing cart and a rider.

"Careful." Karina snatched the hood of my cloak, pulling me off balance so I had to stumble back a step. The cart thumped into a puddle and sent up a spray of muddy water higher than my head, which splashed down on the cobbles where I'd been standing.

I glowered at the wet sidewalk, Corwin teetering beside me. Karina just folded her arms.

"You have got to be the most annoying guardian angel ever," I said, enunciating each word deliberately.

Karina's lips wobbled like she couldn't decide whether to laugh or frown. "You...you think I'm a guardian angel?"

"I think you are frustrating and stubborn and have the most uncanny knack for being in the right place at the right time," I said. "So don't you dare mock my calling and my sacrifice when I try to do the exact same thing. *Viona uchenye* aren't the only protectors out there."

She blinked at me before she finally grunted. "Hmm. Then maybe I should teach you to wield a sword like one."

It didn't mean I'd won the argument. But she hadn't either. And at this point, I'd accept a draw.

CHAPTER FIVE

A *dom'ychist* attendant poured tepid water over my head, and I sang the ritualistic words of my cleansing through chattering teeth. "O'in forgive me. O'in wash me. O'in work in me and make me new."

The prayer rang hollow against tiled walls, nearly lost in the splash of water.

My thoughts always failed to stay on track at this point. Why was I asking Their forgiveness? I'd done nothing wrong. Unless it was wrong to help someone who was hurting. But every healer knew that wasn't true. It was only the Law that said we were unclean after touching blood. And the world that thanked us for our sacrifice and our sin.

A threadbare towel swung in front of me and I took it, careful not to touch the attendant who handed it to me. I stood and stepped from the worn metal tub and wrapped the thin towel around my soaked, secondhand shift.

The clatter of my movements echoed against the cracked tiles, and below me, clear water trickled through a drain in the floor. The attendant could have heated the water. She could have stoked the coals in the braziers at the edges of the room, but apparently, a healer who sullied herself to help a blood mage's goat didn't deserve such luxuries.

I tried to remind myself that this was still a far cry better than the last time I'd gone through the Blood Rites. Then I'd had only myself, a bare rock for a shelf, and a mountain spring I'd had to skim the ice off.

I'd already thanked Evgenia profusely. She had no reason to pay for my visit to the *dom'ychist* since the person I'd healed wasn't even part of the caravan. But she'd insisted, and since I wouldn't have been able to afford even this place on my salary, I hadn't argued. Much.

The attendant opened the door, and I stepped into another dim room lined with water-stained benches. "I will collect you after your time of contemplation and reflection," the attendant said, voice loud in the quiet room.

"Thank you," I said.

I settled myself on a bench as she walked through a door on the opposite wall.

This was the part where I was supposed to think of my sins and the nature of forgiveness. Except, what had I done wrong? The attendant would say it was helping a blood mage's goat. Karina would say it was walking into a situation I couldn't get out of.

Both of them would be right, but not in the way they thought.

My sin wasn't helping someone who didn't deserve it. It was the secret desire, the temptation that slid under the good intentions and rotted them from the inside out.

My thumb slid under the wet sleeve of my shift and found the raised edge of the first scar. There was my sin.

I lay under the blanket in my rented room in Valeria, biting back tears. This week had been bad. We'd had an early cold snap in the fall and every joint below my waist ached with it. I could barely bend my knees or fit my swollen feet into my shoes.

Knowing there was nothing left, I whispered the last words of a spell and twisted my fingers in the appropriate configuration. But spells needed power, *vytl*. And only a wisp of it answered my summons. I'd used everything nearby, and the spell failed in the empty air, the released components stinging my hands as they dissipated.

I curled into a ball, my head too heavy to lift. Exams loomed tomorrow and I couldn't even stand. If I didn't pass my tests, I couldn't continue to take classes. And how could I expect to be a healer if I couldn't get out of bed some days?

O'in help me, I needed another answer. I needed energy and healing. I needed *vytl*.

No. I could do it. I just had to push through.

I nudged the covers out of the way and rolled to the edge of the bed. Squeezing my eyes shut against the stabbing in my knees, I levered myself to my feet and paused to catch my breath. Just one more step, then I could collapse in my chair.

I fumbled for the edge of the desk, misjudged the distance, and knocked a glass to the floor. It shattered in a burst of sound and crystal, and I lost my balance and fell, palms skidding across the floor.

I landed in a heap and curled in on myself, crying. I couldn't even get across the room; how would I ever be a healer?

I lifted my hand to see a single drop of blood on my palm and a jagged bit of glass sticking from my skin. With a gasp, I pulled it out.

It was kind of funny, laying on the worn rug, watching the shining blood well up and trickle across my palm. In the notes I'd been trying to get to, there was a list of all the natural sources of *vytl* in the world. There was the usual: plants and, to a lesser extent, the earth and rocks themselves. But there were others as well. Animals. And humans.

More specifically, their blood.

Blood released *vytl* into the world.

Staring at my hand, I called up my spell again. Just as an experiment. Just to see what would happen. I squeezed my fingers, letting the blood slide between them. You couldn't see *vytl*. It was an invisible force. But I could imagine it drifting up into the air, filling my room with power.

I inhaled as the threads of the healing spell strengthened and held. It was such a small spell in the face of my illness, but it worked this time. And...and this wasn't bad. It wasn't like I was hurting anyone. It was helping me study, that's all.

Still, it wasn't quite enough. I couldn't stand yet, and I didn't want to drag myself into my chair.

Without thinking too hard about it, I let my hand creep for my healer's bag, which lay beside the bed. Within arm's reach. My fingers closed around the smooth haft of my healer's knife.

Everyone who grew up in Ballaslav would tell me the name for what I was doing. *I* knew what I was doing. But surely something so evil would *feel* evil. It wouldn't feel like curiosity. Or relief.

Mabushka would kill me.

But Mabushka had always been strong. She didn't know what it was like to need more. To reach deep and find yourself empty.

I wasn't changing anything about myself to do this. I wasn't accepting that evil into me. I just needed a boost. Something small and easy to get me through to the next day.

If it was awful, I'd stop. If it didn't work, I wouldn't do it again.

I pulled a roll of bandages out of the bag first. No reason to be an idiot about this. My knife's edge gleamed in the candlelight.

I laid it against the skin of my wrist and closed my eyes. Mabushka always said, 'if you have to close your eyes to do something, maybe you should think about it twice.'

Best not to think of her right now.

I sliced down.

Da'ermo, I'd expected pain but not quite like that. The knife clattered to the ground as I spoke the words of the spell again, gathering the newly released *vytl* from the air. Power rushed through me, and I took a deep clear breath as the pain in my legs faded.

Now, I could sit up straight. A healing spell for swelling

leaped from my tongue, and I laughed as my feet returned to their normal size and color.

I wrapped the bandage around my wrist and gathered my scattered notes. There was still time to study for my exams. I stood and stumbled to my desk, ignoring the tears pouring down my cheeks.

I deserved the shivers that shook my body in the dim room of the *dom'ychist*. That had been my sin. And this was my punishment.

I'd thought I was so clever. I'd thought I could do what thousands of mages had done before, but I could do it without becoming someone evil. I'd thought I was strong enough. Good enough. Could anyone be more self-deluding than me? I'd stayed at the University long enough to know there was no spell to turn back time. No way to go back and fix what turned out to be the biggest mistake of my life.

I could only go forward. Go home and start over. And hope and pray Mabushka and Eira could forgive the truth once I was finally brave enough to tell them.

The attendant opened the door, holding out a sprig of hyssop tied with a white ribbon.

I stood, wiping my cheeks and eyes and walked out the door.

CHAPTER SIX

Two weeks to home had felt like a lifetime back in Elisaveta, but as we neared Darayevo, the time seemed to stream past me until the caravan stopped on a muddy track just a couple hours from town.

"You won't stay and eat one last meal with us?" Evgenia said from the door of the heart's blood wagon.

I fastened my satchel and smiled ruefully. "Home is less than an hour's walk west," I said. "I'd like to surprise my grandmother and sister for dinner."

Evgenia's eyes softened. "Of course. You be safe in the woods from here to there, all right? Maybe I should send Karina with you, in case there are bandits."

I shook my head. "They'd be looking for richer targets than me. I've left the supplies under the bunk for your next healer."

Evgenia bit her lip. "If you ever need a job again," she said. "You know most of our route now and where to find us. You're always welcome."

Her kindness made a lump in my throat. The woman knew hardly anything about me but she'd given me a place in her caravan and treated me like family.

"Thank you, *sudinya*," I said and gave her a quick curtsy. "For everything."

Her mouth screwed up. "Oh," she said and surged forward to envelop me in a hug before I could dart away. "Who will I fuss over without you here?"

"The whole caravan I'm sure. And Aleksei will be here soon, right?" Karina had called her mamat back when I'd first met them, and it had only grown more appropriate. Evgenia had that no-nonsense attitude mixed with a healthy dose of care that I remembered from my own mother.

She pulled back and nodded, all business again. "You'd better get going if you want to get there before nightfall. I'll go rouse Pyotr and make sure he sees you off."

She bustled from the wagon, and I took one last look around, strangely reluctant to leave. Was I checking to be sure I hadn't left anything behind? It's not like I had much to misplace. No extra stockings or errant underwear. My satchel was packed, a little heavier from Evgenia and Pyotr's generous salary.

I smoothed the blue and yellow checkered quilt on the bunk and took out the present I'd made for Aleksei. Hopefully, the toy would help him feel more at home with the caravan. I settled the stuffed gray dog on the pillow and left the wagon, closing the door behind me.

Pyotr gave me a gruff hug and told me to be careful. As I walked down the line of wagons stopped on the road just for me, the driver who played the fiddle grinned and tipped his hat. Ivan leaned over from the heart's blood wagon seat and called a spirited goodbye, and the *viona uchenye* gave me their own individual salutes of respect.

Karina stood at the corner of the main road and the one that led into the woods where my grandmother lived. She pointed down the muddy track. "Stay on the ground beside the road. You're less likely to get your boots sucked off that way."

I rolled my eyes. Everyone who grew up in Ballaslav knew that.

"Keep your ears open. Just because you're not carrying anything doesn't mean someone won't try to take what's left."

"I'll be fine, Karina."

"Sure you will," she said. "But if someone grabs you from behind, you stomp on their foot, like this, and when they let go, you slam the heel of your hand into their nose, like this." She took my hand to demonstrate.

I pulled away with an exasperated sigh. "Why are you imagining me set upon by thugs, ruffians, and men who want to steal my last reyev?"

She shrugged and her face turned sheepish. "I was trained to plan for the worst."

I rubbed my hands down my skirt, feeling like there was so much more here than what we both let settle on the surface. I'd imagined her as my angel, but I hadn't really tried to talk to her since we'd bickered in Zhivko.

Karina rubbed the back of her neck and glanced at me. "Look, I know we haven't really seen things the same way, but stay out of trouble. Remember the trick with your hand."

She turned to leave.

"Not much of a goodbye," I said.

She paused. "No, it isn't. But then we might see each other again, right?"

I crossed my arms as she walked away. Maybe I wasn't the only one to blame for not becoming friends. Did the *viona's* training addle their brains?

I shook my head on the mystery and headed off down the track. Behind me, the drivers called out, the wagons creaked, and the caravan started moving again.

I kept to the edges of the track where the ground was firmer as Karina had suggested. In the years we'd grown up here, I'd always walked between Mabushka's and Darayevo. This turn of the road gave me a shortcut, though. At the scummy pond fondly called "Suka's Mistake," I turned to cut through the woods. I'd get there with pine needles on my cloak, but I'd arrive before dark.

I raised my nose and sniffed the air. From here, I ought to be able to smell the woodsmoke from the fire and whatever Mabushka was cooking for dinner.

I frowned. That was woodsmoke all right, but old and damp smelling. Had Eira not dried the wood properly again?

I leaped the small creek that backed up against the yard and peered between the trees. Why were there no lights? And it was so quiet. Usually, Eira sang while she cooked and Mabushka grumbled about not being able to hear herself think.

I fetched up against the back fence and stared, my mouth dropping open.

"No," I whispered.

Blackened timbers speared the sky where our roof had once been, and the walls had crumbled to charcoal.

I tumbled over the fence and raced to the ruined house. "Mabushka!" I scrambled up the cracked foundation stones and pushed through fragile walls, my hands turning black from the soot. "Eira!"

The fireplace still stood, though dark and cold now, and I recognized the copper kettle gleaming from the ashes. "Mabushka." Fist-sized cinders crunched under my boots as I sifted through the wreckage, searching for signs of my sister and grandmother.

What would be left? My heart stuttered. Bones? Bodies? *Pohomzhet da ma Baud.* Had the fire taken the house that quickly? In the night? Would they have had time to get out? Maybe I'd find them at one of the neighbors.

My hand clenched my bodice over my chest. Yes. That's where I should look. I shouldn't panic. I shouldn't assume the worst.

The light had faded while I'd searched and, now, I stood in the burnt ruins of our house in deepening twilight. Purple shadows reached for me from the crumbling corners, and I tripped over the slanted edge of our table as I tried to make my way out of the house.

A rustling in the woods caught my attention as I righted myself, and I froze where I stood. Was that a figure standing between the trees or a sapling that I didn't remember? For the first time, it crossed my mind that this might not have been an accident. If someone had burned the house down on purpose, they could have come back to finish the job.

I peered into the woods, but nothing moved.

A whispered voice behind me made me jump.

"It was someone calling. I'm sure of it."

I turned. A dirt path led from our front door to the main track into the village. A couple of dim shapes stood on that path now.

"Hey, don't go poking around our house," another voice said. "Haven't you done enough damage?"

I gasped. "Eira?"

A pause. "Reyna?"

I stumbled out of the burnt wreckage as my fair-haired sister rushed forward. We collided on the blackened front step, throwing our arms around each other. My breath shuddered against her shoulder as relief swept through me. She was warm and solid and alive.

"I thought you were dead," I said, my voice thick. "I thought you burned with the house."

"Reyna, what are you doing here?" Eira pulled back, not out of my arms but far enough to peer into my dirty face. I could well imagine what tears and ash had made of it. "You were supposed to be gone at that University for years."

Her blue eyes matched mine, but she'd started wearing her gold hair in braids pinned to her head, like Mabushka.

"I—I failed my exams," I said. That lie was easier right now than the truth.

Disappointment and censure filled her eyes, and she opened her mouth.

"Where's mabushka?" I said before she could say anything that would make me regret coming home.

Eira's lips thinned, and she glanced over her shoulder. "We...have to talk about that."

I followed her gaze. A young man stood on the path, staring at me. Dark hair curled around his ears, and his hand rested on a broad hunting knife in his belt. He glanced behind me as if he expected someone else to be standing there, too.

I raised an eyebrow at Eira, who flushed in the twilight.

"This is Vitaly," she said. "He moved into his uncle's house, the old Romosk place just after you left. I've been staying there since...Come on. You must be tired. I'll tell you everything at Vitaly's."

"Eira."

She stepped out of my reach and skipped down the step to Vitaly's side.

My fingers clenched, and I concentrated on uncurling them. Mabushka couldn't be dead. Eira wouldn't be treating this so lightly if she were. Would she?

I followed them. Stan Romosk had been our nearest neighbor our entire childhood until he'd up and left right before I'd gone to Valeria. I hadn't known he'd had a nephew. You could see their house from ours when the lights were all lit and vice versa, I imagined.

Vitaly pushed open the door, which stuck a little bit, and cast an apologetic look at me. "Sorry, it's probably not what you're used to."

"She's used to what I'm used to," Eira said. "And besides it's loads better than it was before. Look, you can see the floor now."

Vitaly circled the one-room house, lighting candles while Eira cleared a small table and bade me sit.

"Vitaly's done so much with the place since he came. The roof doesn't leak anymore, and the chimney only whistles when the wind blows from the north."

"Eira." She was a whole year younger than me, but she babbled like a middle-aged housewife. How long did she expect to put me off? She had to talk to me sometime.

"Still, you should have seen it before I got here. Bachelors," she said with a sniff.

"Eira!"

She jumped, her eyes going wide.

I sighed and rubbed my forehead. Maybe this was as hard for her as it was for me and talking about anything else was the only way for her to deal with it.

"It's nice," I said. I could see her touch in the spotless copper pot hanging over the fireplace and the bright rug I remembered her braiding before I left. I frowned. Her favorite shawl lay across the end of the one bed tucked in the corner. "Where do you sleep?"

Vitaly set the biggest candle on the table, his face gone red in the light.

"In the bed, of course," Eira said.

Vitaly cleared his throat. "I sleep on the floor by the door."

Eira gave him a smile and leaned toward me. "He's been a perfect gentleman, Reyna," she whispered. "I promise. And it's not like you were here to defend my virtue."

I winced. Eira hadn't wanted me to go to the University in the first place. She'd argued that I was being selfish and my place was here, with my family. And given everything that had happened here and in Valeria, she was right.

I put my head in my hands. "Eira, what happened?"

Eira's face fell, and Vitaly pulled up a stool to sit next to her. He whispered something in her ear, and her mouth firmed. "Men came at night," she said. "Almost a week ago now. We were asleep, and they pulled Mabushka and me from our beds and out to the yard." Her voice caught, and she buried her head in her hands.

Vitaly murmured to her, his arm around her shoulders.

When she finally spoke, my pulse beat in my ears. "They had such strange eyes. Even in the torchlight, I could see the red. They wanted to know where you were." Her gaze focused on me. "Their leader kept asking for my sister. Said you'd come back eventually. Why were they looking for you?"

I shook my head in bewilderment. Why would the blood mages here want me? How could they possibly know what I was? What I'd done?

"What happened then?" I said, fighting to keep my voice from shaking.

"Vitaly came." Eira smiled at him. He blushed again. "I broke away from one of the men and ran toward the woods. And Vitaly was there. Reyna, he was amazing. He kept them from getting me."

"I couldn't keep them from burning the house, though," Vitaly said, brow furrowed.

"We watched," Eira said, head bowed.

"Why?" I said. "If they were looking for me, why burn the house?"

"They didn't want you to have anywhere to go."

I chewed my lip. I knew what she was saying, I just didn't want it to be true. "Eira, where's Mabushka?"

"They took her," she whispered. "They said if you wanted her back, you'd have to go get her."

CHAPTER SEVEN

"Why do they want you, Reyna?" Eira said as I paced Vitaly's little cottage from one wall to the other.

"I don't know. It could be...it kind of makes sense that they'd be connected." The two worst parts of my life entwined. "But how would they know? Unless..."

Luka. I'd told him all sorts of things in our time together, including where I'd lived and the family I'd left behind.

"Reyna?"

I shook my head. I did not want to have this conversation. Not now.

Eira huffed. "Right, because being all moody and mysterious is really helpful right now."

I glared at her, but she was right. "I got into some trouble in Valeria with some...not nice people."

"You think it's related."

I frowned and moved to the little window, shuttered now that it was dark. "It's the only thing I can think of. But I don't know how it could be. They're all back in Valeria."

And it didn't matter who these men were anyway. They had Mabushka. And I had no choice.

I stopped pacing and snatched up my woefully empty satchel.

"What are you going to do?" Eira said.

"What they want," I said. "I assume they told you where I should go to get Mabushka back."

Eira bounced up from her chair. "Are you going to blast them away?" She twiddled her fingers in a mockery of spellwork.

"Eira." I rolled my eyes. "I'm a healer. Not a battle-mage. I'm going to go in there and talk to them."

"And then what?" She put her hands on her hips. "Ask them nicely to give Mabushka back? If they want a ransom, we don't have the money to pay. Unless you acquired some wealthy patron down south."

I scowled and opened my bag so she could see the meager store of coins at the bottom. "I was broke by the time I made it over the mountains. If they want a ransom, all I have to trade is myself." And I would if they'd take me.

Eira's shoulders slumped.

Vitaly stood and took a cloak from a peg by the door. "I can show you where they hide. But I don't think you should go alone."

Eira snatched a gray cloak from another peg. "She's not going alone. If they want her, they'll have to take me, too. And of course, you're coming to protect us." She grinned and stood on tiptoe to kiss his cheek.

I pressed my lips together to keep from laughing at Vitaly's face. He really must have been a gentleman. Otherwise, he wouldn't blush hard enough to set the house on fire every time my sister flirted with him.

Eira and Vitaly led the way through the dark forest, past the Yaralev's house, and the Gesparo's, all just a little different than I remembered. Enough to make me jump when they appeared before I was ready for them.

We passed the looming bulk of the sawmill, the creek gurgling past the wheel that would drive the saw during the day. It sucked and slurped its way down past our burned house.

Several minutes later, the trees thinned and the moon illuminated a pile of rock we'd climbed and explored as children. Air moved through through the stones with a low moan. We'd called it *Dya'val dal Kuchnya*. Devil's Kitchen.

Vitaly pointed to a crevice between two large stones that leaned against each other like a doorway to hell.

"Inside is a—"

Eira rolled her eyes. "She knows what's inside, Vitaly. Genadi Yaralev blocked us in one summer. It took us the whole day to find the other opening in the back and squeeze out. We went home crying and Papa stormed over to the Yaralev's. I thought he was going to kill Genadi."

"I'd never seen him so angry," I said, focusing on the memory, not on the creeping feeling of horror. As though I'd already walked through the stone doorway and the walls were closing in around me.

"I don't think he'd ever seen you so frightened." She moved closer to me. "You don't have to go in alone. I'll be right next to you, all right?"

I gave her a weak smile. The experience trapped underground hadn't affected her at all. I was the only one carrying baggage from Genadi Yaralev's prank.

But I wasn't a child anymore, and I'd learned a trick or two since I was eight. I spoke a word and twisted my fingers and a ball of mage light appeared over my outstretched palm. I was a healer primarily, but useful spells weren't picky about who used them.

Despite Eira's brave words, she stepped closer to my light. Vitaly grinned sheepishly.

"Guess we won't need these," he said, digging in his breeches pocket and producing a box of matches.

I bit my lip. "I don't think you should come with us, Vitaly."

His lips hardened and a muscle in his jaw jumped. "Of course I'm coming."

"She's right," Eira said, surprising me. "They're not expecting you. You could scare them into doing something to Mabushka. You stay out here and guard the door. If something happens and we need you, we'll yell."

Her wiles didn't work on him this time. He shook his head. "I'm not letting you go in there alone."

"And I'm not letting you risk Mabushka's life."

They glared at each other. An owl hooted behind the pile of rocks and his stance relaxed a fraction. "Fine," he said. Though he didn't seem happy about it. "But be careful."

Eira snorted, and I just kept myself from doing the same. What else would we be?

I stepped forward with my light and ducked to avoid hitting my head on the stone above me, Eira so close behind me she nearly tread on my boots.

Two paces in, a shiver of *vytl* raised the hair on my arms. They must have set a ward spell to warn them of someone's approach.

"They know we're coming," I said.

The stone passage closed in and my breath came in shorter and shorter gasps. I looked up and smacked my head on an outcrop. My breath hissed through my teeth as I rubbed the spot gingerly.

Eira put a hand on my shoulder, and I took a second to catch my breath. This place had stood solid for as many years as I had been alive, probably many more. It wouldn't come down around our ears just because I felt like a bug in a jar. The light bounced off the irregular walls and finally dropped away into the interior cavern.

I stepped from the passage and forced away my shivers. It was better here where the walls sloped away. The men who'd made this place their home had dug out the soft silt underneath and the interior was much bigger now. Crates and bedrolls littered the edges of the cave, evidence of a lengthy habitation.

"Mabushka," Eira whispered behind me.

Several men lounged against the back wall of the cavern. In front of them, directly in the center of the open space, stood a table. One man sat there, his hands idly playing with the ends of a long rope. Mabushka sat tied to the other end.

"See, Eira," the man said with a toothy grin. "I told you she'd be back."

Eira flinched and took a step sideways, placing me between her and the man. His rough breeches and patched coat told me he was a worker at the mill. The rust-red ring around his brown eyes, barely visible in the dim light, told me he was a blood mage.

"I'm here," I said. "Now what do you want?"

The man raised his dark eyes to the ceiling before he leaned toward Mabushka. "Leave home for a while and they forget all their manners, don't they?"

Mabushka sat ramrod straight in her chair. Her gray-brown hair straggled from the braids she always wore pinned to her head, but her blue eyes blazed.

"Reyna, be nice to the nasty blood mage," Mabushka said, her Ballaslavian still tinged with a Valerian accent.

The man glared at her. "Let's start over." He gave me a mocking half-bow from his seated position. "I'm *Dryg* Emil."

I wouldn't call any man "friend" who kidnapped my grandmother and terrorized my sister. But I had to play his game for now. "Reyna," I said.

He used his boot to push an extra chair my way. "Have a seat."

"I'm comfortable where I am, thank you."

He shrugged. "Have it your way. Just thought you might like to rest your feet."

"I only plan to be here as long as it takes you to tell me what you want with my family."

He sighed. "You obviously haven't read the script. I'm supposed to give you the whole recruitment spiel. Magic and glory and freedom and all that."

"Why don't you skip to the good parts?"

His jaw clenched. "I'm a member of an organization. A powerful organization the rulers of this country would do well not to anger."

I raised my eyebrows at this ragtag little band of kidnappers. "I can see that."

His lips thinned. "And we need people like you."

"Broke and desperate?"

"Smart and mobile." He quirked a smile. "Though desperate helps, too."

I waved a hand around the cave. "And what does your organization do? Besides lurk in shadows."

"We gather the power we deserve. The power the rest of the world is too scared to use."

I went still, the humor fleeing our conversation like a startled cat. A draft ghosted through the cavern from the tiny back entrance, and Emil's smile grew, sending a shiver down my spine. My gaze scurried over the men lining the back wall. Every one of them had the rusty red ring around his irises.

Blood mages were notoriously defensive about their power. They never worked together, never shared. When the miller shorted you your flour, you told your friends "he shares like a blood mage." When he was hung for weighting his bags with lead, you shook your head and said, "he succumbed to a blood mage's greed."

When I'd walked in here, it hadn't occurred to me what it meant that a *group* of blood mages had kidnapped my grandmother.

They were working together.

Toward what?

"I'd like to take my grandmother home now." It was worth a shot.

Emil sighed. "And I'd love to let you take her, Reyna. I

can see where you get your manners. But see, my organization is short on recruits this month."

"Let her go and you can have me."

His lips pulled in amusement as Mabushka made a distressed noise in the back of her throat. "That's very generous of you, but it's not really what I want."

I blinked. I'd been sure... "What do you want, then?" I said through my teeth.

He lifted his hand and one of the other blood mages stepped forward to place a leather folio in it. "I need a messenger."

He held the folio out to me.

I swallowed. "Why me? Why not my grandmother, or Eira, or anyone else in the world?"

He tilted his head at Mabushka. "This one's creaky, and that one's..." He considered Eira, who cowered behind my right shoulder. "Flighty. We wanted someone more reliable."

"And what's in these messages?"

"Just plans. Communications. Things we'd rather not have the *viona krovaya* aware of."

There was a lot more to it than that, or they'd have picked anyone they came across. But I was afraid to push. Afraid of what they might know about me and what they might tell. I didn't want the *viona krovaya* looking too close at me, either. That was probably a large part of why they'd picked me.

"Are you missing the script again?" Emil said. "This is the part where you say, 'why would I ever work for you?'"

"I've read ahead, and I think I know the answer to that already." And that's why they wouldn't trade me for Mabushka. They needed her to keep me in line.

"Oh, but it's so fun to threaten." He flicked a slim, sharp blade from a sheath at his waist and laid it against Mabushka's hand. Her thin skin puckered with the pressure. A drop of blood welled up, and Emil closed his eyes and breathed deep.

The trickle of released *vytl* made every blood mage in the room stand at attention. I swallowed down bile.

"Do we have a deal...*Dryg* Reyna?"

The despicable choice raged within me. Except it wasn't really a choice. Save myself or save Mabushka? Their claws sank deep, dictating my actions.

But how could I do anything—even something so innocuous—for those who'd thrown away the basic laws of humanity? How could I even brush against that evil when I'd finally escaped it?

I'd lost so much of myself to it already, and spent so much of myself to get away from it, I couldn't see how there was anything left for it to cling to.

But alongside the duty and the self-sacrifice, a shameful hope sprang up. If I joined them, I could work to free Mabushka. If I joined them, I could save her.

If I joined them, I could feel the power flow over my damaged skin again. Touch it, taste it, succumb to its sweet sickness.

I buried that thought as deep as I could and kept my eyes on Mabushka's frightened face.

I stepped forward and took the folio from him. "We have a deal."

CHAPTER EIGHT

Karina stayed in the narrow back passage of the cave while Reyna and her sister left with the folio. Through the jagged space in front of her, she could see the blood mage, Emil, and Reyna's grandmother.

The old woman glared at the man. "She's too smart to be caught by you for long."

Emil laughed. "My dear, Adelle, Reyna created her own trap and walked right into it."

Adelle's jaw clenched. "What do you mean?"

"You should ask her next time you get to see her."

As the band of blood mages settled down for the rest of the night, Karina slowly and carefully wormed her way down the passage toward fresh air. She moved so her boots and the leather of her jerkin didn't scrape the rock and alert the *ispor'chennai* below.

Near the top of the passage, she found the slight whorls in the dirt indicating a spell had been placed there. As she'd done the first time, she dug in her pocket and pulled out the simple wooden button that served as her spell focus. She pressed her thumb to its surface and whispered the trigger word.

Her spell released a burst of *vytl* that disrupted the ward spell, and she crawled across before it could recover. A trick that was as expensive as it was useful.

Karina squeezed carefully through the opening in the rocks and into the bright night. The moon had glided high overhead while they'd been down in the bowels of the earth, and she used its light to retrieve her weapons from the nearby rock where she'd stashed them. She didn't like leaving her axes behind, but the passage had been too narrow for them.

Safely back in the trees, Karina paused to take stock.

So, Reyna was trapped into working for the very blood mages who had kidnapped her grandmother. Didn't that just take the shine off a brand-new blade?

Well, if Reyna wanted to honor her agreement and stay mobile, she really only had one option.

Karina set off toward Darayevo.

I stepped off the stone bridge that spanned the creek and breathed a sigh of relief when I saw the lights of Darayevo glittering in the dark. Even at four in the morning, there were lanterns and torches to guide a weary traveler to civilization.

"Ugh, a piece of ice just stabbed me through the hole in my boot," Eira said behind me. "Why couldn't we have waited at Vitaly's until morning?"

I closed my eyes and counted to ten. I remembered now

why I'd been so anxious to go to Valeria in the first place, and I was having a hard time remembering why I'd fought so hard to convince Eira to come with me now.

We'd gone back to Vitaly's after we'd emerged from the *Dya'val dal kuchnya* and sat around his table, staring at the folio.

"I have to go back to the caravan," I'd said. "It's the only way I'll have the money or the opportunity to get where they're sending me."

"At least you have a contact," Eira said. "Someone you said would hire you again."

"I want you to come with me."

Eira blinked, then she sat back and crossed her arms. "No."

"Eira."

"I'm not the one who likes leaving home," she said. "You are."

My mouth firmed. "That's not the point."

"There are things for me here." Her gaze lifted to Vitaly, who raised his chin.

She was seventeen and she thought she was in love. *Pohomzhet da ma Baud*, who was I to say she wasn't? I wouldn't laugh at her feelings, but this wasn't the time for one of Eira's stubborn fits. If I said no, she'd say yes, just because it was the opposite.

"Eira, if you stay, I can't support you."

"I'm not asking you to."

"Then who will? Do you plan to live here? Is Vitaly ready for a wife?"

Eira bit her lip and gazed up at her protector. Vitaly's face went white, then red.

"I— I—," he said. "Eira, you know I— but I can't—"

Eira dragged in a small surprised breath and turned from him.

My jaw clenched. *Da'ermo*, I'd only meant to point out the obvious logic of Eira's decision. I hadn't meant to damage their fragile romance. "He can't now," I said. "Just not yet. Right, Vitaly?"

Vitaly looked torn, but Eira didn't meet his eyes. *Pohomzhet da ma Baud*, I was only a year older than her. I wasn't supposed to be her matchmaker. That was Mabushka's job.

Vitaly fell to his knees beside Eira. "Go with your sister," he said.

She gave a little cry.

"You'll be safer."

She shook her head, and he cast me a beseeching look.

I took a deep breath and spoke quietly but with as much conviction as I could put into my voice. "If they come back and take you, too, think what they could make me do for them."

"You—You're worried about me?" She peeked at us through her lashes.

Vitaly nodded vigorously. I just held her gaze. It wasn't an exaggeration. If the blood mages took my sister, too...they could order me to burn the world, and I would die in ash and fire trying.

As we left Vitaly's cottage, I felt like the evil baron dragging Svetanka from Anastasy's arms. Vitaly stood at the edge of the road, watching us walk away. We'd only gone twenty paces when Eira whirled from my side and raced back to Vitaly. She flung her arms around his neck and planted her lips on his.

Before he could raise his arms or do more than blink, she'd sobbed and run back to me.

Two hours later, the complaint about the ice was the first thing I'd heard her say.

"Caravan's keep a really tight schedule," I said. "I don't know when they were planning to leave Darayevo, but I don't want to miss them. We'd never catch up." And I'd never find another one that didn't want to check my arms before hiring me.

I glanced at her scowling at her boots as she traversed the rutted road.

"Was that your first kiss?" I said.

"Yes," she said, her voice sullen. "Don't laugh, it's the best I could do."

"I wasn't laughing."

"I'll bet you had loads more practice while you were down south. Do Valerian boys kiss better?"

"I—I don't know." I'd never kissed a Valerian. I glanced at her again. "What was it like?"

She thought for a moment. "His nose was very cold."

I did laugh at that, and she joined me.

Darayevo's caravansary was a step down from Elisaveta's but not the worst we'd seen in the two-week journey from the mountains. The caravans were parked in neat rows in a field on the edge of town, and the big building housing the caravan services was lit up even at this hour.

I asked the sleepy boy holding down the desk where the Grigorsyn caravan was parked. No need to go through the director if Pyotr and Evgenia would hire me again directly.

The sun poked a cautious ray over the horizon as we made our way down the rows of wagons. Cooks were wide awake as their bleary-eyed companions began to stir.

Pyotr manned his pot as usual, the others just emerging out from under the wagons, yawning and stretching in the gray light. Evgenia passed her husband and gave him a peck on the cheek before she saw us and cried out.

"Reyna, what are you doing here?"

I'd planned my story, everything I needed to say, but it all dissolved at the sight of Evgenia's open smile. My lip trembled, and she must have seen a great deal of the truth written across my face.

"Sit, *mushkai*. Have some breakfast." She pulled us to a bench and fetched us two steaming bowls of *memka*.

"I'm sorry, Eva," I said. "You probably thought you were rid of me—"

"Stop that. Tell me what happened."

"Mabushka's gone," I said. "I don't know what to do."

"Oh, *mushka*," she said, sinking to the bench beside me. "I'm so sorry."

"I got home and— and—" Emotion clogged my throat, and I stopped before I started crying. The relief of seeing Eira had circumvented the grief for my home, but now it came back, flooding me so I couldn't speak.

"The house burned," Eira said, flatly.

I swallowed and gestured to her. "This is my sister, Eira. I'm sorry, Evgenia, I didn't know where else to go."

"Here. Of course you should have come here. You know we need a full-time healer, and your sister is welcome, too. You need time and a place to rest and recover."

"Thank you, Eva."

"Have you been walking all night? You can rest in our wagon today. We won't leave Darayevo until tomorrow morning."

Pyotr and Evgenia's wagon was painted with blue and red-feathered birds. They swooped and soared up and down the walls and across the ceiling. Instead of two narrow bunks with a small aisle between, their wagon had one large bed that took up more than half of the space.

"Why did you say that about Mabushka being gone?" Eira said. "She's going to think she's dead."

I pressed my hands to my cheeks as if I could keep myself from flying apart. "I couldn't very well tell her the truth. 'By the way, Evgenia, my grandmother was taken by a group of deranged blood mages who are forcing me to run messages for them.' This way she won't ask questions."

"Might be a little awkward if we ever get Mabushka free and they meet."

I rubbed my forehead. "We'll deal with that when we come to it. We should get some sleep."

Eira sat on the end of the straw mattress and fingered the worn blanket. "It's a little cramped," she said.

"We should be grateful," I said. "Employees sleep under the wagons usually."

"In the mud?"

"It's usually frozen by then," I said with a wicked grin. "The caravan is for transporting goods, not people. There's a couple of wagons for travelers who can pay, but they can't afford to have wagons just for employees to sleep in."

Eira shivered before curling up on the left side of the bed. "And you thought I'd be safer with you. Watch me catch pneumonia and die in less than a week."

I rolled my eyes. "You're not going to die of pneumonia."

She snorted with her eyes closed and rolled over so I couldn't see her face. A clear sign we were done talking.

I settled myself on the other side of the bed and waited while her breathing evened out and her shoulders relaxed. But sleep didn't come for me.

I stared at my satchel which held the damned folio that had taken hold of my life. I'd had no other choice, but that didn't mean I could just ignore the way it made my insides twist.

This association would kill me. And not just because I'd be arrested if the *viona krovaya* ever figured out I was carrying messages for a blood mage rebellion. It would bring me back to the place in myself I'd fought so hard to leave behind in Valeria. Already I could imagine the slime coating my skin, invisible to everyone but me. The others would go on as before, talking with me, laughing with me, all the while oblivious to the fact that I was rotting from the inside, spreading my filth around to my unsuspecting friends.

I buried my face under my arm. I'd already compromised so many people. Evgenia, Pyotr, Karina, Vitaly. Eira.

I slept fitfully for a few hours, the noises of the caravansary waking me every few minutes, while Eira snored gently beside me. When the sun slanted through the tiny window and fell directly on my face, I gave up and rolled off the bunk. Eira dozed on, and I let her sleep. At least it would keep her from thinking about Vitaly.

The two had grown very close while I'd been off making stupid decisions and it made me feel...itchy, like a hair stuck in a shirt. Was their love real? Or was it just the first brush with feelings that were actually returned? Maybe I was just nervous because I hadn't been there to see them meet, to see them flirt, and fall in love.

Eira made decisions on a whim, and I was the one to run after her with the well-laid plans. Maybe I was just playing the role I'd grown used to.

Except I'd given up that role when I'd left her here alone with Mabushka. And I'd come back to find Eira had grown up while I'd been away.

I slipped out the door of the wagon.

This early in the afternoon, the caravansary was deserted. Pyotr and Evgenia were off taking care of caravan business while the drivers and the *viona uchenye* took advantage of their last day in town.

The only one left to stand casual guard over the wagons was Karina. The young woman stood with her back to me, arms raised over her head, fingers stretching toward the sky. Then she slowly bent in half, bringing her nose to her knees.

I glanced at my feet. I probably couldn't even touch my toes if I tried.

"I guess you were right," I said as she straightened gracefully. "About us seeing each other again."

I half expected her to jump in surprise, but I should have known I couldn't sneak up on her. She twisted, putting her hands on her hips and grinning.

"I guess I was," she said.

I rolled my eyes when that seemed like all she wanted to say. I sat on one of the benches surrounding the fire and pulled my cloak around my shoulders.

"What are you doing?" I said.

"Stretching."

"Why?"

She spread her legs and bent sideways, one arm over her head. "Keeps me limber in case I need to fight today."

"Let me guess, you have exercises that keep you quick and strong, too."

"Yep."

"And after you do those, you'll sharpen your axes, just in case."

She stood up and tilted her head. "Your point?"

"Do you do anything other than fight?"

She opened her mouth, but I spoke over her response.

"Or prepare to fight?"

She snapped her mouth shut, and her lips quirked in a self-deprecating grin. "My patron picked me out when I was eight to become *viona uchenye*. I started on hand-to-hand combat and self-defense immediately. When I'd mastered those by age twelve, I picked up my axes. They trained us in history, so we would not repeat our mistakes, literature, so we would know how people think, and philosophy, so we could defend ourselves with words as well as weapons."

She held out her hand palm up. "It leaves very little time for other activities."

"Is that typical?" I knew about the history and the

weaponry. I'd had no idea about all the rest of it. "Does every *viona uchenye* start so young and train so hard?"

She fiddled with the cuffs of her sleeves. "Not all. I was somewhat special."

I'll bet. You could tell by the way she moved. I planted my chin on my palm. "Still, everyone needs a hobby."

She tilted her head. "Why?"

I was beginning to see why she was so strange. All that training, she'd probably had little time to practice all that knowing how people think and defending herself with words stuff.

"Because having a purpose is important. But so is having time to think and gather your thoughts. The body needs rest and relaxation as much as it needs discipline. Surely your teachers knew that."

"Yes, but my patron...she works twice as hard as anyone. If she can do it, so can I."

I sighed and glanced away, wondering how long I could hold a conversation with someone so intense. My disease had taught me the value of rest. What would be drastic enough to teach Karina that she couldn't drive herself so hard without breaking down?

"Sometimes," she said, her voice heavy with reluctance, "I like to dance."

I turned back in time to see her spin in the air and land lightly on her toes with one arm curved before her and the other raised over her head. She grinned at me.

I snorted. "Probably because it helps you fight or something stupid like that," I muttered.

She threw back her head and laughed. I liked the way she

guffawed as if she didn't care what people thought of her or her teeth.

Someone cleared their throat behind me. "Delivery for the Grigorsyn caravan."

I turned.

A boy about my age stood next to one of the wagons, a canvas rucksack thrown over his shoulder. The sun lit up an amazing amount of red in his blond hair, and his blue eyes crinkled at the corners with good humor. His features weren't perfect, his nose was a little big for his face and one of his front teeth was crooked, but he grinned like he had the world's best joke he just had to share.

For the first time since Luka, my breath hitched, and I suppressed the urge to check my hair. Was it sticking up in funny places after my fitful nap? Great, I probably looked like a rooster.

His eyes darted between me and Karina, and his grin tilted. "Are Pyotr and Evgenia around?"

I blinked. "Yes," I blurted. "I mean, no." I flushed. Talk much, Reyna? I stood and brushed off the seat of my skirt. "They're at the caravansary taking care of business before we leave."

"Ah, so they must have left you in charge." He twitched his eyebrows at me.

I spread my arms to include the muddy ground, the benches, and the fire-pit. "Welcome to my domain." Thank O'in, my brain finally turned on. "My castle," I indicated the wagons. "My kingdom," the fire-pit. "And my loyal body-guard." I gestured to Karina, who had settled back down onto a bench. Her eyes narrowed.

He nodded with approval. "I like it. And of course, no kingdom would be complete without a fair lady and a traveling minstrel." He pulled his rucksack around to the front and held it like a lute. "Your favorite song, my lady?"

I giggled, which snapped me out of the playful banter. Good God, was I flirting? Flirting had always been Eira's thing, not mine. Even with Luka, I'd never...

I cleared my throat. "I think my favorite song would be a little hard to play on that canvas, don't you?"

Thankfully, he sensed my retreat and backed away from the danger as well. "Probably," he said and slung the bag back across his shoulder. "Doesn't mean you can't pretend." He winked at me.

I couldn't help chuckling. I was in so much trouble. I crossed to the other side of the fire-pit and leaned down to Karina. "Help me out."

She sat back and crossed her boots. "I think it's more fun to watch. Just what are you trying to do exactly?"

"I don't know," I whispered. I straightened and turned back to the boy whose grin was falling a little. "I can collect your delivery. What is it?"

The full force of his humor returned. "Me," he said.

I couldn't resist. I slapped my forehead. "Oh, of course. Now I remember. We placed an order for—" Tall, blond, and funny. "Someone like you."

"Yeah?" he said. "So I fit the bill?"

I pretended to look him up and down. "I suppose. We need someone to make us laugh." I stepped up to him and measured my height against his. My head barely crested his shoulders. I pulled his arms out from his sides. "And we can always hang the laundry on you to dry."

He laughed. "I'm also good at lifting things."

"Hmm," I said skeptically. "We'll see." What had possessed me? I'd never been this good at talking to boys. It was just that this guy's grin invited me to join in.

At least he was a complete stranger I would never see again.

"Aleksei!" Evgenia cried behind me.

The boy and I spun to see Evgenia and Pyotr racing toward us.

"Mamat," he said and ran to Eva. He picked her up and swung her around before settling her back down in the mud. Then he extended his hand to Pyotr. "Patepf."

Evgenia turned to Karina and me. "Karina, Reyna," she said. "You've met our son, Aleksei?"

He really was the delivery. Heat flared in my cheeks. Wonderful.

CHAPTER NINE

Eira eventually emerged from the wagon before dinner. She'd combed her gold hair and re-braided it, and she looked much fresher than I after her long nap. The caravan's denizens trickled back into camp one by one or in groups to sit around the fire while Pyotr stirred his pot. Did he know how to cook anything that didn't have its origins in that stockpot?

Eira came to sit next to me, and Karina glanced up from her place on the bench beside us.

"Karina, this is my sister, Eira," I said. "Eira, this is Karina. One of the *viona uchenye* who protect us on the road."

Karina nodded and Eira perked up. "You're *viona uchenye*? Our favorite tales growing up were of Anastasy Sergeisyn."

Anastasy, hero of the five cities. Anastasy and Svetanka, greatest couple in Ballaslavian history. He'd been *viona uchenye* before O'in had chosen him as a holy warrior.

"I imagine reality differs somewhat from the tales," I said.

"Unfortunately," Karina said. "For some reason, no one stands around waiting to write songs about my exploits. I think I must be doing something wrong."

"Maybe you're guarding the wrong people," I said offhandedly.

Karina's breath huffed white in the night air, her eyes trained on my face. "Maybe I'm not."

It had been a joke, but faced with the quiet fire in her gaze I couldn't help remembering all the arguments we'd had on the way from Elisaveta. The way she only seemed to have one speed: breakneck. The way her protective streak felt smothering sometimes.

We could have been friends. But our relationship felt like trying to reach out and catch the hand of someone riding by on a horse. So close, only to miss at the last second.

Probably for the best. One less person I would disappoint when they learned the truth.

I glanced away in time to catch Aleksei heading toward us and drew in a breath. Speaking of...

"Who's he?" Eira whispered.

"Pyotr and Evgenia's son," I said. "He just rejoined the caravan here in Darayevo." The way Evgenia had talked about him had led me to assume he'd be much younger. I'd also assumed that this would be his first time with the caravan. It had become clear very quickly I'd been wrong. Aleksei had grown up traveling the roads with the caravan. His recent absence had been temporary though no one seemed to want to talk about why.

He stopped in front of us and nodded at me. "My mother

tells me you helped her get ready for my arrival, Reyna."

I flushed. "I just mended some blankets. That's all."
Please, don't let him have found it. Please, don't let him—

"Oh." His grin flashed. "Because I found this guy. He seemed to be quite at home on my bunk." He pulled the stuffed dog out from behind his back.

"*Da'ermo,*" I said under my breath. Eira cast me a curious glance.

"I just thought maybe you might know where he came from."

"No, idea. Sorry," I said a little too quickly. "But I'll take him if you don't want him. Maybe Victor would like him." I stood and reached for the toy.

He yanked it out of reach. "No, no. He and I are getting along fine." He held the dog in the crook of his arm and stroked its head. "Victor wouldn't like the competition. He'd have this guy apart in two seconds flat. I think Biter should stay with me."

"Biter?" I said. "That's not—" I ground my teeth on the rest of the sentence. What did I care what he named the stupid thing? It had gotten me in enough trouble already.

He settled the dog on his shoulder and raised his eyebrows at me. "What were you going to say?"

"Nothing," I said. "I'm sure he'll be very happy with you." O'in help me, I almost envied the thing.

Why wasn't Eira chiming in with something flirty and distracting? She was good at that. It was like magic the way she spoke and turned heads. I glanced down at her, but she was playing with the edge of her apron and staring off into the distance.

I swallowed. She really must be in love with Vitaly if she was so distraught that she didn't even notice another cute boy standing right in front of her. Maybe I really had ruined her life when I'd forced her to come with me.

"Reyna, Eira," Evgenia said, making me jump. She stopped behind our bench and put a hand on Eira's shoulders. "You getting settled in?"

"Yes, *sudinya*," Eira said, her tone and gaze still faraway.

"Aleksei, have you met Eira? Reyna's sister?"

Aleksei executed a florid bow, saving the dog from falling off his shoulder at the last minute. "*Verdey drogoi, mushka.*"

A flash of jealousy burned in my chest, but Eira just nodded at him.

"*Spaasebo*," she said.

Evgenia's eyes fell on the dog as Aleksei adjusted it on his shoulder. "A new friend?" she said.

Aleksei grinned. "A stray," he said. "He wandered into the caravan, and I figured he could use a home."

I flushed again.

Evgenia chuckled before turning to me. "We're thinking about renting another wagon for you and Eira to share at night."

My mouth gaped. "Evgenia, you don't have to do that. I can handle the ground, and Eira will be fine."

She patted my shoulder. "It's no trouble. And what if your condition flares up again?"

I choked, but Aleksei spoke before I could protest again.

"Reyna is right, Mamat."

I glanced at him.

"Why can't they just use the heart's blood wagon? It's perfect."

Evgenia looked at him like he was missing the point. "It's yours."

Aleksei rolled his eyes. "Mamat, I told you, I'm not going to use it. I've slept under the wagons with the others since I was twelve.

"But now it's different."

His mobile mouth hardened, every trace of humor disappearing. "How?"

Evgenia sputtered. "You need time to recover. You shouldn't push yourself."

"I'm fine," Aleksei said through his teeth. "I told you, nothing's changed." He turned to me and Eira. "You should use the wagon. It will stand empty otherwise."

Aleksei turned on his heel and strode away. Evgenia cast us an apologetic look and went after him.

I rubbed my hands up and down my arms. What exactly had happened in the months since he'd been with the caravan? Whatever it was, he obviously didn't want it interfering with his life. Sounded familiar.

Karina snorted. "Well, if you don't take the wagon, I will. I'm kind of tired of freezing my ass off at night."

Two nights later, shouting woke me from a nightmare where I'd been drowning in blood, glorious blood, and I thrashed and rolled out of my bunk.

"What is it?" Eira asked, fear clearing the sleep from her

voice. "What's wrong?"

I grimaced in the dark of the wagon and stood to throw open the shutters of the little window. "Sounds like an attack," I said.

"An attack? Who would attack us?" She threw off her covers and put her stockinged feet on the floor.

"Bandits stalk the caravans, especially this time of year. They steal the grain and other supplies. Why do you think we travel with the *viona uchenye*?"

Eira knelt on her bunk to peer out the other window. Nothing moved outside. A couple of scraggly trees stood nearby, wreathed with mist, but there was no sign of fighting except the muffled noise.

The shouting stopped, and I stumbled to the door, running into Eira who'd had the same idea. Outside, the paying travelers from the other wagons stood in the cold darkness, the drivers forming rings around them.

The drivers allowed us through, and I pushed my way to Corwin, hands wrapped around my elbows. "What happened?" I asked him in Valerian.

"Don't know," he said. "There was all this shouting. The guards went in that direction, but I haven't heard anything in the last few minutes, have you?"

I shook my head.

We jumped as more shouting sounded from the forest on our right, this time familiar voices raised in alarm. I recognized a couple of them and caught several snatches of conversation.

"East is clear."

"So is North."

"—just a scratch. *Da'ermo*, should have moved faster." Karina's voice.

I pushed past the drivers and raced toward the circle of wagons.

"Reyna?" Aleksei's bulk rose out of the dark on my left. "Stay in with the drivers until they've called the all-clear."

I shook my head. "Someone's hurt."

I passed the wagons, Aleksei following me, but I didn't have to traipse into the woods to find my patient.

Two of the other *viona uchenye* emerged from the trees carrying a cursing Karina between them. My shoulders relaxed a fraction. If she had enough breath to curse, it couldn't be that bad.

I raced forward to meet them. "What's wrong?"

"Don't," Karina said, holding out a bloody hand to keep me at bay. "You'll have to go through the Rites if you touch me."

"O'in save me from pretentious *viona*, we are not doing this again. You've made your sacrifice, now allow me mine."

"Reyna—"

"No." My hand slashed through the air. "You are going to sit there, and you are going to shut up until I am through with you. If you try to send me away again, I will have one of them gag you." I glared up at the *viona* supporting her. The one nearest me, a man as old as Mabushka, gave me a hearty wink.

Karina gaped, but she stayed silent, either because of my threat or because I'd shocked all the argument out of her. Either way worked for me.

She clenched her jaw, and I hissed in sympathy as I

found the large gash across her thigh, just above the knee.

The rush of *vytl* released into the world by her blood staggered me, and I sat back on my heels breathing hard. I wanted to reach, to gather, to use. It was there already, what harm was there in collecting it? It would just go to waste otherwise.

I bit down hard on my tongue and shook my head to ease the temptation. I would not do that. I could not. Karina's steady gaze made me flush and bend my head to my task.

"You're lucky," I said. "This is relatively shallow. But it will need stitches."

"Stitches?" Her voice cracked on the word, and I glanced up at her.

"Don't tell me the big bad *viona uchenye* is afraid of stitches."

She glared at me from under her sweat-soaked bangs. "Afraid is the wrong word."

"What's the right one?"

"Scared," the older *viona uchenye* offered.

"Terrified," another said.

"Shut up," Karina said through her teeth. "I'll take more stitches than any of you combined."

The older *viona* bit his lip on a smile, and the other looked away, whistling.

"Reyna?" Eira said behind me.

I glanced around to see Aleksei, Evgenia, Pyotr, and Eira watching from a safe distance. "She'll be fine," I said. "She'll have an impressive scar to show off to all the boy *viona*."

Someone snorted behind me while Karina sputtered.

"Is anyone else hurt?" I asked.

"No, *lubonitsva*," the older *viona* answered.

"Eira, will you grab my kit from the wagon?"

"How about some clothes while I'm at it?" Eira said, cocking her hip.

I glanced down at my insubstantial shift and cleared my throat. "That would be helpful."

"You cannot touch anyone else until you are cleansed," one of the other *viona uchenye* reminded me.

I nodded. With my hands covered in Karina's blood, I could hardly argue the Law. "Eira can follow us to our camp and leave them just outside. I'll need my kit before then anyway."

Eira scurried off and returned moments later with my things in a bundle under her arm. The *viona uchenye* lifted Karina between them and set off. One had gone on ahead to set up their separate camp. The older one held me back with a hand on my arm.

He jerked his chin at Karina. "She talks big," he said quietly. "But we're pretty sure this is her first real job. Go easy on her, all right?"

I gave him a mock sigh. "I suppose if you insist."

He chuckled, and I followed him.

We set up a very primitive camp out of sight of the caravan. Eira dropped my things on the ground and retreated to a safe distance while I retrieved my kit.

"Be careful," she said when I'd straightened.

I hid my shudder. She didn't know how appropriate her words were. Karina was strong, and the *vytl* released with her blood was potent and tempting.

"I will," I said. "Go on back to sleep. I'll see you

tomorrow."

The other *viona uchenye* had begun the Rites in the stream next to our camp while Karina sat propped against a tree. I knelt beside her and rummaged through my kit for a bottle of clear liquid, a needle, and thread. I handed her a pair of scissors.

"Can you manage to cut away your pant leg?" I said.

She grimaced. "I only have one other pair of breeches."

"I'll mend them for you, I promise."

She made an unhappy noise through her teeth and cut a nice neat hole in her pants for me to work through. I bent to examine her wound, and before she could ask what I was doing, I'd poured the liquid over the gash.

"*Da'ermo,*" she said. "What's in that?"

"Witch hazel, hyssop, lots of alcohol."

"Is that why it burns like *venaka?*"

"You could drink it on LongNight to stay warm." *Venaka* was clear, colorless, and odorless and when it was passed around on LongNight it made you feel like you could breathe fire. Traditionally, it was served in tiny glasses. Because one sip was all you needed.

I pulled a long piece of silk thread from my spool, and Karina's eyes widened. "It might be better not to watch this part," I said. "I couldn't find any numbing creams in Zhivko."

A muscle in her jaw leaped. "Just do it," she said and screwed her eyes tight against the sight.

I worked as quickly as I could, sewing her skin back together, ignoring the feel of her blood between my fingers. There were spells that would hold the wound closed, but I didn't dare use any of them with her blood staining my hands red. A normal healer would have no trouble, but I'd do irrevocable damage if I tried it.

Carefully, I cleaned my hands and the wound and wrapped a clean white bandage around her leg. Only when all the blood was gone did I place my hands on the bandage and whisper spells of cleansing and healing, to ward off blood sickness and allow her to heal faster.

"Thank you," Karina said.

I looked up, but her eyes were still closed. "You're welcome."

"I know I can be...difficult," she said.

I shrugged as I packed up my things and then realized she couldn't see the gesture. "You're a little intense, I guess."

"My patron calls me focused. I've trained for so long, I don't really know how to be..."

"Normal?"

Her eyes popped open. Then she winced. "A friend," she said.

I blinked.

She sighed. "This is going to sound really stupid."

"Try me," I said.

She picked at the ragged edge of her breeches. "I really wanted you to like me. But I didn't know how to be normal. I guess I kind of blew it."

I almost laughed and then realized she might take that the wrong way. "Lucky for you, I'm not really into normal."

She jumped. "What?"

I shrugged. "I tried it once. But I wasn't very good at it. I'm better at straying from the path, making things harder for myself."

Her hazel eyes examined me. "Maybe if you had someone to help pull you back from the edge, you'd do better."

I raised my eyebrows. "Are you volunteering?"

She closed her eyes, and her head thunked against the tree behind her. "I've been volunteering since I met you. I think you've just been saying no."

I drew in a breath. She didn't even know what she was offering, but she extended it like a gift. If I took it, I'd have to trust her. At least a little. But could I trust someone else when I didn't even trust myself? If I was honest, I was partly the reason Karina never found a grip when reaching for me. I couldn't afford to let her get close when my past threatened everyone around me.

"We can help you with the Rites, *mushka,*" the older *viona* said, making me jump. "If you're all done."

"Thank you," I said quietly.

They helped Karina to the stream, and I supervised while they settled her as comfortably as possible on the bank. The ritual was the same whether you performed it in a *dom'ychist* with attendants to help or the wilderness with only your companions.

We dabbed drops of blessed oil on our foreheads to signify the purity of our thoughts, on each wrist to signify the purity of our deeds, over our hearts to signify the purity of our hearts, and finally on each eyelid to signify the purity of our souls. I always felt like a fraud when I dabbed my eyelids.

As one of the others poured water over my head, I recited the words. "O'in forgive me, O'in wash me, O'in work in me and make me new."

Cleansed and dried, we huddled beside the fire for our time of meditation and reflection.

After the *domy'chist* in Zhivko, I was struck by the difference in the *viona uchenye*. The attendants in Zhivko had made me feel ashamed of my actions. They'd been callous and rough.

Out in the woods, with no luxuries except those we'd brought, the *viona* were...gentle. Accepting. As we sat around the fire, one asked another about the fight. Someone shared something personal. And before I knew it, they'd extended their easy camaraderie to Karina and me.

Here, their sacrifice was accepted. Celebrated. And by extension, so was mine.

I hadn't chosen poorly. Healing someone wasn't a crime. It was a gift.

Like the one Karina was offering me.

"Listen," I said quietly to Karina while the others murmured around us. "I'm not...I'm not saying no anymore."

Her expression didn't change as she stared into the fire, but beside me, her arm tensed. "You're not?"

"No." I blew out my breath. "But if you're going to be my friend, you can't be my mother, too. You can't protect me from my choices. And you can't keep me from making them."

She tipped her head, and her mouth pulled sideways. "But I'm your guardian angel."

I flicked her leg, close enough to the stitches to draw her attention, far enough away so I didn't actually hurt her. "Even angels have their limits, apparently."

She winced. "Fair enough. It's a deal."

CHAPTER TEN

"Go," Evgenia said, pushing Eira and me from the caravan site. "Go have fun. That's an order from your employer."

"Are you sure—" I started.

"I'm not really in the mood—" Eira said.

"Bah." Evgenia tossed her head at the other employees already drifting into town. "Young people belong at the faire. Now go have fun."

"Thanks, Mamat, don't mind if I do." Aleksei slid around her outflung arm, kissed her on the cheek, and danced away before she could catch him.

"I didn't mean—" she started. "Aleksei, are you sure you should be—"

"Don't worry, Mamat, I'll make sure they have fun." Aleksei took Eira and I by the shoulders and started walking.

Behind us, Evgenia sighed and waved goodbye.

"Aleksei," I said. "You don't have to come with us. We don't even really want to go."

"Come on. Who doesn't want to go to a faire?" He leaned in to whisper. "Besides, if I don't take you, she won't let me out of her sight."

As we walked down the rows of wagons I glanced at him out of the corner of my eye. Rare sunlight picked out the red highlights in his hair. "Why is she so protective?"

"'Cause I'm special," he said with a wink.

I rolled my eyes.

Eira leaned over to whisper in my ear. "Maybe she's not trying to protect him from the world. Maybe she's trying to protect the world from him."

I opened my mouth to respond but then saw Karina leaning on a makeshift cane at the end of the row. Waiting for us.

"You shouldn't be walking," I said, eyes narrowed.

"It doesn't hurt anymore," she said. "And besides you said a little exercise would be good for the leg. Help it to heal properly."

"Reyna," Aleksei said with an admonishing frown. "You're not going to make our valiant protector stay home while we have all the fun."

"Besides," Karina said, limping forward with her stick. My feet slipped and slid in the mud, but she still managed to plant her feet like a stalking predator. "We had a deal."

"What deal?" Aleksei said.

"Yeah, what deal?" Eira looked between us.

The deal was just that I wouldn't say no to being friends as long as she didn't smother me in over-protectiveness. But that meant I couldn't turn around and smother her in return.

I sighed. "Fine, but if you tear your stitches out, I'm not redoing them."

"Of course not," Karina said. "You'll just watch me bleed to death."

"Try me," I said as she turned and limped along with us.

I kept my gaze on the dirt track ahead, misshapen by an army of wagon wheels. I stumbled over the uneven ground and winced as the odd gait jarred my knees and hips. The familiar pain wasn't enough to keep my mind off the real reason I didn't want Aleksei and Karina tagging along, though.

Emil, the blood mage, had given me specific stopping points along our route. Places where I was expected to pick up more folios. The faire in town was the next stop on my list. This was the only sign of civilization for miles, so I wasn't that surprised.

Now I was going to have to figure out how to find the blood mage's contact without alerting Aleksei or Karina.

Bad enough I was endangering their souls. Now I risked getting them arrested as well.

I hadn't given much thought to walking the whole way to the faire, but by the time the brightly colored awnings and tents rose in front of us, my knees sent little lightning flashes up and down my legs and I could feel my feet swelling in my boots. I breathed through my nose, lips tight, and tried to ignore the pain.

Aleksei slapped his hands together. "Well, *mushkai*, what do you want to see first?"

I glanced down the row of stalls where they faded into the actual town. Emil had said I could identify my contact by

the red. It probably meant I would be meeting with a registered blood mage. Here, out in the open, where everyone
could see.

"Look, they have a menagerie." Eira pointed to a series of
cages tucked back behind the tents, where a troop of dogs
chased colored balls through the dead grass.

She dragged us that way. I didn't protest too much. It was
easier to follow her than try to think of ways to slip away.

A whole flight of Torracan parrots perched on a raised log
outside one of the tents, their bright red and blue plumage
glinting in the sun. They made us laugh by singing an off-beat
version of the national anthem.

But the rest of the menagerie was a little disappointing.
Just a couple of thin wolves behind their thick cage bars and a
deer with a patchy pelt. I tried not to look at the bars of the
cages and see the walls of the Bastion, the legendary prison
where blood mages, murderers, and other traitors were sent.

"Come on," Aleksei said, quietly. "They're making me
sad."

He steered us back toward the main thoroughfare, and
my sister started drifting down the way, perusing the wares
laid out on rickety tables.

I wandered across the dried ruts with her and ran a hand
along a stall sporting hand-made trinkets and blown glass
balls. I picked up one of the glass ornaments. It was a beautiful scarlet with a loop on top. I could imagine it hanging
from the window in the heart's blood wagon, sending blood-
red beams across the walls. I shuddered and put it back.

"What's wrong with it?" Aleksei said from behind me as I
moved on.

"Nothing. They're gorgeous," I said. "I just don't like the color."

I glanced down the line of stalls again and sucked in a breath. From this angle, I could see a booth about halfway down draped with ostentatious red fabric.

Red was only reserved for blood mages and *viona krovaya* in regards to clothing. There was nothing that said a vendor couldn't decorate a stall with red. Still, it was a bold move considering the associations most people had with the color.

I bit my lip. Aleksei stood beside me, sorting through a craftsman's tools on the table beside us, and Karina limped toward us from the menagerie, surprisingly fleet across the ragged ground.

Before Aleksei could follow, I slipped over to Eira, who stood at a jeweler's stall. "I need your help," I whispered in her ear. "I need you to distract Aleksei and Karina."

She frowned, lines pulling from the corners of her mouth. "What? Why?"

I gave her a significant look and jerked my head at the vendor down the way with the red cloth.

Her mouth parted, then firmed again. "You're actually going through with this?" she hissed.

I pulled on her arm, checking the area to be sure no one heard her. "What else am I supposed to do? They have Mabushka."

"You know she wouldn't want you risking yourself for her."

"Well, she's not here right now, is she?" I asked, then wished I could take the words back as Eira's face fell.

I rubbed my eyes. "Do you have a better plan?"

She scowled. "No. And you know it. Fine. I'll distract the others. But get it over with, okay?"

"Fine with me," I muttered as she stalked across the road to take Aleksei's arm. I tried to ignore the way her hand on his elbow made heat pool in my gut and hurried across to the red-draped stall.

A woman in a sturdy brown dress and stained apron stood behind a counter packed with bottles and phials, seemingly unaffected by the astringent pall that hung over her stall.

"U-um, a 'friend' sent me," I blurted out. There were probably more subtle ways to work it into conversation, but I wanted to be away as quickly as possible.

Her eyes widened, spreading a network of wrinkles around her light blue eyes. Eyes that were devoid of the rust-red ring of the blood mages. I almost leaned forward to be sure, but here in the bright sunlight, she wouldn't have been able to hide it.

"Of course," she said, taking my awkward code-phrase in stride. She reached under the counter and slid a folio of battered leather across.

I snatched it and slid it under my cloak. I was about to run, having discharged my duty, but something made me pause. She didn't wear a cloak. She didn't have the ring of Blood Lust. And her stained sleeves were pushed up high enough I could see her forearms were clear of any scars.

Not a blood mage.

Was she like me? Trapped into helping men like Emil? Blackmailed, tricked, or otherwise beholden?

I shifted back toward the counter, a cascade of empathy

making my chest tight. Her eyes stayed sharp on me as I picked through the bottles lining her stall. Some things were labeled. Others I held to my nose and sniffed.

"Anything you want for the caravan?" Aleksei's voice said over my shoulder.

I squeaked and fumbled the bottle I was holding. Eira stood with Karina a couple of stalls down, her expression swinging from apology to exasperation and back again.

I forced my breathing to calm and gave her a little nod. He couldn't have seen anything. Not if he was still standing there grinning.

"Actually," I said and held up the little green bottle for the woman. "Willow bark and mint?"

She nodded, a smile twitching at her lips. "And yarrow for potency."

"What's all that mean?" Aleksei said.

"It numbs pain. I've been looking for some. Karina could have used it last week." I looked back at the woman. "Is this the only one?"

She shook her head and reached to take the bottle from me. "You don't want that one, *lubonitsva*," she said, stooping to rummage under the counter. "The stuff out here is watered down. For those who don't know the difference."

I raised my eyebrows. "I see."

She glanced up at me and sniffed. "Glass is expensive," she said. "And fools are rich." She stood, pulling a large wooden canteen and a cloth bundle with her. She shifted the useless bottles aside and laid them out carefully.

"This is the real stuff. Kept for those who know what they're doing."

I took the canteen and dabbed some of the liquid on the back of my hand. My skin grew cold, then tingly, then numb.

I couldn't help smiling. Even knowing I'd never be able to afford it all. "How much?" I said anyway.

She sized me up and down. "Five copper reyevs"

Aleksei plunked five copper coins down on the table with a jingle.

"What?" I said.

He shrugged. "It's for the caravan, right? When I accidentally chop my foot off gathering firewood, I fully expect to be dosed with the good stuff."

I eyed his legs. "You're in the habit of cutting off limbs?"

He shrugged and grinned. "Accidents happen."

I gathered up the numbing agent and nodded my thanks to the woman. She returned the gesture. It felt...friendly. An acknowledgment, even though we both knew it would be safer to keep our distance.

Aleksei juggled two packages already—clearly, he'd kept busy with Eira even if it hadn't lasted as long as I'd hoped—and he insisted I add the numbing agent to his load. Since I was still trying to hide the folio under my cloak, I didn't argue too much.

"I think I should get back," I said. My knees trembled already, and it wouldn't be long before I couldn't ignore the dull ache creeping through my limbs.

"Already?" Aleksei said. "Come on, at least get some fried *memka* with me."

With him? Was he asking me specifically?

But before I'd done more than open my mouth in

surprise, he called across to Eira and Karina. "Who else wants fried food?"

Good, I told myself as he loped off, following the smell of oil and dough. *You don't want whatever he's offering. Friendship is one thing, but you've had the other before and remember how that turned out?*

I should have turned around and headed back for the caravan. I knew what my legs were telling me. The joints ached and I felt like I could hear them creaking. But a rebellious piece of me insisted on following Aleksei. Something in his smile, in the way his eyes sparked when he told a joke, drew me deeper than I wanted to go.

I made it to the end of the vendor stalls before my knees gave out, and I sank to the ground with a groan. Turns out I wouldn't have made it back to the caravan even if I'd tried. I squeezed my eyes shut as I forced air between my clenched teeth.

"Reyna?" Karina limped up behind me. "Reyna, what's wrong?"

She tried to crouch next to me.

"Don't," I whispered. "You'll tear your stitches."

"Da'ermo," Eira said. She had no problem kneeling. "How bad is it?"

I gauged the swelling in my knees and feet and grimaced. "Bad." Even my hips were complaining.

"Karina, get Aleksei. I'll head to the caravan and see if Evgenia has some warming bricks."

"Thank you," I said but they were already away.

People streamed beside me, giving me looks before shuffling out of the way. No one wanted to approach and find out if this was the type of illness that would make them go through the Rites.

"Whoa, what happened?" Aleksei said, kneeling in the mud beside me. I tried not to think what his mother would say about the knees of his breeches. "I was only gone two minutes."

"She has some kind of illness that takes her in bouts like this," Karina said, behind him. "We should get her back to the caravan."

"It sounds much worse when you say it like that," I muttered.

Without hesitation, Aleksei dumped his packages in my lap, then slipped his arms under me and hoisted me aloft.

Heat flooded my cheeks. "You don't have to—" I said.

"What? Show off for a pretty girl?" He winked. "No, I'm pretty sure there's a rule that says I have to."

My flush deepened. The only one to call me pretty had been Luka. Next to Eira I was "just Reyna" and that had always been fine. Mabushka called me clever, Mamat called me steadfast, and Papa had called me his songbird. Why did all of those seem so drab all of a sudden?

"Go," Karina said when he hesitated. "I'll follow."

"This happens a lot?" Aleksei said as he started for the caravan.

"Often enough," I said. I didn't really want to get into how I'd hoped to one day be rid of the curse but that not even the best healers could do anything.

"So who heals the healer?"

I had just enough energy to huff a laugh. "The healer herself mostly."

"Then why aren't you? Or can't you do spells while riding?"

I gulped. I always hesitated. It wasn't just now. "I don't want to waste it all on myself."

"I don't understand," he said. "Don't you get the energy for spells from the world?"

"Yes, but you can still run out if you're reckless, especially up here in Ballaslav." My curled fingers gestured to the barren land around us. Some trees marched up to the edge of town but mostly harsh open plains greeted us beyond the caravans.

"Taking care of yourself isn't reckless," he said.

I closed my eyes. "It is when you're a healer." I swallowed against the knot in my throat. "Look. When I was ten, sickness took half our village. I helped Mabushka care for our neighbors. We fought for them for so long. Used up nearly all the *vytl* in the area. And then my parents got sick."

"Oh."

He was silent long enough that I wondered how far we could possibly be from the caravan and opened my eyes again.

"I'm sorry," he said as the heart's blood wagon came into view.

"You can put me down here," I said. "No one needs to tuck me in."

He set me down on the step, then took the packages from me. "I understand why you hesitate," he said. "But is it any better if you collapse before you can help your patients? Healing isn't all magic, is it? Sometimes it's just being there for them."

I gaped at him. He wasn't a healer. He was a caravaner. But somehow, he'd just put his finger exactly on why I'd wanted to be a healer in the first place. As if I'd forgotten it. Or buried it too deep.

He handed me one of his packages. "This one's for you. I hope you like the color better."

I pulled back the cloth edges and blinked at the blue glass ball in my palm. Just like the one I'd been admiring, only this one wouldn't remind me of blood. It looked like the sky in Valeria.

"Aleksei, you didn't have to."

He grinned. "No, but that's what makes it special, right?"

He turned and left me on the step holding his beautiful present and blinking in confusion. I watched as his strawberry blond head and broad shoulders disappeared around a wagon.

Eira ran up with a couple of steaming bricks held in a towel. "What's wrong?" she said. "Why are you still out here?"

She was right, my joints screamed at me to lie down, to curl up under the covers and let the day go by so I could start over some other time. But for that moment, it had been more important to watch Aleksei walk away.

I shook my head and pushed into the wagon. Eira fussed over the bed and the bricks and ushered me under the covers as gently as Mabushka.

I grabbed her hand as she tucked the blanket around me. "Eira, will you hang this in the window for me?" I handed her the glass globe.

She frowned. "I was going to close the shutters so you didn't get chilled."

I shook my head. "I want to see the colors. Please?"

Her lips twisted, but she found some spare twine under the bunk and strung it through the loop on top, then stood on her bunk to hang it in the open window.

"Aleksei, huh?" she said as if continuing another conversation.

"Don't say it like that," I said. "It doesn't mean—It was just a gift. He saw me looking at them and thought it would be nice."

Eira rolled her eyes. "Reyna, men buy pretty things for women when they want to say, 'hey, I like you' but they don't know how."

I snorted. I hardly considered myself a woman, and Eira was even younger than me. Aleksei might be attractive, funny and extraordinarily kind as far as I could tell. But I'd been fooled before. I curled around my aches, both real and remembered, and hid my face from my sister.

"How do I make him stop?" I whispered.

She huffed a laugh. "Why would you want to? Come on, Reyna. Aleksei is cute. And he's the heir of a fairly successful caravan. Who are you holding out for?"

"I'm not holding out for anyone," I said. "I just don't want that right now."

She sat on the edge of my bunk and tucked her feet up under her skirt. "Did you meet someone in Valeria?"

"No," I said. Yes.

She raised her eyebrows at my quick response.

"Look, it wasn't like you and Vitaly," I managed to mumble. "I—I'd rather not talk about it."

She hesitated before finally nodding. "All right," she said. "You don't have to." She stood and moved toward the door. "But if it was really that bad, things can only get better with Aleksei, *isavit?*"

She turned the latch and slipped out, closing the door behind her with a gentle click.

I slipped the fingers of my left hand under my right sleeve and touched the scars on my wrist. She didn't know the truth, and *pohomzhet da ma baud*, it hurt not to tell her. If I did, she would know. She would know it wasn't worth it to get close to anyone ever again.

I stumbled down the street, the towers of the University rising ahead of me. I shivered, though the cool autumn air wasn't even close to the frigid temperature I was used to. My head spun, causing the cobbles to tip under my feet, and I caught myself against the wall of a nearby bookshop.

I dragged in a couple of desperate breaths. I still felt like I wasn't getting enough air.

This wasn't from my curse. The aches and fatigue had disappeared with the rush of power I'd taken in the moment I'd sliced my wrists this afternoon. It was only as I'd raced to class that black had edged my vision, and I wobbled on my feet.

I pushed myself off the wall, staggered, and careened into someone on the street. Their hands closed around my arms, and I raised bleary eyes to an intent face with a fringe of blonde hair.

"You..." she started, but then her hands slid down my arms and caught on the bandages beneath my sleeves. I yelped in pain.

She glanced down, and her eyes went round. Blood soaked through my sleeve. *Da'ermo*, I hadn't noticed that before I'd left. I couldn't show up to my lecture bleeding.

Her gaze met mine again, and she snatched her hands back, staring at her palms. My stomach roiled. I staggered away from her horror, distancing myself from what I'd done, who I was now. Her blurry figure receded behind me until I could squeeze my eyes shut and pretend it hadn't happened. No one had seen. I was still safe.

My toe caught the edge of a cobble, and I fell. I leaned my forehead against the sidewalk, too woozy to do anything about it.

"Miss, are you all right?" The voice spoke with a Ballaslavian accent but the words were Valerian.

I groaned inarticulately. Fantastic, Reyna. Running from one person, only to attract the attention of another.

"Miss? *Da'ermo*, no wonder she collapsed. Look at this." Someone picked up my arm, and I was too weak to pull it away.

"Come on, Luka. She's just a goat."

"No, look at her eyes." Someone peeled back one of my eyelids and I flinched away.

"So, she's a selfie. Even more reason to leave her. They're crazy."

"I'm not going to let her bleed out on the street like this. Besides, she looks like she's from Ballaslav."

The world went gray and fuzzy after that, and when I woke I wasn't in the street anymore. Wrinkled linen pressed against my cheek and my fingers flexed against the bedding. I rubbed my eyes, taking in the late afternoon sunlight stained blue and green and orange that slanted across a small, crowded room.

Books were piled in every corner, against every wall, and in some cases spilled across the floorboards.

A boy stood with his back to me, sorting through a stack of older texts, unbound and handwritten. I pulled the sheet up further, wondering if I should clear my throat to get his attention. But he heard the rustle of the bedding and turned, eyebrows raised.

"Hello," he said. The colored light came from a partially obscured stained-glass window and turned his black hair blue. He gave me a delightfully crooked smile. He looked about eighteen.

I glanced around the room, but no one lingered in the shadows to save me from strange men. "What time is it?" I said, checking surreptitiously to be sure I was still dressed under the sheet.

He grinned, one side of his mouth pulling sideways, as the bells in the University clocktower struck the hour.

I groaned. "*Da'ermo*, I'm so late." I threw back the sheet and tried to stand, but the man stopped me and pushed me back down. My heart beat faster.

"Whatever class you were headed for is long over, *mushka*," he said.

I glanced at him sharply. "You're from Ballaslav."

He nodded and turned to the bedside table piled precariously with more books and a plate of bread and cheese. "Yes, though it's been a couple of years since I've been home. Eat this. It will help build up what you've lost."

I eyed the plate dubiously. Would he try to drug me if I was already in his house under his power?

He laughed at my look. "I carried you here, bound your arms, placed every healing spell I know on you, and let you sleep in my bed. If I wanted to do more than help, it would be far too late for you to object."

I tilted my head. "Why did you help me?"

He reached out to touch the bandages around my wrists. "Because I've been where you are."

I flushed and pulled my arm away, remembering the horror of the girl on the street. "You don't understand. It's not like that."

"I do. You are both the user and the used."

I blinked at him. "How—?"

His gaze flashed to my face and away again. "Your eyes."

My fingers reached up to touch my cheek. "What?"

His eyes narrowed. "You don't know?" He stood and strode to a cluttered table on the opposite wall. "The *vytl* we draw from blood is different. More potent. Infused with the life of the person it comes from. When we take it in, we are imbued with that difference."

He turned, a wooden mirror in his palm. He handed it to me.

Goosebumps ran up my arms as I took in my reflection. My blue eyes widened so I could easily see the thin red ring that surrounded my irises. I swallowed down bile. I'd changed myself. My actions had left a physical mark. First the scars. Now this.

My hand trembled. He'd said, "we."

He sat back down and met my eyes without shame. The same red ring surrounded his brown eyes.

"It's called the Blood Lust," he said. "And it only shows up in those who have recently drawn *vytl* from blood. It goes away after a few days of abstinence. But that's how I knew what you've been doing."

"It's just for energy," I said too quickly. "I've been so tired here. With all the lectures and everything, it's hard to keep up."

"I know," he said, voice soothing. "I'm not judging you. But there are better ways to get energy."

I pulled my knees up and hugged them. "All the healers say they can't help. This is the only thing that does."

"I didn't mean you have to stop." He hesitated. "Most take their strength from others."

I shook my head hard enough to loosen my hair from its braids. "No. That's the only thing that makes this bearable. I'm not hurting anyone else."

He stared at me solemnly for a moment before speaking. "Then you need to at least take care of yourself," he said, reaching for my hand again. "Use the healing you know to close the wounds when you're done. Be sure they're clean. If you're untidy, you're dead. Do you know about the blood sickness yet? The one specific to blood mages."

I shook my head. Blood sickness sounded bad.

"I can tell you about that one later." His fingers stroked

mine, as though unconsciously. I didn't pull away. The worst had happened. Someone had learned my secret and it was all right. Comforting even. His gaze wasn't filled with horror. Disgust didn't mar his features. My breath came easier, and the knot in my chest loosened.

"Are you a student at the University, too?" I asked.

He smiled. "I learned everything they could teach me. But most of this..." He gestured to my bandaged wrist. "I had to muddle out on my own."

I bit my lip. "I didn't know there was much more to it."

"When you learned your first spell, did you automatically know the best way to go about it? Or did you barely get it to work those first few times?"

"All right," I said with a rueful smile. "I might have jumped on the ice without knowing how thick it was."

He laughed, hearing a phrase from our homeland. "Exactly. There's much more to know."

I looked up at him through my eyelashes. "And you'd teach me?"

He gave me that crooked grin again and my heart thumped in my chest. "Only if you tell me your name first."

I had to clear my throat. "Reyna."

His thumb stroked my knuckles. "Nice to meet you, Reyna. I'm Luka."

CHAPTER ELEVEN

"Wait, wait, say it slower," Corwin said, frantically digging for the parchment he carried in his satchel.

Aleksei reached out to pull the Valerian aside so he didn't get run over by a cart. "*Verdey drogoi, Ser Corwin.*"

Corwin didn't even look up at the busy street as he scribbled in his notes. "How do you spell it?"

Aleksei's gaze went blank. "Um..."

"I'll write it down for you some time, Corwin," I said. "It means 'solid roads.'"

"And this is a traditional Ballaslavian greeting?" Corwin said, head tilted in question.

"I've only heard caravaners use it," Karina said.

Instead of answering, Corwin paused to gawk at a passing funeral procession while the rest of us stepped back and nodded to the mourners. Black horses marched down the cobbles, broad feathers waving from their bridals.

Eira took my elbow and leaned into my ear to speak in

Ballaslavian. "Why did you let him come along? He's going to be like this all the way to the *yshkiniva*."

I glared at her. It wasn't like I'd wanted any of them to come along. But that's what I got for asking Evgenia if the caravan could drop me off in town while a bunch of busybodies listened in.

"You could have said something," I hissed back at her. "Kept them all from following me. Corwin wouldn't have noticed if it hadn't been for all of you."

Eira jerked back. "If you really have to do this, I'm at least not going to let you do it alone."

I raised my eyes to the sky, asking O'in for patience.

"What can't she do alone?" Karina said behind my shoulder.

I jumped, but Eira gave her a bright smile. "Entertain Corwin."

Karina pursed her lips. She walked beside us with barely a trace of a limp in her step. Maybe *viona uchenye* healed faster than the rest of us. Or maybe it was just Karina.

"I know what you mean," she said with a shudder. "He makes me feel like a bug in a jar."

"Leave him alone," Aleksei said, slinging an arm over her shoulder. "I think it's cute seeing the way everything's new to him. Kind of like a puppy."

I beamed at Aleksei. He understood, at least.

Karina sighed and shrugged away from Aleksei. She grasped Corwin's arm and steered him away from the funeral procession. "Come on, *mulnik*," she said in her accented Valerian. "We only have an hour or two before Evgenia and Pyotr leave us to seek firmer roads."

Everyone winced. The fall weather had left the roads frozen in mighty ruts one day and pocked with puddles deep enough to swallow a cow the next. It was easy to see where the caravaners got their saying.

A modest *yshkiniva* rose between a butcher shop and the attached *dom'ychist* on the other side of the street, and we darted across the muddy ground. Two little towers rose on either side of the columned portico, making the entrance seem far grander than the two-story building actually deserved.

I glanced around, searching for a trace of red. According to Emil's note, this was where I'd find the third folio I was supposed to pick up.

Nothing but drab colors on the buildings, browns and grays and the occasional blue. And the only man lingering in front of the *dom'ychist* wore a stained white shirt. The rare sunlight caught fresh pox scars on his face as he cast anxious looks toward the *domy'chist* door.

Aleksei stopped, then gestured up the steps toward the *yshkiniva* to let the man go first. But he shook his head and stepped out of reach.

"Don't touch me," he said. "I was ill, and I haven't been cleansed yet."

Aleksei's friendly expression didn't waver. "Is the *domy'chist* closed then?"

The man flushed and shook his head. "They told me I need...need hyssop."

Understanding passed between us like a breath of wind. He obviously didn't have the money for the herb and the *domy'chist* attendants wouldn't let him in without it. I had some tucked away in the healer's kit under my bed, but of course, it didn't do any good there.

"Here, friend," Aleksei said and dug in his pocket. He pulled out three copper reyevs.

The man started to shake his head, but Aleksei tossed the money to him, forcing him to catch it or let it roll into the mud. He caught it.

Aleksei gave him a nod and strode up the steps to the *yshkiniva*.

"Thank you, *ser*," the man called to Aleksei's back before he darted to the door of the *domy'chist*.

"That was nice of you," I said, hurrying to catch up to Aleksei. My knees twinged, but as long as we didn't go wandering around town, I'd be all right until we returned to the caravan.

Aleksei shrugged off the compliment. "It's no more than anyone else would have done."

I hid a smile. Not true. Most people would have rushed by, ignoring the man while he was unclean.

Inside the *yshkiniva*, a short colonnade stretched to either side of us, separating the foyer from the central courtyard. A small fountain splashed in the tiled space beyond the columns underneath a dusty glass dome. On the far wall, a pair of double doors led to the Court of Absolution.

"Now what?" Corwin asked. His hushed voice still rang in the quiet space.

Eira rolled her eyes and stepped up to the fountain. "O'in forgive me. O'in wash me. O'in work in me and make me new," she sang and dipped her hands in the basin where the water pooled. She touched a dripping finger to her forehead, each wrist, her heart, and her eyelids.

"You can stay here in the Court of Supplication," Karina said. "But that's as far as you can go."

Corwin frowned as Eira moved through the courtyard toward the big double doors. "You mean I can't go in?"

Karina shrugged. "Sorry. It's the Law."

I waited till Eira had slipped through the doors before I said, "I'll stay with him."

Aleksei's brows lowered. "Are you sure? I could..."

I shook my head and smiled brightly. "It's all right. I don't mind." And it would be a lot easier to sneak around just Corwin than my sister and Karina. Even Aleksei looked askance at me already.

Karina paused at the fountain like she wanted to protest, but Aleksei shrugged and joined her to perform the Rites.

"What's back there that you want to hide?" Corwin asked.

I sighed. "We're not hiding anything. It's protection of a sort. You can only go into the Court of Supplication if you've been cleansed recently. And you can't be cleansed unless you want to convert."

"I can't even peek?" he asked as the others disappeared through the double doors.

"There are places we can't go either," I said. "Beyond the Court of Supplication is the Court of Priests. Only the local *otepf* is allowed in there. It's where he talks directly to O'in."

"And I take it that's another protection?" Corwin asked. I half expected him to snort in derision, but he was digging out his notes again.

"Actually, yes. Every Court of Priests is a little different. Because O'in's presence manifests in different ways. Sometimes it's a bottomless pool. Sometimes it's fire or a whirlwind. But there's one thing that's always the same. The priests always go in with someone to pull them out. Because anyone who steps into O'in's presence might not come out again."

Corwin stared at me, pen poised over his paper. "You're kidding."

"I'm not."

He shook his head. "Your religion is a harsh one."

I winced. He wasn't the only one to think so.

He bent his head, sketching a rough outline of the *yshkiniva*, and I used his distraction to slip away and out the front door. I rubbed my arms in the sunlight on the front step of the *yshkiniva*, as if I could rub off the source of my guilt. Even standing in the Court of Supplication, I fouled the place.

A flash of red caught my attention and my heart sank. A young woman, a blood mage, stood in the shadows between two shops on the other side of the street. She met my eyes deliberately and gestured.

My contact. I'd know them by the red Emil had said.

I sucked in a bracing breath and stalked down the stairs and across the street.

"Yes?" I said, stopping at the corner of the alley. I didn't dare get any closer.

She held a leather-bound folio out, bridging the space between us. I glanced at her hands. She wore a pair of gloves but a single stark scar stood out on her bare wrist above the edge.

I took it reluctantly. "Thank you," I said and started to turn.

"Wait."

I didn't want to. I wanted to run and pretend none of this was happening. But a plaintive note in her voice made me hesitate.

"Please, you have to help me."

I pressed the folio against my side, under my own cloak, and braced my other hand against the brick wall next to me. "Help you what?"

"Help me get into the *yshkiniva*."

I gasped and whirled around. "You can't."

She held out her hands. "I just want to pray. That's it. I just want to talk to O'in again."

I couldn't help meeting her eyes. They were a clear brown, with no ring of Blood Lust. Just like mine. The only difference between us was the cloak. She'd been caught. She'd been registered, and I hadn't.

I dropped my gaze. "I'm sorry. I'm not going to help you get in. Just pray out here."

She lunged for me, and I shifted back with a yelp. "You don't understand," she said. "The priests say I can't be clean. But I only did it that once, and I'm sorry for it. I don't want to be damned. I don't want to die of the blood sickness."

"I'm sorry," I said again. I had no idea what else to tell her. If I'd known how to fix any of that, I wouldn't be here.

She kept coming, and I stumbled back, tripping down

into the street with a jolt that jarred my knees and hips. I winced.

"Reyna?" Aleksei's voice came to me from the top of the *yshkiniva* stairs, and I glanced over my shoulder. He stood with Eira and Karina and Corwin.

Great. Wonderful.

I hurried across the street, away from the blood mage, a part of me cringing at my cowardice. All she wanted was what I had. Anonymity and a connection with O'in.

Behind me, she sobbed, and I could hear her following.

Three *dom'ychist* attendants dressed in shapeless undyed cotton tunics with firm expressions flowed from the *dom'ychist*. I paused on the steps as they intercepted her in the street.

"Please," she said, eyes on me. "Please."

The attendants' scowls didn't change. "Leave now," one of them said. "You endanger all by being here."

Her eyes filled with tears, and I wondered if anyone else noticed they were clear.

When she didn't move off right away, the attendants stooped and each snatched up a large stone from the edge of the street.

The blood mage covered her face before she turned and fled.

A movement beside me made me start. Aleksei had skipped down the steps to my side, his brow twisted and his lips drawn back in a snarl. He lurched to the street and grabbed up his own rock. He cocked his arm back to heave it at the retreating blood mage.

My breath hitched even as I stood frozen.

Karina lunged to grasp his arm and snatched away the deadly projectile. She scowled at Aleksei and nodded at the attendants who had dropped their rocks without following through on their threat.

Aleksei swore and jerked his fist from her grip before turning to stride in the opposite direction. His reaction was so violent I was almost surprised he didn't spit on the street in contempt.

It was a common reaction. The appropriate, even expected, reaction to the sight of a blood mage, especially one who was trying to enter such a sacred place. But I hadn't expected to see it from Aleksei. Aleksei who had refused to gawk at caged animals, who had spoken tolerance for Corwin, and who had given an unclean man his chance for redemption.

I shuddered and drew the edges of my cloak closer, hiding the folio beneath. If he thought that poorly of a new, obviously repentant blood mage, what would he think of me?

"For a country that reviles blood magic," Corwin said as we turned to follow Aleksei, "you certainly have a lot of them."

"Ballaslav doesn't have very much *vytl*," I said, head down to watch the ruts in the road. "The energy that powers spells. It comes from the world around us. Living things, plants, and animals." I gestured around at the bare mud and rock of my homeland. "We don't have a lot of that. And snow dampens what we do have."

"So we have less energy for a mage to work with," Karina said, frowning at the streets.

"Exactly. More and more mages turn to blood magic to power their spells."

"Even when blood makes them unclean in your religion?" Corwin said.

"Some people will murder for just the hint of a little more power," Eira said.

"They're not all murderers," I said, a little too quickly. "Some take *vytl* from animals. And some only cut themselves."

Karina gave me a funny look, and I flushed. Before I could think too hard about it, she'd gone back to scanning our surroundings. I didn't know what she thought could creep up on us out here. The space between the town and the caravansary was bare except for some stunted trees that had already lost their leaves.

Corwin frowned. "But the punishment is universal. Ostracism?"

Eira shrugged. "Basically. You can talk to a blood mage, but you can't touch them without having to go through extensive Rites. And no one's going to hire one."

"How can you tell you're talking to one?" He held up his hands when Eira frowned and opened her mouth. "I know, I know, the cloak. But what if they just didn't wear the cloak? No one would know they were a blood mage."

Eira's mouth dropped open in horror, and Karina's lips thinned.

"No Ballaslavian would be so selfish," Eira said.

I fought off a wave of nausea at Eira's words and the disgust I heard in them.

Corwin shrugged. "In my experience, every human is selfish, no matter where they come from."

Eira shook her head. "You don't understand," she said as I swallowed and controlled my expression. "Blood mages can never be cleansed, so they will always be barred from O'in's presence. Every time they touch someone, everything they handle, is unclean. Unregistered blood mages aren't just dangerous because they hurt people. Unregistered blood mages endanger everyone's souls." She tossed her hair over her shoulder. "Like I said. No one would ever be that selfish."

I wished she was right. But I'd made the coward's choice, and now I had to live with it. And every time I came across another blood mage or took one of their folios, I had my face rubbed in it.

I had to get away from Emil and his mages. But the only way to do that would be to free Mabushka from their clutches.

CHAPTER TWELVE

I tried hard not to think of Aleksei when I sat in the open door of the heart's blood wagon and watched the last of the caravan pass into town. I held tight to the doorframe as we bounced along the rutted street. Clearly whatever had happened to him, whatever made him late to join the caravan and had made his mother so protective, had involved a blood mage.

I didn't dare ask him for details. My eyes were clear but my sins lay too close to the surface to chance an errant question stealing my freedom. Especially while I was still tangled up in this mess with Emil.

My other hand rested on the folios while I scanned the streets for a good place to jump off.

"I don't like you going alone," Eira said from over my shoulder.

I stifled a sigh and refused to turn. We'd had this conversation half a dozen times already and it never went well.

"I know. But someone has to keep the others from

wondering where I am. You have to distract Karina and Aleksei."

"I wouldn't have to distract them if you weren't going anywhere."

I closed my eyes. "Eira—"

"Wait. Listen to me. If you lure the blood mages to the caravan, Aleksei, Karina, and I can help you fight them. We don't have to do their dirty work for them anymore."

Heat raced along my nerves leaving a chill in its wake. "No!" I said. "No, we're not telling anyone."

"Reyna—"

I spun on the wagon step, meeting her eyes. "No. Now you listen, all right? What happens to Mabushka if we try to fight the blood mages head-on? The whole reason they have her is so they can hurt her if we do anything. We can't fight them. Not directly at least."

Her shoulders slumped, and she sank down on the edge of the bunk. "We can't work for them forever."

I pushed myself to my feet and crossed the wagon to take her hands. "It's not forever. I'm going to find out where they're keeping her. We need more information if we're going to free her."

She jerked in surprise. "Free her?"

"We want the same thing, Eira. I just...I'm not a warrior. I'm not an *Izavital* like Anastasy or Svetanka. O'in didn't give me a holy sword to smash through our enemies. We have to do this our way. It may be slower. But it's safer."

She gave my fingers a little squeeze before she pulled them from my grip and crossed her arms. "I still think we'll need some help."

I pursed my lips and blew out my breath through my nose. She wasn't wrong. And it wasn't her fault the very thought made my stomach knot.

"After I find out where she is. All right? Then we can make plans and maybe trust someone who won't turn us over to the *viona krovaya*."

She blanched, and I felt a zing of shame for bringing up my greatest fear and making it hers.

"I have to go." I had specific instructions for the folios, and if I lost the blood mages's trust for a moment, I lost the chance to find Mabushka.

"Promise you'll be careful," she said to my back.

I bit my lip at the door. "I will." Then I slid down into the street and away.

It took me almost an hour to find the large well-lit inn at the end of a street full of banks. I'd expected some dingy little pub sharing a wall with a tannery or something equally as squalid, but this was a strange luxury. Expensive oil lamps gleamed on either side of the door, their brass polished to a high shine, and wide windows gave me a clear view inside, where well-dressed patrons ate and played cards.

I checked Emil's note one more time. Then the sign out front.

THE RED NOBLE

This had to be a mistake. I didn't belong in a place like this and neither did anyone associated with Emil.

A man in a deep maroon coat with gold buttons leaned against the corner of the building and watched as I wavered on the opposite curb.

Finally, I shook my head. There must be another "Red Noble" a couple of streets over. Maybe I should have checked the neighborhood closer to the caravansary.

The man lit his pipe as I passed him and tipped his hat to me. "*Dryg* Reyna," he said.

Shock rocked me back on my heels. "What did you call me?" It was what Emil had said. Friend.

He just smiled and stuck his pipe in his mouth. "You have what was passed to you?"

I gave him a stiff nod and moved to hand him the folios I'd carried beneath my cloak, but he shook his head and straightened up. "This way."

He led me, not to the front door, but to a service entrance in the alley beside the inn. I balked on the doorstep. Attention would get me into trouble and I couldn't imagine anything worse than walking into an inn full of nobles. But I'd told Eira I would find out where Mabushka was. So I stepped in.

The fanciest place I'd ever set foot in had been the University in Valeria. And that had definitely been a place of study and work, not leisure, even if the towers and the gardens had felt rich.

The Red Noble made me feel like a mouse in a ballroom. Through an open door, I could see patrons sitting in their thick brocades, jewels glinting in the light. Even the servants' corridor gleamed.

"Where are we going?" I asked my guide as he moved deeper into the building, past a bustling kitchen and a private meeting room.

"To the Red Nobles' best kept secret," he said.

At the very end of the hall, a tall man dressed in a rust-red uniform stood beside a nondescript door. A black club hung from his belt.

I pulled the edges of my cloak around me and shrank against the wall, chin down as the *viona krovaya* swept us with his gaze. *Da'ermo,* had the man led me into a trap?

My guide gave the *viona* a saucy wink and pressed a coin into his palm. The *viona* just grunted and stood aside to open the door.

I gaped as my guide gestured me through. I scampered ahead, keeping my questions behind my teeth, and the *viona* closed the door fast enough to catch my heels.

Another hallway stretched before me, not as clean or well-lit but with more rooms branching off, and from the sound of it, another common room at the far end.

"After you," my guide said with a smirk and a bow.

I lifted my chin and started down the hall. The other one had smelled of perfume and roast mutton. Here, the sizzle of fried *memka* made my stomach growl.

A woman crossed the hall in front of us, and I faltered. Her red cloak swirled around her feet as she turned to see who was coming up behind her. Her red-ringed eyes narrowed, and she raised her nose and sniffed, something about my appearance disagreeing with her. She turned and twitched the edge of her scarlet cloak up over her arm with a practiced gesture and sailed away. If I hadn't known better, I'd think she was flaunting her shame at me.

At the end of the hall, a room opened in front of me, and I jerked to a stop on the edge of the jaunty pool of light. Red cloaks filled the room, casting a scarlet haze across my vision and a shadow over my heart. Hundreds, thousands of blood mages all in one room, looking at me with their red-rimmed eyes, judging me, reminding me of my crime and the black smear on my soul.

It took me a moment to blink and take a deep breath and finally see that there were only about ten or so mages, all in the red cloaks. I just had never seen so many in one place before. And scattered among them were others in plainer, less condemning colors, some with the eyes of blood lust and some without.

Only a few had looked up at my entrance and now they went back to their games and their conversations and their food, bored with the frightened girl in the dark blue bodice and tan skirt standing frozen in the hallway.

"Welcome to The Lancet," my guide said from behind me.

"What is this place?" I said through the lump in my throat, but already I could see another street through the thick wavy glass of the front windows. Two inns sitting back to back, one in a respectable part of town, the other on a street I'd think twice about frequenting at night. And someone had thought to build a door connecting the two.

"Sometimes we need a place to be ourselves," the man said, moving around me to gesture at the common room.

"And sometimes someone doesn't want the local *otepf* or *yshkiniva* to know they met with a blood mage." He gestured back the way we'd come. "So they can go into a respected establishment and come in here without worrying about who will see and comment and judge."

I gripped the frayed ends of my sleeves. "And the *viona krovaya* just let them come through?"

He snorted. "The *viona krovaya* will allow just about anything as long as enough coin changes hands. Come on, *mushka*," the man said with a little laugh at my wide eyes. "Volksyn wants to talk to you."

Again, I was tempted to drop the folios and run, but there were too many blood mages between me and the door. And there was a corrupt *viona krovaya* at my back. I wasn't sure which was worse.

I just had to find Mabushka. All I had to do was play along until someone slipped and told me where they were keeping her.

The man led me to the stairs that climbed the far wall to a second-story balcony looking out over the common room.

There the walls opened onto a sitting area filled with worn sofas and an armchair that looked like it had fallen off the back of the trash wagon.

The woman I'd seen in the hall stood with her back to me, talking to someone seated, and her voice cracked out like a whip. "*Dryg* Emil said she was recalcitrant."

"And I said I'd handle her," another voice said. A familiar voice. "You gave me the job, so let me do it. Trust me, Mamat. I know what I'm doing with Reyna."

The woman sniffed and turned, and the man leading me

stepped aside so I could see who sat on the sofa. Black hair gleamed in the lamplight, brown eyes danced with good humor, and a puckered scar across his face screamed at me to run.

My heart jumped in my chest, and I spun toward the stairs. Away, away, I had to get away. Before he caught me, before he changed who I was and made me doubt my sanity. Again.

A hand snapped out and caught my arm, pulling me back from my frantic flight. I looked up into the woman's red-ringed blue eyes. Her fingers dug into my skin, nails catching on the edges of the scars crisscrossing my forearms. A slow smile spread across her face as though she felt them and knew what they meant.

"Going somewhere?" she said, voice sweet and sticky like honey.

I hated honey.

I gulped, my throat bobbing loudly in the sudden quiet. Even the noise in the common room had faded, so we stood in a perfect bubble of silence, everyone waiting for something.

"Hello, Reyna," Luka said, his sweet smile greeting me as it had every day for a year in a warmer, greener place. "You look so white, *lublenni*. Here, sit." He stood and the woman tugged my arm so I had no choice but to move across the intervening space and sit beside him on the sofa.

It wasn't until I was settled that she finally removed her hand and stepped away from me. I shivered and rubbed my arm.

Her lips twisted in a sneer when she saw my gesture.

"Thank you, Mamat," Luka said with a frown at the woman. "I'll take it from here."

"If she mucks this up..."

He cut her off with a scowl. "Yes, Mamat."

"*Sudinya* Volka," my guide said. "Perhaps you can help us with a dispute downstairs."

The woman raised her chin and allowed the man to lead her away, but I got the impression Luka would be hearing more later. This woman would never let a couple of men distract her from saying her piece.

I remained focused on Luka with the vague thought that I shouldn't turn my back on him. My eyes caught on the scar that crossed his left eyebrow and curved down his cheek. It was still red and raw looking. Only seven months old. It almost gave him a rakish, dashing look. Almost.

I shuddered. "What do you want with me, Luka?" Now I knew it wasn't an accident they'd found my home and taken Mabushka. Before I could almost believe I was just a random recruit, but not anymore. If Luka was running this operation, he wanted something specific with me. Something that would help him get this little rebellion he was orchestrating off the ground.

His lower lip stuck out. On a less mature man, I'd have called it a pout. "Would you believe me if I said I missed you, *lublenni?*"

My jaw clenched and my eyes strayed to the scar again. "No. And don't call me that."

His lips thinned, and he rubbed the puckered skin. "I guess I wouldn't either."

"You kidnapped Mabushka."

"How else was I supposed to talk to you? After...everything...Well, I didn't think you'd ever want to talk to me again."

"You've got that right."

His jaw worked. He always ground his teeth when he was frustrated. "*Blenni—*"

"I said don't call me that."

He rolled his eyes. "Reyna then. Look I wanted to bring you in on this sooner. But I knew you wouldn't want to see me, so I had to improvise."

"Bring me in on what? Luka what the hell are you trying to do here?" I gestured down the stairs at the blood mages congregating below. "Stage a rebellion? Send Ballaslav back into the *Krovaya Epohka*?"

He sliced his hand through the air, stopping me. "This is nothing like the Bloody Epoch," he said. "We don't want to overthrow anyone. We just want the freedom that's been taken from us."

"What do you mean?" I said, though I was pretty sure I knew already.

"We want to make blood magic legal."

I shook my head even as my stomach fluttered. "You can't. It's not just against the law. It's against the Law. And that's been around since even before the *Krovaya Epohka*."

"Then maybe it's time for a change," he said, spreading his hands. "I hoped you'd want to help."

He was talking literal blasphemy. "O'in isn't going to change Their mind about blood magic."

He sat forward. "I'm not talking about O'in. I'm talking about Ballaslav. Ballaslav just doesn't have enough *vytl*.

That's the way the world works. But our government punishes those of us who would reach for more than the world gives up."

I shook my head, making my braid swing. "It's not just looking for more than what the world would give and you know it. Blood magic makes spells more powerful." Overpowerful in a lot of cases.

He threw up his hands. "What's wrong with that? What's wrong with wanting to do more?"

"How about the fact that it kills us in the process," I said quietly.

His hands dropped back into his lap. "A sacrifice many of us are willing to make. Just like you make a sacrifice every time you heal someone."

My jaw clenched. "It's nothing like that."

"No? What about those nobles next door? They would use you for blood magic. And the *viona krovaya* who let you in, he'll be the one to register you. By taking your blood. They use us for blood magic and then punish us for it. Do you think that's fair?"

I swallowed down the nausea that rolled up my throat. "I figured I made myself pretty clear seven months ago. Why do you think I'd change my mind?"

He reached out to stroke my forearm with his finger. "Like you said, it's been seven months. You must be getting pretty desperate."

I wrenched myself away from his touch and stood abruptly. I couldn't run, I still had to find Mabushka. So, I strode to the railing and peered down at the common room.

"I meant what I said, Luka." My fingers gripped the

banister hard enough to turn my knuckles white. "I'm not using it again. Not ever. Not for anything."

His face fell, and he ducked his head.

"It hurts people just so you can have a little more power," I said. Maybe he'd listen to me this time. "I have plenty of power for the things I'm doing. I don't need more. Not when the cost is so high."

"Broken bones and split fingernails," Luka scoffed. "What happens when someone lays dying at your feet Reyna and your disease leaves you nothing to give them."

I spun toward him. "How dare you?" I whispered. "How dare you use that against me?"

"That's why I thought you could help." Luka stood and moved to join me at the rail. "You understand what it's like to need more than the world gives. You know when to be satisfied and when to strive for more."

He reached out to touch my hand again. This time I didn't pull away. "You know what it's like to struggle in secret. Better than any of the ones down there. They were caught because they weren't careful enough."

"So, they're useless to you, now," I said. The red cloak made them conspicuous. The *viona krovaya* would be watching them constantly. The ones who weren't corrupt, that is.

Luka shrugged. "I wouldn't say useless. But far less mobile, yes. You haven't been registered. You can move freely."

"I still could be watched. What happens when they know I've been meeting with blood mages?"

He shrugged. "Then you disappear until you're not

watched anymore. If you haven't been registered, you can't be tracked."

I glanced at him sidelong. "What do you mean tracked? They follow you?"

"Why do you think the *viona krovaya* take your blood when they register you? They keep it so they can always find you. Even control you."

My eyebrows lowered in consternation. "Isn't that just another form of blood magic?"

Luka nodded with enthusiasm. "Exactly. The government condemns us for using blood to power our spells and then turns around and uses it to control us. The hypocrisy makes me sick."

He didn't look sick. He looked gleeful. Like he'd won the argument already.

I pressed my lips together, staring at my feet.

"So, it really doesn't matter if you wear the red or not."

"Of course not." Luka tweaked the edge of my plain brown cloak. "You should know that." He leaned his elbows on the banister and stared up at the ceiling. "All I want is to create a place where we can practice our craft without fear. Where we can gather enough power without restriction to do the things we have to, help the people who need it. Is that really so bad?"

He made it sound normal. Honorable even. And the people below didn't seem all that sinister now that I wasn't caught off guard. Several were only children, drawn into blood magic by someone older and less scrupulous.

But I'd been down this path before.

I shook my head. His expression lightened, and I realized he thought I was answering him.

"No, Luka," I said so he couldn't misunderstand. "I know all that, and I know that it's wrong."

"Why?" he said.

He was going to say more, solidify his argument or something, but I didn't let him.

"Because it changes people," I said. "And not in a good way. It changes how they think and how they value life. I don't want to be that kind of person, Luka. And I don't want to encourage anyone else to be either." I turned to face him. "My answer is no."

He looked genuinely regretful. "I thought you'd feel that way," he said. "That's why I took precautions." He pulled a white cloth from his pocket. A sharp pang went through my chest before I could even see it clearly.

Blood smeared the white linen, staining it a dull red. I knew blood very well by now and this blood sang to me. A part of it flowed through my own veins and pumped through my heart.

Mabushka.

I lunged for the cloth. "What have you done to her?"

He whipped it out of my reach and tucked it back in his pocket. "Nothing. She had a nose bleed. Nothing serious. I offered to throw this away for her."

Now I recognized one of her handkerchiefs. There would be a little Valerian A embroidered in the corner. My first attempt at fancy stitching. I'd given it to her for LongNight six years ago.

I swallowed. "What are you going to do to her?" He

claimed a noble purpose, but he was no better than the authorities who took blood to track a mage. With that scrap of linen, he could do anything he wanted to Mabushka, even at a distance. I'd thought maybe he had brought her here, but now I realized she could be anywhere.

"Nothing. So long as you don't do anything stupid. Assurance, Reyna. This is just assurance." He patted his pocket.

I ground my teeth. Did I have any choice? I'd promised Eira I'd find something we could use. But all I'd done was get myself mired deeper than before.

"What do you want me to do?"

CHAPTER THIRTEEN

The caravan had only stopped long enough to drop off a wagon load of grain before continuing on the road. Evgenia and Pyotr wanted to get to the winter capital before the court moved for the season. Fortunately—or unfortunately depending on my mood—that fit with Luka's plans, too. He wanted me in Post da Konstantin and had promised to contact me as soon as we arrived.

But by the time I'd extricated myself from The Lancet and The Red Noble, the caravan had rolled out of town to camp on the edge of the Howling Bog, which stood between us and the capital. I had to hitch a ride three miles down the road with a chatty tinker in his jangling cart. When I hopped off in sight of the caravan's cooking fires, my ears rang from all the clanging pots and pans and tools that hung behind my head.

I touched my satchel, where I'd tucked Luka's next assignment and shivered. A few snowflakes fell, and I sniffed the air. There'd be a foot of snow on the ground by morning, and I was immensely glad Eira and I would be snug in the heart's blood wagon tonight. The others would all be hunkering down under their wagons, layering padded quilts between themselves and the frozen ground.

Two figures stood between the wagons, silhouetted by the fires, a lanky dog sitting beside them. Eira and Aleksei from the shape of their shadows.

I blew out my breath in a sigh and stepped toward them.

"You made it," a voice said behind me.

I yelped and whirled around. Karina coalesced out of the darkness, and I clutched my chest, willing my heart to slow down. "You scared the muck out of me."

Karina limped forward. "Sorry. Eira told us you had to run an errand in town."

I frowned at the stiff way she moved. She'd been walking completely normal the last day or two. She shouldn't be limping, unless she'd overworked herself and the muscle ached. What was she doing out here anyway? Had she followed me again?

Her eyes went wide as I stared at her. "What?" she said, glancing around.

I shook my head. She wouldn't be so calm if she'd seen what I was doing. She probably was just out here standing guard and the cold made her leg stiff. "Nothing," I said.

"Reyna," Eira said, coming toward us. "Are you all right?"

It was all she could say with Karina and Aleksei present, but I understood what she meant. Had I learned where Mabushka was? Could we fight against the blood mages now?

I winced. "I'm not great. But it's nothing serious."

Her mouth twisted in a way that said she'd get the rest out of me later.

"Patepf's stew will change that," Aleksei said with a grin.

"That bad, huh?" I said and smiled at him.

"That good. He found some wild truffles nearby. He says they'd have been ruined by the morning."

Victor barked, making Eira and I jump.

"Stupid dog," Eira said with a shaky laugh.

But Karina squinted into the stand of trees nearby. The same place where Victor was looking.

"What is it?" I said, but Karina held her hand up for quiet.

Victor barked again and took off into the trees. Karina rushed after him, her gait lopsided but determined.

There was a growl and a short sharp yell from the trees.

"Victor's caught something," I started to say just as Eira dashed past me, following Karina into the darkness. "Eira! What are you doing?"

I raised my eyes to the sky before following her. This wouldn't be the first time I'd had to bail Eira out of some trouble she'd run into head-first.

Aleksei pulled even with me. "Reyna, go back to camp. *Da'ermo*, has everyone gone daft?"

"I'm not leaving Eira. Where are the other *viona uchenye?*"

"Defending the camp. Where they're supposed to be. Unlike some people."

"Hey, this wasn't how I expected my night to go, either."

His smile flashed bright in the darkness. "What were you imagining?"

I flushed. I don't know why. All I'd imagined was some dinner and my bed.

We skidded to a stop where the trees tapered away at the edge of the swamp. Victor leaped and growled at the base of a pine, claws scrabbling at the bark while Karina peered up into the branches, a bemused look on her face. Eira stood beside her, hands over her mouth.

"Well," Karina said with a little smirk. "It's a little stringy but maybe Pyotr can make something of it in his stewpot."

"Very funny," a voice said from the branches. "Call the dog off, I'm no bandit."

"Vitaly," Eira said, voice high and breathy.

Karina whistled for Victor, who ceased growling and hurried to sit next to her. Vitaly tumbled out of the branches with a great deal of thumping and cursing. He must have used up every ounce of the little bit of speed and agility he had getting up there without the dog taking a chunk out of him.

He'd barely put both feet on the ground when Eira flung her arms around his neck and planted her lips on his. Vitaly hesitated only a moment before he drew her into his arms and kissed her back.

I opened my mouth, about to say something to remind my sister she had an audience. But if the boy had followed her all the way from Darayevo and they still felt this way after almost a month apart, then they deserved their reunion.

Karina waited, her head cocked at a quizzical angle.

"Wow," Aleksei said.

"I know," Karina said. "How can they breathe?"

"They're like two puzzle pieces. Look at the way they fit."

I cleared my throat. "Eira?"

There was a muffled grunt that could have come from my sister.

"Why don't you introduce Vitaly?"

No response.

"Right," I said instead. "Vitaly, this is Aleksei, son of the caravan leads. And Karina, one of our *viona uchenye*."

Vitaly's hand raised in a little wave, but he didn't lift his face from my sister's.

"Karina, Aleksei, this is Vitaly. Eira's...er."

"We can see," Aleksei said. "Maybe more than we wanted to."

Behind Eira's head, Vitaly might have winced but now she had a hold of his ears, and I don't think he dared pull away lest she take them with her.

"What do you suppose he wants?" Karina said, voice baffled.

"Obviously Eira," Aleksei said.

"Hey." I elbowed him. "That's my sister you're talking about."

"Sorry," Aleksei said. "It was too easy."

"Vitaly helped Eira when our house burned down. I guess he must have followed her here."

Aleksei's smile turned sappy. "Aw. They're like Anastasy and Svetanka. No wonder they fit."

I rolled my eyes and pulled my hood up. The snow was starting to gather on the branches of the few trees, lining them in white.

"What?" Aleksei said with a wiggle of his eyebrows. "Don't you believe in romance?"

I opened my mouth but my answer caught in my throat. I'd thought I'd found my own Anastasy once. But he'd turned out to have more in common with the evil baron than the golden hero.

"Yes, well, I supposed he'd like to stay by Eira," I said. I directed it at Vitaly, but it was Aleksei who answered.

"I'll talk to Mamat," he said. "She's always talking about getting a farrier to travel with us. Maybe I can convince her he's good with horseshoes."

That caught Vitaly's attention when nothing else had. He pulled away from Eira and stared at Aleksei, mouth open and eyes wide. "Really?" he said. "You'd do that for me?"

Aleksei shrugged. "Who am I to stand in the way of true love? Are you any good with horseshoes?"

"He'd have to stop kissing long enough to see them," Karina said with a pointed glance at Vitaly.

Vitaly flushed a bright, painful-looking red, but he raised his chin and tucked Eira under his arm. She snuggled against his chest. Good grief, this was getting ridiculous.

Karina's eyes narrowed before she finally shrugged and turned away. She didn't see because her back was turned but Vitaly beamed as though he'd won something important before he went back to kissing my sister.

I wondered if Vitaly regretted his choice a couple of days later as he stumbled over the low brush at the edge of the road and splashed into the bog. Anyone else would have cursed, but he just sighed and pulled himself out with a squelch.

Most caravans traveled around the Silmaran Fens, also known affectionately as the Howling Bog. But one of our drivers, Ivan, had grown up nearby and carried a map of the firm ground in his head. Using his knowledge, Evgenia and Pyotr could shave off an entire week of travel by going through the bog instead of taking the safer route to the south.

I wished they hadn't this time. The fens had been used by blood mages during the *Krovaya Epohka*. They'd lived and worked here, using it as a staging area from which they could assault the capital. And the fens still reeked of blood and violence even four hundred years later. Any mage passing through could feel the weight of bloody history even if they couldn't see the *vytl* that had been released here.

It was hard enough keeping my spells from drawing extra *vytl*. Here, with the memory of blood, they would be even more dangerous.

Awful for a healer, but it made me wonder if there were any blood mages who still used this place as a home. Over any other place in Ballaslav, spells would be the most powerful here in the fens.

Although right now, the physical nature of our surroundings was our biggest problem. This wasn't the first time Vitaly had stumbled, tripped, or splashed in the time he'd been with us. The boy was a clutz of the finest order. It was a wonder he still had all his limbs attached.

He was also terrible with horses, and I was pretty sure Evgenia had noticed. But she hadn't said anything yet. Maybe she'd noticed his devotion to Eira and was keeping the truth to herself for now.

I glanced at Eira, beside me on the wagon seat, and

jerked my head at Vitaly, who was emptying the muddy water from his boot.

She sighed. "I know, I know. But I'll hurt his feelings if I insist he ride with us. Everyone else walks."

"We camp here," Ivan called down the row of wagons. "Don't move until I come show you where the good ground is."

"No problem," I muttered, wrapping the leads around the seat beside me. Normally, Ivan drove the heart's blood wagon, but since he was playing native guide, I'd taken his place. Mostly it just meant keeping the shaggy horse directly behind the wagon in front of us, but I kept worrying it would take it into its head to bolt into the bog.

Ivan carefully arranged every wagon in the train, ensuring each wheel stood on firm ground. If any of them sunk even a little, we'd have to hack them free in the morning from the frozen mud. The horses had to be picketed on an island a few hundred feet away and be protected from the same danger. The rest of us set up camp as the drivers and the *viona uchenye* unhitched the horses and led them to safe ground.

There was a crash and Vitaly grabbed desperately for the stack of bowls he'd knocked over. I rubbed my temples as Eira rushed to help him pick them up and inspect them for mud. I wished them luck. There was mud everywhere.

The basin of water for the Rites had to be refilled four times before everyone had made it through the line. The muck got under your fingernails, into your boots, and between your toes. I was hard-pressed to find a spot of my clothing clean enough to wipe my hands with. The hard slog and subsequent dirt and mud had taken their toll on our spirits. We were quiet as we settled around the fire with our bowls, with only the occasional splash and slurp from the bog breaking our silence.

Then one of the drivers pulled out his fiddle and the mood lifted in anticipation. He put his bow to the strings and played a couple of bars of music. Several people grinned as they recognized the first stanza of the ballad. The player raised his eyebrows at Aleksei.

Aleksei shook his head with a smile. "Do you know how long it's been since I sang Anastasy?"

"Probably as long since I've played it," the fiddler responded. "But we found a Svetanka for you." He jerked his head at me without causing a break in the music.

I held up my hands. "I'm not very good. Maybe Eira..." I glanced at my sister who had no compunctions about singing for strangers, but she was nuzzling Vitaly and not paying any attention. Blegh. Good for Eira, finding a love as sweet as that of the legendary couple, but did they have to flaunt it while we were eating?

Aleksei was looking at me, a challenge in his eyes. "I'll sing it if you will," he said.

I started to shake my head, but the fiddler launched into Anastasy's first stanza and Aleksei raised his voice in song.

I swallowed and fought to keep my eyebrows from climbing into my hair. Aleksei's rich tenor reached across the fire and plucked at memories of sitting beside our little hearth in the cottage, listening to Mamat and Papa sing about two lonely hearts finding each other over and over again even as the world strove to keep them apart.

Anastasy's part came to a close and the fiddler played the bridge between. I chewed my lip as Aleksei grinned at me. I hadn't agreed to anything, but I couldn't leave Anastasy without a Svetanka.

I opened my mouth and sang Svetanka's response to Anastasy's proposal. And if Aleksei's Svetanka was a little wobbly, he had only himself to blame.

Off to the side, Corwin scribbled madly as Karina translated in his ear.

When we got to the chorus, Aleksei joined me and took the melody while I took the harmony. I had to admit, we sounded good together. Maybe Eira was right about the whole confidence thing. She and Vitaly had taken a break from staring deeply into one another's eyes to cuddle cheek to cheek as they listened to the music.

I turned away from them and nearly broke the line of harmony to laugh as I saw Evgenia and Pyotr doing the same thing. Aleksei caught my gaze and rolled his eyes.

The next time around, Aleksei took the harmony, throwing me off for a moment before I found the melody below him. Papa had never sung that high.

As we drew the ballad to a close, the fiddler pulled out the last haunting chords and let them linger in the night air.

"So which part of that wasn't supposed to be very good?" Aleksei asked me.

In the moment of silence before I could answer, there was a splash and a quiet nicker from one of the horses. Aleksei and several of the drivers spun toward the island where they were picketed. There was another nicker, this time moving away from us.

"The horses," Aleksei said and shot to his feet.

Karina was already off, splashing between the mist-shrouded hummocks. The rest of the *viona uchenye* and the drivers followed her.

"Are we under attack?" Vitaly said.

Evgenia and Pyotr lurched upright. "Horse thieves. Stay here," Evgenia said, pointing to the fire. "In the circle of wagons. We'll make sure the *viona* chase off any horse thieves."

I stood, my gaze darting between the two of them as they slipped into the bog after the others. They'd said to stay put, but sitting there with Corwin and the rest of the passengers felt too much like waiting for the ax to fall.

I glanced at my sister, who sat alone now. "Where's Vitaly?"

"Standing guard," she said, gesturing to the circle of wagons.

I frowned. "Is that such a good idea?"

Eira bristled. "You want to be the one to tell him no?"

I raised my hands in defeat. "No, of course not."

But I was going to get my healer's kit, just in case. It would be just like Vitaly to slip into the bog and break an ankle while the others came back unscathed.

Beyond the circle of firelight, mist shrouded the little snow and slush-covered hummocks. I couldn't see anything through the fog. It even muffled sound.

I rounded the corner of the heart's blood wagon and came face to face with a stranger. He froze, red-ringed eyes wide with surprise, his hands on the tarp of the nearest wagon. Another figure rustled through the next wagon down the line.

The horses were just a decoy.

I spun and raced for the fire. "The grain!" I called into the bog. "*Viona,* to me. They're going for the grain."

A flying weight hit me from behind, and I went down with a thud. For the moment, I was glad that mud had softened my fall.

I twisted and saw the blood mage scrabbling for a knife. I swung my fist at him, but I couldn't get my elbow back far enough to put any power behind it.

They'd lured everyone away with the horse theft, leaving only Eira and me and a few passengers to defend the grain. A frantic glance beside me showed Eira scrabbling for some sort of weapon. I bared my teeth in a grin. My sister may have been headstrong and impulsive, but at least that meant she would always be there for me with a frying pan or a... flaming firebrand?

The fiery log came down, glancing off the side of the blood mage's head, striking him on the shoulder. I used the moment of distraction to knee him in the groin the way Mabushka had taught me, and when he reeled back, I thrust the heel of my hand into his nose the way Karina had taught me.

He lunged back, clutching his face, and I staggered to my feet. Eira reached for me, and I grabbed her arm. The blood mage stared at the blood coating his fingers, and the ring around his eyes grew wider as his nostrils flared.

Uh oh. Great job, Reyna. Give the blood mage the very thing he needs to be even more powerful.

I drew in a deep breath and clutched Eira's hand. The mage raised his eyes to mine and smiled.

"Eira!" Vitaly appeared out of the mist, stumbled over Eira's discarded firebrand, and crashed into the mage, taking him to the ground. His feet tangled in the other man's limbs, and he lashed out in panic. Vitaly's boot clipped the mage's temple and our attacker went limp.

We gaped at Vitaly, who stared at the mage with horror. Two more bodies lay in the shadows between the wagons. I didn't remember anyone taking them out. Had Vitaly's clumsiness saved us all?

Three of the *viona uchenye* burst into the firelight, weapons drawn. They stopped when they saw the bodies.

"O'in save me, did I kill them?" Vitaly said.

A *viona uchenye* went to each one of the bodies.

"Nice work," the nearest one said. He narrowed his eyes at Vitaly while someone else clapped the young man on the shoulder. He looked sick to his stomach.

"What's happening out there?" I asked the *viona*. I couldn't see anything beyond the mist.

"The horses were a decoy," he said. "If these are the only ones who went for the grain, then it's over. The others should be getting back soon, and we'll take stock."

Right, then I really might need my kit. I went back to dig through the heart's blood wagon, for real this time.

"Reyna," a voice called. I spun and nearly knocked into Karina, who had pulled herself up out of the muck and onto dry land. "Reyna, I heard you call." She seized my arms, her eyes wide as she checked for damage. "Are you all right?"

"I'm fine," I said. "Vitaly saved us, if you can believe that."

She didn't laugh with me like I'd intended her to. Her eyes tightened a fraction.

"Were you really that worried?" I said. "I didn't know anything could frighten you." Well, besides stitches.

She hesitated a beat before chuckling and pulling away. "You'd be surprised..."

"Reyna." Ivan splashed through the water, bits of thin ice floating away from his movements. "We've found Aleksei. He's hurt."

I sucked in a breath and snatched my kit from the open door of the wagon. "Where?"

"You'll have to come to him. I've left torches to mark the way. I'll show you."

I slid off the island into the frigid water that swirled around my knees. My skirt and cloak dragged along behind me, slowing me down.

Karina splashed behind me. Seriously, she was more loyal than a dog.

Ivan led the way across the swamp through water up to our waists. Mist wreathed the torches stuck in the hummocks along the way, giving them glowing halos.

The murmur of voices told me we were close, and I hopped to the last hummock where someone had stuck a couple of torches into the mud and the reeds. There was a huge splash and a neigh, and a frightened white horse lunged out of the water beside us. I gasped and dodged backward as the driver scrambled to keep a hand on its halter. Then driver and horse disappeared toward the caravan almost as fast as they'd appeared.

On the wet ground ahead, Ivan and Evgenia knelt beside a third figure.

I dropped to my knees beside Aleksei. His white face stared up at the night sky, and he struggled to draw breath.

"What happened?" I said. His hand clutched his chest, and I moved it so I could unbutton his shirt. I hated to do this in the cold air but who knew what damage I would cause by moving him, especially through the evil footing of the bog.

I expected one of the others to answer, but Aleksei gasped out, "Horse—kicked me."

"I'll kill the stupid creature," Eva said, wiping her eyes before clasping Aleksei's other hand.

"She was—frightened, Mamat," Aleksei said.

"Stop talking," I told him. He could barely breathe, let alone speak. A livid bruise marked his chest just under his heart, and I fancied I could see the hoofprint.

"Probably broke a rib or two," I said. "He'll be fine." I hoped. It was possible the broken rib had punctured his lung, considering how much trouble he was having. But saying so out loud wouldn't make Evgenia any easier to deal with.

"Can you fix it?" Eva said. "What do you need? We'll get you anything."

"Blankets," I said. "And a stretcher. We'll have to get him back to camp once I'm done with him, and I don't want his body dealing with the cold on top of trauma." I swallowed but didn't let Eva see how nervous I was.

O'in, please don't let me muck this up.

"Ivan, you heard her," Eva said.

I shook my head. "You should go, too, Eva."

"I'm not going anywhere," she said in the steely tone that moved dozens of drivers to carry out her will.

"You can't help him by staying, *sudinya*," I said, matching her tone. "But you can help him by going. I need time and space. Karina will guard us."

Aleksei squeezed her hand. "She said—I'll be fine, Mamat. Give the lady what she wants."

Eva's jaw hardened, and I raised my chin. Finally, she nodded. Swiftly, she leaned down and kissed Aleksei's forehead. "*Ja lublenn tevya.*"

Aleksei rolled his eyes. "Ugh, right when—I can't duck."

"Be sure everyone makes it into dry clothes," I said as she and Ivan moved off. "I don't want to see any frostbite in the morning."

I waited until she'd disappeared from my sight before touching Aleksei's shoulder. "Thank you."

He jerked his chin in a nod. He'd closed his eyes and sweat trickled down his temple.

"Why didn't you want her around?" Karina said.

"Family complicates things," I said. "They get in the way, ask questions. They care too much. Aleksei, you've broken a rib. It's pressed against your lung, that's why you're having such a hard time breathing. I'm going to have to put it back in place before you can be moved."

His throat bobbed, and his eyes opened long enough for him to glance at me. He nodded.

"If I'd realized all I had to do to get you to shut up was to break a bone, I'd have done it a lot sooner," I said.

He cracked a small smile.

I laid out everything I'd need in a neat line on my bag.

"Have you ever done this before?" Karina whispered in my ear.

I bit my lip. "Once. On a dead rabbit."

Aleksei's eyes shot open.

"But you'll be fine," I hastened to assure him. "I was the best in my class."

"Which you didn't finish," Karina pointed out.

I glared at her. "You're not helping. Look, go stand guard or something. I can't do this with you watching me."

"Right," she said and took off into the mist. A splash told me she hadn't gone far.

"All right," I said, more to myself than to Aleksei. A broken limb could be set with strength and knowledge. But a broken rib had to heal on its own or get a little help from magic.

Thank O'in there wasn't any blood. The corruption in my veins would make my spells draw *vytl* from blood whether I wanted them to or not. Which was why I'd been so careful with Karina's wound.

I still had to worry about the excess residue from the fens, but if I was lucky, the blood mages would have used up enough in this area to make a difference.

I rubbed my half-frozen fingers together and took a deep breath. I'd done this spell back in Valeria before I'd ruined my life. I knew I could do it. I just had to concentrate.

A pull here, a nudge there. Strength and pressure to keep the bone from sinking back against the lung tissue. A pain block on this nerve and some gentle guidance for the stressed blood vessel. And once the rib was in place, a binding to keep it there.

Even with the swamp's bloody past, my spells drew only the normal *vytl* needed. But the corruption in my blood always wanted more power. No matter the consequences.

My hands shook in reaction. I wanted it. Badly. Luka had been right. It had been so long since I'd felt powerful. But this healing required precision, not power.

Just a little more. The binding had to stay long enough for the bone to start to knit by itself.

But I was exhausted. My knees ached on the cold ground, and I could feel them swelling, getting hot and achy. I faltered, the spell sputtering against my fingers in reaction. I would just have to end it, elegant or not.

I closed my fist and yanked, cutting off the end of the spell in a messy knot.

The spell dissipated, and I sank back on my heels, a headache pounding in my skull. I checked my work, touching the fading bruise on Aleksei's chest, testing the binding spell keeping his rib in place. Everything looked all right.

"Is it done?" Aleksei said, voice rough and groggy.

"You can sit up. Carefully." I helped him as he propped himself up on an elbow.

"Hey," he said. "It doesn't hurt."

"The spell is keeping the rib in place, and it will keep the pain at bay for now."

Without thinking, I brought my shaking hands to my face and rubbed my eyes. Thank O'in I'd made it.

Aleksei's hand reached out and took my wrist, closing around the place where my sleeves had fallen to reveal bare skin. He turned it over, and his thumb brushed the edge of a scar.

I gasped and pulled away, my heart thudding. What had I done? Months of hiding and one careless gesture had ruined it all.

He would look at me the same way he'd looked at the girl outside the *yshkiniva*. He'd sneer and throw rocks at me and he'd be right.

"I—It's not what you think." I yanked the edges of my sleeves down. "It's not—I'm not—*Da'ermo*, please—please don't look at me like that."

"No, Reyna. It's all right," he said, voice soft. "I understand."

I clutched my elbows to keep my hands from shaking. The words didn't make any sense. "You do?"

His mouth twisted, whether it was from humor or pain I couldn't tell. "I do. I have them, too."

He pulled up his sleeves, and I stared. Three scars marred each of his forearms, almost mathematical in their precision.

My fingers stole to my mouth as blood rushed in my ears. Scars. He had scars. Each one a perfect leftover from the knife.

"You were a victim, right?" he said.

My gut clenched. "What?"

"Your eyes are normal. They bled you for one of their sick spells, didn't they?" He reached out and ran a finger down my forearm.

He thought I was a victim. He didn't look at me and see an abuser. I gagged and nearly puked all over him.

His fingers closed over mine.

"I know what it's like," he said, not meeting my eyes.

"Someone I thought was a friend—more than a friend—used me. He did that to me just for a little bit more power."

I swallowed down bile, trying not to imagine Aleksei's face in place of another in my memory.

"The worst part is how long I let him do it," he said quietly. "I thought maybe...maybe I could change him."

"But you couldn't," I said. I hadn't even realized I was going to speak. His story...I could have written the words myself. From either perspective. From the one who was bleeding...and the one who cut.

Deep lines slashed the corners of his mouth and eyes. "You can't change a blood mage. I know that now." Finally, he met my eyes again. "You haven't been through the Rites, have you? It's why you're hiding."

My breath shook in my chest.

"I don't blame you, you know. They weren't...weren't pleasant. We're taught that the Rites are for washing away sin, but it wasn't even my sin I was paying for. It was his. And now everyone looks at me like a victim."

Splashing indicated the return of Evgenia and Ivan, and Karina's voice rose in greeting.

"I won't tell," Aleksei said. "No one has to know if that's what it takes to make you feel safe again."

He said it so gently, with so much understanding behind it, I had to turn my face away and scrub my cheeks with my hands. I wanted him to understand. I wanted the words he said. But I wanted it after the truth. Not the continuation of this impossible lie.

CHAPTER FOURTEEN

"Welcome to my new home," Luka said, opening the door with a flourish.

I hesitated on the threshold of the very Valerian looking manor located just a few blocks from the University. "Your family paid for all this?" I said, stepping across the gleaming marble floor into the foyer. It was a far cry from the attic room Luka had lived in until the week before.

"Nice, isn't it?" He strode to the long balustrade that curved up the stairs. "I was thinking of inviting a few friends over tonight to try out the wine cellar."

I made a face. "Are you sure your parents would be all right with that?"

He laughed. "No. But they're not here, are they?"

His reckless grin invited me to share the joke. I could only shake my head with a smile. I cared too much about what my family thought to try something like that, but it was just like Luka to beg forgiveness rather than ask permission.

"Well, I hope you have fun," I said, checking out a door that led under the grand staircase.

Luka's hand flattened against the door at eye level and he pushed it closed as he leaned beside me. His gaze centered on me, making me shiver. The red ring around his irises glittered in the bright sunlight streaming through the hall. I licked my lips.

"I thought maybe you'd like to stay," he said.

"I'm...I'm not sure." I didn't really like his friends. They were all a little louder, a little rougher than I found pleasant. I was getting used to the red in their eyes, but I didn't always like the jokes they told. Too many of them felt like cruelties disguised as humor.

"Please?"

"I have exams I have to study for."

He sighed and tweaked my chin. "Smart and beautiful. I guess I can't complain since it's one of the things I love about you."

My breath caught. "You do?"

"Isn't it obvious?" he said, voice pitched low as he reached to twine his fingers with mine.

Well, yes. But no. I didn't know how to recognize when a boy was interested in me. Eira was the one who drew all the attention. This was entirely new territory. And he hadn't tried to kiss me yet. Because he was too much of a gentleman? Or was there some other reason?

"You know, there are plenty of other things we could do besides inviting your friends," I said. I wasn't quite bold enough to meet his eyes while I said it. But I pulled a little on his hand, drawing him closer.

He was better than the boys he called friends. He wasn't cruel. He'd stopped to help a girl bleeding on the street and now look at us. I just had to convince him of that.

"Yes, but I wanted to show you off," he said. The fingertips of his other hand brushed a fall of hair back from my face. "I want them to see the kind of girl I've snagged for myself."

I flushed. He *was* proud of me, then.

"Say yes, please?"

Maybe if he saw me in comparison to his friends, he'd realize just what kind of people they were. "A-all right," I said.

His eyes crinkled at their corners, and he slid his hands up my arms, stopping on the bulky bandages wrapped around my forearms. "What's this?"

I shrugged and pulled away from him. "The cold this morning made my legs ache. I just needed a little extra healing this morning. Don't worry, I took care of it."

It was even easier now than it had been a month ago. With every cut, more and more power poured into my spells. The corruption in my blood didn't just allow me to draw more power, it reached out for it, demanded it. The corruption might have been hurting me, but it was also the only thing keeping me strong.

He frowned. "If you would just find a goat, you wouldn't have to take care of it."

"You know I hate that word." I stepped away from him, my heels ringing in the empty hall. "I don't want to hurt anyone but me," I said.

He opened his mouth, and I turned to put my hand

against his chest. "Luka please," I said. "I don't want to fight about this."

He scowled, lips tight with frustration. There was one way to keep him from arguing. I wasn't the bold one. Eira was. But perhaps this once I could follow her example.

I stood on my toes, slid my hands around the back of his neck and pressed my lips against his.

I curled on my bunk in the heart's blood wagon, a thin and very expensive piece of paper crumpled in my hand. Luka had given me the communication spell before I'd left him at The Lancet. "So I can contact you," he'd said with the grin I'd fallen for over a year ago.

The paper had remained blank as we'd rolled closer and closer to Post da Konstantin, and I'd had the brief insane hope that maybe it was broken and I could ignore Luka and his plans forever.

Not so.

Just this morning, words had appeared scrawled in Luka's careless handwriting.

Reyna, I need you.

Even now the words made my heart leap as they always had. The nausea that followed, however, was new.

On the edge of Post da Konstantin, you'll meet a blood mage named Sergei. He has a package for you. He's too conspicuous to get it across the city, but you will be perfect to bring it to me.

Below the note was a rust-red thumbprint. The blood didn't just call to me, it sang. As if I needed a reminder that he held Mabushka.

Thoughts raced round and round, making me dizzy enough to bury my head against the pillow.

I was only valuable to Luka as long as I remained unregistered. The moment I donned the red cloak, my movements would be just as restricted as every other blood mage.

And maybe when that happened, he'd let Mabushka go. There wouldn't be any reason to control me anymore, so he wouldn't need to keep her.

But to gain Mabushka's freedom, I would have to turn myself in. I would have to acknowledge that I'd spilled blood; I would have to admit to myself and the world that I'd corrupted myself for power.

A tear slipped down my temple and soaked into the quilt beneath my head. I could save Mabushka. I just had to give up the rest of my life to do it. My fingers spasmed on the paper.

Coward. User. Sinner. It didn't matter what names I called myself in my head, I remained frozen on the bed.

I was everything I called myself and more. Aleksei thought I was a victim. But I was worse. I was a conspirator. A cohort. A blood mage, no matter that I hadn't touched a drop in seven months. All because I wasn't brave enough to say no to Luka.

I pushed myself upright and wiped the tears from my

face. Crying wouldn't solve anything. If I wasn't willing to end Mabushka's imprisonment the right way, I would have to push forward into the wrong way.

I opened the door of the wagon with the same thought I'd had in my head since I'd crossed the mountains into Ballaslav.

Let's get this over with.

Evgenia and Pyotr had given everyone four days off, now that we'd reached Post da Konstantin, so it wasn't hard to slip away from the caravansary with some of the drivers who headed into the city for some fun. Once again, I left Eira behind to keep certain people from following.

This time, Luka's note had given me an address, a building where I was supposed to meet this man, Sergei. He'd also included an ominous afterthought: bring a bribe.

I found the place at the edge of the city, in a district full of tanneries and slaughterhouses. I could well imagine blood mages making their home here where the air was filled with the feel of tainted *vytl*.

I stood outside the building, my jaw going slack as a kind of numbness spread along my limbs.

This wasn't a house. Or even a business.

This was a *viona krovaya* guard post. Two of them stood outside, dressed in their rust-red uniforms and the doorframe was painted a messy scarlet.

I tried to swallow, but my throat was too dry. My feet wanted to run, and I had to tell them sternly that Luka wouldn't have sent me here just to get me caught. He still needed me and he needed me mobile.

The bribe. This is what I must need it for.

I ground my teeth. He couldn't have said something? Anything more that would have warned me about what I was walking into?

I gathered the edges of my cloak so I had something to clench and marched across the muddy street.

The *viona krovaya* gave me calculating looks, one with a smirk and the other with his lip curled in a grimace.

I opened my mouth and to my horror only heard a squeak. Quickly, I cleared my throat and tried again.

"I need to see a man called Sergei?" I said. It still didn't sound confident, but at least the words had come out this time.

The one on the left with a patchy blond beard rolled his lips between his teeth before spitting on the doorstep. "Yeah?"

That wasn't particularly helpful. "Do you...do you have anyone here by that name?"

He cracked his neck. "Yeah."

I huffed, more annoyed now than scared. "What would it take to see him?"

"More than a couple of questions," he said and the other guard chuckled.

I enjoyed being laughed at as much as the next girl. I tore my purse from my belt and shoved it into his chest. "That much?" I said.

He snatched at the purse before I could let it fall to the

front step, and he poured the coins into his other hand. My meager wealth all spent on Luka's ridiculous plan.

The *viona* closed his fist over the money and stepped aside with a mocking bow. "My lady…"

I sniffed and thrust my nose in the air to tell him exactly how I felt about that and stepped into the guard post.

It wasn't much more than a squalid little room cut in half by floor-to-ceiling bars and a cell door. On the one side stood a chair that looked perfectly ordinary until you realized it was bolted to the floor and had leather straps around the arms.

I shuddered.

Behind the bars, a man lounged across a long bench, his chin covered in dark stubble and his hair straggling into his eyes. He watched me as his fingers braided and unbraided a bit of leather no longer than his finger.

"Well, hello," he said, voice surprisingly even given his appearance and situation.

"Are you Sergei?" I said. I couldn't imagine he'd say no. There was literally no one else here.

"I am."

"Luka sent me." Then I bit my tongue as I realized he might think I was here to rescue him.

He coughed, curling forward over his knees. "Yeah, I figured someone would be by soon," he said when he'd caught his breath. "Seeing as I'm about to be registered. He can't do much with us once we're registered."

My gaze flicked to the chair. Dark stains marred the wooden surface.

"It's all right. I won't hold it against Volksyn. Won't have long to hold it against him anyway."

My breath went shaky. "How...how much blood do they take?"

He chuckled which caused him to cough again. "Enough. Enough to use against you. It's the corruption that lets them track you. But that's not why I don't have long."

He held out his sleeve so I could see the flecks of blood left by his cough. The blood sickness. From the look of it, he must be in the last stages.

It had taken me months in Valeria to realize that when Luka talked about a blood mage's corruption, he meant it literally. The corruption allowed us to draw more power from blood. But in the end, it was what killed us. The more blood you used, the faster you died. A good healer could hold it off for a few years, maybe even a decade. But no longer.

"You're dying."

"Yeah."

I hesitated. "I can help. I'm a healer."

"Not even magic can heal the blood sickness, *blenni*, but thanks for offering."

"I know that." I wanted to snap but didn't have the heart to. "But I can make it not so painful."

He flipped the hair from his eyes and pinned me with a prideful glare. "I've earned my pain, *blenni*. Learn from me and don't let it go this far. And if you do, don't get caught. Now take what you came for and go."

He jerked his chin at the other side of the room where a satchel lay on a rough table. Then he leaned back against the bench and closed his eyes. Conversation over.

I swallowed once more before darting across the room to

snatch the satchel. And then because Mabushka had raised me to be polite no matter what, I said, "Thank you."

I tucked the bag under my cloak and made it to the door.

Where the bearded *viona krovaya* stopped me with a hand planted across the open doorway.

"Where are you going?" he said.

"What do you mean?"

He leaned close enough I could smell his breath. He'd die from the rot in his teeth unless he got a healer to see to them soon. "You can't just leave. There's a toll. Every time you cross the threshold."

Ice flowed through my veins. "But I gave you everything I have already."

"Everything?" He grinned at his fellow. "That's too bad."

My stomach lurched. I could offer to heal his teeth. Or maybe he had a rash he didn't want anyone else to see. But from the way he leered, I didn't think he was going to accept anything I'd willingly offer.

"Maybe not everything," a voice said from the street.

I gasped, relief winning out over consternation.

Karina tossed a pouch to the nearest *viona*. Then grasped my arm and hauled me out of the guard post while he was busy fumbling with the strings.

I went with her willingly enough, but two blocks away, she still had hold of my wrist. By then my heart had stopped racing, and the panic gave way to a raging heat that beat in my cheeks.

"Karina." I tried to yank my arm from her grasp, but she held tight and glared over her shoulder. "Karina, did you follow me?"

She dragged me to the mouth of an alley and a familiar figure jumped at our appearance.

"Eira. What are you doing here?" I said, each word its own storm.

"We could ask you the same thing," Karina said, finally releasing my wrist.

My gaze darted between the two of them, Eira blanching in the face of my wrath and Karina crossing her arms to lean against the wall. "Eira, what did you do?"

It was Karina who answered, considering my sister couldn't seem to do more than stare at her shoes. "She knew you were in trouble and asked for help."

"I couldn't let you go alone," Eira said. "And Karina's good at this sort of thing. We agreed that we would need help."

"I asked you to wait," I hissed at her, my fist clenching in the fabric of my skirt. "You know why we had to wait. How much did you tell her? *Da'ermo*, Eira. You could have ruined everything."

Eira flushed and opened her mouth.

"She didn't tell me anything, *malvo o'in*," Karina said, her gentle voice doing more to deflate my anger than Eira's protests. "Just asked me to help her follow you and protect you."

Malvo o'in. Misguided one. It was the same thing she'd called the blood mage in Elisaveta. I winced away from the pity.

"You want to tell us what you were doing?" she said. "Maybe we can help."

"I know what she was doing."

I spun as Aleksei's voice bounced off the walls of the alley. He stood silhouetted against the street.

"*Pohomzhet da ma Baud*," I said, throwing my hands in the air. "Did you tell the whole city?"

"I didn't tell him, I swear," Eira cried. "Only Karina."

"She didn't have to tell me," Aleksei said, stalking toward us. He clutched Luka's communication spell in his hand, my instructions still visible against the pale paper.

My stomach dropped, and I put my hand to my hip where my own bag would normally hang. I'd meant to bring it with me, but I'd decided at the last minute that I wanted my hands free. I'd left it in the heart's blood wagon.

"She didn't have to tell you because you went through my things," I snapped, the blood rushing to my face.

"Mamat wanted to straighten things up for you. As a favor. She'd have found it if I hadn't." He thrust the paper at me. "I assumed you'd rather she didn't know what you've been up to."

I fumbled to grab the paper before it fell in the slush of the alleyway.

"I'm being pretty patient," Karina said, still leaning against the wall. "For the last time, what's going on?"

I opened my mouth, ready to lie, to defend myself, to extricate Eira. I wasn't sure which. But the words didn't come.

"She's working with blood mages," Aleksei said, turning from me to face the *viona*. "Stealing for them." He whirled back to me. "I know they've hurt you, but you don't have to keep doing their dirty work. You can walk away. You don't have to be their victim anymore."

I flushed when Eira and Karina turned their gazes on me, confused and pitying respectively. I'd thought I was doing the safe thing, or at least the safest thing left to me. But it was all going to pieces around me.

"It's not what you think," I said. My voice was as weak as my argument.

"Then tell us what it is," Aleksei said, and I was surprised he didn't wave his hands over his head in frustration.

"I can't," I said.

"Why not?" Karina said.

I just shook my head.

"They have Mabushka," Eira said, voice harsh in the silence.

"Eira!" What was she doing?

"They burned our house and took Mabushka. They told Reyna she has to work for them or they'll kill her."

Aleksei jerked back before turning to me, a question in his eyes. Karina didn't look surprised. She just gazed at me with a steady expression. I had little choice now, thanks to Eira's outburst.

I swallowed and uncrumpled Luka's communication spell to show them Mabushka's thumbprint. "It's her blood. To prove they still have her. I wanted to find out where they were keeping her so I could rescue her."

Aleksei and Karina looked at each other.

I shook my head. "I know what you're going to say and the answer is no."

"What were we going to say?" Karina said.

"You're going to tell me to do something about it. To fight

back. Well, Eira's already tried that argument. But I'm not doing anything to risk Mabushka's life."

Aleksei stepped closer and put his hand on mine. "But you aren't alone anymore. We'll help you."

"You're actually in the best possible place you can be," Karina said. "This blood mage trusts you. Or at least he thinks he controls you. So long as you're clever about it, he doesn't have to know you're working against him at all."

My eyes narrowed. None of them understood. Even Eira didn't know how dangerous Luka was. Or how well he knew me.

Aleksei stepped close and whispered so only I could hear. "Do you want to be under his control forever?"

It wasn't rhetorical. He met my eyes and asked the question seriously, like he knew how I'd reacted when Luka said he needed me.

"I know the answer isn't easy," he said. "He'll always have some part of you that you can't get back. But you don't have to let him have any more of you."

He was right but in a way that was twisted and warped from what he meant.

Most of me hated Luka, hated him for what he'd turned me into, hated him for what had happened in Valeria. But the rational part of me knew how much of that was my own fault. I knew how I'd thrown myself at him, how desperate I'd been.

And there was still a small, hidden, loathed part of me that loved him and wanted what he offered. Every day I had to fight it off and stuff it back down under the disgust and fear and guilt. They didn't understand that his control extended far deeper than Mabushka's thumbprint on that paper.

And that was the problem, wasn't it? I let him keep that part of me. Over and over I gave in to it. I'd never be free of him or the blood until I cut that part out of me and burned it.

I tossed the satchel at Karina. "This is what he wanted. I didn't want to look in it. I didn't want to be a part of it."

"But if we know what he's planning, maybe we can anticipate and counter his moves," Aleksei said as Karina plunged her hand into the satchel and pulled out a bracelet.

"What is it?" Eira said.

Karina stood as if frozen, the broad silver cuff embossed with brass glinting between her fingers.

Aleksei peered at it. "Are those spell markings?"

I took a reluctant step forward. Inlaid bronze wire formed intricate patterns that I only recognized because of my time at the University. "I think so," I said. "Though they're much more complicated than anything I've ever worked with."

"It's a key," Karina said.

The rest of us glanced at her.

"How do you know?" Aleksei said.

"I've seen it before. As a part of my training. This is the key to the Bastion."

I took a sharp sip of breath. The Bastion, Ballaslav's most famous prison. Last home for murderers, thieves, and unrepentant blood mages. Post da Konstantin had been built on the icy shores of the Bay of Yulslav. The Bastion stood on the opposite shore, a looming black presence in the mists of the bay.

"The bracelet is a spell focus. It belongs to the warden," Karina said. "With the appropriate key words, it will allow a small party through the wards protecting the Bastion." Karina chewed her lip. "Do you know how expensive a piece of magery this is?"

I took the bracelet from her and turned it over in my hands. "Luka wanted this," I said.

"He must be planning to break someone out," Karina said.

"Or steal something," Aleksei said.

Karina gave him a disparaging look.

Aleksei shrugged. "You don't know."

"And neither do we," Eira said, chewing her bottom lip.

"We'll have to disrupt his plans somehow," Aleksei said. "When we find out what they are."

"How do you know he'll tell me?" I said. "I'm not exactly high up in his organization."

"He trusted you with this," he said. "Maybe he'll trust you with the rest."

"And if he does, you're going to tell us this time," Karina said. "Right?"

They still didn't understand what Luka was capable of. But they were already too deep. By following me, they'd placed themselves squarely in the middle of it. And if they had a stake in my problems then it seemed only fair to let them help solve them.

I sighed. "Right."

CHAPTER FIFTEEN

In the end, I sent one sentence back to Luka via his communication spell.

I have it.

Now we just had to wait. Only this time I wasn't waiting alone.

"Are you mad at me?" Eira asked as we climbed into the heart's blood wagon, leaving Karina and Aleksei chattering outside.

I slumped on my bunk and rubbed my eyes. "Why did you tell them about Mabushka?" I finally said.

She shut the door and sat down opposite me. "Aleksei was really mad," she said, voice quiet.

My jaw clenched. "Yes."

She shrugged. "I didn't want him to be mad at you."

My hands stroked the worn quilt on the bunk over and over. Eira had always been the one to act without thinking.

She was the impulsive one, and I kept expecting her to be the impulsive one. But then she said something that proved she not only thought before she acted, she'd been thinking of me.

"It doesn't matter if he's mad at me," I said, fingers clenching on the bedspread.

She bent her head to meet my eyes. "I'm not blind, Reyna. You like him."

I shook my head.

"Why not?" she said, misinterpreting the meaning. "He's nice and funny. He's not as good looking as Vitaly, but he's not bad. Why won't you admit it?"

A couple of months in love and she thought she knew everything about it. "It's complicated, Eira. The...the last time I felt this way, it didn't turn out so well."

She tilted her hea. "I knew you left someone in Valeria."

"If only he'd stayed there," I said.

She sat back with a smug look.

Da'ermo, I couldn't believe I'd said that out loud.

She drew her legs up onto the bed and rested her chin on her knees. "You want to explain that?"

No.

Yes. The way she waited, eyes steady and serious, reminded me of Mabushka. And for once, I wasn't afraid of what my sister would say.

I mirrored her position. "I met someone, but...I didn't know what he was really like. Or, well, I guess I did, but I ignored it. I wanted him to be a certain way so I pretended everything was all right."

"Your judgment is usually pretty good," she said. "He couldn't have been that bad."

"Believe me, he was." I held out Luka's communication spell.

Her eyes widened as she looked at the page that held my answer. "That's him?"

I tossed the paper on the tiny fold-down table at the back of the wagon and hugged my knees tighter. "I mucked up, Eira," I said. Maybe I should tell her the whole ugly truth. All I had to do was roll up my sleeves. If anyone could understand my mistakes, it would be my impulsive sister.

I opened my mouth, but before I could speak the com spell flashed and new words scrawled across it in Luka's handwriting.

Eira followed my gaze. "What does he say?" she whispered.

Reluctantly, I reached for the sheet of paper.

Well done, blenni. Would you like to free your grandmother? Meet me at the northwest docks three days from now at sundown. Bring the satchel.

"Do you think he really means it?" Eira said, reading upside down.

"If he does, it's not without a whole lot of strings attached." There was still an entire blood mage rebellion Luka was planning, and after going to such lengths to secure my help, I didn't see him relinquishing it that easily. Still...

"It's still a chance," Eira said, standing suddenly enough to make the wagon sway. "I'll get the others. Karina will know what to do at least."

I clutched my cloak to keep it from flapping in the icy breeze coming from the north. This particular wind was called the Shaker's Breath, named for O'in's eternal adversary. He reigned over the cold, dark, and above all lonely plane where sinners were exiled after death.

Sometimes I wondered if the name didn't have a far simpler origin in the fact that it made you shake and shiver in your boots.

Water lapped at the foot of the docks, breaking up the ice that had formed around the pylons. In less than a month, the entire bay would freeze over and stay that way until summer.

The docks were mostly deserted this time of night, but a couple of workers stacked crates beside a tavern on the waterfront, light spilling out of its big windows onto the cobblestones in front of me. As I passed, one of them dropped his burden and cursed.

I glanced over my shoulder, trying to spot the armed shadow I knew must be moving between the buildings. Karina had promised to follow, to keep me safe even among blood mages.

I couldn't spot her. But that didn't mean she wasn't there.

Three cloaked figures waited for me at the northwest pier. My steps slowed as I approached them, peering under their flapping hoods, looking for a familiar face.

Luka turned at the sound of my boots on the cobblestones and smiled. "See, Mamat," he said. "I told you she wouldn't let us down."

Sudinya Volka sniffed and looked me up and down.

"That remains to be seen," she said. I was struck by how melodic her voice was. She'd make a better Svetanka than I ever could. "Do you have it?" She held out her hand to me. Her scarlet cloak took the opportunity to rip free from her other hand and wave in the wind.

Da'ermo, we would be spotted for sure. And it didn't matter how corrupt the *viona krovaya* were, if I was caught associating with registered blood mages, no bribe would protect me. They'd find the scars; they'd find the truth.

I pulled the satchel out from under my cloak, where I'd carried it close to my body, and threw it to her. She caught it deftly, despite the surprise, and reached inside to pull the bracelet out. She held it up so the silver flickered in the lamplight.

The last figure drew his hood down, and I recognized Emil from the *Dya'val dal Kuchnya*.

"Good to see you again, *Dryg* Reyna."

I clenched my fists at my sides. "Where is my grandmother?"

"Safe enough," he said and tapped his fingers to his forehead in a mocking salute. "She sends her regards."

My lips pinched.

"Enough," *Sudinya* Volka said. "This is genuine. Our window is closing; we leave immediately." She gestured sharply and the men fell in line behind her.

So much for Luka being the voice of authority in this little rebellion.

The blood mages clambered down into a small skiff, tied below the pier. Luka stood, one foot up on the side of the boat and held out his hand to me, courteous as any noble.

I kept my hands under my cloak. "You said I could have my grandmother back."

"And you can. As soon as our work here is done. That was the deal, Reyna."

"Who are we breaking out?" I said.

Luka froze, face carefully blank. "What do you mean?"

My gaze flicked to the opposite side of the bay where the Bastion loomed. "A fair trade, right? My grandmother's life for one of your people," I said. "Who is it?"

A shadow crossed Luka's face for a moment before he beamed at his mother. "See? Smart and beautiful."

My chest ached.

Volka was not as amused as Luka. She straightened and speared me with her gaze. "Get in the boat. Now."

Her tone made my knees quake, and I bent to scramble into the bobbing vessel. I cast one longing glance behind me, wishing I could tuck Karina into my pocket somehow. She wouldn't be able to follow us across the bay, not without being spotted.

Emil took up a pair of oars and rowed us away from the lights of the wharf. I huddled down on my bench, hoping to use the sides of the boat to break the wind. It howled over the water here where there was nothing to break its course. Waves sent sprays of saltwater into our eyes and soaked through our cloaks. The boat bounced from crest to trough and back to crest, making my stomach churn.

Just as I began to wonder if they planned to row the entire way across the bay, Emil stood and hauled up the triangular mainsail. After that, my stomach settled a bit. We still bobbed from wave to wave but the motion was smoother.

Even as I huddled away from the wind, *Sudinya* Volka sat straight and proud in the bow of the boat, her cloak wrapped around her like a bloody shroud.

"Why do you wear the red tonight?" I said. "Won't it draw attention?"

She glanced at me out of the corner of her eye, and for a moment, I thought she would turn away and ignore my question. "Some of us wear the red with pride. Some of us don't shy away from the consequences of power."

"It will kill you, you know. The blood sickness always kills."

"Not before I've done my work. It wouldn't dare."

My next shiver had nothing to do with the Shaker's Breath.

The little skiff fairly flew across the bay and long before I was ready, the Bastion rose in front of us like a hulking dragon hunched over its pile of gold. Carved from an ancient outcropping of obsidian through magic and ingenuity, it gleamed black against the glacier behind it. No one escaped the Bastion. It was impossible to tunnel out and even if you made it out the doors, there were only two places to run: the bay, which was patrolled regularly and the glacier, where men froze and died without anyone knowing where they fell.

A staircase of black stone descended into the water ahead of us. When the bay froze over you would be able to step from the ice onto the first step, but now we tied the boat to a pole that rose from the water beside the steps.

The four of us jumped the short distance. My boots skidded on the slippery rock, and I would have fallen into the icy bay if I hadn't flung myself across the steps.

Volka looked down her nose at me before striding up the staircase, her cloak sweeping over my fingers.

Luka extended a hand, but I ignored it and picked myself up off the ground.

At the top of the steps, a lowered portcullis stabbed the stone under our feet with a hundred wicked points, keeping potential jailbreakers out and whatever we were after in. This was the fortress that Post da Konstantin was named for. Konstantin himself had built it to guard the shores of the newly formed Ballaslav from barbarian raiders well over a thousand years ago.

Volka stepped up to the bars. Were we seriously just going to walk in the front door?

A figure appeared behind the portcullis and Volka greeted the man by name.

"Akim," she said.

"*Sudinya.*" The man, dressed in black, picked his teeth as if he let blood mages into the Bastion all the time.

Volka held up the bracelet, and he stepped back. I expected the portcullis to rise with a groan or at least the grind of ancient machinery, but instead, a little door in the bars swung open, large enough to admit two people at a time. Volka stepped across with Emil, and Luka grabbed my arm to follow them.

As we stepped under the breached portcullis, a shiver of magic swept across my skin, leaving goosebumps in its wake. It had to be the ward that protected this place. Volka had made it recognize us with the bracelet.

"See what our power can buy us?" Luka said in my ear,

gesturing to the complicit guard who stood back to let us into the stronghold.

Akim finally flicked his fingers as if he hadn't found anything interesting in his teeth and jerked his head at us. "We don't have long," he said. "If any of the others see us, we're dead. And I'm not risking my neck for you, so remember that. If we're caught, you're on your own."

"You've made that clear," Volka said and followed the man through a small door in the rock wall.

I let out the breath I'd been holding. My plan wouldn't have worked if they'd managed to buy every guard in the Bastion.

Between Karina, Aleksei, Eira, and I, we'd decided the only way to get rid of Luka was to get him caught. Waiting wasn't working. I knew better than the rest of them that Luka didn't mean what he said about releasing Mabushka. Even if he did, he would find some other way to keep his hold on me.

Luckily, I'd just walked into a prison full of guards who had experience bringing down blood mages. Shouldn't be too hard to disrupt this caper and get the rest of them caught without getting caught myself, right?

I stifled a snort. This was going to go so well.

Karina had promised to come rescue me if everything went sideways and I ended up arrested. But while I knew she would kill herself trying, I doubted she'd be able to get there in time to keep the authorities from uncovering my arms and my secret.

So I just had to escape an inescapable prison.

Akim led us through a warren of black corridors. I kept craning my neck, trying to see cells and the criminals locked inside, but there was nothing except seamless rock walls stretching on and on. Every now and then, the glassy surface was broken by a line of script chiseled in an arc up the walls and over our heads.

I reached out to touch one and stopped myself. It was a spell. I couldn't pause long enough to read it, but Akim saw me looking and chuckled.

"No magic allowed in here under the wards, *mushka*," he said. "It'll trigger every stasis spell in every cell and corridor. Nothing gets in or out when they're up."

I blanched. Healers used stasis spells to keep patients stable while they were moved or if they were in too much pain to withstand treatments. We always made sure they were unconscious while they were held because the feeling of being trapped in a bubble of air was claustrophobic at best and induced insanity at worst.

My knees twinged while we walked. The swelling hadn't been too terrible this morning, but this much exertion wouldn't be good for them.

Finally, the black walls opened into a large room without a ceiling. A dome of stars stretched overhead and the Shaker's breath whistled across the opening. The walls curved around on either side of us, meeting on the opposite side of the room.

There the rock had been carved into a massive face and a gaping mouth that opened onto darkness.

Akim turned to grin at us. "Welcome to the Reckoning Chamber. Where the fates of all sinners are decided."

Volka didn't look impressed.

Luka pointed at the mouth. "What's that?"

"Not everyone survives the Bastion," he said with a shrug. "The stiffs go down there and the depths take them."

"And...and what's the Reckoning?" I said, not sure I really wanted to know.

"The final punishment for murderers, thieves, and anyone who uses blood for power. This is where we take their humanity."

"We don't need a tour," Volka said. "Where is he?"

Akim shrugged again and pointed to a piece of the polished black wall. I saw no difference between it and the rest of the wall, but Volka stepped forward, held out the bracelet, and said a couple of words while pressing it against the glassy stone.

The wall vanished, leaving a recessed space the size of the inside of a wagon. A man stood with his back to us, his hands clasped behind him.

I gulped. The cells had been here the whole time, each person shut inside a black glass case waiting for execution or the "final punishment," whatever Akim meant by that.

"Aleksandr," Volka said.

The man turned as if surprised, and I was struck by his stark black hair and the shape of his features. An older, more rugged version of Luka.

The man smiled and reached to take Volka's hand.

"I knew you'd come, *vozlublenni*," he said and kissed her palm.

The corner of Volka's mouth lifted, and she reached up with her other hand to cup his cheek.

"Always," she said. They smiled into each other's eyes before Volka turned back into the main room, all brisk business. "We have one more task to finish. Where is the beast?" she asked Akim.

He frowned. "You're sure you can control it?"

Her eyes flashed, and even though the red ring was dimmed without sunlight, the air crackled with her ire. "I'm sure."

"Right," Akim said, swallowing audibly. "Very well. Lilliathanon, you have company."

The moonlight shone down through the open ceiling onto a table in the middle of the room. It cast a long shadow on the floor.

The shadow moved. It rippled and pooled and surged upward into an impossibility standing in the middle of the room. A large black panther stalked toward Volka, red eyes fixed on her figure. Then it sank back to the floor and morphed into a huge snake that glided forward. And at last, it flowed upward and settled into the shape of a large human towering over Volka, edges indistinct but those eyes still glowing red.

I stopped breathing.

"Human," the thing said.

Volka inclined her head. "I have a deal to offer you."

"What is it?"

"Freedom," she said.

It tilted its head and stooped to look at her closer. "I am free."

She raised her eyebrows. "You are? I beg your pardon, I thought this was a prison."

The thing glanced around. "Yes, but I am no prisoner."

"No, you're their executioner."

It tilted its head. "It is a thing I am good at."

"But you want more," she said.

"How would you know that?"

"You only have the freedom to feed when they want you to, on whoever they bring you. I will let you feed whenever you like." She gestured to Emil who shifted from foot to foot beside the wall. "A gift. To prove what I say is true."

Emil's eyes widened as the creature turned its orange gaze on him. "What?"

The shadow sprang across the space, and I had time to do no more than raise my hand. As if I could stop whatever was happening.

Emil screamed as the creature's claws closed on his arms, drawing blood.

I covered my face.

"Still want to play by the rules, Reyna?" Luka said in my ear.

I turned my shoulder, but Luka shifted closer.

"This is how the good guys keep us in line. They make impossible rules and when we break them...They feed us to him."

He took my hands from my face, and the first thing I saw was Emil, hanging limp from the creature's claws, twitching.

"What happened to him?" I whispered.

"It took his memories. Everything that made Emil a person, it stole away from him."

I yanked my hands from his grasp. "And you think that's supposed to convince me you're right? Luka, nothing you say will make me come back to you."

He drew back, his jaw clenched and his face white.

"Nothing, huh? You're still pretending you're better than the rest of us. Still lying to yourself about all of it."

He gestured around us, taking in the polished walls, the carved mouth, even the creature. "You belong here, too, you know? Or are you lying to yourself about that as well? If we don't win, you'll end up here. With the rest of the blood mages...and murderers."

CHAPTER SIXTEEN

"Luka," I said, pushing through the door of the dining room. "I got your message."

He looked up from his place at the table where he'd spread out a bunch of papers. When he saw me, he scooped them up and tucked them into a leather folio.

I smiled at him from under my lashes. I'd seen Eira do the same thing to great effect before. "Couldn't wait to see me again, huh?" I sidled up to his chair.

"We have a problem, Reyna." He pushed his seat back and stood, making me skip back a couple of steps.

"What do you mean?"

"You said you were being careful. Didn't I tell you how to cover your tracks?" He stalked toward me.

I retreated from him until I fetched up against the sideboard. "I was. I mean, I am. Luka, what is this about?"

"Someone's been asking questions about you. Getting too close to the truth. Reyna, I can't protect you anymore."

Fear stabbed through my chest, and I clutched the ends of my sleeves. He'd been protecting me? "From who?"

His jaw clenched and he turned. "Follow me."

I followed him through the house to the door under the grand staircase. I'd never been down there before, but now he opened the door and descended the steps. I hesitated a moment before grabbing my skirts and following him. A mage light of dim gold bobbed over his head, and I had to hurry to stay in the pool of light. I wished he would take my hand. It was cool down here and his warmth and comfort would be welcome.

He hadn't told me everything would be okay.

At the bottom of the steps, racks of wine bottles glinted in his light as we passed. From deeper in the cellar came a rasping pain-filled gasp.

Luka's light splashed on the wall at the end of the corridor illuminating a set of ill-made bars. Here in the depths of his home, he'd built a makeshift cell. Was this where he was planning to bring his goats? *Da'ermo*, had he already done so?

A figure sprawled on the floor of the cell, chest rising and falling with irregular breathing.

The light swept over her face, and I gasped.

"Professor Benson," I said, grasping the bars. "Luka, let me in there."

Without a word, he unlocked the tiny door, and I slipped inside and fell to my knees beside my favorite teacher. A dark stain spread across the sleeves of her gown and pooled on the earthen floor beneath her. So much blood. Her face was pale from the loss.

I grabbed her arms, trying to staunch the bleeding with my hands.

"*Pohomzhet da ma Baud.* Luka, what have you done?" I glared up at him. "How dare you bleed her?"

"I was trying to protect you."

I formed the signs for the first healing spell that came to my mind.

"She knows, Reyna," Luka said behind me.

I paused, my heart beating faster.

"She knows about you, about what you've done, how you've been getting by. You heal her, you let her go, and the Valerians will know soon after. They'll arrest you, Reyna."

Professor Benson's eyes fluttered open. Surprise clouded her features for a moment, before it was replaced by accusation.

My hands shook.

No, no. I hadn't wanted her to know. I hadn't ever wanted to see her look at me like this.

I had to help. I was a healer. Wasn't I a healer? She'd lost so much blood. She'd be gone soon. I didn't have much time.

But I'd be arrested. After this mess, she'd make sure of it. They'd take me away from Luka. They'd lock me up here so far from the ice and snow I'd grown up with. Or they'd send me back to my homeland to wear the red. Either way, I'd be disgraced, cut off from Eira and Mabushka.

My fingers curled into fists. O'in help me.

No, no, I couldn't pray to him, not with this in front of me. Even if all my prayers had been rote before, this one could never be, so I just wouldn't pray it.

Was I seriously considering trading her life for my freedom?

"No," I snapped.

"Reyna, she'll—"

"She'll live," I said. "And, yes, she'll tell. But I'm not going to let her die."

I cast the most powerful healing spell I knew, waiting for her wounds to close, the blood to stop flowing. It would be plenty with all the extra power I could control now.

Instead, she cried out and arched back against the dirt floor.

"What?" I lunged forward to clutch her shoulders, to hold her steady as her whole body shook and her eyes rolled back in her head. "Luka, what's happening?"

"She's dying. Your spell stripped all the *vytl* from her blood, and now she's dying."

"No! No, I healed her!"

"You're a blood mage, Reyna. Your spells will always seek out the *vytl* from blood first. You can't pick and choose."

I'd done this? Professor Benson convulsed, and I held her head to keep her from hurting herself against the cellar floor.

"Why didn't you say something?" I sobbed. "You knew what I was going to do." I didn't expect an answer. It didn't matter anyway. I should have known. Professor Benson herself had taught me enough about healing spells and the drawing of *vytl* that I should have been able to guess what my bloody corruption would do.

I couldn't escape what I'd made myself into. The need that beat in my ears any time blood was in the air. The sickness that flowed through my veins. The spells I'd never be able to use on a patient again because I'd risk killing them.

I closed my eyes, cutting off the sight of her face twisted with pain and spasms. "I'm sorry."

She gasped again and tears spilled over my cheeks filling my throat with bile. "I'm sorry. I'm sorry. Forgive me, I'm sorry."

No one would ever forgive me. I couldn't forgive myself as I refused to watch as she breathed and bled her last.

Luka stood in the Reckoning Chamber in the Bastion with that memory reflected in his eyes, and I hated him for it. I'd done most of this to myself. But I knew now why Luka hadn't warned me. He'd been there for every step I'd taken down the path. He'd walked in front of me, urging me onward through the twilight. Because he'd wanted to change me, the same way I'd wanted to change him. He'd wanted me to accept my place as a blood mage. And he'd made the path smoother to that end.

The scar crossing his eyebrow and cheek wasn't nearly enough in payment and justice.

I had something more in mind today.

"I'm a healer, Luka," I said in response to his comment all those months ago. "I choose to be a healer."

"You already chose," he said. "You can't go back now." He shook his head as if washing his hands of me and stalked away to greet his father.

Good. My plan might not have been ideal but it was the

best I could do. It was time for my own reckoning.

Volka turned, the shadow creature matching her movement. Emil lay listless on the floor.

Let these people get what they deserved.

"We're done here," Volka said, holding out her hand to Aleksandr. "Let's get out of this place."

Akim had anticipated her and was striding away. They moved toward the open corridor, Luka following them.

No one was looking at me.

I whispered a spell under my breath. It didn't matter what. Little *vytl* was to be had in rock and ice, but there was just enough to power my tiny healing spell.

Just enough to trigger the wards.

Aleksandr stepped through the doorway and froze as the first stasis spell sprang up. He hung there, foot raised for a step, mouth curved in a smirk, motionless and trapped.

The sound of bells tore through the air, making me cover my ears.

"No!" Volka said and whirled around, eyes wide. I sunk back into the shadows against the wall.

Akim stood on the other side of the stasis spell staring open-mouthed at Aleksandr.

Volka threw out her hands to the bought guard. "Help him. Please."

Akim shook his head. "A deal's a deal, lady. I'm not getting caught with you."

Volka screamed as he took off down the corridor. She swore and spat, but didn't dare get any closer to the stasis spell lest she get sucked in. Luka ran to her side as the shadowy creature swarmed toward them.

I hurled myself across the room. The mouth carved into the opposite wall gaped dark and jagged as I shot between its teeth. My prayer as I fell through into the abyss was simple. "O'in help me."

I dropped.

I would have screamed but the fall stole the breath from my lungs. I reached out but only felt smooth walls race by my fingertips. Something harder than wood but softer than stone clipped my foot, and I grabbed at it as I fell past. For a moment, I found purchase against whatever was wedged in the shaft. Hanging there in the darkness, gasping in fear and exertion, my fingers recognized the shape of an elbow and a shoulder.

A frozen corpse. My fingers spasmed, and I fell again, the corpse ripping my cloak away, nearly strangling me in the process. I expected to hit the bottom with a splat, but the shaft curved, breaking my second fall gently and sending me racing toward a pinprick of light.

The chute spat me out into the frigid night air, and I had a split second to register the stars wheeling above me before I hit the water.

A thousand needles of ice stabbed me, and I flailed against the freezing water that threatened to send me into a panic. I had just enough sense to hold my breath as odd, random facts about shock and hypothermia spun through my head.

A hand grabbed the back of my bodice and hauled me up. My head broke the surface of the water, and I gasped.

"That was the best exit strategy I've ever seen. Like a cork popping from a bottle."

"Karina?" I said. The rest of my question was lost in spluttering as she hauled me into a boat the size of a bathtub.

"In the half-way frozen flesh," she said, grinning at me.

I shuddered. "Don't talk about frozen flesh."

She pulled her cloak from her own shoulders and flung it over me. "Do you have a spell to dry you out? We've still got to make it across the bay and the wind's up."

I couldn't dry myself out, but I could warm myself up. My teeth chattered as I spoke the spell. Steam rose from my soaked clothes as Karina unshipped the oars and began rowing.

I looked up to take in where I'd managed a nearly miraculous escape. A hole in the polished obsidian let out right next to the seam where the Bastion butted up against the neighboring glacier, cliffs of ice glowing blue in the moonlight. The glacier curved here, leaving a small inlet protected from the wind and the swells. I didn't want to think of how many frozen corpses lurked beneath us in the depths.

"What are you doing here?" I said, as soon as I could form the words around my chattering teeth. "Not that I'm ungrateful for your perfect placement and timing, but wasn't I supposed to meet you at the *yshkiniva* with Eira and Aleksei?"

She gave me a look as she rowed. "Did you really expect me to stay behind?" she said. Then she shrugged. "I thought it might be fun to find a way to sneak into the Bastion while you found the best way out." She glanced over her shoulder. "I was thinking of climbing up through that hole just before you shot out of it."

I couldn't help laughing, but I stopped before it became

hysterical. I'd made it. Luka and his mother were trapped behind me, and I was free. Relief made my limbs weak.

It took us nearly an hour to row back across the bay. By then, my muscles had frozen tight and my joints ached with it. I nearly screamed when I had to unlock myself from my position in the bottom of the boat.

I just had to get to the others, I told myself. I could rest then.

The *yshkiniva* we'd chosen as our meeting place was three blocks over from the docks. We'd had no way of knowing how long I'd be in the Bastion, and the *yshkiniva* was the only place that kept its doors open at all hours of the night but wasn't likely to be crowded.

I barely kept up as Karina trotted up the steps. This *yshkiniva* was a bit grander than the last one we'd been to. The court of supplication lay under a glass dome and a man-made stream gurgled in a tiled trough in the floor in place of the fountain.

Eira, Vitaly, and Aleksei sat on a bench just inside the door under the dome. They jumped to their feet as soon as they saw us.

"Reyna!" Eira got to me first. "Are you all right?"

"I'm fine. I just need to sit down." Whether from the cold, or the long walk through the prison, or the long drop at the end, my legs complained with voices louder than the klaxon bells of the Bastion.

As soon as I'd collapsed on the bench, I wove every pain block and healing spell I knew around my traitorous limps, hoping it would drive away the spikes of pain driving through my knees and feet. They'd be swollen and tender in the morning no matter what I did.

The doors to the Court of Absolution opened, making me jump, but it was only the local *otepf* blinking sleep from his eyes as he pulled his stole on over his shoulders.

"Can I help you, my children? Do you need a priest?"

Eira cast a narrow-lipped look at me before she dragged Vitaly with her to intercept him.

Aleksei knelt in front of me. "How did it go?"

"I'm alive," I said between spells. "And I'm free, so I'm going to say it went great."

"So," he said. "Was it a jailbreak? Or did they want to steal something?" He glanced at Karina.

"Jailbreak," I said. "A double one, actually. They went in for a prisoner and...something else." I wasn't sure how to describe the shadow creature.

Aleksei frowned, and Karina grinned as she held out her hand. "I told you. Pay up."

He ignored her. "How did you escape?"

I shuddered. "Let's just say you don't want to touch me until I've performed the Rites."

Someone pushed through the doors to the street. "Aleksei," a familiar voice said.

"Oh no," Aleksei groaned.

I winced. "What is your mother doing here?"

"Aleksei, do you know what time it is?" Evgenia said, planting her hands on her hips. "You know you shouldn't be out so late. I've had to chase you across half of Post da Konstantin." Then she caught sight of me and all the scolding fell from her face. "Reyna, you look awful. What happened?"

"I, uh, fell in the bay."

"*Sudinya*, may I help you?" The *otepf* approached, hands spread, a perplexed frown creasing his brow. Eira rolled her eyes behind him.

"Oh, no. I'm sorry they've been bothering you, *otepf*. I've just come to collect my wayward children."

I leaned my head back against the wall and closed my eyes, letting Evgenia's babble wash over me. I still had to find some dry clothes and perform the Rites before I could return home with them, and eventually, I'd have to figure out how to find Mabushka now that Luka was caught, but for now, I was content to sit still for five minutes and breathe.

The door of the *yshkiniva* slammed open, releasing a blast of wind through the Court of Supplication.

I shot upright.

Luka stood framed in the doorway. His mother stood beside him, red cloak swirling around her feet, eyes livid as they found me sitting on the bench. A creature made of shadows and darkness stalked between them looking like a large, spectral dog.

No, no, no. He'd been caught. I was supposed to be free of him. Unless...I glanced at the shadow creature. Unless it could change into something with wings. *Da'ermo.*

My friends froze, staring at the group that dared to step across the threshold.

"You can't come in here," the *otepf* said. He flung his hands out to indicate the Court. "This is a holy place. The least you blasphemers can do is respect it."

Luka ignored him and strode toward me, as I struggled to my feet.

"You triggered the wards," he said, voice low and poisonous. He leaned toward me, his face inches from mine so I could see the ring around his irises, dull in the dim light.

I swallowed. "Why would I do that?" I said. "I had as much to lose by getting caught as you."

"But you didn't get caught. You escaped. Quite handily, too."

My heart thudded in my chest as his murderous gaze swept over me. "Now my father is back in that place. They won't risk him escaping a second time. They'll kill him now." He lowered his chin. "Maybe we should make it even."

He spun, facing my companions. Karina waited, feet planted on the tiles, while Aleksei held an arm in front of Evgenia and Eira huddled beside Vitaly.

My chest seized, and I couldn't breathe. "Luka, please," I whispered.

Karina chose that moment to strike, her axes coming easily to her hands as she leaped from her standing position.

Volka intercepted her with a stun spell that took Karina square in the chest. She went down with a crack and a clatter on the tile floor. Volka stepped forward to finish the job.

I rushed to Karina's still form, sliding the rest of the way on my knees.

"Stop," Evgenia said, stepping forward. "I don't know what's going on, but this has to stop."

Luka caught her against him. "I really wish you hadn't done it, Reyna," he said, his arm around Evgenia's throat. "Because now I have to make sure you never do anything like it again."

He drew a club from his belt and struck her on the

temple.

I cried out as Eva crumpled. Aleksei yelled and reached to catch her.

I was a healer, not a battle mage, but I climbed to my feet and threw every spell for numbness and pain I knew at Luka, who deflected them easily.

The *otepf* rushed for them, yelling, "I'm calling the *viona krovaya!*"

Luka laughed. "No matter. We're done here, anyway." He gestured for his mother. "Mamat, come away."

His words halted Volka before she could kill Karina. She glared at me and planted her boot in the *viona's* ribs before she turned to follow her son out the door.

"Reyna," Aleksei called as Luka disappeared into the night. Snowflakes blew past the open door. "Reyna, what's wrong with her?"

I fell to my knees beside Evgenia. Her pulse beat erratically against my fingers, and I brushed back her hair to examine her skull. A livid bruise, already black and dark purple against her pale skin, spread across her temple. The bone shifted underneath my careful touch.

"Her skull is broken. She's probably bleeding into her brain." Tears clogged my throat as I went through every healing spell in my head and came up empty. None of them were powerful enough to fix this. "She's dying."

His eyes widened as he met my gaze across his mother's body. "She can't die. It was just a bump, wasn't it?"

I shook my head. "The bone here is too delicate."

He clutched her closer. "Why would he hurt her?"

He hurt her because of me. I had to be taught a lesson,

and he'd chosen Evgenia as an example.

I readied a spell to stop the internal bleeding, knowing it wouldn't be enough but unwilling to sit back and watch her die.

"Reyna, you have to do something," he said. "You're a healer."

"I'm trying, Aleksei," I said quietly, refusing to rush the most important healing I'd ever done in my life.

My fingers twisted, forming the spell, and it settled weak and ineffective against her temple. Another one to reset the thin bones of her skull which only managed to piece together one or two fragments.

"It's not enough," I said, voice hollow through my tears. I needed more. The spells themselves would help, but only if they had more power behind them.

Karina stirred and Eira rushed to help her sit up.

"Reyna, hurry. Do something." Aleksei's knuckles were white where they clung to Evgenia's shoulders.

"I can't," I said, my voice rising as my throat tightened. I met his grief-stricken eyes.

"You can't let her die."

The words struck me, carving into my chest. I couldn't let her die.

I couldn't let her die even if the cost was my freedom.

I shook my head. Why did I hesitate? What had I been doing for the past seven months? Hiding from everything I'd ever done; everyone I'd ever hurt? Was this freedom? And was it worth Evgenia's life?

No. It wasn't.

I'd left Valeria because I'd wanted to keep the last shreds

of my life and my choices. I hadn't realized I'd already lost everything. I'd lost Eira and Mabushka. I'd lost my homeland and my salvation. I'd lost my chance at ever finding someone to live my life with.

I'd lost it all the moment I cut myself open to pass a test. Professor Benson's death had only proved it.

Across the tile floor, Eira and Vitaly stared at Evgenia, while Karina's groggy gaze remained fixed on me. The *otepf* hovered behind them, wringing his hands.

I looked down at Evgenia's face, her chest slowing with her irregular breath. Luka's blow had left no blood. Whether he'd done it intentionally or not, he'd left me with only one choice.

I drew Aleksei's knife from his belt, and before I could rethink my decision, I drew the edge of the blade across my left arm, cutting through fabric and skin.

At least I would no longer be a coward.

I inhaled at the sharp familiar pain, my hands shaking not with fear or weakness, but with anticipation. A sick sort of relief flooded through me, weaving pain with pleasure.

"What are you doing?" Aleksei said, horror lacing his words. Blood ran down the inside of my arm, dripping into the stream of water meant to cleanse, turning it red.

My vision swam, and I shut my eyes to block out Aleksei, Karina, and Eira. I gathered Evgenia into my arms and reached.

Glorious *vytl* flowed through my spells, unfettered, and filled the air around me. I breathed deep and healed Evgenia, knitting bone, healing tissue, and condemning myself to eternal damnation.

PART TWO

CHAPTER SEVENTEEN

Karina stepped off of the snow-packed street to avoid a sleigh full of noisy young men and women heading out of the city for ice skating, snowball fights, or whatever it was young people did around the holidays. She didn't know. In her life, LongNight had always meant a brief respite from training and an even briefer visit from her revered patron before her studies resumed with a vengeance.

She spotted a red cloak, stark against the snow, at the end of the street, and her heart leaped. *Let this be her*, she prayed. It had been three months now. She'd never lost track of her for this long before.

The girl wearing the red darted across the street and pushed open the door of a butcher shop. Karina sidled up next to the building and knelt, pretending to tie her boot while her ears strained to hear.

"You're late," a gruff male voice said, disparagingly.

"I'm sorry," another voice said, and Karina sagged, her

entire body singing with relief. "It's hard to go even a couple of blocks when kids throw rocks at you."

"Quit your whining. You chose your sin. The day's entrails won't shift themselves."

"Will you actually pay me this time?" she said. "I haven't eaten since yesterday."

"Money comes at the end of the week. You know that."

"What about the message I left with you? Have any other blood mages accepted it?"

A guffaw. "Never thought there was anything worse than a blood mage, but you must be it. None of them want to talk to you."

A door banged, and Karina straightened and crept to the corner of the alley beside the butcher. The girl pushed through the back door with a sack that leaked blood across the snow. She heaved it into a cheap wheelbarrow before trundling it away down the packed snow.

Karina followed. She was certain now, even though the girl kept her hood up to hide her face. There was something in her gait, a hitch that spoke of pain as familiar to Karina as the voice had been.

The girl dumped her burden in the offal pits at the edge of the city. She hesitated, then Karina winced as she climbed down into the pit to rummage through the rotting entrails and other castoffs for something edible.

She finally climbed out with a dried apple core in one hand and a few bits of moldy bread in the other.

Karina had to stop behind a tanner and press a hand to her chest, hoping to ease the pain. The girl walked alone, but her back remained unbowed. Her determination was shackled by the red cloak she wore, but she still searched, still fought, still rebelled. It would be ten times harder to find her grandmother now that she was registered, but Karina could tell she hadn't given up.

By the time the girl disappeared into a squalid building at the edge of the harbor, the sun had dipped below the horizon.

Karina studied the timber-framed house with its crumbling plaster and the door that hung half off its hinges before she circled around to find a drainpipe in the back. She shimmied up, then swung a shutter open and dropped to the floor inside just as the girl appeared at the top of the stairs, unfastening her cloak.

They stared at each other a moment, hazel eyes meeting blue. Blue that was clear of the dull red ring that had been there the last time they'd looked each other in the eyes.

The other girl swallowed. "Karina," she said.

"Reyna."

Reyna shook her head and let her hands fall to her sides. She wouldn't remove her cloak now that someone untainted stood in the same room. It was the Law.

"What are you doing here?" Reyna said, glancing around the large room. Too many bunks crowded the space, mud and slush covered the rough floorboards, and ashes littered the tiny hearth set into the far wall. Several bodies lay under thin blankets or red cloaks. One or two sat on the floor or their bunks, their heads hanging listlessly. No one acknowledged the intruder.

"I came to see you," Karina said.

"Why?" Reyna moved to one of the bunks and tossed her

apple core and moldy bread into a small dinged pot that hung from the post.

Karina moved with her. "Because we're friends." She crossed her arms. "Or at least, I thought we were. Did that change because we found out your secret?"

Reyna snorted. "It did for everyone else. Aleksei was pretty quick to abandon me."

"What about Eira?"

Reyna's jaw tightened, and she grabbed the pot holding her meager dinner.

Karina dug in her pouch and pulled out a paper-wrapped pastry. She offered the nut and honey-covered bread.

Reyna drew herself up. "Don't taunt me, Karina. I'm a blood mage, unclean. Everyone and everything I touch is unclean. You'll have to go through the Rites just for coming here."

"Your eyes are clear," Karina said.

The other girl turned her shoulder, hiding her eyes. "Doesn't seem to matter to anyone else. Besides, if I'm caught doing blood magic again, it's the Bastion for me. And I doubt I'll get out the same way a second time. Unless it's as a corpse."

Karina tossed the pastry on the bunk. "Eat the damn thing, Reyna. I know for a fact it's more than you've had to eat in days."

Reyna spun to stare, brow furrowed in confusion. "Have you been following me again?"

"Guardian angel, remember?"

Reyna's face crumpled, and she rubbed her eyes. "You don't have to feel sorry for me, you know? I—I chose this."

"I know." Reyna would never know how well Karina knew that.

Reyna stared at her.

Karina let her.

The other girl finally sighed and sat on the bunk to snatch up the pastry and tear into it. "Back with the caravan," she said, her voice faltering with some emotion she struggled to hide. "You said you didn't have a lot of experience with friendship."

Karina leaned on the bunk opposite her. "So?" she said.

"I feel obliged to tell you it doesn't usually extend this far. Aleksei's reaction was the right one."

Karina pretended not to notice the way her voice broke on his name. "He wasn't the one that called the *viona krovaya* on you," Karina said quietly. "That was the *otepf.*"

"No, but he didn't do anything to stop them either."

Neither had Karina, but Reyna was too polite to point that out to her face.

She'd meant to. She'd had the whole thing planned out in her head for months, and then when it had finally happened, she'd been too sick from Volka's stun spell to think straight. She could only watch as the blood swords dragged the girl away. Taking Karina's heart and soul with them.

And by the time her head had cleared, Reyna had disappeared into the system. Karina could have gone to the *viona krovaya* and used Reyna's registered blood to track her down, but that had seemed like a violation of the privacy and choice that Reyna held dear.

She hadn't wanted to be protected from her choices.

Reyna finished the pastry and spent a long time licking the honey from her fingers.

"There's more where that came from, if you want it," Karina said, studying her features. "I have a job for you."

Reyna snorted. "Right. I think I'll pass."

Karina blinked. "You haven't even heard what it is yet."

"I don't have to." Reyna sighed. "No one wants to hire a blood mage unless it's for something really awful. The things no one else wants to do because they'll have to go through the Rites. But we're already unclean so it doesn't matter to us. Am I close?"

Karina opened her mouth once or twice before responding. "Yes," she finally said. "But this would be a different kind of awful than anything out there." Karina gestured out the window.

Reyna at least looked interested at that. "What kind of awful are we talking about?"

"You've seen the corruption in the *viona krovaya*." It wasn't a question.

"Yes," Reyna said. "Bribes aren't even the worst of it. Nobles work with blood mages all the time and the *viona krovaya* just look the other way."

"If you come with me, you'll be working to root out the corruption that Luka's rebellion is spreading."

Reyna straightened on the bunk, her eyes bright and focused. "Why me?"

"Because you're still trying to get Luka caught."

Reyna's mouth fell open. "How...how do you know that?"

Karina shrugged. "It's how I found you. Rumors of a

blood mage looking for Luka, looking for other blood mages to connect with."

"How do you know I didn't want to join him for real this time?"

"Because he still has your grandmother," Karina said. "And because you got caught and registered on purpose. Didn't you?"

"I..." Reyna dropped her gaze to her hands. "Yes."

"Because Evgenia was dying."

"Because Evgenia was dying, because I didn't want to be his pawn anymore, because I was tired of lying."

"What if you weren't his pawn anymore? What if you went back to him as an equal? Do you think he'd take you?"

Reyna stood and paced down the length of the bunk and back. "Do you know what you're asking?"

"It's already what you're trying to do, isn't it?"

Reyna rubbed her forehead. "He...he set me up to get caught. He knew exactly what he was doing when he tried to kill Evgenia without using blood. I either had to let her die, which he knew I wouldn't do, or I had to use blood magic to save her, revealing myself in the process. He did it on purpose. And then he still kept Mabushka as a hostage."

"He wants you for something."

"He wants me for something. So, yes. Yes, I do think he'd take me back. I just don't know if I want to go."

"Would you rather stay here?" It was a serious question. If Reyna chose to stay in this squalor, picking through scraps and handling other people's trash, Karina would still follow her. But she knew the girl better than that.

Reyna still hesitated.

Karina stood and adjusted her cloak before reaching for the window. "Meet me at the west end of Archon's Bridge before dawn tomorrow morning."

Reyna looked at her out of the corner of her eye. "I haven't said yes, yet."

"Then say it."

"Karina," Reyna said and paused.

Karina waited while she found the words.

"You're not that terrible at this whole friendship thing. Just so you know."

There really wasn't any way I was going to say no to Karina. Like she'd said, this was just a better way to do what I'd already been doing. I just needed a few hours to work myself up to it. Luka had broken me in more ways than one and it didn't matter how much I tried to guard my heart and my life, he just kept breaking me.

Time to return the favor.

The lamps at the end of Archon's Bridge burned low by the time I hurried up the street the next morning. The sky went gray, then pink behind the Winter Palace that stood on the hill, while the city and the frozen bay beyond remained dark and brooding. I deliberately turned my face away from the looming blackness of the Bastion. Now that I knew what was inside, I even more desperately didn't want to end up in there.

At the end of the bridge, I tucked my hands under my armpits and stamped my feet to keep warm. The red wool cloak around my shoulders had gone thin and ragged in the three months since my registration, and it wasn't like anyone particularly cared if a blood mage went to sleep in the cold and never woke up again.

Well, maybe one or two people cared about this blood mage. My lips curved against my better judgment. I told myself not to get my hopes up. Karina had a lot to work against to make this plan work. But it was hard to tell my heart to slow down when I'd finally talked to someone who treated me like a real person for the first time in three months. Every interaction before that had been with the untainted, who scorned me for my poor choices, or other blood mages, who scorned me for my clear eyes.

A sliver of sun shone over the horizon and there was still no sign of Karina. She could just be late. She could have run up against opposition. Maybe whoever she worked for now didn't want to hire a blood mage.

Or maybe she'd decided against the entire plan.

I glanced back toward the city, the buildings going wobbly as tears pricked my eyes. I couldn't go back. I hadn't told Karina how close to breaking down I'd been the moment I'd seen a friendly face. My life now was doing almost as good a job of breaking me as Luka had. The hunger, the shame, the loneliness.

I missed Eira.

I hadn't spoken with her since the day my blood had flowed onto the floor of the *yshkiniva*. I'd turned away and hadn't dared look at her as they'd dragged me away.

I followed her now, the way Karina still followed me, apparently. She worked herself to exhaustion every day for a seamstress four blocks from my bunkhouse. But I never tried to contact her. She'd gone into debt to pay for the Rites, and the seamstress she worked for took all her wages in payment of that debt. Poor Eira. She hated sewing.

Vitaly had followed her, still loyal to Eira as Karina was to me. But he was stuck in the same muck, paying for the Rites and left in debt because of it.

I cringed and leaned against the balustrade of the bridge to look down at the frozen river that flowed from the Howling Bog into the bay. How awful would it be to throw myself in? As awful as walking back into the city? At least throwing myself in the river would provide an end.

"It wouldn't help, you know," Karina's voice said beside me. "I'd follow you there, too."

I hid my smile against my arms as I swallowed down the tears that sprang to my throat. She'd come. O'in bless her, she'd come.

"One day I'll figure out how you move so quietly," I said.

I raised my head, then gasped and staggered back a step, my heart racing in reaction.

Karina wore the rust-red coat of the *viona krovaya*, a black club hanging from her wide belt. The last time I'd seen one of the blood swords this close, they'd taken my blood for registration. Most of the scars on my body were put there by me, but there were one or two that were new.

"What is it?" she asked, brow furrowed. Then she glanced down. "Oh. Oh, of course. I'm sorry, I didn't think to warn you. Where we're going, every blood mage is paired with a *viona krovaya* as a precaution. I figured it would be better if you worked with someone you already knew."

"Better," I said through numb lips. I forced myself to take a deep breath and relax my muscles which had gone taut. "Yes, better." She was right, it would be. But I could tell it would be a long time before the mere sight of that uniform didn't make my stomach clench.

"Was—" I started, then had to clear my throat. "Was this a promotion?" That came out better.

"Sort of a sideways one," she said. *Viona krovaya* were picked from the ranks of the *viona uchenye*. Since Karina could already claim intimate knowledge of at least one blood mage, that had probably helped the process along.

"Are you ready?" she said.

I held out my empty hands. "It's not like I had anything to pack." Everything I'd owned had been burned. Fire was the only thing that could cleanse a blood mage's corruption. Even our bodies were burned after we died.

Her lips twisted in what looked a little like pain. "I figured," she said as she turned and started across the bridge. "I took the liberty of finding you some things. I didn't think you'd mind."

I ignored that as I stared over her shoulder to the massive edifice on the hill, silhouetted by the red and gold sunrise. "Karina...just where are we going for this job?"

She glanced over her shoulder and cocked her thumb up the hill. "Where do you think?"

The Winter Palace. Two towers topped with round peaks framed the main hall with extensive wings sweeping to either side. I'd heard the gardens behind it were the most beautiful when they were snow-covered. Having grown up in a small cottage in a small village outside of the small town of

Darayevo I'd never even thought of the possibility of seeing them from the inside. Eira had dreamed and imagined and dragged me into her fantasies of wearing beautiful dresses and dancing with handsome men in mirror-lined halls.

Pohomzhet da ma Baud, what exactly had I agreed to?

An hour later, all I could think was at least Karina hadn't tried to dress me up in the ridiculous ribbon bedecked finery Eira had always imagined. I wore a sensible blue skirt and bodice with a clean shift underneath and new boots since mine had been worn through before my arrest. I wondered how much money she'd wasted on these things that she would have to burn after I'd used them. Had she gone into debt the way the others had? She'd even found me another red cloak, one that wasn't stained from my time in the slush filled streets of Post da Konstantin. This one was even lined in rough velvet.

"Karina, who am I working for?" I said, rubbing the little fibers back and forth between my fingers.

She hesitated for the briefest of moments. "It's complicated. In the end, you're working for my patron, who is trying to suss out the blood mage rebellion."

I gave her a narrow-eyed look. "If your patron is here in the palace, what were you doing working for a common caravan?"

She tilted her head. "Gaining experience. They don't let just anyone work up here on the hill. That's one of the reasons why we'll have a public employer. Someone else who doesn't know what we're really trying to do. It'll help us fit in."

"Us?"

"Yes. Since I'm supposed to keep you from tainting anyone."

"And track me down if I run."

Another pause. "That too."

"And what's our employer's name?"

"He is the Baron Fyodor Iosif Ruriksyn."

"Baron," I said flatly.

"Yes."

I remembered the Red Noble backed up against a tavern full of blood mages. I remembered the nobles who hired blood mages to do their dirty work while the *viona krovaya* pocketed bribes to keep them quiet.

"Luka's rot has spread here, too, hasn't it?"

Karina shook her head, then nodded. "It's worse than that. This is the heart of Ballaslav. The rest of the country follows where the court leads."

"So it starts here," I said.

"It can end here if you can convince Luka to let you back in."

I squared my shoulders. "Then let's get to it."

She led me down the narrow corridors obviously used by servants and those who provided special services to the nobility, like Karina. We passed into broader hallways lined with artwork, plush carpets, and windows that faced the bay and the city. I clutched the edges of my cloak so it wouldn't brush anything. Would they have to burn the carpets after I'd walked over them?

At the far end of the hall, I caught sight of what had to be some sort of princess. Decked out in silver fabric with bows down the front of her split skirt and feathers in her hair, she looked like she was on her way to a ball.

Karina saw my look and rolled her eyes. "Some people have no taste," she said. "Silver went out of style three years ago. If you can't afford to keep up with the times maybe you should be building up your estate, not gallivanting around at court."

"I think she's beautiful," I said wistfully as the woman disappeared through a large arch in the wall we followed. "Since when do you like fashion?"

"You'd have to be dead not to notice it at court. If you thought she was something, wait till you see what's through here." Karina stopped at a bare spot on the wall.

I glanced at it and realized it was actually an unobtrusive door set into the plaster. Karina pushed the latch and shouldered the door open, letting out a wave of noise, voices raised in conversation and laughter.

I started to follow her and stopped short on the threshold, staring around at the pageantry. Even in the city, I'd never seen so many people so well-dressed in one room. The colors blurred before my eyes, and I fought off a wave of dizziness.

"The Little Court," Karina said, looking at me. "This is where those not invited to the Regal Court gather and do business."

"What kind of business?"

"Oh, there's the actual kinds of business, like trade contracts and the like, and then there's 'women's business' like securing husbands and brokering political alliances." She squinted into the crowd. "Your employer has to be in here somewhere."

I opened my mouth to start saying that there was no way they'd want a blood mage in the Little Court, but I bit off my protest when a lady dressed in blue taffeta sailed by, a blood mage and their *viona krovaya* trailing behind her.

Clearly, the rules were different up here on the hill.

I caught sight of an *otepf* with a large pointed hat the same color as his stole standing at the edge of things. He stared at the blood mage with a pinched frown. I wasn't sure what the colored stoles signified, but I was pretty sure purple was really high up in the priesthood.

At least Karina had brought me through a side entrance where no one noticed our appearance and not through the enormous archway I'd noticed down the hall. There, a man clad in red and gold broadcloth with a big floppy hat and the screaming golden eagle of the Konstantin heirs embroidered on his front called out the names of those who entered. His voice was swallowed by the din but no one seemed to mind as they swept inside and joined the throng.

Karina didn't lead me along the edge of the room like I'd expected, she just waded through the middle. I trotted along behind her, casting anxious looks around me. But the crowd parted, whether because of Karina's determined stride or because of the color of my cloak, I couldn't tell.

Karina stopped abruptly. "I don't see him," she said. "But that's his valet. Wait here while I see what's up."

I opened my mouth to protest, but she was gone before the words could form. Some sort of grand dowager or matriarch towered over me and eyeballed my red cloak. I squeaked and stepped aside. Someone cried out that I'd trod on their foot, but when I turned to apologize, they scowled and strode away from me.

A hand took my elbow and steered me to an ebb in the crowd where no one threatened to run me over. "I've found it best to read the movement of courtiers like the tides of the sea," my rescuer said. "And move with them rather than against them."

"Corwin," I said, recognizing the little Valerian man who'd traveled with the caravan.

His gaze cleared with recognition. "Reyna," he said. "What a pleasure." He swept me an elegant bow. "I see you've gone up in the world, too." He gestured around us at the Little Court.

I clenched my jaw and drew my cloak around me. "Not exactly," I said. "You shouldn't be speaking to me. Though I notice your Ballaslavian has gotten a lot better."

He waved a hand. "You're not damned according to my religion," he said. "The Almighty won't mind me talking to you."

"As I recall, blood magic is still illegal in Valeria."

He reached out to brush his fingers down the edge of my cloak. "And you seem to be paying the price. Ostracizing you isn't going to make any difference as far as I can see."

"So, are you staying with the Valerian ambassador?" I asked, diverting the tone of the conversation.

He brightened. "Yes. He doesn't have a lot of time to devote to showing me around, but that just means I have more time for my own studies."

I noticed the crowd around us moving and splitting just as something over my shoulder caught Corwin's gaze.

"Yesofya Ekaterin Borislava Konstantinadoch, Grand Duchess," the herald said behind me.

I gasped and whirled around, coming face to face with a woman about Mabushka's age dressed in an elegant blue-green gown, her iron-gray hair pulled back in a loose chignon.

"Your Excellency," Corwin said.

CHAPTER EIGHTEEN

I froze, caught in the Grand Duchess's blue-eyed stare. I had to be imagining it but for a moment it seemed as if her gaze sharpened, then softened as it rested on my face.

For the first time in three months, I forgot myself. I forgot what I'd done and how the world saw me.

Until she said, "*ispor'chennai.*" Tainted.

Even then she didn't sound disgusted. She sounded like she was sad she had to remind me of my place.

I gasped and scrambled back out of her way. Who was I to stand there staring at the Grand Duchess, breathing the same air she breathed? I ran into someone and felt Karina's hands close around my arms as the ruler of my country raised her chin and swept down the long room to a pair of double doors in the far wall. Half a dozen ladies followed in her wake and four guards dressed in stark white uniforms trimmed with gold.

The one in the lead, a bald man with an eye patch, glared at me as he passed.

"*Viona semaya*," Karina whispered in my ear. "They guard the Grand Duchess and her family."

My knees trembled, either from all the walking I'd already done today or the unfiltered gaze of Ballaslavian royalty, I wasn't sure which.

"Let's get out of here," Karina said.

"Gladly." My voice sounded as weak as my legs.

I gave Corwin a little wave as Karina steered me out of the Little Court, her hand on my elbow. As soon as we were out the door, I shook myself and pulled my arm from her grip.

"You shouldn't touch me," I said.

She rolled her eyes. "I'm *viona krovaya*, now. The Rites are part of my job description. Your new employer mucked things up by spending the morning in his suite, but if we hurry, we can catch him before he leaves for lunch."

"You said he doesn't know what I'm here for, right?" I pushed myself to keep up with her, ignoring the pang of pain in my knees. I'd be limping before the day was through.

"He's just here to lend credibility to your presence."

I snorted. Credibility for a blood mage. What a joke.

"He doesn't know who you're really working for. No one can know who you're really working for." She gave me a significant look over her shoulder.

I rolled my eyes. "Karina, I don't even know who I'm really working for."

"My patron," she said shortly. "You'll meet her tomorrow." She stopped in front of an ornate door in an even more ornate hallway. "She's a very busy woman. She wants to see you face-to-face, but we have to fit into her schedule."

I opened my mouth, but Karina had already raised her fist to knock.

A voice bade us enter, and she opened the door to let me through.

"*Zaluzhennai*," Karina said. "I have brought your new mage."

A man stood up from a massive desk in the center of the room. My overall impression of him started with round and gradually included red. He was rotund enough that if I laid him out on the plush carpet, I'd be able to roll him. And his face had gone florid under his carrot-colored hair.

Karina bowed. "Reyna Sofya Daryadoch, this is Baron Fyodor Iosif Ruriksyn."

"Thank you, *viona*," the Baron said. He reached into his pocket before shaking Karina's hand, making no effort to hide the two silver reyevs he passed to her in the process. "I think you can leave your charge here while we get acquainted. I won't let her get up to any mischief."

I was pretty sure this was strictly against the rules, but Karina pocketed the money and left without a word. She did send me a pointed glance over her shoulder I interpreted as "don't screw this up." I wish I knew how.

"So, *ispor'chennai*," he said, coming around his desk. "I understand you're a healer. University trained?"

"I...didn't finish." In the streets, *ispor'chennai* had been spat at me, a combination of curse and insult. Here, though, it seemed to be more of a title.

He smiled a sly smile. "Ah," he said. "You moved on to acquire a different set of skills. I see."

"I am still an adequate healer," I said, drawing myself up.

"Wonderful," he said. "I find myself ailing more and more in these winter months. If only the court stayed south. Elisaveta is much more hospitable to men of my...stature this time of year."

I could already tell if the Baron just abstained from certain excesses like sweets and wine and maybe the cigars burning in his ashtray, half of his complaints would resolve themselves in days. But even if I was here as his healer, I doubted he'd listen to me. Such men usually didn't.

"And, of course, I expect the utmost devotion in my staff," Ruriksyn said. "When it comes to my health and wellbeing you should not consider yourself confined by certain strictures your kind normally faces."

I raised my chin. "You mean blood magic." Might as well get it out in the open. I already hated the way this man trotted around his meaning like a lady through a muck strewn pasture.

Ruriksyn winced. "I suppose if you must say it out loud, we could call it that."

"But you'd rather not."

"I'd rather forget the whole thing, but..." He raised his hands in a "what can you do" gesture.

"But you brought me here, anyway," I said.

"Yes, well. Some of my staff are not so devoted." His eyes flicked over my shoulder, and I couldn't help turning to see.

Another blood mage sat on a low stool in the corner of the lush office. She kept her pale hands folded in her lap and her gaze lowered. Her hood was down, revealing a mass of curling brown hair barely contained in a braid.

She didn't look up as she said, "Blood magic is blasphemy."

The baron sighed as if she'd refused to do him a trivial favor. "Sometimes blasphemous things are necessary. Why should I risk my own soul when there are those willing to stand between me and damnation?" He put his hand to his heart and bowed to me, the respect in his gesture belied by an obvious wink. "Thank you for your sacrifice."

My hands curled into fists under the safety of my cloak. I actually agreed with the girl in the corner, not this jolly man with a rotting heart.

But if this was where Luka's rebellion was taking root, then this was where I needed to be. And I needed word to get back to Luka. To lure him closer so that one day I could topple him from his high ground.

And it all started here, in the corrupted heart of my country.

I swept my cloak around me in the best bow I could conjure. "I'm happy to serve."

He grinned and clapped his hands together. "Excellent."

Just then, the door opened. "Someone to see you, *Zaluzhennai*," Karina said.

I straightened and found myself staring into a set of familiar blue-green eyes. They widened in shock, looking much the same as they had the last time I'd seen them. Only then, the dominant emotion had been horror and disgust.

Aleksei Pyotrsyn recovered faster than I and raised his chin as the shock cleared from his face. I ducked my gaze before I could see anything worse replace it.

"Ah, *Ser* Pyotrsyn," Ruriksyn said. "I assume you've come to discuss that shipment you'll be handling for me."

"Yes, *Zaluzhennai*. Do you have our contract?"

Da'ermo, it was good to hear his voice, even if it was only a step above a growl.

"A moment while I find it." Ruriksyn retreated behind his desk.

Aleksei turned to me, almost reluctantly. "*Ispor'chennai*," he said.

I expected to shudder at the insult in his voice, but it was a bit of a relief to hear myself called what I knew myself to be. And if anyone deserved to call me tainted it was Aleksei.

I felt Karina step up behind me. Aleksei's eyes shifted to her. "Karina," he said. "You're moving up in the world."

Karina shrugged. "Sorry, I left you short one *viona*. Someone else needed me more."

Aleksei grimaced. "I see that." His gaze shifted back to me. "Does she come when you whistle?"

My hand shot out to hold Karina back, but she just shrugged. "I've been called worse."

Ruriksyn's eyes followed our display avidly, and I flushed to think what he made of the exchange. "I see you are already acquainted with my new healer."

Aleksei turned an instant too late to hide his pain. "She was one of our permanent staff before..."

Before I'd thrown it all away. The sky was bright with the bridges I'd burned behind me.

"Then maybe you can tell me whether I've made a good choice in hiring her," Ruriksyn said.

I winced and Karina stiffened. If he was looking for my

references, I could have pulled in Eira and half the caravan. They'd give me the same hurt filled review as Aleksei.

Aleksei squared his shoulders and shot a glance at me I couldn't read.

"I think her methods and ability to tell the truth are heinous," he said. "But she's probably the best and most dedicated healer I've ever seen."

My mouth dropped open.

Ruriksyn smiled. "Well, then. I guess I should be glad I hired her. Heinous methods and all. Anya, you may show Reyna and the *viona* to their room."

The other blood mage stood up, movements graceful, face still downturned, and led us deeper into the baron's suite. I cast one look back at Aleksei before I followed.

The next day, Karina woke me at an ungodly hour and led me through empty hallways. Apparently, her patron was busy and important enough that the only time we could meet with her was before the rest of the world woke.

She left me in a small receiving room and disappeared again quickly enough I couldn't even ask her what to expect.

I bit my lip as I surveyed the room. Would they have to burn one of the footstools if I decided to sit on it? This room was a little more out of the way than the others I'd seen so far and much less grand than the baron's suite, with a merry fire burning in the grate.

I was just about to risk sitting down when the door

opened, and Karina slipped in. She bowed and backed up with an air of obsequiousness I'd never seen before.

A figure pushed the door further open and followed her into the room.

If I had managed to sit, I would have leaped to my feet.

The Grand Duchess of Ballaslav, Yesofya Ekaterin Borislava Konstinadoch stepped in and gestured for Karina to close the door behind her.

Karina did so, then darted around her so she could grab one of the armchairs and drag it into place for her.

This was Karina's patron? I didn't know a swear appropriate for the shock coursing through me.

"Can I bring you anything, *Prevoshkedohva*?" Karina said as soon as her butt hit the cushion. "Tea, coffee, breakfast?"

The Duchess smiled up at her. "I'm fine, Karina. Why don't you sit?"

Karina's eyes widened at her informality, and she glanced around the room. She finally settled on dragging a footstool over until it sat just behind and to the left of the Duchess's chair.

I simply stood.

"Reyna," the Grand Duchess said, voice surprisingly soft. There was unexpected emotion behind my name.

I'd half expected her to call me *ispor'chennai*.

"*Prevoshkedohva*," I said, taking my cue from Karina. It meant 'excellency,' but for all I knew, a Grand Duchess could be called Supreme High Godmother.

"Would you care to sit?" Elegance and courtesy infused every word and gesture, even when she spoke to someone like me.

I followed Karina's example—though probably for different reasons—and perched on the edge of a footstool. Just in case they had to get rid of it afterward.

After that, she seemed to be at a loss for words. Perhaps the normal protocol failed when it came to speaking to a blood mage.

Someone tapped politely on the door, and I jerked in surprise when it opened. Should I hide myself? Surely the Grand Duchess wouldn't want to besmirch her reputation by getting caught conversing with a blood mage.

But she smiled when a middle-aged man poked his head around the door. "Am I interrupting?" he said.

"Not yet," the Duchess said. "You're just in time for introductions. Reyna, this is my son, Mikhail."

Prince Mikhail Dimitri Radomir Konstantinsyn, her son and the heir to her empire, stepped inside and nodded politely. I leaped to my feet and bowed. I expected Karina to do the same, but she remained on her stool, looking up at her patron with starry eyes.

Mikhail stood taller than most men, his back still straight and strong despite the gray creeping through his dark hair. A smile touched his wide mouth.

A series of tragedies over the last twenty years had slowly whittled away the Grand Duchess's large family, leaving her with Mikhail as her sole heir. Court gossip had become common knowledge throughout Ballaslav that he was looking for a wife, and every eligible woman in the country (plus some not so eligible) had flocked to court, hoping to become the next Grand Duchess.

I looked back and forth between the two people I'd

thought myself most disconnected from and wondered not for the first time what I was doing here.

The Duchess seemed to understand my confusion. "At my age," she said, "a ruler must include her heir in every minute detail, just in case she isn't around the next morning." She smiled ruefully at her son.

"May it never be so, Mamat," he said, with his own version of the same smile. He turned his gaze on me again and tilted his head in question. "I trust you are enjoying your time in court, Reyna."

I chewed the inside of my cheek and wondered just what I was allowed to say to the ruler of my country and the leader of said court. "I'm not sure how to answer that," I said. It seemed easier to be truthful.

The Duchess's lips twisted. "I'd appreciate your candid observations."

Very well. "Candidly? You seem to have an infestation of blood mages."

She and Mikhail exchanged a glance. "Then you've already noticed my problem."

My fingers curled around the fabric of my cloak. "And you want me to help with that."

She regarded me carefully. "I think you are in a unique position to do so, yes."

She wanted to use me. Just like Luka. In this case, I actually wanted to do what she said, but it didn't change the fact that people only ever saw me as a tool.

"What do you think I can do?" I said.

"I think you can help me flush out the rot," she said. I got the impression this woman never pulled her punches. "You can ingratiate yourself with the others of your kind, find out their plans, and point out their ringleaders, so I can exterminate them."

"That's easier said than done," I said. "I'm not popular with that group right now."

She glanced sidelong at Karina. "I was led to believe you had some sort of connection with their leader."

Just how much did she know about me? I looked pointedly at Karina, who winced.

I frowned. "With Luka. Yes."

"Can you infiltrate his operation again?"

"I...I think I can convince him, yes. But this will be dangerous," I said. "It may look like I've hit bottom, but I still have some very important things to lose."

She nodded. "I see."

Karina frowned. "I don't."

The Duchess's lips twitched with amusement. "Reyna is looking for some sort of compensation."

Did she find my situation amusing? I cocked my head to look at her. "In other words, what's in it for me?"

"Reyna!" Karina said, aghast.

I shot her a glance. "He still has Mabushka. I'm not doing anything to provoke him without good reason."

"I could say this is your patriotic duty to your country," the Duchess said. "But I don't think my country has treated you very well in this matter."

I blinked. That wasn't what she was supposed to say.

"I can't free your grandmother," she continued. "I don't have the resources to spare for one lost woman."

"I figured," I said. "I want something else that's well

within your purview." I'd been thinking of her since Karina had led me up the hill the day before.

"Try me," she said.

"I want you to bring my sister here. Find some excuse. Make her one of your ladies or something. Anything to get her out of the city and out of debt." I braced myself for her refusal.

"Done," she said.

I swallowed my response. I hadn't expected her to agree so quickly. Maybe I should have held out for more.

"And Vitaly," I added.

"What?"

"She probably won't come without him. So, find a place for him, too."

She shared a look with Karina, who gave her the slightest shrug.

"Anything else?" the Duchess said.

Enough gold so I'd never be hungry again, my degree from the University, Professor Benson's life back, and freedom from the red cloak that had lost me the regard of those I cared about the most.

"Nothing," I said.

"Then we have a deal?"

"We do."

CHAPTER NINETEEN

M y fingers curled against the gilt-encrusted wall as I peeked around the corner into the next corridor. About halfway down, a parade of footmen in royal livery carried furniture in and out of an open doorway while Eira stood outside clutching the tiny bag that was her poor excuse for luggage.

"Why don't you go in?" Karina said over my shoulder.

I jumped. "Seriously, stop sneaking up on me," I said, one hand going to my pounding heart.

"Maybe you should get used to the fact that I'm always going to be here."

"Lurking?"

Karina raised her eyebrows and eyed my position in the hallway. "What do you call what you're doing?"

I opened my mouth, then snapped it closed. "Um..."

"Why don't you go say hello?"

I closed my eyes and spun away. "She doesn't want to see

me, Karina. I'm the reason she's spent so many months suffering."

"You don't know that for sure."

My hand slashed through the air. "Let her have her space. If I go in there, she's just going to throw a shoe at me or something."

"I would if I had a spare," Eira said from behind me. "But I don't, so I guess you're safe for now."

I whirled to see my sister standing at the corner, hands on hips.

"Come in or not," she said, turning to retreat into her room. "But don't just stand there. I don't really want people seeing a blood mage hanging around my door."

"Wouldn't do much damage in this court," Karina muttered.

I hesitated before following Eira. Inside the room, I fought not to let my jaw drop. The little room I shared with Karina in Baron Ruriksyn's suite was bare and cramped compared to this. Chandeliers hung from the high ceilings dripping with crystal, and the tall windows let in the fierce winter sunlight, which slanted across a set of blue uphol-stered sofas.

"I take it you're the reason a royal footman showed up at the shop this morning to practically drag me here," Eira said, placing her little bag on a side table that dwarfed it. "He said I'm to become one of the Grand Duchess's ladies. I don't...I don't even know what that means."

"It means you'll be a lady in the royal court," I said. "You'll be important, respected. I thought you might like it."

She whirled on me. "So you dragged me here, throwing away everything I've built the last few months? I only just started earning back my wage. I finally have enough to buy myself a new apron. How am I ever going to afford the clothes and things a lady needs? Or am I supposed to follow the Grand Duchess around looking like this?"

She gestured down to her stained brown kirtle.

My lips pressed together, and I clenched my fingers in my skirt. I hadn't thought of it like that. How stupid could I be to think I could just bring her here and everything would be all right?

Karina examined her nails from the doorway. "Check the closets," she said.

"What?" Eira shook her head.

"Check the closets."

Eira frowned and stalked to one of the ornately carved doors in the far wall. She threw it open and stood staring at the wealth of fabric hanging from the rod. "What—?"

I'd never seen my sister at a loss for words.

Karina shrugged before addressing me. "Your employer's not an idiot. You told her to bring Eira here and make her a lady. She knew exactly what Eira would need to fit in and be comfortable, and she took care of it. Did you think she would try to cheat you out of her side of the deal?"

"What deal?" Eira said, turning toward me, her hands full of fabric.

It was my turn to shrug. "It's nothing." Karina had specifically said no one was supposed to know who I was working for.

Eira glared. "It's not nothing. You worked for Luka in

order to keep Mabushka safe. What awful thing are you doing to give me a place here?" She dropped the gown she'd been holding to plant her hands on her hips.

"This isn't like that," I said.

"It's exactly like that," Karina muttered.

I scowled at her. "Stay out of this."

Eira threw her hands up in the air. "Why can't you just leave me alone? You left for Valeria easy enough. Now everything's mucked up and it's all because you came home."

"I wanted you to be safe," I said, arms stiff at my sides. "I don't want to have anything left to lose. Not my pride, not my freedom. And not my family."

She raised her chin. "Vitaly would have kept me safe. But you took me away from him again."

We stood glaring at each other, breathing heavily.

A knock rang through the tense silence. With a nonchalant motion, Karina opened the door.

Vitaly grinned on the doorstep, wearing an immaculate set of palace livery. "Good morning, my lady." He swept Eira an elegant bow made slightly ridiculous by the way his hair flopped into his eyes. "I'm to be your footman."

"Reyna knew you wouldn't want to be separated," Karina told Eira, who held her hands to her mouth. "So she asked for a place for Vitaly as well."

Eira's eyes sought mine.

I managed to unlock my jaw long enough to say, "I just want you to be happy."

I didn't let the silence stretch this time. I turned and stalked out of the room, making Vitaly leap out of the way.

I was right. I shouldn't have come. She didn't appreciate

what I was trying to do for her. Maybe she would have been safer if I'd just left her in the city.

But no. With Luka still out there, he could have just as easily kidnapped my sister next.

"Where are you going?" Karina said, hustling to catch up with me.

"To fulfill my side of the bargain. Where do the blood mages gather when they're not working?"

Karina chewed her lip, then jerked her head. "Come with me."

She led me through the halls into a section of the palace that was obviously used by the servants. Bare walls passed and the worn floorboards weren't even covered with rugs.

At the end of the hall, the walls opened up to form an antechamber where several *viona krovaya* sat playing Beggar's Chance.

Karina jerked her chin when I hesitated. "They're through there," she whispered, indicating a door in the far wall. "I'll stay out here. Maybe these brutes will have something interesting to say."

I had to wade through the card game and the idle *viona* to get to the door, and I gulped down my nerves. A couple of them glared, but even more of them leered.

It almost made me falter. Luckily, my blood still pulsed from Eira's anger, and I made it across the room before I could balk.

Instead of knocking, I grasped the handle of the door and stepped in without an invitation.

Five blood mages lounged in a room full of castoff furniture. All of them looked up at my entrance. Three sat at a table playing dice, and two conversed across a tray of drinks. One of the two not playing dice stood to greet me with a wide smile.

"Well, hello there." The blood mage was only a couple years older than me and had black hair slicked down with too much oil. "I haven't seen you around before. What's your name, *blenni*?"

I opened my mouth to say something, torn between "hey, handsome, how do I join this little club?" and "back off, your gaze is making me greasy."

Before I could choose, one of the others playing dice narrowed his eyes.

"Don't get your hopes up, Fedor," he said. "She's the one who got Aleksandr locked in the Bastion."

"Dear Aleksandr," I said as the friendly blood mage backed away in disgust. "How is he?"

"Not well," the one at the table said. "Considering he could be free if it weren't for you."

"He could be dead," I said, voice harsh. "But he's not. Why? Oh, that's right, because I helped break out the executioner." I strode forward, ignoring their protests and sat on the sofa where Fedor had leaped up at my entrance. "Or did Luka forget that little fact?"

"From what I heard, you didn't work with him willingly," the woman across from me said.

"Well, he did kidnap my grandmother to coerce my cooperation. How would that make you feel?" I pretended to pick the lint from my cloak where it lay over the cushions, but my focus remained on them.

Her eyes narrowed. "Your point?"

I smiled at my lap. "Things change."

"They can't have changed that much. Your eyes are clear. You haven't drawn *vytl* from blood in months. You belong with Anya over there."

She gestured to the corner where another blood mage sat so quietly I hadn't even noticed her when I'd come in. It was the girl with the curly hair. The other blood mage who worked for Baron Ruriksyn.

Anya didn't look up, hands clasped before her. It looked like she was praying.

"I haven't drawn *vytl* from blood because I don't want to die any faster than I have to," I said. "I'm smart enough to find other ways to get what I want and only use the extra power when I need to."

The woman's lips pursed like she'd sat on a hedgehog. "What do you want?"

"I want to talk to Luka," I said. "I assume you have a way to contact him. Mine was taken when I was caught."

"Why should we trust you?"

"You shouldn't," I said, hoping it was the right tactic. If not, I was burning my one chance at this. "Luka tried to manipulate me to get me to work for him. Never trust someone who's being coerced. That's why I want to do things differently this time. I want all in."

They stared at me.

"Why?" Fedor said.

"Like I said. Things change. I used to believe the Law was fair. Even when I was on the wrong side of it, I believed it was right and I was wrong. Then I was registered. I didn't realize how much I could suffer for something so 'fair.'"

"Right, you've suffered." He laughed in my face. "A cushy job in the palace after only three months in the city and you expect us to—"

I sprang to my feet and yanked down the edge of my bodice so the long, jagged scar that crossed my collar bone and traveled over my heart was visible. "This was the least of what I suffered at the hands of the *viona krovaya*. This was how they chose to take my blood for the registry. My only crime was trying to help someone I cared about and they savaged me for it." I pulled my clothing closed again and straightened with as much dignity as I could muster. I turned from them and lowered my head and my voice. "Every friend I had turned on me. Because I healed someone. Does that sound fair to you?"

They glanced at each other, but no one spoke. I sensed I was losing my chance. Time for a different tactic. I had one more option to win their trust. "I don't care if you don't believe me. It's Luka I need to talk to." I started for the door. "If you get the chance, tell him the *viona krovaya* know about The Red Noble and The Lancet," I said. "They're headed there to clear them out."

Fedor frowned. "How do you know?"

The Duchess, Mikhail, and I had agreed that this would be information worthy of my return to Luka, but all I said was, "You don't think I'd come back to him empty-handed, do you?"

I reached for the door handle.

"Wait," he said behind me.

I stopped and smiled while my face was still hidden.

There was a pause. "Maybe you should sit down."

CHAPTER TWENTY

It took most of a week to convince the blood mages that I wasn't going to turn right around and report them to the *viona krovaya*. But now that Eira was safe, I could be patient.

Every now and then, I spotted her from across a room or down a hall, following in the Grand Duchess's wake with her other ladies, like a gaggle of geese. I tried not to be jealous when I saw Eira's bright head bent to hear what one of her companions said. It was good she was making friends. I had no right feeling left out just because our relationship had never been that easy.

Finally, Fedor told me Luka wanted to talk, and I slipped away from court to meet the other blood mage in the bowels of the palace. Karina came along, as always, guiding me down a long set of wide steps to the cellars.

"What's down here?" I said.

"Mostly storage," Karina said. "Lots of wine. They say there's a hundred secret passageways and tunnels that start here below the palace."

"Are there?" I asked.

Karina shrugged. "I've only found five."

I glanced at her sidelong. "Did you grow up here? With the Grand Duchess as your patron?"

Karina rubbed the back of her neck. "I did. At least some of the time. Mostly, I was training." She darted ahead before I could ask her anything else about her childhood or lack thereof. "You'll like this." She gestured ahead where the hall opened into a foyer, not as grand as those upstairs but still elegant in its simplicity. A large space stretched out, broken by two rows of wide columns. It wasn't empty—an *otepf* stood arguing with a cloaked blood mage while their *viona krovaya* watched—but my gaze was caught beyond them. A pair of carved doors stood open on the far wall, depicting men in armor, women in flowing robes, and armies marching across the wood.

"What is it?" I said. Just past the doors, I could make out a long hall lined with obsidian and white marble.

"The Hall of Heroes," Karina said, voice hushed. "It's where all the *Izavitals* in Ballaslav's past have been anointed. Sort of a cross between an *yshkiniva* and a museum. Very old, very important, very holy."

The raised voices finally caught my attention. The *otepf* standing in the door of the Hall threw out his arms as if to keep the blood mage back. It was the same man I'd seen in the Little Court with the purple stole.

"You may not enter here, *ispor'chennai*. It is forbidden."

"I only wish to pray," a quiet voice responded, and I recognized Anya, Baron Ruriksyn's reluctant blood mage.

"Who will you pray to, for O'in has abandoned you? You

are cut off from Them and rightly so." He took a step back, into the blackness of the hall, and slammed the beautiful doors in her face.

Anya's shoulders slumped for a brief moment before they set, resolved. Then without hesitation, she knelt where she was, on the doorstep and folded her hands in front of her.

The *viona krovaya* following her sighed and moved off to lean against a wall and pick his fingernails as if he was used to this behavior.

I chewed my lip, then stepped forward, footsteps quiet against the worn flagstones. I stopped close enough to Anya that my cloak brushed hers.

She didn't look up.

"Why do you torture yourself like this?" I asked. "According to the *otepfs,* we are damned. There is nothing we can do to change that."

"As you say," she said to the floor. "According to the *otepfs*. But I don't believe they have the authority to keep me from O'in. I will continue to pray until I hear from Them or until the blood sickness finally takes me."

I stepped back, shaken by the simple conviction in her tone. I hardly prayed anymore, but then I'd long since stopped expecting an answer.

"Reyna," Fedor's voice rang around the columns of the foyer. "My friend, you made it."

The blood mage with a propensity for too much hair oil slung his arm around my shoulders and cast his gaze at Karina and the other *viona*. "We won't be long." He tossed a silver reyev to Karina, who pocketed it with a nod. She'd done almost as much work establishing herself as a *viona* who was willing to be bribed as I'd done convincing the blood mages I was one of them.

Fedor winked and steered me deeper into the palace depths. But as soon as we were out of sight, he snatched his arm from my shoulders.

"Thank you for trusting me," I said.

"I don't," he snapped, and I stumbled. "I don't trust blood mages who cut themselves, and I don't trust ones who get their fellows captured."

"Luka got himself captured," I said with a bravado I didn't feel. I lifted my chin. "He should have known we couldn't just walk into the Bastion and walk back out again."

His eyes narrowed in the dim light of the hallway. "I also think you're a liar."

"Then why are you doing this?"

"Because I know how much Luka is obsessed with you. And he'll be angry if he finds out you want to talk to him and I didn't let you."

He spun on his heel and stalked off, leaving me scurrying to catch up. Obsessed? There'd been a time when we'd been in love. And he'd certainly gone through quite a bit to get me on his side, but just because he wanted to use me didn't make him obsessed.

We passed an open doorway to a storage room, and I glanced inside. Two men stood taking inventory of the boxes and crates scattered around the room. I gasped as I recognized Aleksei.

Fedor noticed. "Don't worry about them. As long as they don't follow us, we'll be fine."

Aleksei looked up as we passed, meeting my eyes with a

jerk of recognition. I stepped quicker so the wall cut off his accusing gaze.

Deep underground, Fedor finally stopped beside another storage room. It seemed nondescript until I crossed the threshold and felt the tingle of a ward on my skin.

In an empty corner stood something large covered with a cloth.

Fedor stepped up to it and pulled the fabric aside with a flourish so it floated down to pool against the ground, revealing a standing mirror.

Without prompting, Fedor stepped up and laid his hand against the gilt frame and whispered the words of a spell. Spell markings crawled around the edges, lighting up as they went until the glass between them shimmered.

I gasped. "A communication spell?" I knew they could be cast onto mirrors as well as paper, but the process was so complicated and expensive that most mages never bothered. Com spells on paper were so much more affordable and easier to use.

Fedor glanced back at me with a smirk. "We stole it from the Grand Duchess. Only one in Ballaslav apparently."

The glass warped and bent, making me dizzy, until finally, it smoothed out, like a hand had run over it, pushing out the folds. And suddenly, instead of a reflection of us and the storage room, I saw a reflection of another place entirely. Luka standing beside a table laden with books, a window behind him casting light into his black hair. It reminded me so much of the first time I'd ever seen him that I had to catch my breath.

"Reyna," he said with a smile.

I swallowed, holding on to the thought that the last time we'd faced each other he'd forced my hand and ended my life as I'd known it.

"Luka," I said and was proud when my voice didn't break.

"You look well, *blenni*."

I looked like a blood mage, but I had a sneaking suspicion that that's what he meant. "I wanted to talk to you."

"So I've heard."

His smirk remained fixed, and I wanted to smack him for it. "I want to join you," I said instead. "Like you wanted in the first place."

He dropped his gaze to examine his fingernails, making me grind my teeth. "And why do you think I would I want you back?"

The words stabbed at me, but I forced myself to take a mental step back and breathe. I knew he was bluffing. Fedor had told me as much when he'd said Luka was still obsessed with me.

I'd planned for this. From the moment I knew what I was supposed to be doing for the Grand Duchess. For longer if I was honest with myself. I'd been imagining what I would say to Luka since he'd left me bleeding on the floor of the *yshkiniva*. I couldn't say much of it now, but I could capture that anger, that confidence. I could show him that I wasn't the same girl he'd manipulated and coerced, loved and lost. I was strong. And I was angry.

I planted my feet and crossed my arms, making myself bigger. "Because you wanted me to be registered. This fits into your plans."

His eyes narrowed. "How do you figure?"

"You forced the issue. You knew I wouldn't let Evgenia die, and you made it so I would have to use blood magic to heal her. With half a dozen witnesses looking on. You wanted me to do it. And I did."

He held my gaze, and I refused to tremble. Finally, he shrugged. "All right, you caught me. I set you up to be registered."

"Why?"

He straightened, his mobile mouth pressed into a thin line. "Because I wanted you to see what your life would be like if you actually lived by all the rules you pretended to follow. I wanted you to see the truth of what you are."

"Mission accomplished," I said. "I've seen the truth. I fell into your trap and came out the worse for it. Now what?"

"Now you're free to be a real blood mage."

My fingers dug into my elbows. "I want more freedom."

He nodded. "I thought you would. Fedor will let you know what you can do—"

I held up my hand to stop him. "No."

"No?"

"No. I don't want to be your pawn anymore. If I'm going to do this, I'm going to be your partner. I'm all in, Luka. Are you?"

He tilted his head. "I am," he said, but he still looked confused.

"Then prove it," I said, hiding the way my heart hammered in my chest. My normal caution was urging me to shut up, to take what he gave, and not push him too far. But that had gotten me squat in the past. Luka didn't value anything he hadn't fought for. So I'd make him fight.

"I want Mabushka," I said.

"Reyna—"

"Partners," I said again, slower this time. "You can't hold onto her and still trust me. And I know you want to trust me. Either you give her back to me or I'm walking away. Because I'm not working with her kidnapper."

"You'll have to give me more than just trust, then," he said, and my heart jumped when I realized he'd just taken the first step toward agreeing to my terms.

"Of course," I said as if I'd expected that. "What do you want?"

"You're there in the palace," he said.

"Yes."

"Well, why don't I bring your grandmother to you? Sound good?"

I sucked in a breath. "You want me to get you into the palace."

His lips curled, the strange mix of pleasure and menace making my stomach clench. "You get us into the palace in a week's time, and I will bring your grandmother and hand her over to you personally. No more tricks, no more blackmail. We'll be partners. Just like we were meant to be."

"Done," I said, hardly thinking through the implications. I'd work them out later with Karina and the Grand Duchess.

"Done," he said quietly. "See you in a week, *blenni*."

Fedor stepped forward to end the spell in a shimmer of glass.

"Well, it looks like you got what you wanted," he said with a sneer.

"Yes." Mabushka. I'd have Mabushka back within the week as long as Luka kept his word. I could wait that long. "I'm going back. My *viona* gets antsy when I'm gone for too long."

He just snorted and turned to gather up the cloth at the base of the mirror.

I hurried through the cold halls, my hands tucked under my armpits, my mind racing. I had to talk to Karina. And the Grand Duchess.

A figure stepped out in front of me, and I squeaked as I stumbled back to avoid a collision.

"Reyna," Aleksei said.

"Don't you mean *ispor'chennai*?" I said before I could stop myself.

Aleksei winced, and a brief pang of regret hit me.

"What are you doing here?" I asked.

His brow scrunched. "Inventorying the cargo we're carrying for Baron Ruriksyn. Why?"

I glanced over my shoulder. No sign of Fedor yet, but he couldn't catch me standing here talking to Aleksei. He already didn't trust me.

"No reason," I said and moved to push past him.

He danced out of the way so my cloak wouldn't even brush him. "What?" he said. "You don't want me to know you're working with blood mages willingly now? You don't have to worry. The whole palace knows. How's Eira feel about it, by the way?"

I stopped and rocked back on my heels. "She's safe. That's all that matters."

"She's not talking to you, is she?"

"That's none of your business, Aleksei," I said quietly. "Just leave me alone. That should be easy. You hate blood mages."

"I hate myself. For trusting you. But you saved Mamat's life."

I whirled to see his expression. He didn't look angry. He looked...conflicted as he ran a hand through his strawberry blond hair. "I can't make that work in my head with everything I know about blood mages."

Behind him, Fedor crept up the corridor, and I held my breath.

Aleksei stepped closer. "What are you doing with them, Reyna?" he said quietly. "You've already lost your soul. Are you willing to sacrifice your pride, as well?"

I straightened. "I lost my pride the day you begged me to heal your mother then sat there stupid while I paid the price. You did nothing while I was dragged off to be registered."

He threw his hands in the air. "What did you want me to do? What could I have done differently?"

"Nothing. I'm a blood mage. This is my life now."

"You're a healer. No matter what color you wear." He reached out, almost brushing the edge of my cloak.

I swallowed. Harsh words I'd been prepared to deal with, but this? I looked away to protect myself from the intensity of his gaze and caught sight of Fedor. His left hand had drifted toward the knife I knew he carried hidden beneath his cloak, and his right hand had curled into the first gesture or a spell which would leave Aleksei bleeding on the ground.

Pohomzhet da ma Baud, he would kill him.

I only knew one way to protect him at this point. I couldn't get him under the Grand Duchess's wing, like I had with Eira. "Don't pretend to know me," I said and swept my hand up as if to knock him away. He reeled back to avoid contact. "Your friendship was so cheap that you abandoned me the moment the blood swords took hold of me. Go away, Aleksei. Go back to your mother, and I hope every time you look at her, you remember her life belongs to me."

He reared back, and I forced myself to watch as his face crumpled. He ducked his gaze and stepped around me to leave the depths of the palace.

Fedor stepped up beside me, swamping me with the smell of his hair oil. "Is he going to be a problem?"

I kept my face tight and controlled, betraying nothing. "Not anymore."

Karina led me up the central keep of the palace to the very top where the Crown Hall perched.

The large room was lined with windows, which looked out over the city, the bay, and the Bastion on one side and all of Ballaslav on the other. A gleaming parquet floor reflected the mural on the ceiling which pictured Anastasy glowing with holy light as he reached for Svetanka. His love writhed in the grasp of the Shaker, twisting so she could reach back, fingers just short of brushing Anastasy's.

I gaped at the scene as Karina hurried past like she'd seen it a million times. Maybe she had.

At the end of the Hall, stood a pedestal where the Eagle Crown of Ballaslav lay on a velvet cushion. It wasn't much to look at considering it had sat on the head of forty-nine monarchs before Yesofya had taken the throne. Konstantin, the namesake of this city, had been the first to declare himself Grand Duke instead of King. He'd claimed to be a simple man, saying that the best monarch cared more about their country and their people than about the title before their name and the metal on their head. Every monarch to sit on the throne after him had continued the tradition.

The coronet was made of bronze and consisted of a simple band, decorated only by a wing-spread eagle, its eyes two glittering rubies.

"It's just sitting there where anyone could grab it," I said, glancing around the empty Hall.

Karina snorted. "Not unless they want to lose a hand. The Eagle Crown is bound to the blood of Konstantin. Only the Grand Duchess and her chosen heir can touch it without being burned to the bone. There's a whole ceremony that has to take place when the monarch names an heir. They slit their thumb and let the 'Eagle drink' is what I've heard."

I stared at the crown. "Oh," I said, imagining a million bloody thumbprints marring the gleaming surface.

"It's why we've never had any pretenders or usurpers in our line of monarchs like Valeria and Minosa have had."

Behind the pedestal stood another mural, a huge map of Ballaslav.

Karina stepped up to this and slid sideways, disappearing

between Elisaveta and the mountains that separated Ballaslav from Valeria.

I gaped. Then I stepped forward and peered around the cleverly disguised doorway. The map had been painted in such a way as to hide the distortion in the wall.

Karina beckoned me into a corridor lined with more windows, a bridge spanning the empty space between the two main towers of the palace. We hadn't gone far when Karina turned off the corridor to another door. She knocked politely and waited for someone on the other side to call "Enter" before she opened it.

Inside, Prince Mikhail sat at a desk that would have taken three strong men to move, his hands folded over the stack of papers in front of him.

"*Mushka* Daryadoch." He nodded to me. "*Viona* Karina. *Prevoshkedhova* will be along shortly. But we didn't want to wait considering how important your news is."

"Thank you, *Vysovechova*," I said. I'd gotten Karina to tell me all the appropriate titles for these people.

He gestured to a chair, but I shook my head. It didn't feel right to sit in front of a prince.

Karina placed herself against her customary wall and crossed her arms. When this charade was finally over and I could go home, I would be lonely without her lurking in the background of every conversation.

"Karina said you contacted the leader of the rebellion. Luka Volksyn."

"Yes, *ser*. And if you'd like, I can tell you where the stolen communication spell is being hidden. The big mirror with all the gilding."

Mikhail jerked. "The blood mages have it?" He sighed and made a note. "I'll just add that to the list of things I didn't know I needed to take care of today."

"I'd leave it for now. If you retrieve it, then they'll know I'm working for you. Besides, you'll have bigger things to worry about."

His considerable attention swung back toward me. "Oh?"

"Luka wanted me to get him into the palace," I said.

Behind me, Karina gasped. Mikhail froze, his pen dropping from his fingers.

"Do you know why?" he managed to ask.

I spread my hands. "I can only think of a couple of reasons he'd want to get in here, and it's not to ask *Prevoshkedhova* nicely to change the Law."

"You think he is staging a coup."

"It seems a bit early for it. There are still plenty of people who oppose him. But I think we should be ready for that possibility. He's obviously planning something, and I'm not the only one he trusts."

Mikhail nodded, looking thoughtful. "We've thought for a long time that he must have someone here in court, someone close to *Prevoshkedhova*, feeding him information."

"You mean, someone besides me?" I raised an eyebrow.

He smiled ruefully. "Someone besides you."

It was odd. He reminded me of someone so strongly, I felt inclined to trust him with no second thoughts. Maybe it was my dad, though they looked nothing alike. Papa had been short and blond. Mikhail was built like a dockworker, all shoulders and muscle. I wondered how he stayed that way, sitting behind desks all day.

Still, as much as I trusted him, I had come here for a reason. "There's one more thing I want. Since I'm telling you all this."

He watched me quietly and I braced myself for a scathing rebuke and an argument that would make me question my decision.

"Are you always like this?" he said, voice full of sympathy and curiosity. "So calculating? Because you don't have to be. Not with us. *Prevoshkedhova* and I aren't trying to cheat you or hurt you. We're trying to help you."

I stared at him. He and the Duchess were two of a kind. Neither ever responded the way I expected.

I turned my gaze to the window and the snow flurries beyond. "I've had to be. Ever since Luka took Mabushka, I've had to wonder how every action might hurt her."

"Maybe it's time we fixed that," Karina said from behind me.

Mikhail's eyes flicked to her.

I held my breath. Then puffed out my cheeks. "He's bringing her here. I made a deal with him. If I help him get into the palace, he will give Mabushka back. But I need your help to make sure it happens."

Mikhail gestured for me to continue.

"I'm not a warrior. You'll have *viona krovaya* and *viona semaya* to keep Luka's coup from succeeding, but I want you to promise they'll help me get Mabushka away from him before he can hurt her."

"If it's a choice between your grandmother and the throne, Reyna, I don't know if I can make that promise."

I shook my head. "Just...let us try. Please?"

Mikhail focused on Karina. "It'll be tricky, luring him in far enough to trap him and freeing the grandmother. Think you can do it?"

Karina met my eyes with a grin. "If I don't, I'll eat my axes."

CHAPTER TWENTY-ONE

The stairs to the cellar were too dark, the lanterns extinguished for the night, and I was reminded of the night I'd followed Luka to a cell where he'd stood back while I ruined my life.

I hurried through the dark, refusing to think about how similar my situation was now.

Karina's waiting upstairs, I reminded myself. I'm not doing this alone. I have a plan.

A circle of light ahead made me pick up my pace. Fedor must already be at the river gate with the other blood mages, preparing for their coup.

A figure stepped between me and the light, and I cried out.

"Reyna, it's me."

I clutched my chest as my heart pounded against my ribs. "Aleksei?"

Two more shadows coalesced out of the dark. "And Eira and Vitaly," Aleksei said.

"*Pohomzhet da ma Baud*, what are you doing here?" A murmur from ahead told me the blood mages had heard my cry and were debating the wisdom of investigating.

"We're here to keep you from mucking up your life even more," Eira said.

I glared at Aleksei even though he wouldn't be able to see it in the dark. "You dragged her into this? How dare you?"

"I wanted to help," Eira said, and I could imagine her lifting her chin in defiance. "Reyna, why do you keep going back to them?"

"You don't understand—"

"We do," Aleksei said. "All blood mages are the same. Once they've tried it, they can't tear themselves away, but we can help you. You don't have to keep going back to the blood."

The nimbus of light was headed back our way. *Da'ermo*, I was so close to freeing Mabushka, and they were going to ruin it. And Aleksei, the *ublyduk*, had dragged Eira out of her safety and placed her squarely in the middle of Luka's coup. I could kill him.

"That isn't what this is," I said.

"Then tell me you're not working with the blood mages. I want to hear it."

I opened my mouth, then snapped it shut on my response. I couldn't lie to him, and he knew it. But I also couldn't tell him the truth. Not yet. Karina had said I couldn't tell anyone who I was working with. If they'd even believe me now.

"If you muck this up, Aleksei—"

"Don't do this, Reyna," he said and glanced at the

approaching blood mages. "Look there's only three of them. We'll help you take them."

Three blood mages. Three friends. I was the one who could tip the difference either way. It would have been nice if I could take them up on the offer.

O'in help me, everything was going sideways. How could I protect them all? Mabushka. Eira. Aleksei. They were all in danger because of me and the choice I had to make. Luka had promised that as long as I did my part, there would be no killing. I hated that I had to trust him on that, but it was Mabushka's life at risk right now.

"I'm sorry," I said. It sounded too much like the poor apology I'd offered Professor Benson as she'd bled out under my hands. "I'm sorry. Help!" I raised my voice on the last word. "Help, there's too many of them!"

My call brought the blood mages the last few feet, bringing their light and their magic with them.

Aleksei gave me a sad, torn look before he wrenched himself away from my grasp and went for Fedor. I guess I should have been grateful he didn't want to hit me, even if I'd just betrayed him.

The other two blood mages went for Vitaly.

No one had to attack Eira. She stood against the wall with her hands over her mouth as tears streamed down her face. I turned away from her before the emotion clogging my throat turned into my own tears and gave everything away.

One of the blood mages grabbed Vitaly from behind, but the footman flailed and one of his fists caught the mage across the side of his head. He went down, and Vitaly turned to tackle the other. They fell in a tangle of limbs, and I winced as Vitaly's clumsy elbows and knees battered the mage.

Meanwhile, Aleksei was locked with Fedor. I whispered the words of a numbing spell and Aleksei tripped over his own feet to land in the dirt of the cellar. I rushed to hold him down as he twisted on the ground. He'd bitten through his lip.

He raised a hand to wipe the blood from his face, and he looked from the smear of red to me and back again.

I inhaled, feeling the power released into the air by the spilling of his blood. My hands shook as I grabbed his wrists, but I refused to cast a spell with Aleksei's blood so close.

"Please stop," I said. "Don't make me hurt you."

"Too late," he said, quiet and defeated.

"Enough," Fedor said, calling up a stun spell between his hands before he hit Vitaly with it.

Vitaly jerked and grunted and managed to bash the back of his head into the other blood mage's face as he finally went still.

The female blood mage cried out and held her bloody nose. In the light of Fedor's mage globe, the red ring around her eyes pulsed and grew wider.

Fedor shook his head and stooped to make sure Vitaly was finally subdued. Then he glanced around at the battered blood mages, Aleksei lying beneath me, and Eira weeping in the corner.

"This is just great," he said. "Now what do we do with them?"

"Bring them with us," I suggested.

The woman growled. "It'd be faster just to kill them."

Fedor's hand slashed through the air. "Luka said no blood, remember?"

"It's a bit late for that," the woman said, her voice thick from her broken nose.

"Bring them," Fedor said through his tight jaw. "If we need the blood later, we'll have some readily available."

His words sent a chill down my spine, but I stood and dragged Aleksei to his feet. If Karina and I did this right, then it would never come to that.

"Is everything ready?" Fedor asked me, holding his mage light high so he could peer into my face. "Where's your *viona krovaya*?"

"I made sure she'd be stuck in the privy with the runs for the rest of the night," I said.

"Liar," he said low and venomous. "Your eyes are clear. You haven't drawn power from blood in weeks at least."

I glared back at him and put some steel in my voice. "I'm a healer, *ublyduk*. I don't need magic to take my revenge on a body. Now, are we doing this tonight? Or would you like to wait until your boss dies of the blood sickness?"

He sneered and gestured me forward into the dark.

We herded our prisoners ahead of us, Eira and Aleksei burdened by Vitaly's limp weight. I couldn't tell if he was unconscious or just really out of it from the stun, but from the murderous looks Eira kept shooting me, I guessed he wasn't in great shape. I'll heal him myself when this is all over, I promised her silently. Let's just make it to the next step.

The cellar air grew colder until we reached an archway. Beyond a wrought iron gate lay a snowy hill sloping down to the edge of the frozen river, where sledges docked for deliveries during the day. The moon reflected from the pale snow while the wind pulled at our clothes.

A figure passed between us and the view.

"About time," Luka said.

I fumbled the key from my belt pouch and unlocked the gate. Luka stepped in, nearly a dozen hooded figures crowding in behind him.

He stopped beside me. "It's good to have you back, Reyna," he said quietly and caressed my cheek with his thumb. His fingers drifted under my chin and tilted it up.

I knew what he wanted. I met his lips with mine, ignoring the way my stomach curled with disgust. I counted to five in my head and drew back as soon as I felt it was safe.

"Now I believe there's something you owe me," I whispered.

"She's here," he said against my lips as blood mages clattered in around us, anonymous in their hoods. "You can say hello as soon as this is finished."

"Don't you trust me?" I said, daring.

"I trust you. But I don't trust her. She's been very vocal this whole time. She'll remain gagged until we're sure it's safe."

A muffled noise behind me made Luka draw back and squint into the darkness. "What's this?" he said, his voice lowering. "There's a few too many of you here, aren't there?"

"We had some trouble along the way," Fedor said. "We had to improvise."

Luka raised his eyebrows as he recognized our prisoners. "A nice little reunion," he said. He smiled at me, the scar across his cheek flashing in the uncertain light. "It's too bad I didn't have time to think of a fitting gift. I guess watching as Reyna and I bring in a new epokha will have to be enough."

"We could have done this just as easily without her," Fedor said.

They could have, yes, but it wouldn't have fit with Luka's plans. He was still fixated on getting me alongside him. I didn't really want to look too closely at that, not while Aleksei stood just feet away.

"You couldn't have gotten everyone to the Grand Duchess's private suite," I said instead. "I can." I tilted my head coyly at Luka. "That is, if that's what you'd like?"

He pinched my chin. "Smart and beautiful, as always."

I let out my breath as Luka unwillingly drew himself away from me and led the way through the cellars. I was glad when the light went with him and a cloud went over the moon so I couldn't see Aleksei's face.

I hastened to catch up to Luka, and he put his arm around me. "I missed you," he whispered in my ear. "I really wanted you to be a part of this, and I was worried you'd never forgive me."

Thanks to Karina's intervention, the halls of the palace were dark and clear as Luka and his blood mages stalked through them like they owned the place.

I led them to the top of the palace, where a wide foyer stood outside the Crown Hall.

Luka frowned at the huge double doors. "This doesn't seem right."

My heart thumped. He couldn't stop now. Karina's trap would remain unsprung.

"It's the Crown Hall," I said.

"Isn't that a little public to get to the Grand Duchess's suite."

"There's a passage behind the mural that leads across to the other tower. It's actually the back way, if you can believe it." I just avoided wincing. I probably shouldn't have phrased it like that. "It's a big empty room, Luka. Trust me." *Please don't let him see the irony in that last part,* I prayed.

"I do." He leaned in to kiss me again.

I splayed my fingers against his chest. "Then maybe after all this is done, I can show you my favorite spot in the palace."

"Where's that?" he said as I drew away toward the door.

The dungeons, if we had any. I smiled over my shoulder. "You'll see."

I opened the door and stepped inside as if to show him there was nothing to fear. The black panes of glass marched down the halls as clouds covered what little moonlight there'd been outside.

After an overlong heartbeat, Luka finally led his people into the Hall. I waited at the door, theoretically to make sure everyone made it inside okay, but really, I wanted to be sure every single mage he'd brought was caught in the trap. The last one passed me, giving me a funny look, and I slipped inside after him.

At the far end of the dark hall, Luka stepped onto the dais beside the Eagle Crown.

From behind the altar, Karina stood up. Around the room *viona krovaya* boiled out from behind the curtains and tapestries and statues of past monarchs. Thirty *viona*, the entirety of the palace contingent that Karina could trust, had managed to hide themselves in an empty room.

Luka's red-ringed eyes went wide, and he threw up his hands. "It's a trap," he called. "Get out. Reyna..."

I met Luka's eyes across the room...

And slammed the doors behind me. I threw the lock with a click that echoed in the dark.

Realization dawned in Luka's eyes as the first *viona krovaya* moved and the tableau was broken.

The fight was short and painful for Luka's mages as the blood swords countered them exactly the way they'd been trained. They used clubs and fists, weapons designed to incapacitate without drawing blood. And they were ruthless. With their own souls forfeited, they cared about nothing, except subduing the mages.

Some had to be stunned or bashed on the head to get them to stop fighting, but others saw the way things were going and laid down without protest.

Two minutes later, every blood mage lay on the ground with a *viona* standing over top of them.

Mikhail strode down from the dais, Karina at his side. "Good work," he said. "Round them up."

"Wait," I said. "Mabushka! Mabushka, where are you?"

Eira jerked where she stood with Aleksei and Vitaly off to the side of the room, but I wasn't watching her. I was looking for a response to my call.

There, one of the hooded figures on the ground had started struggling at the sound of my voice. I rushed forward and pushed the *viona krovaya* away before I dropped to my knees beside the figure. I yanked away the enveloping red cloak and tore off the hood. Mabushka blinked up at me, hands bound and mouth gagged. My hands clutched her arms, and I bowed my head in relief.

She grunted and raised her bound wrists imperiously. My smile wobbled, perilously close to tears.

"Your knife, please," I said to the *viona*.

He grunted at my tone of demand. As a registered blood mage, I wasn't allowed to carry a blade. He was well within the law and the Law to refuse, but he pulled a small knife from his belt and handed it to me, hilt first.

As my fingers closed around it, Eira hit the ground next to me. "Why didn't you tell me she was here? Was that what all this was about? *Da'ermo*, Reyna, if you'd just told me—"

"How could I tell you with them standing right there? If you'd just stayed away like I wanted—"

Mabushka pulled the gag from her mouth as soon as I had her hands free. "Shut up, both of you. Muck on a stick, you'd bicker as hell froze over." And then she burst into tears and threw her arms around both of us, heedless of my red cloak and what she knew it must mean.

That unconscious gesture of acceptance undid the months and months of fear and doubt I'd been tangled in, and I clutched her tightly. If her shoulder was a little wet when I finally pulled away, she wouldn't say anything.

I'd have stayed there all night, but I felt eyes on us and looked up to see Mikhail and Karina waiting for me. Aleksei stood awkwardly behind and to the side of them. I cleared my throat and wiped my nose surreptitiously on my sleeve.

"No *viona semaya*?" I said to Karina. "They didn't want any of the fun?"

"The family swords only protect the Duchess's family," Karina said. "So that's where they are." She jerked a thumb over her shoulder at the only two *viona* in gold-trimmed white. Mikhail's protectors standing by the wall.

Mikhail nodded at the surrounding blood mages.

"Which one of these is Luka? I'd like to arrest him myself."

As I pulled away, Mabushka sagged alarmingly.

"Are you all right?" I said.

She pulled her arms back from us and pushed herself up. "I'm fine," she said, voice less robust than I remembered it being. "It's just been an exhausting couple of months."

I exchanged a glance with Eira. Mabushka had always been strong. I'd have said she didn't even know the word exhausting.

"You go," Eira said, quietly. "I've got her for now."

Vitaly knelt beside her to help. He'd seemed far worse on the walk from the cellars, but now he grinned at me and lent his renewed strength to Eira and Mabushka. I shook my head. Maybe he was part bear. There were legends of men who borrowed the strength of polar bears in the northernmost parts of Ballaslav.

I stood and turned to survey the room. Where had I seen Luka last? A quick check near the altar revealed Fedor, but no Luka. Neither did the rest of the room.

"He's not here," I said. Karina and Aleksei, who both knew what Luka looked like, had been searching as well and now they shook their heads, confirming my thought.

"Could he have gotten past you?" Mikhail asked Karina. She'd started off between Luka and the hidden door, but it had been a very confusing two minutes. "Where was he headed?"

The blood drained from my face. "The royal suites. I even told him how to get there."

Mikhail didn't wait for Karina's protest. He took off toward the Duchess's rooms. I raced after him. If Luka had managed to get past us, what would he do to her? Had he been planning to assassinate the Duchess this whole time? Would he try for it in a last-ditch effort now that his plans had been foiled?

We reached the door of her rooms, and my breath caught in my throat when I saw the hall was empty. The *viona semaya* weren't at their posts.

"Mamat!" Mikhail called. He threw the door open and strode in. "Mamat!"

"Here."

He visibly relaxed when he heard her voice, shaken but hale and healthy.

We found her in her bedroom, standing in a dressing gown as two *viona semaya* prowled the corners of her room. Her hair flew in every direction and her nightgown was askew, but she seemed unharmed.

Mikhail rushed to her side. "Are you all right? What happened?"

She patted his hands away. "I'm fine. I'm not...not sure what happened."

"You called for us, *Prevoshkedhova*," one of the *viona* said. "But when we got here, there was nothing."

"I heard something. I was waiting up to hear the news

from the coup, and I thought maybe one of the blood mages made it this far."

"Maybe he tried to get in and couldn't," I said to Mikhail.

"You didn't capture the ring leader?" the Grand Duchess said.

Mikhail winced. "No."

She put her hand on his. "Perhaps now all he wants is to escape," she said. "Maybe we should let him."

"What?" Mikhail's eyes widened. "Mamat, he must be caught."

She shook her head. "He's defeated. Let him slink off to lick his wounds."

"*Vysovechova*," a *viona* said from the doorway, face a sickly shade of white. "Blood mages have attacked the Bastion."

"What?" Mikhail snapped, spinning.

"The battle rages even now."

"This...this was a distraction," I said, bile rising in the back of my throat. "Volka sent Luka to distract us here while she took the Bastion."

"It'll take more than a dozen angry blood mages to take that prison," Mikhail said. "And we've fought him off here."

I shook my head. Luka was still out there, possibly escaping, and we were just standing here. "We need to catch him. Then we'll have our own hostage. Volka's son."

I turned on my heel and raced for the door, blood pounding in my ears.

"Reyna, wait!" Mikhail called behind me. "You're safe from him. This isn't your job anymore."

Like hell it wasn't. Luka was my mistake. The mistake

that had followed me over the mountains and corrupted my homeland. He'd even dared follow me here into the heart of my new life. I wasn't letting him flee.

If I were Luka, how would I escape the palace? Not through the front door. Would he be stupid enough to leave the way he'd come in? He had to assume I would tell the blood swords about the river gate. But he had a good head start.

I made a split-second decision and headed for the cellars. If he went out the front door the *viona krovaya* would catch him. I hoped he went the other way. I wanted to be the one to lock him away for good.

The river gate banged in the wind from the storm outside, hinges squealing in protest. The snow that fell sideways was what we called False Hope. It was more slush than snow, hinting at a balmier time to come, but there would be no summer for months yet.

I dragged my cloak around me and raced out into the sleet. A figure slipped and slid beside the dock while a team of dogs wearing clawed boots for traction waited with a sledge on the frozen river. They had probably brought the mages here, and now Luka would use the same means to escape.

I stopped struggling with my cloak, picked up my pace, and flung myself down the hill at the figure. I struck him at shoulder height, and we went down together, tumbling across the ice and fetching up against the pylons of the dock.

He kicked himself free of me and stood panting. "Reyna," Luka said. "O'in take me for a fool, I trusted you this time."

"That was the idea," I said, hauling myself to my feet,

using the dock to brace against the wind. The slush soaked through my cloak, making me shiver.

"Why are you being so stupid about all this? Why can't you just accept your role in all of it?"

"Because your way isn't better, Luka." We both had to shout to be heard over the wind and the hiss of the sleet. "It hurts people."

He raised his eyebrows and opened his mouth in mock surprise. "Oh, you want to talk about hurting people. Well, you should really talk to that Grand Duchess of yours about that."

He turned to tuck the edges of a bundle down into the sledge as if I was going to let him get away.

"What do you mean?" I said.

"The executioner we took from the Bastion, you know what it does?"

"It took Emil's mind," I said. "I was there, remember?"

"It steals memories. It reaches inside a person and takes everything that makes them an individual. They don't remember their name, their history. They don't remember the ones they love or hate. They can't even remember how to eat or that fire is hot. My uncle burned his hand so bad after the Bastion they had to cut it off. That's what she does to the worst blood mages. She strips them of their humanity, leaves them an empty husk, and then sends them back to their family to be a horrible, constant reminder. It's worse than death, Reyna. At least death has an end. That's what we're fighting."

"And you think that justifies taking blood from innocent people?"

"No, I'm just telling you that no one is better than anyone else. Not even you."

"Fine!" I threw up my hands. "I'm a blood mage. I took blood. I killed—" I choked, unable to say it. "Is that all you wanted? I admitted what I was the day I healed Evgenia, so why can't you leave me and my family alone? I wouldn't have done any of this," I gestured back toward the palace that rose behind us in the gloom, "if it hadn't been for you. I don't care if you take all the blood in the world as long as you leave us alone. Isn't that enough?"

"You don't understand." He lurched toward me and grabbed my arms. I wasn't sure if he was going to hit me or kiss me. "You've never understood. It's not about having enough blood. It's about having the right blood. I don't, but you do."

Cries from behind us made him swear and pull away. I spun to see Mikhail burst from the river gate followed by Karina and what had to be the entire palace contingent of the *viona semaya*.

I turned back to Luka...who was making his escape down the river on his sledge.

"Reyna!" Mikhail slid to a halt beside me. "Are you all right?"

"Fine," I said, dazed by the worry in his voice. Shouldn't he have been more concerned about Luka's escape?

"At least you're safe. What were you doing haring off after him by yourself?"

What did he care? Why would the Prince of Ballaslav come looking for one lowly blood mage?

It wasn't until I saw Karina pounding up with her

brethren that I knew the answer. The *viona* that marched out into the storm didn't wear the rust-red of the blood swords. They wore the white and gold of those that protected the Duchess's family. And as they staggered to a halt at the sight of me, Karina fell into place at their head. Her red uniform stood out from theirs, but the way she held herself among them—more comfortable than she'd been with the *viona krovaya*, more at ease than she'd ever been with the other *viona uchenye* of the caravan—told me where she belonged. This was why she'd never fit in with any of them. Because she was meant for better things.

She was meant to guard royalty.

CHAPTER TWENTY-TWO

Mikhail bundled me off to Eira's suite and disappeared before I had a chance to ask him anything important. I slammed through the door, my stomach churning along with my thoughts.

Eira jumped as I strode into her rooms. Vitaly scrambled to shut the door behind me while Mabushka turned where she lay on the couch.

I wanted to fuss over my grandmother, to make sure she was all right, tend to her hurts, and then curl up in her lap and ignore the storm inside and out. But I couldn't tame my heart and mind long enough for that.

"What happened?" Eira said, a throw pillow clutched in her hands. "You look like you've seen Anastasy's ghost. Did you catch Luka?"

"I—No," I said as she tucked the pillow behind Mabushka. My mouth opened and closed. What did I tell them when I knew nothing for certain myself?

"He got away?" I hadn't noticed Aleksei standing

awkwardly in the corner, as if he'd followed them all in here and then hadn't figured out how to leave yet.

"Not before throwing ice on the fire," I said.

Eira's brow furrowed. "What do you mean?"

I stalked over to grasp the back of the couch opposite Eira and Mabushka. I stared at my white knuckles.

"Who am I, Karina?" I didn't have to check to know that she'd followed me all the way from the river gate. She would be there behind me, leaning against the door or the wall, her arms folded, her sharp eyes taking in everything. Just like always.

After a moment's hesitation, she said, "Why are you asking?"

I turned to glance at her. She was positioned almost exactly as I'd imagined her. "Something Luka said."

She tilted her head. "What did that *ispor'chennai* say?"

"He said this whole thing is a matter of having the right blood. And that I had the right blood."

She opened her mouth, but I could tell what she was about to say, and I interrupted her before she could speak. "Don't lie to me. You've been lying to me this whole time, and I'm not falling for it anymore. So I'm asking again, who am I? And for that matter, who are you?"

Her hazel eyes met mine, and we stared at each other for several long moments.

I could tell when she made her decision. She blew out her breath and raised her chin.

"I started training as *viona uchenye* when I was eight. Two years later I was set apart as *viona semaya*."

Eira's mouth dropped open, but since I'd guessed as much down by the river gate, I didn't flinch.

"But...but when you joined the caravan you were *viona uchenye*," Aleksei said from his corner. "Were you kicked out or just hiding?"

"Let's call it hiding," she said. Her eyes hadn't left my face.

"Why?" Eira said. "Why go out on your own?"

"I wasn't the only one."

"What do you mean?"

Karina's gaze shifted to Vitaly. Eira followed the look and turned to her erstwhile beloved, her confusion morphing into horror. But he didn't return her look.

He glared at Karina. "Don't you dare."

"If I'm going down, I'm taking you with me," Karina said.

"What is she talking about?" Eira said. "Vitaly?"

"Tell her the truth," I said.

As we watched, his back straightened and his shoulders squared. Suddenly, I realized how tall he was. Gone was the lanky, awkward young man we'd traveled with. This man moved with the same supple grace as Karina. He moved like a fighter.

"I don't understand," Eira said, even though I was sure she did. Her voice had grown small and quiet. "The *viona semaya* protect the Duchess's family. That's their sole purpose."

Karina nodded, her eyes back on me. "When we were first training, we were each assigned one member of the royal family to guard and protect and lay down our lives for. That's what we've been doing."

All this and she still hadn't said it.

"Who are we?"

"Reyna Sofya Darya Konstantinadoch," Karina said. "And—"

"Eira Ekaterin Darya Konstantinadoch," Vitaly said.

"Named for your mother, your mother's mother, and the many times great grandfather who founded this city."

I sat on the couch before my knees went out from under me. I'd guessed, out there in the snow. Mikhail reminded me of my mother, not my father. His sister. And I could see her face in the Duchess's when she stopped being regal and took a moment to be a grandmother. But it was something entirely different to have it stated in such reverent tones by a girl you thought had been your friend.

Sleet hissed outside, leaving streaks across the tall dark windows. Mabushka laid her head back against the couch.

"Did you know, Mabushka?" I asked.

"I did," she said without raising her head.

"Why didn't you ever tell us?"

Finally, she sat up and shrugged, completely nonchalant in the face of this world-altering news. "Your mother gave that up before you were ever born. Darya didn't want that for herself, and she didn't want it for you two. She was very happy living in a cabin in the woods with your father. It shouldn't have ever been an issue." She glared at Karina and Vitaly in turn.

Karina shrugged. "*Prevoshkedhova* was happy to leave it at that," she said. "When Darya left, the Duchess had five children and three grandchildren. After accident and treason took two of them, she decided that all of her offspring and their children needed her protection, whether they agreed to it or knew about it at all. That's when we were selected. If all had gone according to plan, you'd never have known what we were."

I winced. She didn't see what was wrong with that at all.

Eira was looking glassy-eyed.

"And I thought I'd have to work up to meeting royalty," Aleksei said with a short laugh.

I glared in his direction, and he swallowed it with a cough.

"How does this change things?" I said. I didn't know how to voice the feeling that my entire world had shifted twenty paces to the left.

"It doesn't," Karina said. "You've always been who you are. It's just, now you know about it."

And learning about who I really was didn't change the mistakes I'd made. Maybe before Valeria, before the blood, the Duchess would have been able to welcome me into her court. But not now with my best feature being a red cloak. She'd made that pretty clear already, always meeting me in secret.

Maybe it would change things for Eira, though. Eira wasn't tainted by association. Not yet. No one knew we were related here, and we could keep it that way.

"Eira..."

Before I could finish, Eira burst into tears.

Vitaly rushed to her side. "What is it?" he said. "What's wrong?"

"I thought—I thought you loved me," she said, her voice

just short of a wail. "But you don't. I was just your assignment."

Vitaly's face went white. "No—no, that's not it at all." He reached for her hand. "Eira—"

"Don't touch me!" Eira leaped to her feet, throwing off Vitaly's hand, and ran to her room and slammed the door.

"Eira!" Vitaly fetched up against the door, but she'd locked it behind her. "Eira, please, it's not like that. Listen to me."

Karina snorted. "That's why you're not supposed to get involved with the one you're guarding. It blurs the lines."

My jaw clenched, and I glared at her. "She has a point."

Her brow furrowed. "What?"

I spun away before she could see my pain. When she'd come to find me in the city, the red cloak had meant nothing to her. I hadn't realized then how much her loyalty had meant to me until now, when I knew it was all just a part of her job. She didn't care about me. She cared about my blood. Just like Luka.

"Even Luka knew who I was before I did," I said, hoping she didn't notice how thick my voice had gotten. I paced to the window to stare out at the False Hope slashing against the glass. Karina remained beside the door, watching me warily.

What did Luka want in the palace? Did he want to take over Ballaslav with me to lend him legitimacy? Did he want my blood for something bigger?

But he'd left without me, and he hadn't tried to take me with him.

It was easy to see him standing beside the sledge, his arms

thrown wide and his hair blowing in the wind. The memory was still so fresh. He'd had something there. Something packed away under a blanket.

"Luka stole something," I said out loud. "Whatever he wanted to do originally, he managed to steal something from the palace and get away with it."

I had to figure out what it was. It was probably the key to whatever he was planning. Especially now that the palace coup hadn't worked.

Karina stepped forward, eyes eager. "We can retrace his—"

I spun to cut her off. "I'm not talking to you, right now."

She jerked back. "What? Why?"

I rolled my eyes heavenward. "Why do you think?"

Vitaly still leaned against Eira's door, whispering into the wood, and Aleksei stared at the floor, the ceiling, everywhere except Karina or I.

I knew by now I couldn't stop Karina from following me. From protecting me the way she'd been *assigned to,* but I damn well didn't have to talk to her. Not when nearly every word out of her mouth so far had been a lie.

Instead of returning to Baron Ruriksyn's suite that night, I curled up on Eira's other couch. I slept through the entire morning and a bit of the afternoon the next day and woke just as livid and worried as I'd gone to sleep. Vitaly still slumped against Eira's closed door while I checked on Mabushka. She slept fitfully, and I cast a simple sleep spell to help her before

I left and went stalking toward the Grand Duchess's apartments.

No one had bothered to tell me what was going on at the Bastion despite my involvement, so it seemed like I'd have to find out for myself.

Karina followed me like a shadow. She still wore her rust-red uniform, and I wondered if being *viona krovaya* trumped being *viona semaya* in some ways. Whatever her duties now included, dark circles sagged under her eyes as if she'd stood guard the whole night.

This time I approached the Grand Duchess's office overtly. I didn't creep through the private passage from the Crown Hall or hide my destination from the few nobles and servants I passed. Luka already knew I was working against him. It wouldn't hurt anything except the Grand Duchess's reputation if people knew I was seeking her and her heir.

A pair of *viona semaya* stood outside the door of the office, and I recognized the blonde woman that normally accompanied Mikhail. Neither of them stopped me as I raised my fist to bang on the wood.

Without waiting for an answer, I thrust the door open. Mikhail stood at the desk amidst a flurry of activity. Footmen and aides in military garb hurried around him.

An *otepf*, the one in the purple stole that I'd seen my first day in court and the one who'd treated Anya with such contempt, stood from a chair beside the door and advanced on me, a scowl pulling at his sagging jowls. "You can't come in here, *ispor'chennai*. You ruin everything you touch."

I rolled my eyes. As if I didn't know that. The words were

getting old. "I'm not tainting anyone just by talking to them, *otepf*. And I'm not leaving until I've said what I came to say."

Mikhail glanced around at the sound of my voice and raised his chin. He met my eyes for a moment before gesturing to the people around him. "Leave us, please," he said, voice full of quiet authority. "Another minute or two won't make a difference either way. You, too, *Otepf* Eriksyn."

The *otepf* sputtered as the swarm of people carried him with them out the door, and Mikhail and I were left in silence.

"Reyna," he said. "I don't kick the head of the priesthood out for just anyone. I wasn't aware we had an appointment."

"We didn't...uncle." I sat in the chair opposite him without waiting for him to offer me a seat.

His eyebrows hit his hairline, and he folded his hands in front of him, giving me his undivided attention. "Ah," he said. "That."

"Yes, that."

"I assume Karina told you." He glanced at my bodyguard who had arranged herself behind me somewhere. I didn't bother to look.

"I made her," I said.

I heard Karina shift self-consciously. How strict were her orders not to tell us the truth?

"It's...not a problem," Mikhail said, and I imagined Karina relaxing the tiniest bit. He opened his hands toward me. "If you're not here to confirm your suspicions..."

"I want to know why you kept it from me. From us. Eira's pretty upset, too."

"It was not our choice. Your mother, Darya, did not want

this life for you. She thought it corrupted people. I loved my little sister very much, even if I didn't agree with her, and I wanted to respect her last wishes."

"But you brought us here anyway in the end. Why? Because I'd already done a bang-up job of corrupting myself without your influence?"

"Because no matter what your mother wanted, you're family, and it seemed like you could use some help. And I believe that as much as our parents love us and we respect them, eventually one has to leave the house and make one's own decisions and mistakes."

I slumped in the chair. "I guess I've got that part right."

He shifted uncomfortably. "We can't do anything about that." He gestured to my cloak. "The Law and the *otepfs* are pretty clear about it. But I know *Prevoshkedhova* and I would like to get to know our nieces and granddaughters better. Especially for Darya's sake."

I sighed. That was actually more than I'd expected. The situation was awkward, to say the least. I was now that shameful relative you invited for LongNight dinner but always hoped wouldn't show up.

"You can at least acknowledge Eira," I said. "She won't make the head of the priesthood froth at the mouth."

He ducked his head to hide a grin. "They're all a little on edge right now. We lost the Bastion last night."

"What?" I sat up just as the door opened, and the Grand Duchess swept in.

"Reyna," she said when she saw me. She cast a confused look at Mikhail.

"She knows," he said.

Her brows lowered. "Who...?"

I glanced at Karina, who had turned white.

"She guessed," Mikhail said without a twitch.

Karina relaxed, her face regaining some of its color.

I braced myself for the Duchess's version of the "honoring Darya's wishes" explanation.

I didn't expect her to rush forward, grab my hand, and yank me out of my chair and into her arms, but that's exactly what she did.

"Mamat, the Rites," Mikhail said, rising from his chair in alarm.

"*Da'ermo* on the Rites," the Duchess said, making me choke. "I want to hug my granddaughter finally." She drew back far enough to look into my face. "I'm so sorry we've had to do this. I wish it didn't have to be this way."

"It's all right," I said, wondering how hard I was allowed to tug so she would let go. "It's the Law. I understand."

She finally let me draw away. "I'm not sure I do anymore. Something is wrong when I can't even acknowledge my long-lost granddaughter."

Mikhail sat back down, a frown settling on his brow.

"From what I understand, I wasn't exactly lost," I said. "You knew exactly where to send a bodyguard." It hadn't been an accident when Karina showed up to tell Blagoy the caravan needed a healer. She really had helped me get the job.

"Yes, well. I'm glad we have you now. You were immensely helpful last night against Luka."

"Apparently, not helpful enough," I said, gesturing to Mikhail. "I didn't think they'd be able to take the Bastion."

"Surprise mostly," Mikhail said. "We were so focused on keeping them from taking the palace, we didn't anticipate a simultaneous offensive."

"So all those blood mages and murderers are loose?" I said.

"No, we arrived early enough to lay siege to the prison. So at least they're holed up there. We'll take it back from them. I will call up three contingents of *viona krovaya* and supplement them with the army to storm the place—"

"No," the Duchess said, picking up a figurine of a shepherdess from the mantel and examining it. "I want most of the *viona krovaya* to remain here. We can't afford to lessen the protection of the palace. One contingent will certainly be enough to pry the *ispor'chennai* from a place they aren't familiar with."

Mikhail stared at her. "I'm not sure I agree, Mamat."

"Don't underestimate Luka," I said. "I think he took something with him when he escaped last night."

Mikhail's gaze sharpened on me. "What was it?"

"I don't know. I just know it had to be important."

The Duchess replaced the figurine, then waved an airy hand. "We will have the palace searched. But I think it's unlikely he made it out with anything truly valuable."

I frowned. Luka wasn't interested in value, only power. Again, I was stuck with people who didn't understand Luka the way I did.

Well, if she didn't take his threat seriously, then I would. I could trace his steps as well as anyone and figure out what he'd taken.

CHAPTER TWENTY-THREE

I crossed the bridge between towers, the sun coming clear and stark through the windows as the palace spread below us. Back to the Crown Hall, back down through countless stairs and hallways lined with paintings, mirrors, and carpets. Down through the depths of the cellars, past the Hall of Heroes with its carved double doors depicting the stories of *Izavitals* through the ages. Past the storeroom where the Duchess's stolen mirror stood under its covering. All the way to the river gate, which stood locked with a brand-new padlock.

I stood chewing my lip. Then turned around and went back the other way, paying closer attention to the objects we passed. Was anything missing? Out of place? For a man who only cared about power, what would he steal from a palace full of valuables?

I climbed the stairs slowly, my knees and feet aching with the effort. At the top, I stopped to check the swelling and found the skin around my knees hot to the touch.

"Reyna," Karina said from my shoulder.

I held up my hand before she could say anything or offer to help. I cast a quick spell to relieve some of the inflammation and winced as I stood. It was enough to keep me upright after climbing all those flights, but I still limped down the hall, swaying gingerly on my feet.

In the Crown Hall, I stopped before the pedestal that held the Eagle Crown. I kept my breathing steady as I stared, studying the spread wings as the ruby-eyed eagle glared at me.

"What if he took it?" I said.

Karina snorted. "Oh, now you're talking to me?"

I scowled at her and she rolled her eyes before stepping forward to stand beside me.

"He couldn't have," she said.

"But what—"

"I told you, it burns anyone who touches it."

"He has blood magic. The corruption in his blood gives more power to his spells than any normal mage could ever draw. What if he found a way around the protections? How would we know this isn't a fake?"

Her lips pressed together in a thin white line, and I was glad for a moment that she believed me for long enough to consider it.

Then, quick as a stooping hawk, she reached out to lay a finger on the crown.

"What are you doing?" I cried as she yanked her hand back and hissed.

She cradled her fingers against her chest, face white. "Checking."

"I was asking if there was a spell or something that would tell us," I said. "I wasn't asking you to touch the damn thing."

She grunted. "Only way to be sure."

I took her arm and gently pulled it toward me. She spread her fingers to reveal angry pink skin fading to white around the edges. "It's real," she said. "If I actually tried to lift it, it would take the skin off."

"Ick," I said and reached into my belt pouch for a phial of generic salve and a little roll of bandages. I didn't have to worry about running out of numbing agents or how expensive they were here. Baron Ruriksyn had made sure I had everything I needed.

"I thought you were mad at me," she said as I spread the salve across her fingertip and wrapped it with a clean white cloth.

"I am. But that doesn't mean I'm going to let you stay in pain." I tied the bandage off with a little tug to prove my point and spun on my heel.

"Where are you going?"

"I can't figure out what he stole. Not without more information, but there's someone here who might know more. Mabushka has spent months with him."

"You think he would just tell her his plans?"

"No, I think she's clever and observant and mad as hell. Maybe he underestimated her."

As I rounded the corner into Eira's hallway, I caught the flash of silky skirts and ducked back a step. Several of the

Duchess's ladies sailed out of Eira's door, and I made sure to stay out of sight.

One of the women tripped over something outside Eira's door and they all laughed, their voices ringing down the hall. I waited until they'd cleared out before making my way down the carpet.

Vitaly lay across Eira's doorway, his arms crossed over his chest and his head pillowed on his jacket. He frowned up at us.

Karina fought back a grin. "She kicked you out?"

"Shut up," he said to her. "This is all your fault."

"Not all," I said. "You could have told her the truth from the start."

"Our orders were very specific. We were supposed to protect you. Any way we could. We were not supposed to reveal your true identities."

"We also weren't supposed to get romantically involved," Karina said. "That's the first rule of the *viona semaya*. Loyalty and faithfulness without emotion."

"Get off it, Karina," Vitaly said. "You can't tell me you didn't get emotional."

Karina flushed.

"I'm a better guard because of how I feel," he said. "I may never get any closer than the hallway ever again, but I will always choose her. Her life is more important than mine, not because some Grandmaster assigned her to me. But because without her, my life is nothing. I will always stand between her and the world."

I pressed my lips together so I wouldn't embarrass him by breaking into a sappy smile.

Karina rolled her eyes. "Right, well, we need to see her, so could you stand maybe to the left of the world."

He closed his eyes to resume his nap, his lips lifting in a small smile. "You'll have to go through me to get to her."

"Gladly," Karina said. She leaned over him and opened the door. Then she planted her boot in his gut and walked over top of him.

Back at the caravan, I'd gotten the impression Karina found Vitaly vexing. An awkward bundle of adolescent male. Now I wondered how much of that was sibling rivalry. If they'd trained together most of their lives, they were probably as close to brother and sister as you could get.

I opted to step over Vitaly, rather than on him, holding my cloak so it wouldn't catch on his clothing.

Mabushka sat on the window seat, a forgotten book in her hand, while Eira moved toward the bedroom. She stopped long enough to see who had gotten through Vitaly, but when she saw it was Karina and me, she sniffed and continued out of sight.

"What was with the ladybirds?" Karina asked Mabushka.

My grandmother sighed and leaned back against the wall. "The Duchess is making an announcement later and they came to make sure Eira knew about it."

"What sort of announcement?" Karina said, with a frown. "The *viona semaya* weren't informed."

Mabushka shrugged. "Beats me. Something important. But it's not like anyone tells me anything tucked away in here."

Karina glanced at me, and I snorted. "I'm not going to

pretend to know what's going on in *Prevoshkedohva's* head," I said.

Karina frowned. "What does that mean?"

"You didn't think she was acting strange this morning?"

Karina drew herself up. "She's allowed to act however she wants to act."

"But why was she being so...I don't know, weird?" I said. "She practically ignored us for years, now all of a sudden she's sickly-sweet. Like the ideal grandmother, if your ideal grandmother bakes cookies and lets you stay up past your bed time."

Mabushka smiled with her teeth. "You can make your own damn cookies."

I grinned and leaned toward her. She reached out and tugged me the rest of the way into a side-armed hug. But for her, it felt natural.

"I mean it," I said. "She was being odd."

Karina bristled. "She's busy. She runs a country. Maybe she doesn't really know how to be a grandmother and also be a monarch. She's just trying to make you happy."

"Yeah, well, if she asks, I liked her better as a monarch. It's a little late for her to be all hands-on. Especially when I'm wearing this." I flapped the edges of my cloak at her.

Karina dropped her gaze. "She would never ask me. And I would never presume to give her advice."

"Speaking of..." Mabushka said and took the edge of my cloak from me. "Should we talk about this?"

I gulped and tried to pull away from her, but she kept her grip on my shoulders.

"If we have to..." I said.

"I think we have to. Luka told me some."

Karina, showing a little bit of tact for once, backed off far enough to stand guard over the room but not be within earshot.

"Now, what happened?"

I unclenched my jaw. "I thought Luka told you."

"I'd like to hear it from you."

I still wanted to pull away, to put some distance between myself and her reaction, but she wouldn't let me go. And Mabushka had only ever tolerated the Law. She'd taught it to Eira and me as a courtesy to Mamat, but I wasn't worried about losing her because I was tainted. I was worried about losing her because I'd disappointed her.

"I made mistakes, Mabushka," I said quietly. "A lot of mistakes. And now...I can't get away from them. Everything I ever wanted, it's all gone. My life is gone."

In the circle of her arms, I couldn't escape the waves of grief that I'd pushed back for so long. I couldn't look ahead and concentrate on the next thing. I couldn't ignore the presence of the past in my life.

I covered my face, unwilling to look her in the eye.

"Nonsense," she said in my ear, voice gravelly and dear. "Your life isn't gone. Just changed. Mistakes don't destroy us, they change us. Usually for the better in some way."

I snorted. "Not this time."

"You're here, aren't you," she said, gesturing to pale blue walls and crystal chandeliers. "You know the truth about yourself. You're fighting against your demons. What did I always tell you when you failed a healing spell?"

"Do it again. Do it again until you do it right."

"That's all life is, hon," she said. "Doing it over and over again until you get it right."

I wiped my eyes.

"It's harder when your mistakes manage to hurt other people, but it's a hard you've gotta deal with. And considering that you managed to get me away from that bastard, I think you're doing pretty well."

I didn't know what to say that would tell her how she'd reached inside me and burned out all the fear and shame. I'd spent so long worrying about what she'd say and think when she learned the truth. I shouldn't have. I knew my grandmother. Her wit and wisdom had picked me up and dusted me off my whole life. How dare I be afraid of it?

I cleared my throat and gave her a squeeze. She took the hint and loosened her grip enough to let me sit back a little.

"That's what I wanted to talk to you about," I said. "Luka took something while he was here. You were with him for months. Do you know what he might have been after?"

She shook her head even before I got my hopes up. "He didn't spend a lot of time in the house where he kept me. Mostly made his blood mages keep me in line. The only time he came to talk was to mock me."

I winced.

She straightened up on the window seat. "Not that I was completely useless while I was there. I listened as much as I could, and I know the names of the ones the blood mages were working with."

"You do?" I blinked at her. "Mabushka, that's really helpful." If I'd had more time with the blood mages before Luka's coup, I would have tried to do something similar from this side.

"Do you have a pen and some paper?" she said. "It's not a short list."

She was right. By the time she was done speaking, I had a list of about thirty names. Some of which seemed familiar enough I knew I'd heard them before. One stood out.

"Baron Ruriksyn," I said out loud. I sighed. I couldn't actually find it in me to be surprised. Not after the way he talked about blood magic. "I know that one well enough and believe me, I'll be talking to him about this. But these others... Do you think Eira might know?"

"She's spent more of her time in court getting to know people," Mabushka said.

I stood to track my sister down in her bedroom, and Karina started to follow me. I whirled around at the door. "I'm just going to the other room. I don't need a bodyguard there."

She frowned. "How do you know?"

I threw up my hands. "It's an interior room. It doesn't have any windows or doors. Eira might be angry at me, but I doubt she'll murder me. Go haunt someone else for a change."

I shut the door in her face.

Eira stood in front of a full-length mirror, her hands smoothing her dress, a light pink silk thing with a high waist and a gauzy outer layer that made her look like a princess out of a storybook. I guess that wasn't too far off now.

"You look wonderful," I said.

Eira met my eyes in the mirror and scowled. "What are you doing here?"

Great, I'd traded a girl I didn't want to talk to for a girl who didn't want to talk to me.

"I need your help."

She barked out a mocking laugh. "Oh, the almighty Reyna needs help finally? Imagine that."

"What's that supposed to mean?" I planted my hands on my hips.

"Clearly it means nothing," she said, turning to pin me with a glare. "Since you don't even get the irony. What do you want?"

I thrust the list at her. "You've been learning names and titles, I haven't. This is the list Mabushka made of all the people she knows are working directly with the blood mages. Recognize any of them?"

She fumbled for the paper with a frown. Then as she read, her eyes widened and mouth dropped open. "Yes, most of them. Reyna, this is half the court."

My breath caught as she met my gaze, horror crossing her expression.

"*Prevoshkedhova* needs to know about this," Eira said.

"Will you bring it to her?" I said. "I want to talk to Baron Ruriksyn myself."

"Of course, but...be careful, Reyna. If this is true..." She frowned down at the paper, the edges crumpling as her fingers tightened.

"Then we have a big problem," I said. "I know."

✺

Two doors down from Baron Ruriksyn's suite, I ran into Aleksei. I skipped back a step, holding the edges of my cloak close.

"Reyna," he said, then his throat bobbed and he ducked his gaze to the floor.

"Aleksei," I said. I missed his easy grin and his jokes. I didn't deserve them anymore, but I hoped I hadn't snuffed them out in him for good.

We stood there blocking the corridor, looking everywhere but at each other. The last time I'd seen him, my world had shifted drastically. And the time before that, I'd betrayed him to the blood mages. What did you say after something like that?

"What are you still doing here?" I said. "I figured you'd be back to the caravan by now."

"The Grand Duchess locked down the palace after the coup," he said, rubbing the back of his neck. "No one goes in or out until the *viona krovaya* have cleared everyone."

"Oh."

The silence stretched, and I wondered if he felt the weirdness crawling up his spine, too, or if it was just me.

"Reyna, I wanted to apologize."

I glanced up. That wasn't what I was expecting. "Why?" I said. "Afraid of being mad at royalty?"

He jerked his chin. "Wow, you're really hung up on that, aren't you?"

I snorted. "Wouldn't you be? I found out everyone's been lying to me my whole life."

He shrugged. "It doesn't change who you are. Or at least, who I thought you were."

I stared at him.

"I'm sorry I thought you were working with the blood mages willingly," he said before I could think how to respond. "I should have known you had something better planned."

"I'm glad you're so confident in me," I said. "But if I hadn't convinced Luka to bring Mabushka, I would have let them take the palace to keep her safe."

His lips quirked, and he gestured to my faithful bodyguard, lurking behind me. "It's funny you're so angry at Karina for trying to protect you since that's all you seem to want to do for your family."

"I'm not angry at her for protecting me. I'm angry at her for lying to me."

"Like you lied to us about being a blood mage?"

I gaped, then snapped my mouth closed. "That was different."

"Yeah. Her actions just kept you in the dark about what color blood runs through your veins. Yours endangered all of us. To be honest, I don't really know how to think of you anymore. I've misjudged you twice now. Back at the caravan, I thought you were the good and gracious healer. Then I found out you were...what you are. Last night, I thought you had truly embraced that evil. But it turns out you were working against them the whole time. Which is it?"

"Maybe I'm neither of those. Maybe I'm just someone trying to do the best they can and constantly mucking it up."

"That sounds...familiar," he said with the ghost of his old grin. "So, did you find what Luka stole?"

I heaved a sigh. "No, but I think I'm finding what he left behind." I glanced toward Baron Ruriksyn's suite.

He shifted his feet and tugged the edge of his jacket straight. "Er, last night, he seemed very...*you* seemed very..."

I felt the blood drain from my face, and I took a step back. "No. No, I'm not talking about him. Not yet, all right?"

His mouth went round. "Oh, oh no. I didn't mean to ask. I don't want to know. Not yet." He winced. "I just thought, well, obviously it had something to do with you. Maybe you took something from him when you refused to help him."

I rubbed my knuckles absently, but I couldn't think of anything to say.

"I, uh. I was going to see if Baron Ruriksyn had anything else for us to haul out of here," Aleksei said. "Make sure we had everything ready for when they lift the lock-down."

My shoulders sagged. "You might want to reconsider. I just found out he's working for Luka."

"What?" He jerked. "*Da'ermo.* The whole place is rotten." He ran his hands through his hair and paced from one side of the hall to the other. "Without a contract, we can't leave Post da Konstantin. At least, not without losing the money we've already invested."

I rubbed my forehead. "I'm sorry."

He stopped pacing and thrust his hands in his jacket pockets. "Never mind. I'll think of something else. Maybe Corwin has something. He's working with the Valerian ambassador now."

"Maybe they have cargo you can take back to Elisaveta," I said.

"Right." He opened his mouth as if he wanted to say something more but instead settled on, "Goodbye." And he strode off down the hall.

"And I didn't think you two could get any more awkward," Karina said after he left.

"Shut up."

"Really, the bad flirting was kind of amusing, but whatever that was was just painful."

"I said, shut up."

I pushed through the door of Baron Ruriksyn's suite, forgetting to knock, and gasped as I caught sight of him.

The florid noble, loomed over Anya, his hand raised and his face twisted with rage. Anya knelt, holding her cheek.

"Stop," I yelled and threw myself in front of the other blood mage.

I hadn't really thought through my action, only jumped into a situation that was obviously not right. But when the baron's eyes narrowed and he swung his hand back as if to hit me instead, Karina caught the man's hand from behind and bent it backward.

There were definitely some advantages to dragging a *viona semaya* around everywhere I went. Her face betrayed nothing but calm strength as the baron yelped in pain and yanked his arm away.

Karina let him go, though I got the impression that if the threat had been greater, she would have broken his arm first.

The baron glared at her, the folds of his face pulling at his mouth and eyes. Did he know what she was? Or who I was for that matter? I had no idea if Luka had told any of his operatives or blood mages the truth.

"What do you think you're doing?" I said. I glanced at Anya, who was slowly picking herself up off the ground.

"She refused to perform her duties," Baron Ruriksyn said

with a sneer. "And I am free to discipline my staff however I see fit."

"You're punishing her for refusing to break the Law," I said. "You're despicable."

He spread his hands. "Clearly, you don't know how things are done at court. Who do you think is going to stop me?"

"*Prevoshkedhova*," I said, laying out all my cards. "I know you're working for Luka. Hit her again, and I will tell the Grand Duchess where your loyalties lie."

I expected him to shake in his boots. Or at least for his red face to turn white for a change.

Instead, he laughed at me.

"Go ahead. We'll see who comes out unscathed."

A piece of me said I should hesitate. He was too confident to be holding nothing. But *Prevoshkedhova* would never allow this *ublyduk* to remain in her court. "Fine."

"Fine."

CHAPTER TWENTY-FOUR

Evening had fallen by the time I made my way to the Little Court, where I hoped to find the Grand Duchess. Blood pulsed in my ears and made my steps firm against the gleaming floor. But I still hung back against the walls, where I wouldn't be noticed or kicked out as easily.

The Grand Duchess swept through the Little Court as courtiers bowed left and right.

Eira and several other ladies followed. I caught my sister's eye and raised my hand in question. Had she given the Grand Duchess our list? What had she said?

Eira pursed her lips and shook her head just enough to notice.

Beyond her, I caught sight of a tall, lanky footman in the royal livery, moving through the crowd parallel to the Duchess and her ladies, carrying a tray of drinks. Vitaly, as attached to Eira as Karina was to me.

I'd have to get the Grand Duchess's attention somehow. Discreetly. How did you discreetly pull aside the monarch of your country? There was always someone watching. If it wasn't the courtiers, it was the *viona semaya*, who glared at me even now. The one in the lead turned his head, making the lights flash from his bald pate as he kept his one eye on me. The other was covered by a patch.

"Boris," Karina said in my ear. "He heads the *viona semaya* who guard the Duchess."

"I didn't ask," I hissed back at her. How'd she even know I was looking?

Maybe I could slip the Grand Duchess a note. Or send Karina to lure her away. I didn't want to get close with Boris's beady eye on me.

Before I could decide which was the better option, she headed directly for the door beside me. I stepped back and bowed as she passed. Her stiff skirts rustled as she stopped in front of me.

"Reyna," she said. "Will you join us in the Regal Court?"

I made a noise in the back of my throat as I glanced up at her, eyes wide. She'd never even spoken to me in public before, and now she was inviting me into the heart of Ballaslavian government?

I glanced at Eira, who wavered behind the Grand Duchess, but she just gaped.

Karina cleared her throat when I hesitated for too long.

"I...would be honored, *Prevoshkedohva*." What else could I say?

"Eira, too," she said, casting a glance over her shoulder. Then, without waiting for a response, she continued through the big double doors at the end of the hall.

Well, I had wanted to get her attention. Just not that way.

Maybe I'd have a chance to whisper Baron Ruriksyn's betrayal in her ear once I knew what the hell was going on.

Inside the Regal Court, mirrors lined the walls from floor to ceiling, reflecting the light of the chandeliers a thousand times. A red figure flashed beside me, and I couldn't help glancing at an army of Reyna's lined up, my mistake repeated over and over again in endless detail.

I winced and hurried after the Duchess.

A large table made of black wood stood in the center of the long room, balancing the bright gilding from the chandeliers and the mirrors.

Twenty high-backed chairs pushed back as the councilors stood when *Prevoshkedhova* entered the chamber. I recognized most of them from around the palace, though I didn't know their names or titles.

I did recognize the one on the end closest to me. *Otepf* Eriksyn. Head of the priesthood, dressed in his gold robes and purple stole, with his pointy hat on his head.

His mouth dropped open when he saw me, and he drew himself up to protest.

Too bad Mikhail beat him to it.

"*Prevoshkedhova*," he said, his neck stiff and his fingers tense where they rested on the table in front of him. He stood beside the chair on the far end of the table reserved for the heir. "A blood mage in the council chambers?" He glanced at me with an apologetic shrug. "This is unprecedented."

I didn't blame him. The fire of my anger had died as if buried under snow, leaving me cold and uncomfortable.

"That doesn't necessarily mean it's bad," the Grand

Duchess said. She gestured to the chair on her left for Eira and the one on the right for me.

I hesitated. Everyone in Ballaslav knew that the place to the monarch's right was reserved for her confidant. The *Izavital*, if there was one, or a trusted mentor or friend.

"Take your seats, girls," the Duchess said in a voice that would not indulge argument.

Eira slipped into her seat, gracefully arranging her skirts as she sat, letting them pool around her feet.

I dragged the heavy chair back from the table so I could sit, but I didn't drag it back into place, keeping myself behind the Duchess on purpose. Karina settled herself behind my left shoulder, arms crossed over her chest. It occurred to me that maybe that stance wasn't just to make her look more intimidating. It also put her hands closer to the ax hafts that rose over her shoulders.

Vitaly, discreet as a footman, tucked himself in the corner as if waiting to be sent on an errand.

The oldest councilor, who sat directly to my right, curled his lip like I was something he'd pulled off the bottom of his boot.

"*Prevoshkedhova*, I must protest," he said. "She will taint the entire Regal Court."

Otepf Eriksyn nodded so hard I thought his hat would fall off.

"Her mere presence will not taint anything," the Grand Duchess said. "This isn't an *yshkiniva*. Unless, of course, you worship me?"

The rest of the councilors chuckled at the Grand Duchess's joke, but the councilor in question went purple.

"I would commit no such heresy, *Prevoshkedhova*," he said.

I half-turned to Karina to ask who the old man was, but before my lips had even shaped the word, she had leaned forward to whisper in my ear. "Count Yeshevsyn. *Prevoshkedhova's* most trusted councilor."

She certainly wasn't acting like he was her most trusted councilor right now.

"The Count is merely pointing out the Law," *Otepf* Eriksyn said. "It's against the Law for you to associate with blood mages."

"Laws change," Sofya said, lacing her fingers in front of her. "In this case, we needed a change to allow me to introduce my granddaughter, Reyna Sofya Darya Konstantinadoch."

The Count reared back like she'd struck him and the *otepf* stammered.

"Granddaughter?"

"Yes," *Prevoshkedohva* said. "Darya's firstborn. The hundred and fifth daughter in Konstantin's line."

Hmm, good to know. I learned something new about myself every day now it seemed.

"And Eira Ekaterin Darya Konstantinadoch." She gestured to Eira, but their gazes remained focused on me.

I wanted to sink into my overlarge seat as the *otepf's* eyes raked me from head to toe, but I still had my pride. I might have been a blood mage, but I was the descendant of kings. Apparently.

I glanced over to Eira, who sat with her head high, her

hands clasped demurely in front of her. I straightened my spine and mirrored her posture.

The count shook his head. "Granddaughter or not, she's still a blood mage. Her presence profanes this space. What is she doing here?"

I hoped the Grand Duchess would actually answer that one because I wanted to know the answer as well. It would be nearly impossible to mention Baron Ruriksyn to her here with all the councilors' eyes on us.

But one of the other younger councilors spoke up.

"She is serving the Grand Duchess, as we all are." He smiled at me like he was doing me a favor.

"Then she can serve outside, like the rest of her kind," *Otepf* Eriksyn said with a sneer.

The Grand Duchess raised her chin like she scented a challenge. "You can always leave, if my family offends you so much."

She phrased it like he had an option. But she was the Grand Duchess. His monarch. A suggestion from her was to be taken as law until the day you died.

The holy man drew himself up, and his eyes grew wide enough to stand out from his face until he spun on his heel and slammed out the door in a huff.

"Anyone else feel the same?" the Grand Duchess said mildly as if she hadn't just banished the head of the priesthood.

With great aplomb, the count stood, pushing back his chair. He met the Duchess's eyes, but whatever he saw there didn't change his mind.

He followed the *otepf*.

"Well, now that that's settled, *Vysovechova*, you have a report for us."

Mikhail's eyes flicked between the double doors and his mother as if a part of him wanted to go after the councilor and the *otepf*.

Had she really just kicked out her most trusted councilor? Just for me? I wasn't even sure this was something I wanted.

Mikhail finally cleared his throat and shuffled his papers straight. "We need to discuss the situation with the Bastion. The contingent of *viona krovaya* failed to take the prison back from the blood mages." He frowned down at the table. "They were all killed in the process."

"O'in welcome them with open arms," the Duchess said, bowing her head for a moment.

The rest of us followed suit, murmuring the ritual prayer even though we knew they had probably sacrificed their souls in the fight.

"We should send in several contingents of the *viona krovaya*," Mikhail said. "Make sure there are no mistakes and no surviving blood mages this time."

"No," the Duchess said. "We are abandoning the Bastion."

Mikhail blinked at his mother. "What?"

"Let them have it," she said. "It's not worth the fight. And the *viona krovaya* are too valuable to throw away on a prison."

"It's not just the prison," Mikhail said, his tone striking a balance between respect and disagreement. "It's everything that goes with it. Abandoning the Bastion will send a message of weakness when we want to be strong."

"The *viona krovaya* are needed elsewhere," the Duchess said. "But if the rest of you agree to pursue a lost cause, I can't stop you." She surveyed the council. "Does anyone object to my decision?"

Mikhail looked like he wanted to object loudly, but the majority of the councilors around the table shook their heads.

"We must strengthen our position here," the Duchess said. "I will now open the discussion for any ideas regarding our protection."

While I sat and watched as they made their weak plans, I marked each face around the table. Not one of them bothered arguing with the Grand Duchess, not after she kicked out the *otepf* and the Count.

I leaned back in my chair and tried to catch Eira's attention behind the Grand Duchess's back. I didn't need to whisper or wave; she was already watching for me.

I leaned my head toward the councilors and raised my eyebrows in question.

She followed my look, then pulled something out from beside her. She unfolded a piece of paper and, under the edge of the table, tilted it toward me.

It was the list we'd made of all the nobles helping Luka.

I sucked in a breath and mouthed, "all of them?"

She checked again, then her lips thinned, and she nodded.

I stared around the table, but no one was paying any attention to me anymore.

They were all working for Luka. Every last one of them. And...*Prevoshkedhova* had just kicked out the last two who could have defended her. I'd thought we'd won a victory over

Luka when we'd stopped his coup, but somehow, he was more entrenched than ever.

And it seemed the Grand Duchess had opened the doors and invited them in.

As the meeting drew to a close, I sat in my chair behind the Duchess, my fists clenched in my lap. She dismissed the others and stood, everyone rising and bowing as she did. I remained in my seat, eyes down, but she stopped beside me and rested her hand on my shoulder.

"Thank you for joining us, Reyna," she said.

I could almost feel their smirks, every single one of them pleased, not caring if she'd compromised her ideals, her morals, and her very soul for my sake. I hadn't asked for any of this. I didn't want it, didn't appreciate it. I wanted to go home. Back to the small cottage outside Darayevo with Mabushka and Eira before I'd left for school. Or back to Valeria before I'd let a sliver of glass change the course of my life.

The councilors filed out the door, and Eira rose to follow them. I didn't raise my gaze to acknowledge my sister. What would I say anyway?

I almost missed the quiet exchange at the door, when *Prevoshkedhova* responded to one of her councilors, saying, "Of course, it is dangerous for a monarch to have only one heir." And then she was out the door.

Ice flooded my veins and every hair on my arms stood on end. Heir?

She meant Eira. She had to have meant Eira.

But after that council meeting, after being acknowledged before the Court, being defended to her most trusted councilor and the *otepf*, I had a hard time convincing myself.

"I take it I wasn't the only one to notice something odd," Mikhail said.

I jumped at the sound of his voice in the large mirrored room. I'd thought I was alone besides Karina. He'd been still enough that I hadn't even caught his reflection.

Karina shuffled her feet. "You weren't the only one."

"How long has it been like this?" I said.

"I..." He hesitated as he glanced at me. "I can't be sure. She hasn't been herself since the coup, but before that, I noticed something wrong."

He was hedging.

I raised my chin. "How long?" I said.

"Since she approved your transfer here."

I stood abruptly, my cloak catching under the edge of my chair leg. I wrenched it free, ignoring the sound of tearing cloth, and strode to the wall of glass.

"You think I'm responsible?" I said. "That I mucked with her head or something? I'm a healer, *Vysovechova*. I knit flesh and bone. I carve out rotten and diseased tissue, and I bandage boo-boos. I wouldn't have the faintest idea how to go about spelling her." I twiddled my fingers like I was casting a spell.

Mikhail crossed his arms. "I'm not saying you did it magically. But your very existence changes her. You are her granddaughter. And you are a blood mage. We can't get away from it."

"I know. I've been trying for a while now."

"I know you have. You think she didn't ask my opinion

when she wanted to bring you here? I wouldn't have consented if it hadn't been obvious how badly you wanted to change."

I stared at him in the mirror. I hadn't known that.

His voice softened some. "*Prevoshkedohva* and I may see you for who you really are, but the world still sees only your sin. Can you blame her for wanting to fight that?"

He stood and collected his papers before leaving the Regal Court.

"I can blame her," I said to my reflection. I couldn't say I wished they'd just left me alone because Eira deserved everything they'd given her, but there was plenty left over for me to resent. "I don't want any of this. And even if I did, she's betrayed her country for something rotten."

"You speak treason," Karina said quietly.

I spun on her. "You think she's in her right mind?"

Karina stiffened, her gaze fixed over my shoulder. "I'm not allowed to say."

I rolled my eyes. "Come on, Karina. You're at least allowed to think for yourself. You're not just a bodyguard."

"*Viona semaya*," she snapped. "There's a difference, Reyna, even if you refuse to see it. I hold a position of trust and loyalty that you can't seem to understand."

I flushed. "Just because I can see that something isn't right?"

I froze before I could find the words to describe what I'd felt. The Grand Duchess wasn't herself. That's what Mikhail had said.

Pohomzhet da ma Baud, I'd spent the day trying to figure out what Luka had stolen, but he hadn't taken an object.

He'd taken a person, and he'd replaced her with something else.

I lurched forward and grasped Karina's arms. "He took her," I said.

"What?"

"Luka took the Grand Duchess. He replaced her with that thing we freed from the Bastion. That creature, that shape-changer."

Karina wrinkled her nose. "All right, now you're the one who sounds out of their mind."

"I'm not. The thing that escaped from the Bastion with us. It was a shape-changer. You saw it at the *yshkiniva*. It looked like a dog. It's some kind of executioner that steals memories from prisoners. It takes everything that makes them a person. The Grand Duchess was using it to keep the blood mages in line."

Karina drew away, shaking her head. "No, she wouldn't do that."

"She did."

"No!" She raised her hand as if to strike something and froze. "No," she said, letting her hand fall. "I've lived in the palace since I was eight, I've watched her for ten years. I know her. She's kind and just, and yes, she's strict but not to a person's destruction."

"I think you're too close to her," I said. "You see her the way you want to see her."

"I see the truth of her," Karina said. "She cares about Ballaslav. She cares about Mikhail and about her family. She cared about you and Eira even before she met you. So much so that she sent me to protect you. She loves you as her granddaughter. That's what all this is about. She just wants to be your grandmother and you hate her for it."

I stepped back, knowing I'd pushed too far, too fast. Karina believed the best of her patron. Now that she was on the defensive, she'd fight me. She wouldn't believe the truth unless I could prove it to her with something other than words.

CHAPTER TWENTY-FIVE

B y the time I returned to Eira's suite, I had to hold the wall with every step to stay upright. A late night traipsing around the palace with a band of blood mages, followed by a day of rushing to and fro trying to clean up Luka's mess had left my knees swollen and trembling while pain shot through my feet and crawled up my legs.

I'd done too much. But I couldn't stop; there was more to do.

Eira puttered around her sitting room, singing about a Ballaslavian milkmaid who fell in love with a polar bear. Her voice remained clear and strong but the tightness around her eyes told me she was far from relaxed. Aleksei played a game of Beggar's Chance in the corner with Vitaly so at least she'd let him in again.

Eira stopped singing as soon as she noticed me and Karina. I staggered to the couch and collapsed, rubbing my palms up and down my calves and thighs. The friction only warmed them up a little, it did nothing for the pain.

Eira planted herself in front of me as I wove a pain-blocking spell to keep me going.

"The court is infiltrated, isn't it?" she said without preamble. "And the Grand Duchess is compromised somehow."

Aleksei gasped and Vitaly's head came up, his eyes wide. I could imagine him exchanging a look with Karina, but I didn't turn to check.

I started to tell her it was worse. That the Grand Duchess had been replaced. But how would I convince her? Not even Karina believed me, and she knew the Duchess well enough to see the changes.

"We need to fight back," I said, instead.

Eira tilted her head, a spark coming into her eye that hadn't been there a second ago. "That's usually my line."

I huffed a laugh. "You were right. We should have been fighting them long ago, before they ever got close to the palace."

She didn't roll her eyes or say I told you so. She just pursed her lips and nodded. "Right. We're in a good position for it, though. *Prevoshkedhova's* acknowledged us. That means she's given us leverage, and leverage is everything to nobles." She paced to the window and back again. "Who can we use that leverage against?"

I extended a hand, palm up. "Well, the council is clearly out. All the councilors are working for Luka."

"Exactly. We'll have to dig a little deeper. Find the ones who don't like what's going on but are too scared to come forward. And then we make them fight with us."

Months ago, she'd been mooning after Vitaly, and I'd

questioned her judgment on everything. Now she sounded like a general organizing her troops.

"How?" I said.

"We promise them something they want. Power, prestige, money. Whatever we can get our hands on to give. Or we bluff."

I sat back. I started to say that was going to be difficult, but I was interrupted by a knock on the door.

Karina opened it to admit a harried footman.

"*Mushka* Reyna Daryadoch," he said with a formal bow that was far too low. "*Prevoshkedhova* requests your presence in the Crown Hall. Immediately."

I gaped at the window, which was pitch black. The Crown Hall? In the middle of the night? The Crown Hall was used for only one thing and that was holding the Eagle Crown. Unless you were leading a band of blood mages through it during a coup, but we'd already done that.

Like I'd told Luka, it was a big empty room, and if I went, it would just be me, the Grand Duchess, and the crown.

My hands started to tremble.

She was going to name me the heir. She was really going to do it.

I lurched to my feet with a wince to turn on Karina. "Now do you believe me?"

She stiffened. "She just wants to talk to you."

"She's going to do something stupid," I cried and threw my hands in the air.

"Careful," she growled.

Right, insulting the Grand Duchess was not the way to win Karina's belief. "She's going to name me one of her heirs.

Why else would she sneak me into the same room as the crown in the dead of night? Does that sound like the Grand Duchess you know and love?"

Aleksei and Vitaly stood, their game forgotten as they glanced between Karina and me.

Karina's placid expression broke for just a fraction of a second, long enough for doubt to flash across her face.

"I'll prove it," I said. "I'll ask her what she's going to do. If she says she's going to make me heir, then you'll know she's false."

I didn't wait for her to agree. I limped out the door, my gait uneven but as quick as I could make it.

"Reyna, wait," Karina said, hurrying to catch up. "You can't just confront her."

"I can. She acknowledged me before the court. I'm her granddaughter now, and like Eira said, that gives me some power. I can talk to her."

No one waited for me in the empty Hall yet. One lone candle burned on the altar behind the Eagle Crown, its light reflecting off the opaque windows. A carved railing separated the main part of the Hall from the altar and the dais where the crown rested, and I unashamedly used it to haul myself up the short step.

The ruby eyes of the eagle glittered in the candlelight.

"*Pohomzhet da ma Baud*, Karina, I don't want to wear that," I said, and even my hushed voice rang around the room.

"You won't have to," Karina said.

The door banged before I could respond, and another voice carried down the Hall. "*Prevoshkedhova*, we cannot guard your person from outside," it said.

"You may wait out here." The Grand Duchess sounded like she was reiterating an argument she'd already had once. "These two are my closest friends. I trust them with my life and I ask you to do the same."

Three figures preceded the Grand Duchess through the door, swathed in enveloping cloaks. The way the one on the left moved was too familiar.

I grabbed Karina's arm and shoved her down behind the waist-high altar, then dove in beside her.

She started to protest, and I clapped my hand over her mouth. My name died as a squeak on her lips.

"Luka," I whispered against her ear.

She went rigid, and her eyes rolled until she could see my face. Her lips clamped shut under my hand, and she raised her eyebrows. I took the unspoken promise and let her go.

"Well," someone said. "Where is the girl?"

It wasn't Luka who spoke, but I recognized the crisp voice, one used to command. I craned around to peek as Volka threw back her hood and surveyed the Hall with an arched brow. As though she'd been invited to the palace and found the accommodations...lacking.

"She's been summoned," the Duchess said with an airy wave. "She should arrive any moment."

Luka shook back his hood and gazed at the crown on the dais directly in front of our hiding place. I held my breath, but he smiled and turned back to the group.

"Perhaps she dawdles," a deep voice said. The third figure ran a finger along the railing at the edge of the room to check for dust. "Not a promising start to our new *epohka*." Luka's father, Aleksandr, pushed back his hood. The last time I'd seen him he'd been stuck in a stasis spell as I escaped the Bastion.

My hands shook. A false ruler stood in the heart of Ballaslav alongside its most dangerous traitors. And they were waiting for me.

The Duchess glared at Aleksandr. "You chose the pawn," she said. "Not I. This deal of ours is starting to lose its luster." In that moment, as she confronted the family of blood mages, her eyes flashed a fierce orange, clear across the room from our hiding place. Just like the creature from the Bastion.

Karina squeezed my hand. She'd seen. She knew.

"We promised you freedom, didn't we?" Volka said. "Who is freer than the ruler of Ballaslav?"

"Anyone else, I'm coming to realize."

Karina leaned close enough her lips brushed my ear. "You were right. What is that thing?"

She'd barely breathed the words but the susurrus rose and bounced softly off the ceiling as though thunder rumbled in the distance.

Three blood mages and an imposter whipped around to pinpoint the sound.

Volka's eyes darted to the shadowy corners. "Who's there?"

I held my breath and felt Karina do the same beside me.

Luka scanned the room with narrowed eyes while Aleksandr threw his cloak back with a laconic gesture to free his hands. Volka's gaze pierced the dark just above our heads and she stepped forward. Her fingers curled in a gesture I recognized. A killing spell would come when she called.

I shoved Karina's shoulder and jerked my chin at the

opening in the wall behind the altar. She had to get out, to warn someone. Whatever the blood mages were planning, they were going to start tonight.

Her eyes widened, and she shook her head, her lips thinning as she planted herself more firmly beside me.

I ground my teeth and shook my head. Volka was closing in, and she wouldn't hesitate to kill Karina. They needed me, but my bodyguard was an inconvenience.

We couldn't both escape. They'd see us and catch us in the corridor beyond. But if we had a distraction at least one of us might be able to get out.

As if she guessed my thoughts, Karina's fingers reached for my sleeve, but I lunged back and up.

"I'm here, *Prevoshkedhova*," I said, my voice ringing across the empty room. "What did you want from me?" I planted my hands on my hips so my cloak flared, hiding Karina from view and smothering her alarmed hiss.

I spoke to the false Duchess but my gaze came to rest on Volka. She raised her chin to meet my eyes, but she didn't lower her hands as she stepped forward.

I refused to flinch. *Please, Karina. Go get help. Trust me on this.* She'd have to go all the way across the bridge and around the rest of the palace to get back to the front doors where the Duchess's *viona semaya* stood. Could I hold the blood mages off for that long?

"Where were you?" Volka said.

"I came through the passage. Didn't Luka tell you it was there?"

Volka's gaze flicked to her son, who shrugged in assent.

She finally lowered her hands.

"You don't seem surprised to find three blood mages in the presence of the Ballaslavian monarch," she said. "Aren't you frightened?"

I still hadn't heard Karina move from her hiding place, and I couldn't look to be sure. I didn't dare let my eyes or my gaze betray Karina's presence. I had to convince her to abandon her sworn duty of protecting me in order to protect everything else.

"You won't hurt me," I said, loud enough to echo. "You need me for something." I hoped. O'in, please let it be so.

The hem of my cloak shifted in the slight breeze a body made as it moved, and I could imagine Karina cursing under her breath as she slipped toward the hidden passage to the royal suites. My shoulders relaxed a fraction. At least she would be safe.

Before I could celebrate the success, Volka surged forward around the railing, crowding me against the altar. She flicked her wrist until a blade rested in her palm and suddenly the cold edge pressed against my throat.

"Mamat," Luka said behind her. "This will all be useless without her."

Volka's lips tipped in a smirk that made my heart stutter in my chest. "We don't need all of her. Just her blood."

I swallowed, my mouth dry. Why had I been so quick to dismiss my bodyguard again?

Volka grinned and flicked the knife so it slid out from under my chin, leaving a sting and a trickle of warmth.

She stepped away, and I raised a shaking hand to press my fingers to the slice just under my jaw bone. My pulse fluttered under my touch.

"Is everything in place?" Volka said as she strode to the false Duchess.

The shape-shifter raised its chin. "I've made it very clear Reyna is the daughter of kings and has my support. The foundation has been laid and will be carried out by the rest of your operatives here."

Luka took hold of my elbow and steered me three halting steps to the Eagle Crown, which rested on its cushion. My breath came faster with each step.

"No, no, no," I whispered. They meant to chain me to the throne. To the crown that burned pretenders.

Was there a greater pretender than a blood mage sitting on the throne of Ballaslav?

I planted my elbow in Luka's gut, then shot toward the door, urging my legs to carry me even through the pain. I made it ten steps before my left knee collapsed. Even as I cried out, a heavy spell of silence settled around the room, cutting off any noise I could make to alert the guards outside.

Strong hands grasped my arms and lifted me into the air.

"Why don't you cast a spell, little mage?" Aleksandr said. "I want to see your eyes light up with the red."

That's exactly why I didn't dare start any kind of spell. The corruption running through my veins would draw *vytl* from the blood trickling down my neck. And nothing I did would have any effect against them when their own spells swelled with blood magic.

I kicked out with my feet and struck flesh. Aleksandr grunted and shifted so my arms were pinned.

"Try that again," he said. "I still owe you for the Bastion."

I forced myself to ignore his threat and threw my head

back into his face. I had to keep fighting. Karina would be here soon, and all he could do in the meantime was hurt me. I was used to pain by now.

He growled and backhanded me across the face. I fell hard enough to hit my head against the gleaming floor. Everything went white and fuzzy.

When I managed to blink the fog from my vision, Aleksandr was dragging my limp body across the Hall. He flung me against the dais, making the world spin.

I clutched the edges of the step, trying to still the vertigo and the nausea crawling up my throat. Luka knelt beside me, face creased with concern while his mother played with the point of her knife, a smile drifting across her lips.

"That's sweet. She still thinks she can fight," Volka said.

"Get used to it," I said, squeezing my eyes shut. "Because I'm never going to stop fighting you."

She leaned closer, the dull red ring around her irises just visible without sunlight. "Then I'll drag you along with me," she said. "And you'll find out just how much you have left to lose."

My eyes snapped open as my blood went cold. Everyone I cared about lived within these walls, within reach. How had I failed to protect so many people? Mabushka, Eira, Karina. Even Aleksei was trapped here along with everyone else.

While I lay frozen, Aleksandr grabbed my right hand and used it to haul me upright. Volka lunged forward and plunged her dagger into the heel of my palm. I cried out, then bit my lip.

"Was that really necessary?" I grated out.

"I like putting holes in you," Volka said.

I shuddered and decided I really didn't need to be a smart mouth ever again.

The false Duchess stepped forward, its eyes burning a brilliant orange as though it didn't care who saw its true nature anymore. It drew out a small phial of liquid, blood that sang to me of secret bonds. And it was fresh. Less than an hour old.

I raised my head in surprise. The Grand Duchess. The real Grand Duchess had to be alive somewhere if she still had blood to give.

The creature unstoppered the phial and poured the blood over the crown. Inelegant, but if the crown was linked to the Konstantin heirs, it would be effective nonetheless.

The bronze pulsed with an uncertain reddish light, before flashing bright blue as if in recognition.

"Is that what it's supposed to do?" Aleksandr said.

"I believe so," the false Duchess said, staring at the crown with a crease between her brows. "The archives were unclear. There is supposed to be a ceremony, but that's just for the masses. This is the heart of the ritual."

"And now?" Volka said.

The false Duchess seized my bloodied hand so abruptly I squeaked in surprise and pain. The creature dragged my hand toward the crown.

I jerked and fought until my head swam and I hung limp from Aleksandr's arms, not sure which way was up.

Between the two of them, they pressed my palm right over the wingspread eagle.

The bronze warmed against my skin, heating until the

metal seared the edges of the cut Volka had happily gouged into me. My breath hissed between my teeth.

It was over in an instant and the metal cooled as though in apology.

Aleksandr stepped away, and my legs gave out. No one tried to catch me as I hit the gleaming tiles. I curled around my hand, the palm tender and red and the gash cauterized in the shape of an eagle's wing. I took a deep breath, ignoring the way it shuddered in my chest.

"That's it?" Aleksandr asked.

"The process is complete," the false Duchess said. "The Eagle Crown recognizes her."

"See, Reyna?" Luka said with a flash of the grin I hated. "I've made you royalty."

I clenched my teeth as I clutched my burned hand to my chest and pushed myself to a sitting position with my other. "No one will accept this."

Volka smiled so her teeth poked out below her lip, like a fox. "They won't have a choice," she said. "They'll have you, or they'll have no one."

The false Duchess drew herself up. "My obligation to you is fulfilled."

Volka held up one finger. "One more thing," she said. "Then you may run amok if that is your wish." Volka dug in her bodice and pulled out a piece of obsidian, carved into the shape of a flask. "The real Duchess's memories. You can return them to me, then you may take your first victim."

The Duchess's mouth spread in a smile that didn't belong to her, and the creature reached for the dark flask. I didn't see anything pass between them, but the creature's shoulders drooped as if it had just given up a great weight.

Then it turned to me, orange eyes bright in the Duchess's face.

I swallowed, throat dry. In the Bastion, this creature had stolen the memories of Ballaslav's worst criminals. As a sort of executioner, it had stripped them of their minds and their selves. Did Volka and Aleksandr want a mindless pawn to place on the throne?

What did it feel like to lose yourself? Would it hurt? The way Emil had screamed and writhed made it look like the worst thing ever.

I gathered my legs under me. I would not meet my death on the ground.

And then, before my eyes, the Duchess burst into flames.

CHAPTER TWENTY-SIX

The creature wearing the Duchess's face screamed and fell to the floor. Luka stood behind its writhing body. He lowered his hands with a smug smile.

"Mamat!" Mikhail's voice rang through the Hall and bounced off the silencing spells, the echoes sounding strangely muffled. My uncle rushed from the passageway behind the map, either sent here by Karina or alerted by whatever we'd done to the crown.

He skidded to a stop beside the false Duchess's body, now black and twisted while flames licked the floor.

"Mamat," he said again, the agony in his voice making my throat close.

I opened my mouth to say it wasn't her. But before I could form the words, his countenance grew stony, and he raised his eyes to me.

"What have they done?"

He lunged forward and seized my burned hand. I yelped in pain as he spread my palm to reveal the shiny red marks of bronze feathers burned into my skin. The fingers of his left hand uncurled enough for me to see the matching mark on his palm.

His shoulders fell and the corners of his mouth drew down. He looked much older than he had this morning.

Ignoring the pain, I turned my hand in his and gripped his fingers. The blood mages shuffled around us, but I pulled him close, taking that moment to share the only piece of hope I had left.

"It wasn't her," I whispered fiercely.

His eyes widened and, in that instant, I saw a flash of movement and Luka's grin over his shoulder.

"No!"

Luka plunged his blade into Mikhail's back even as I screamed.

Too many things happened at once. At the front of the Hall, the doors flew open, admitting Karina and a cadre of *viona semaya*. Volka cried out, "Hurry, he has a knife!" while her son backed up a step, wielding the bloody blade. Then she and Aleksandr disappeared through the back passageway while the *viona semaya* converged on Luka.

Heedless of the chaos, I lurched forward to catch Mikhail, clutching his shoulders as if I could hold him together by will alone. He sagged, then collapsed against me, and I fell with him, hitting the floor with a soft thud.

Stupid. I'd been so stupid. I should have warned him away as soon as I'd seen him. Of course they would try to kill him. He was the last loose end to oppose their plan.

I pressed my hands to the gaping wound hidden by his clothing, his blood stinging my burned palm.

"No, no, no," I whispered. "*Pohomzhet da ma Baud*, this can't be happening."

I'd thought my life had come apart the moment I'd chosen to heal Evgenia, but I hadn't realized the wreckage could still be washed in blood.

I had to do something. Anything. I was a healer. But even as my fingers unclenched and formed the symbols for a spell, another face in a darkened cellar floated through my memory. Professor Benson, gasping out the last of her life as my spells sucked the *vytl* from her blood.

I choked and yanked my hands back. No, I couldn't cast any of my spells, not with Mikhail's blood creeping across the floor. I'd only kill him faster.

"He needs a healer," I cried, not even sure who would respond. Karina was here somewhere with the *viona semaya* who were scuffling with Luka.

I ripped through Mikhail's thick coat and embroidered shirt to find the wound in his back, but I could already tell from the way his breath hitched that the blade had found his lungs. My eyes burned as I dug through my satchel for bandages and a bottle of witch hazel that I knew would do no good.

If only I could use magic. I could have patched his lung and staunched the bleeding and saved his life, instead of kneeling here on swollen legs while his blood slipped through my fingers. My hands trembled with the need, and I couldn't tell if I craved the blood or the power to do something. Either way was destruction.

Just like with Evgenia, Luka had known exactly what he was doing. Even when I refused to use blood magic, he knew how to control me, my addiction and past mistakes tightening like a noose around my neck.

Mikhail sagged back against the floor and caught my fluttering hands. His eyelids flickered, and he opened glazed eyes to meet my gaze. All I could see in them was the question. Why didn't I help him? Why didn't I save him?

I sobbed, but even as I drowned in guilt, he gripped my hand and smiled as he died.

I bent my head over his chest and wept, the useless bandage unrolling beside us to rest in the pooled blood.

Voices pressed against my ears. I wanted to ignore them, but I heard my name ringing around the vast Hall now that Volka's muffling spell was broken.

I raised my bleary gaze to survey the destruction.

Volka and Aleksandr had disappeared, leaving Luka alone. He stood now between two overlarge *viona semaya*, who gripped his arms so hard he winced. His eyes traveled the length of the Crown Hall frantically, but he didn't find his parents and he met my gaze briefly. His own mother had used him to manage her escape and, from the look on Luka's face, I didn't think it had been a part of the plan.

A crowd of nobles and courtiers had gathered near the door, their murmurs echoing from the dark windows as the *viona semaya* held them back.

Karina stood between Mikhail's body and the twisted remains of the false Duchess, her bronze signet ring, a match for the Eagle Crown, gleaming from the ashes. I couldn't see Karina's face from where I knelt, but her shoulders jerked with every heaving breath she took.

Boris, the Duchess's *viona*, knelt beside me, his mouth

tight and his one eye gleaming at me. A scar ran through his eyebrow and under his thick eyepatch. It pulled now as he frowned. His hand rested on Mikhail's still chest, as though he hoped to feel one final breath.

"What happened here?" he said.

I took a shaking breath and searched the room for some sort of reprieve. There was no one. Except Luka, who stared at me with wide eyes.

Boris followed my gaze. "He killed them?"

"I—yes. But..." What could I say? Luka had been the one to kill them, but the real evil had already escaped. And even if the Duchess was false, Mikhail was not.

"But what, *ispor'chennai?*" Boris growled.

I glanced at the gathered nobles. Every single one of them had been on the list. They all stared at me with varying smirks and smug smiles. And there, behind them, two cloaked figures lurked. Volka and Aleksandr, protected by their crowd of supporters.

Volka caught my gaze and tapped her lip with a long fingernail.

I gulped and turned to Karina. Her face was white and creased with pain but she met my eyes. Then she too gazed out at the sea of traitors. She shook her head just the barest little bit.

"But nothing, *ser*," I said, quietly. "I think the rest of the culprits got away."

"If you're hiding something—"

"I'm not."

Boris stood abruptly and reached for my arm. He yanked

me to my feet, heedless of the Rites he'd have to go through for touching me.

"Boris," Karina said, a warning in her tone.

"Careful," Baron Ruriksyn said, pushing through the crowd. "That's your new Duchess."

Boris jerked. "What?"

The Baron just extended a hand as if to say "see for yourself."

Boris's jaw clenched, and he pried my fingers open. He gasped when he saw the mark on my palm. "How did you manage this trickery?"

"It's not trickery," Karina said, though her lips pulled like she'd swallowed something sour. "She's the right blood."

Boris shook his head and reached for the bronze circlet that lay askew on its cushion. He hissed in pain and drew back to suck his burned fingers.

"You do it," he said, thrusting his chin at me.

I crossed my arms and hugged myself. "No."

He seized my arm and pulled me forward.

"Boris," Karina said, taking a step forward.

"What?" he said, glaring at her. "You don't want it to be true? Don't want to see how far your precious ward has fallen."

Karina's jaw twitched but, finally, she stepped back and gestured for him to proceed.

He placed my hand on the crown.

The bronze warmed to my touch, but it did not burn. Perhaps I should have screamed and pretended to feel pain, but with the traitors arrayed behind us, it wouldn't work for long.

I raised my gaze and met Karina's eyes. She stared at me, a conflicting range of emotion flashing through her eyes before she finally dropped her gaze to the floor.

Boris let go of me with a hiss. "I'll die before I see an *ispor'chennai* on the throne."

"Then you'll die to an empty throne," Baron Ruriksyn said.

"He's right, you know," someone in the crowd said. "We have time before the coronation to figure out what her reign will look like, but there has to be a coronation. The throne can't sit empty."

"The Valerians will take advantage and press north," someone else said.

"O'in will forsake us."

"Better someone from the Konstantin line than a pretender."

Boris watched the crowd, his eye flickering as he took in their words. He might not know that every single one of them was a traitor, but he couldn't miss the way the crowd was leaning. Surely, he had seen the blood mages gaining a foothold in court and realized this was the culmination.

I saw him glance at the other *viona semaya*. And I saw him calculate their odds of fighting this...whatever this was.

He straightened. "I don't know which is worse. An empty throne or a tainted one." He gestured for the other *viona semaya*. "Escort her to her rooms. And may O'in have mercy on all of our souls."

The *viona semaya* formed ranks around me and moved me out of the Hall by the simple expedience of walking forward until I had no choice but to move. As I passed through the crowd, several courtiers broke free to follow along behind us, already chattering about coronation plans. Volka and Aleksandr were among them.

I tried to catch Karina's eye, the lone red uniform among the white, but she walked with her head down, her hands fisted at her sides.

The blood mages had won. Just a day after their failed coup, they had control of the palace. And they had control of me.

CHAPTER TWENTY-SEVEN

They installed me in a spare suite in the royal wing of the palace, just two doors down from the Grand Duchess's old rooms. Boris and a couple *viona semaya* took up residence in an antechamber to serve as my honor guard.

"I vowed to protect the Grand Duchess until I die," he said. "That doesn't change, no matter who wears the Eagle Crown." I didn't like the way he glared at me while he said it. And I wondered just how hard he'd try to stop an assassination attempt. If I died, it left Ballaslav's throne empty, but at least he wouldn't have to make the choice to crown a blood mage.

Less than an hour after they'd dumped me, something thumped on the door to an adjoining suite, and I opened it to find Eira and Mabushka making themselves at home next door. Volka grinned at me from the door to the hall.

"Just wanted to be sure you had all the people you love here together in this trying time," she said, voice smooth and sweet as if she didn't speak poison. She shut the door behind her with a laugh I could feel in my blood.

Eira shook her head. "She's already planning the coronation." My sister turned, her blue eyes on me. "Reyna, what happened?"

I choked, then spun on my heel and retreated back into my suite, unable to answer.

"Reyna." Eira followed me, hands holding her elegant skirt so she could match my stride. Mabushka drifted behind her and immediately found an armchair.

"I don't..." I said. I couldn't force the words out.

There was a polite knock on the door, and Vitaly stuck his head in. Aleksei gave him a gentle shove from behind so they could both step into the suite.

"We heard what happened," Aleksei said quietly.

"Great," Eira said. "I still haven't."

"*Vysovechova* and *Prevoshkedhova* are both dead," Karina said. Her words shook, and I narrowed my eyes. Her entire body quaked where she stood beside my door. "They were killed by the blood mages. But not before they bound Reyna to the Eagle Crown."

"So this is what they've wanted all along?" Eira said. "They've won."

I threw out my hand. "It wasn't her. It wasn't *Prevoshkedhova*. It was a thing wearing her shape."

"That just means the real *Prevoshkedhova* is missing," Karina said, voice rising. "She's out there somewhere, hurt or worse, and we have no idea how to find her." She clamped her mouth shut and swayed.

It occurred to me then that she wasn't mourning the false

Duchess. She was mourning the real one. Of course she was.

"Why didn't you heal them?" Eira asked.

"I couldn't," I cried.

"Too much blood," Karina said. Then she swallowed. "If she'd tried it would have only killed Mikhail faster."

I gasped. How did she know? Then my eyes settled on the rust-red of her uniform. The *viona krovaya* must know some of the details for those they hunted.

She knew the way my addiction controlled me, and she'd just told everyone in the room.

I could feel their eyes, accusing, pitying, questioning, and I gathered my cloak in my hands to stalk across the room. Moving felt better than standing still. It was the only thing I could do. And it felt like running. If I went fast enough maybe I could get away from Karina's sad, blank stare.

Whether she believed it was my fault or not, I'd been there. I'd sat there while Mikhail had died and I'd done nothing. That had to be careening through her mind, slicing through that built-up loyalty, cutting it into tiny pieces.

Eira stepped across to Karina. "Sit," she said. Then when Karina resisted, "There are *viona semaya* all up and down the hall. And Vitaly is here, he'll protect us while you rest."

Vitaly drew himself up. "Eira."

"I don't want to hear what you have to say," Eira said without looking at him. "I just want you to do your job."

His face tightened, and he bowed his head. "Yes, *vozlublenni*," he said quietly.

Eira blanched at the word. It meant beloved. I hadn't heard him call her that before, and the look on her face told me she hadn't either. But she didn't say anything more as he positioned himself by the door, hand resting on the hilt of his knife.

I turned at the wall and paced across to the other side of the room. My knees throbbed in time with each step and I could feel how swollen they were, but I didn't dare stop. I didn't dare let the pain in for one second. I'd just collapse on the floor and sob until I was empty and there'd be no hope on the other side to fill me back up again.

I shuddered again, thinking of my future. A lifetime of sitting on a throne I didn't want with an evil wolf whispering commands in my ear in Volka's melodious voice.

"Go to bed, Reyna," Eira told me as she threw a blanket over Karina's shoulders. "And let Mabushka wrap up that burn." She gestured to my hand, which I kept curled against my chest.

"No." There was a part of me that wanted the reminder. And there was another part of me that wanted the pain. I deserved the pain.

"Why? Do you like looking at it? Do you like thinking of yourself as the new Grand Duchess?"

I gagged. "How can you say that?"

"I'm worried you were tired of wearing the red." She straightened and met my eyes with hers that had gone dull with exhaustion and fear. "I'm worried you might have let him die a little too easily. So you wouldn't have to be just a blood mage anymore."

The blood rushed from my face and back again, leaving me cold and then hot in turn. I lurched forward. "Take it back," I said. "Take it back, now, Eira."

Aleksei stepped in front of me, hands outstretched. "Don't do something you'll regret, Reyna."

Bile climbed up the back of my throat. *Pohomzhet da ma Baud*, did they all think I was capable of murder?

I scrutinized my companions, but none of them met my eyes. Not even Karina. The only one who stared back at me steadily was Mabushka.

I retreated to the bedroom and flung myself down on the lush bedspread. I didn't look up when the mattress bowed under Mabushka's weight. And I didn't look up when she started treating my hand, setting a spell to speed the healing and seal the wound from infection. She didn't mention the way my shoulders shook.

It took a long time to fall asleep despite my exhaustion. And even then, I slept fitfully. The dawn light sent pink streaks across my new ceiling by the time I gave up and just lay there with my eyes closed.

Mabushka snored beside me, and in the other room, I could hear Aleksei singing quietly to himself. I recognized a stanza from Anastasy and Svetanka's ballad. But Anastasy's part sounded lonely and incomplete without a Svetanka.

I threw my arm over my eyes. They burned, dry and hot, all the tears I'd expended last night soaked into the down bedspread.

As the Valerians would say, I was mucked. And all of Ballaslav was mucked with me. The blood mages controlled me, and even if we managed to get rid of them, there would always be someone else out there willing to use my addiction against me. The Grand Duchess of Ballaslav couldn't have such a weakness. Not if she wanted her country to remain free.

I was Ballaslav's greatest enemy right now.

Unless we found someone to be Ballaslav's greatest hero. A hero who could counter me and make sure I didn't hurt anyone or anything.

But no one could counter the Grand Duchess. She was the highest in the land. At least, the highest appointed by men. There was only one higher.

The *Izavital*.

I pulled my arm from my face and opened my eyes, letting Aleksei's lonely chorus sink into me. Anastasy and Svetanka. Joint *Izavitals*, chosen by O'in in a time of strife to save Ballaslav from the Shaker who had disguised himself as the evil baron. Who knew how much of the story was true, but there had been an *Izavital* in nearly every century of Ballaslav's history. Saviors chosen by O'in to guide and guard Ballaslav through hardship.

If war threatened our land, O'in sent a *viona uchenye* to lead the troops. If it was famine, then a wise leader or administrator was designated. An *Izavital* had even guided Ballaslav through the last Darkness when the sun had disappeared from Térne for three desperate months.

Would it even work? *Izavitals* were chosen by O'in. Not man. But what did we have left?

I sat upright and swung my legs out of bed. My knees protested, but staying off them for a few hours had reduced the swelling at least.

I limped from the room, startling Aleksei at the window so that he swallowed the last words of the chorus with a gulp.

Vitaly remained by the door watching over Eira where she lay on one of the couches, curled with her head against the armrest.

Karina lay on the other couch.

I dropped to my knees beside her with a wince. "Karina."

She awoke all at once and shot upright. "What is it?" she said, voice catching with sleep.

"By tomorrow, the blood mages will get their way," I said. "I can kick and I can scream, but in the end, they'll win and I will wear the Eagle Crown. They'll use my family against me and who knows what they'll make me do. What they'll do to Ballaslav through me. No one will be able to stop it."

Karina's eyes tightened. Eira's clothes rustled behind me and Aleksei stepped up, eyes on me.

"Unless we have someone who can counter me."

Karina raised her eyebrows.

"We need an *Izavital*," I said.

Boris buckled his sword belt across his chest and glared across my parlor. "I don't like that she's coming."

"It was her idea," Karina said. She checked her axes and adjusted them the barest little bit.

"She's *ispor'chennai*. Her presence will taint the Hall of Heroes."

"And maybe that will help convince O'in to answer our plea," she said as if that settled the matter. To be fair, it might. It was the only reason I was willing to enter the sacred space. To convince O'in how serious the situation was.

Boris's lips thinned. We'd have to convince him first.

"Besides, we need someone to sing the Rites, and I don't want to have to listen to your attempts."

Boris grimaced.

"If we're taking votes, I don't really like that we have to bring him along," I said.

Karina rolled her eyes at me. "Could we please all try to get along for two seconds? You don't know how an *Izavital* is anointed. Boris does. So he's coming, too."

"Fine," I said, with obvious disdain. Karina hid a smile. For the first time since she'd rushed into the Crown Hall to find Mikhail and the false Duchess dead, she moved with her normal grace as if a weight had been lifted. With a clear goal, she'd shaken free of the black grief that had struck her down last night.

I only hoped I was right about it all. Karina was the perfect choice to counter my reign. She was the one who'd been set aside to guard me and now I'd set her aside to guard Ballaslav.

We just had to see if O'in agreed with me.

Boris ducked his head out my door, then signaled us forward. Vitaly stayed behind to guard Mabushka. Outside, *viona semaya* lined the corridor, but there wasn't a single red cloak in sight.

"Volka didn't leave guards?" I said as I trotted to keep up with Boris.

"She tried. But they don't have any kind of discipline. They got bored after the first three hours and tried to bribe my men to keep watch over you instead." He glanced back at me. "I told them to take the bribe. Now we control what information Volka gets from them."

"Clever," I said.

Boris snorted. "More like lazy. Next I'm going to see if they have any sort of schedule to keep you under guard. I can adjust it so they always think someone else is on duty and we'll be free to move around at will."

Eira met us at the end of the hall. "The way is clear until we get to the Little Court. Then we'll have to go around to avoid some courtiers."

"Easy enough," Boris said. "There's a passage beside it that leads to the kitchens. We can go down from there."

We couldn't afford to be interrupted, not before we'd made it to our goal. And at this point, anyone still in the palace was suspect. The few courtiers and councilors who stood against the blood mages had all fled.

On the main level of the palace, Boris hissed and gestured us through a panel in the wall I hadn't noticed before he touched it. Voices echoed around the corner ahead, and we dove for the dark passageway just in time for Boris to snap the panel shut behind us.

I twisted my fingers in a spell and a dim mage light illuminated the cramped little hallway between walls. Dust tickled my nose, and I resisted the urge to sneeze.

Halfway down a narrow staircase, a wash of fried potatoes and *memka* overtook us, the remnants of breakfast, and Boris led us out of the passage, just feet away from the vast, bustling kitchens. Not only were the cooks busy feeding the palace, my coronation had been scheduled for the next day and they were already preparing the feast that would come after my ascension to the throne.

We scurried past the open doorway, heads down, and turned the corner to find the foyer lined with columns, the carved double doors standing open at the far end. Aleksei stood in the opening, one hand on the door. He waved us over the moment he saw us.

"Hurry," he said. "There have been blood mages through here three times already."

We slipped inside. "What about *Otepf* Eriksyn?" I asked. He wouldn't like finding me here.

"He escaped from the palace last night with Count Yeshevsyn and the other courtiers still loyal to the Law."

Well, at least he wouldn't be bothering us.

Aleksei shut the doors and pulled a large bar across them. It fit into grooves on either side of the doorframe, as if the builders of the Hall of Heroes had anticipated it shielding us from attack someday. Perhaps they had. There was a reason the Crown Hall sat at the top of the palace, where the rulers of Ballaslav could look out over their country, and the Hall of Heroes lay underneath. It was said Ballaslav rested on the shoulders of the faithful, and who was more faithful than O'in's chosen ones?

I turned from the doors, which were carved with scenes of battle and heroism, to survey the rest of the room.

Like an *yshkiniva*, the Hall contained three courts, in this case, separated by two sets of columns. The Court of Supplication that we'd just entered stood mostly empty serving as an antechamber. Someone long ago had chiseled obsidian from the Bastion itself to create a pattern of black and white diamonds on the marble floor.

Karina stepped reverently through the columns into the Court of Absolution, where a dark pool shimmered in the center of the floor.

A carved screen stood between the columns separating us from the Court of Priests. Orange and yellow light flickered beyond it, reflecting from the walls. *Otepf* Eriksyn must have left a brazier burning back there when he'd fled.

I hung back as the others followed Karina into the sacred space. Both Aleksei and Eira gave me looks as they passed, and Boris lifted his lip in a barely contained sneer.

I took a deep breath and raised my chin, but I couldn't help feeling like an intruder. I gathered the edges of my cloak off the ground as if that would keep me from profaning the space. But of course, that was the whole point.

I'd avoided praying since my registration. According to the priests, I was damned and praying would do nothing about that. But if there was ever a time to pray, now would be it.

O'in, are you listening? Ballaslav needs a hero. I need a hero. Karina is the best we have. If I'm supposed to be Ballaslav's greatest enemy, at least make her its savior.

Karina stood before the water, her head tipped back as if she stared at the high ceiling, but I could see her eyes were closed. Maybe she was praying, too. Her breath puffed white in the chilly air. No fireplaces or hypocausts warmed the room. Maybe that's why *Otepf* Eriksyn kept the brazier burning.

Boris lit the candles around the room before he knelt

beside the pool and broke through a thin layer of ice that had formed on the surface of the still water. I shivered, but Karina seemed oblivious to the frigid ordeal she would have to undergo soon.

I knew the stories of past *Izavitals*, at least the famous ones like Anastasy and Svetanka. But the stories only told what happened after Anastasy received his sword from O'in and Svetanka had been gifted her staff. How was an *Izavital* anointed in the first place? And could we force the issue?

I wanted to ask, but I was afraid to even open my mouth.

Boris jerked his head at Aleksei. "Guard the door," he said. "I don't know what will happen if this is interrupted."

Karina finally opened her eyes and smiled at him where he knelt. "Hopefully O'in will be forgiving."

Boris snorted mirthlessly and beckoned Eira closer. He tossed her a thick blanket he'd brought along. "Be ready to wrap her up. If this works, we don't want her freezing to death immediately after."

He cast a glance at me. "You just stay as far away as possible. We don't need you mucking this up with your filth."

"What exactly are we trying to do?" Aleksei said from the door before I could break my silence and snap back at Boris. "How do we get O'in to choose an *Izavital*?"

"Most of the time, O'in makes Their choice clear," Boris said. "But sometimes someone recognizes the need for a savior and they come here. They offer themselves, and O'in gets to decide if they are anointed or not. They accept them or not. It's as simple as that. Now, can we get on with it?"

Karina cocked an eyebrow. "I will if you'd shut up a minute."

Boris crossed his arms and sat back on his heels.

Karina closed her eyes and took a deep breath. "O'in, I'm here."

A finger of air touched my cheek, and I jumped. What the—?

A gust of wind ripped the corners of my cloak from my fingers and made me stagger. The others all gasped or jerked as their clothes ruffled in the unseen wind.

My mouth went dry as I realized the candle flames hadn't even flickered.

What had I expected? I'd been the one to drag us down here. I knew O'in was real, believed it enough to follow the Law even when it expected the impossible. But there was a difference between lifelong belief and the ripple of proof against your skin.

I rubbed the goosebumps on my arms.

Karina gave us a sheepish grin. "I guess I should take that as a good sign."

She stripped off her boots and the rust-red coat that marked her as *viona krovaya,* leaving only her simple linen shirt and breeches to protect her from the chilly air and even colder water.

"O'in forgive me. O'in wash me. O'in work in me and make me new."

I knew it was silly. I knew it wouldn't do any good, but I whispered the words of the Rites with her. The first time I'd done so since my registration.

Karina plunged into the pool.

I gasped as cold rushed over me, as though I had jumped into the water instead. I'd felt this once before when I'd plunged into the bay while escaping from the Bastion. But this time instead of dark, light dazzled my eyes so I saw nothing but white.

Pins and needles stabbed my skin, and I opened my mouth to cry out, half expecting water to flood in. But air filled my lungs even as the rest of me burned with cold. My joints ached with it as every muscle tensed.

"Reyna." A whisper in my ear, singing through me.

I spun, but all I could see was light.

"Reyna." A voice like a thousand bells ringing through the white.

I trembled, fear and longing flooding through my veins, clamping my lips tight and compelling me to answer at the same time.

"I'm here," I whispered.

Warmth poured into me, washing away the cold and soothing the ache in my limbs.

The light faded from my eyes even as the warmth lingered, and I blinked. The dim Hall came into focus around me.

"What did you do?" Boris said, his voice raspy with accusation.

I took a shuddering breath when I realized I stood at the edge of the pool with no memory of moving. Karina stood beside me, dripping onto the marble, her hazel eyes wide. Aleksei stood halfway down the Hall as if he'd raced forward, and Eira hugged the blanket opposite me, her face white.

"What happened?" I said. "Did it work?"

"You got in the way," Boris said, his voice gaining strength. "We're back where we started from because of you."

"No," Karina said, voice hushed. "Look. Look at her cloak. I wasn't accepted, but she was."

I raised my arms, and my cloak, which this morning had been the color of old blood, swept the floor in snowy white folds.

CHAPTER TWENTY-EIGHT

"White," I said, anything more intelligent eluding me. "Why is it white?"

"You're our *Izavital*," Karina said. "O'in chose you."

"She can't be," Boris said. "It's a mistake, an accident."

"Did she go in the pool?" Eira said.

"What?" Boris said.

"I felt the wind. I saw a flash of light. But Reyna never went in the water."

"So?"

"So, why is her hair wet?"

Once Eira pointed it out, I could feel the damp ends seeping into the fabric at my shoulders. I lifted a hand to touch the chilly strands with trembling fingers. For several moments there, I'd felt like I'd plunged into the pool beside Karina. Maybe I had.

Boris's gaze shifted from me to Eira to Aleksei who'd stepped closer to crane his head, staring at the white. "No one will accept an *ispor'chennai* as a savior."

Karina reached out to brush the edge of the cloak. "I think They've made it clear. *Ispor'chennai* no longer."

"She's a mage. She magicked the cloak to make us think that O'in chose her."

"Boris, look at it. Really look."

Boris opened his mouth once more, but then his eyes finally rested on the white fabric and he lurched around the pool to take it between his hands.

I flinched and forced myself to hold still. Boris wasn't the only one studying me. I felt like an albino turkey as wolves circled, trying to decide if I'd taste any different with bleached feathers.

Boris dropped to one knee before me. "I will follow where you lead, *Izavital*," he said, voice hushed. "Forgive my disbelief."

A lump sprang into my throat. Boris hadn't knelt to me even when I'd been declared the future Grand Duchess.

"What did you see?" I said. Whatever it was had to be more important than his loyalty to his future ruler. I took my own cloak between my fingers. The weave was tight and perfect, the white a blinding shade no dye could achieve, but other than that it seemed like a normal cloak to me.

Boris shook his head, so I glanced around at the others.

Aleksei stared at me with a soft, silly smile that I couldn't interpret. Karina just grinned while Eira stood still. My sister didn't smile or frown, but she held her shoulders relaxed, confident without being tense.

I met her eyes.

"I see Mabushka's cabin," she said, then drew a line down the middle of the cloak like she traced a drawing. "In the woods outside Darayevo. Just like how we grew up, but you and I are there with Mabushka and Vitaly. Like we're all a family. It makes me feel like I'm home." She raised her eyes again. "It makes me trust you."

I snorted. "That'll be nice for a change."

She scowled, but Aleksei took over before she could snap back. "I see the caravan. With all the little people." He chuckled to himself. "There's Mamat and Patepf and everyone's happy. Look, it even has the heart's blood wagon."

He grinned just before he caught everyone staring at him.

"I think we must all see different things," Karina said. "Something that means something specific to us."

I wanted to ask what she saw in my cloak, but that seemed like something to leave between her and O'in.

"Like Anastasy's sword," Aleksei said.

"What does a sword have to do with anything?" Eira said.

"Anastasy's sword was a gift from O'in when he became *Izavital*," he said. "And in the ballad, it says he had only to show it to people for them to believe he was O'in's chosen."

I shivered. I wanted to be Ballaslav's *Izavital* about as much as I wanted to be its Grand Duchess.

"But what do we do now?" Eira said. "At least Anastasy was *viona*. He could fight the evil Baron. Reyna is a healer."

"And she's still the heir." Boris stood, catching my attention. "Ballaslav has never had a Grand Duchess who was also *Izavital*. It kind of defeats the purpose."

My fingers twisted together. The heir's scar was still on my palm, but the pain of the burn had disappeared with the ice water's sting.

I chewed my lip as I thought. "I think...I think I'm not supposed to rule Ballaslav."

"What?" Boris said.

"They made me *Izavital* because I'm not supposed to rule Ballaslav." At least O'in and I were in agreement on this, even if we differed on some other things. "We need to find a way to keep me off the throne. I might still be the heir, but the Grand Duchess is still the Grand Duchess. We need to find her before the coronation."

"*Prevoshkedohva* is dead," Boris said, voice flat.

"That wasn't her," I said, shaking my head. "They killed a duplicate. An impostor."

He made a skeptical face.

"Do you know about the executioner of the Bastion?"

He hesitated. "That creature steals memories."

"And it changes shape. I saw it. That's how it impersonated the Duchess. It wore her face and it held her memories. But Volka took them back before Luka killed it."

"And what makes you think she's still alive somewhere? Why wouldn't they kill her?"

He was right. It was a slim hope, but I had to believe they would keep the Grand Duchess around in case something happened to me.

"They used her blood to bind me to the crown. It was still fresh."

He opened his mouth, and I interrupted before he could ask how I knew.

"Believe me. I know blood."

He shut his teeth with a click and extended a hand as if conceding the point.

"So, how do we keep you off the throne?" Aleksei said. "Volka seems pretty intent on crowning you tomorrow."

"We break her power."

"How?" Eira said. "You're just a healer."

"Which means I know how to treat infection," I said with a frown. "You clean the wound, dose it with the right herbs. And if all else fails, you cut out the rot."

I turned to stride around the pool, and they parted to let me pass. Eira passed Karina the blanket and the *viona* wrapped herself in the wool.

"Aleksei, are you still in contact with Corwin?"

"He's still here in the palace, so yes."

"Do you think you could get him to introduce you to the Valerian ambassador? I can't imagine our neighbors will be happy with a blood mage on the throne. They can probably help."

"I can do that. And..."

I glanced at him. "And?"

"I might know where the exiled courtiers are staying," he said, clearing his throat with a sheepish look. "Some have contacted me about smuggling their things out of the palace."

I stopped before the carved door. "Count Yeshevsyn will be on our side at least. Maybe *Otepf* Eriksyn, too. And they can convince the rest. Eira..."

I looked over at my sister, who was making sure Karina was dry before gathering the *viona*'s discarded clothes. I remembered the way she'd walked confidently through court and the way she'd taken charge last night.

"Eira, will you organize them? Once Aleksei has them on our side."

"Are you asking me to plan a coup?"

"I am. Unless you think you can't do it."

She rolled her eyes. "Of course I can do it."

"What would you like me to do, *Izavital?*" Boris said.

"You're sworn to the Duchess," I said, meeting his eyes. "Your first responsibility is to her. Find her and then we'll figure out how to free her."

"What will you be doing?" Eira said.

I huffed. "I'm going to be figuring out why O'in chose a healer as *Izavital.*"

I reached for the door, but Karina stopped me. "You can't go out there like that," she said, gesturing to the white cloak. "They'll know something's different."

"Look," Eira said, lifting the edge of the heavy fabric to show the lining. While the outside was a pristine snowy white, the inside was a deep crimson, the color of fresh blood.

The corner of my mouth quirked. O'in certainly had a sense of humor.

I left my entourage at the door of my suite to fill Vitaly in on everything that had happened under the palace, and I retreated to the bedroom to check on Mabushka.

She dozed on the bed, hands clasped across her stomach, laid out straight and flat. She'd always slept like a piece of wood, and as deeply, too, but with her face white and still, she looked a lot like a corpse.

I tripped across the floor to check her pulse and her breathing. Then sighed in relief.

She was just sleeping. But I'd wanted to talk to her. To show her the white cloak and ask what she saw, what she thought it meant.

It would have to wait.

I returned to the other room to find Karina propped in her usual spot by the door. She'd changed into a dry uniform but had left the coat off this time.

"Where did everyone go?" I asked.

"They have their marching orders," she said. "We don't have long if we're going to get you deposed by tomorrow."

She chuckled, but I couldn't help drooping. Finally, with no one else watching, I could let the last couple hours crash over me. Everything from sneaking through a blood mage infested palace to plunging into the icy depths alongside Karina. I hadn't let myself feel any of it yet.

I collapsed onto the sofa and buried my head in my hands. What in O'in's name—literally—was I supposed to do now? Why had They chosen a healer as *Izavital*? Why had They chosen a blood mage? *Da'ermo*, why had They chosen *me*? With the fate of Ballaslav resting in my stained hands, did I really need anything else to show that I was unworthy of that responsibility?

With a lurch, I stood and tore the cloak from my shoulders, tossing it as far away from me as it would go.

"Should I ask what's wrong?" Karina said, mildly.

"What do you think?" I threw out my hands to indicate the cloak which pooled on the floor, red wrapped around white. "This, this whole thing, this farce, is what's wrong. I didn't ask for this. I don't deserve it. I wanted you to be *Izavital*, not me. I had enough problems being a blood mage and the future Grand Duchess. What does this even mean? Is O'in saying I'm not a blood mage anymore? Did They cleanse my blood, too? Or am I still dying of the blood sickness?"

"I kind of thought you'd be happy," she said when I stopped ranting long enough to haul in some air.

"How is this supposed to make me happy? An honor I didn't earn."

"No one earns it," Karina said. She stepped away from the wall and crouched to pick up the cloak. "Even Anastasy didn't earn it. He became *Izavital* after he failed to rescue Svetanka the first time."

She folded the cloak carefully, leaving the white on the outside. "This is a big deal, yes. But you're not alone with it. Aleksei and Eira are still here. I'm still here."

"Yes, but I can't trust you." It slipped out, but once I'd said it, I didn't want to take it back. That was what it all came down to in the end. I'd trusted her completely once. And she'd lied to me.

I expected her to wince. Or shout and rage. But she stood calmly to lay the folded cloak across the back of the opposite sofa.

"I'm sorry," she said. "You told me once that if I was going to be your friend, I couldn't make your decisions for you. And I broke that promise."

"You did." My hands clenched in my skirt. That was the heart of it.

She sighed, almost like I was being unreasonable. "I'm sorry I did. I should have told you the truth. But I don't think that's your problem with me."

"Then what is?" I said. "I have lots of problems. Please, tell me some more."

A muscle in her jaw twitched as if she clenched her teeth. "You don't want me around because I don't blame you."

"Blame me for what?" The Duchess's kidnapping, Mikhail's death?

"All of it. I don't blame you for becoming a blood mage. I don't blame you for any of the choices you've made that you still can't get over. But you don't want to hear that, because you don't want to be forgiven."

I reared back, sinking onto the sofa cushions.

"You'd rather wallow in this endless guilt because it's easier than accepting that you mucked up and moving on from it. You can do better. But you don't want to do better. You don't want forgiveness."

"How can you say that?" I whispered. Hadn't I been trying to do better since Valeria? This whole time I'd been straining for something more than my mistakes had left me.

"Because some of us have been reaching out, offering it to you from the very beginning, and you won't take it. You've found every excuse to push us away."

I shot to my feet. "You can't offer it because you don't know the whole truth. No one does."

I spun around the end of the couch and paced to the door. I didn't even know where I was running to. Just away. Because her words hurt. There was too much truth in them but not enough truth between us. She didn't know the worst I'd done. She couldn't forgive something she didn't know about, and I would live the rest of my life alone, trying to keep that darkest secret.

I reached the door and grasped the knob.

"I know about Professor Benson," she said to my back.

The world fell out from under me. I only kept my feet by catching myself against the door.

"How...how do you know about that?"

"The same way I knew about the blood mages and the ones that kidnapped your grandmother. I was there."

Slow as an old door, I turned to face her, pressing my back against the wood. "You were there," I said, my voice betraying nothing of the forces inside my heart and mind.

"I've always been there."

"Tell me exactly what you mean by always."

She licked her lips. "I was there when you made the deal with the blood mages. I was there when you found your house burned down. I was there in Valeria before you decided to leave. Just because you can't always see me, doesn't mean I'm not nearby."

I stared at her.

She clasped her hands behind her back. "Even before I met you, I was with you. I was raised to value your life over mine. I studied you, the way you studied medicine. I knew your personality, your strengths, your weaknesses. We even had sketches."

I rubbed my forehead. "How..."

"Stan Romosk. He lived next to you most of your life. He was assigned to you and Eira and Darya before Vitaly and I were old enough to take up our posts."

"And I thought I was joking when I said you were my guardian angel."

Karina winced. "Don't. You wouldn't if you knew how I've failed you."

"Sounds like you never have," I said.

"Once." She rubbed the back of her neck. "Vitaly was right. About my feelings compromising me as much as his do. My duty was to protect you. Not to care about you. But I...I don't know how to do one without the other. The day I left the palace to meet you at the University was the best day of my life. I was so proud to protect you." She wrapped her arms around herself. "And then I got to Valeria."

I gulped and drew in a shaky breath.

"I ran into you in the street. Saw you in person for the first time. And I saw your arms. I saw your eyes, knew what it meant, and I...I broke. I left. I didn't try to find you again because...how could you betray me like that?"

I couldn't swallow away the knot in my throat. Couldn't speak around it either.

"Halfway home, I stopped. I realized I couldn't go back empty-handed. I couldn't return without you. So I went back, angry, to drag you home. And I found Luka's manor after you both left. I found the cellar. And I knew what happened."

Pohomzhet da ma Baud, she did know. She'd *been* there. I covered my mouth.

"You'd already left. There was no one to drag home. And I was alone. Alone with your crimes." She raised her gaze to mine. "But I wasn't angry. I was sad. All the reasons I'd cared about you, everything that had made me proud to be your protector, were still there. Knowing what you'd done didn't change how I felt about you. I thought it would, but it didn't. You couldn't betray me. But I sure as hell could betray you. I left you there and things only got worse. I failed my first and only duty."

"And you've spent this whole time trying to make up for that." I looked back at the last six months as if she shined a mage light on the past. The way she'd distracted Pyotr so I could get the caravan job. The way she'd followed me into the slums of every city we'd stopped in. The way she'd brought me pastries after I'd been registered.

Her knuckles went white where they gripped her arms. "I can't make up for any of it. That's not why I'm here."

"So, you're here because of your duty."

"No." She dropped her hands and focused every bit of her intense gaze on me. "I'm here because this is where I want to be. I know it all, Reyna. I know and I came back. I was assigned to you years ago, but that day, I chose you. I chose not to abandon you. Doesn't matter what you did or what you will do. I chose. And nothing you believe about yourself will change that."

She took up the cloak in her calloused hands and stroked it once before stepping over to hand it to me. "But I'm done trying to force you to take what I'm offering."

She handed me the cloak, a direct contradiction of her words, but I knew what she meant.

I took it from her.

"If you don't want my forgiveness, that's fine. That's your decision, and I promised you could make those yourself. But you can't tell me what I can or can't offer." She adjusted her axes and went to stand beside the door again. "All right?"

"All right," I said. "Any other requests?"

"When this is all over, I'd like you to live a nice quiet life and stop trying to scare me."

I snorted. "You're not afraid of anything."

She huffed a laugh like I'd missed the point. "I'm afraid you'll go where I can't follow."

CHAPTER TWENTY-NINE

Nearly an hour later, Mabushka had woken and Eira had returned. My grandmother and sister sat down in the parlor of the other suite with a tray of lunch and a sheaf of papers. I tried reading over Eira's shoulder, but her notes were all scrawled in her sloping handwriting, which I'd never been able to decipher. And before I could ask her to translate for me, Vitaly let Aleksei through the door. He shucked his coat and rolled up his sleeves like he'd just come in from a hard day's work.

"What news do you have for me?" Eira said, without looking up.

"Corwin is up for some mischief," Aleksei said with a wink in my direction. "It didn't even take much convincing. He likes Reyna a lot."

I flushed, dropping my gaze. I'd missed this side of Aleksei, but flirting with him felt even worse than it had in the caravan. There was so much between us now that couldn't be undone with a joke and a smile.

"He has the Valerian ambassador on board," Aleksei said while Eira scribbled notes. "They're sending someone over to coordinate the details."

"I hope we have some details by then," Eira muttered.

"Won't Volka get suspicious if I start entertaining the Valerian ambassador?" I said.

"Not if it's staged as political maneuvering," she said, aligning the edges of her papers. "He can hint that maybe Valeria is willing to deal with a neighboring blood mage, and while you're supposed to be negotiating border treaties and trade agreements, you can actually be planning your little rebellion."

"All right, good point."

"The others won't be so easy to enlist, though," Aleksei said. "Count Yeshevsyn and the exiled court don't know you as well. You'll have to convince them."

I wanted to say, "Me? But I thought you were going to do it?" But that seemed like the coward's way out, especially when O'in had made it clear this was my job. I still wasn't sure what a healer was supposed to do about any of it, but I had to at least try.

I nodded. "Right. Eira?"

She didn't look up from her list. "I'll cover for you here. If Volka shows up, I'll tell her you ate some bad sausage."

"Gee, thanks."

She shrugged. "There's *viona semaya* all up and down the hall with orders to stall if they see her, and Boris said he was going to mess with the blood mages guard schedule. It likely won't come to that." She took a roll from the tray, broke it in half, and layered some sliced meat and cheese on top.

"Take this. Eat it. You haven't had anything since dinner last night."

"Yes, Mamat," I said with a weak grin and took the food.

I had to tease her, but she was right. My stomach growled as I shoved the makeshift sandwich in my mouth and followed Aleksei through the door. Karina fell in behind as we hurried down the hall.

"Where are we going?" I said with a full mouth.

"Just to the top of the east tower." He pointed through one of the windows lining the hall. The sun glanced from the gold roof opposite us.

"Don't tell me the exiled court is squirreled away in the palace?" I stifled a laugh. They could be right under Volka's nose and she wouldn't even know.

He grinned at me. "Almost, but not quite. There's a special passage that will take us to them."

"Of course there is."

"We'll have to get through the whole palace to get there, though," Karina said. "There aren't any secret ways that I know."

And I'd bet she knew almost all of them.

Viona semaya positioned at intervals down the hall came to attention as we passed. But at the end of the hall, the honor guard petered out and we would have to continue through the blood mage infested palace alone.

Karina took point, creeping ahead of us and directing us down side passages when anyone came close.

At the base of the east tower, she motioned us through a door. I stepped across the threshold before noticing it was a storeroom.

"Wait here," she said. "There're very few places to hide on the way up, so I'll scout ahead and make sure we're clear."

"Karina," I said with a frown. She was leaving me in a small enclosed space with Aleksei?

"Relax. I doubt you'll kill each other before I'm back."

That wasn't what I was worried about.

She shut the door on my protests, and we were left in the darkened room lined with shelves full of sheets and fluffy pillows. Alone, with a boy I'd betrayed in so many ways. We hadn't spoken together really since our awkward conversation outside Baron Ruriksyn's suite.

I shuffled my feet, but there wasn't a lot of room to retreat. Not unless I wanted to bring an avalanche of linen down on my head.

Aleksei cleared his throat but then didn't seem to have anything to say. And I realized it was because he wasn't the one with something that needed to be said.

I'd never actually apologized. To him or to any of them for the things I'd done. Karina was right. I was afraid of what they'd say. I was afraid they'd still hate me. But I was also afraid they wouldn't. I was afraid of their forgiveness, so I'd never asked for it.

"I'm sorry," I said into the quiet darkness. My hands wrapped around the edge of the shelf behind me, anchoring me.

"For what?" Aleksei said. My eyes adjusted to the darkness until I could just make out his expression.

"For everything. I'm sorry I dragged you and your family into my mess. I'm sorry about your mother. I'm sorry about the Rites. I'm sorry I betrayed you to the blood mages. I'm sorry—"

He shifted closer and the air moved. He raised his finger as if to press it against my lips and froze a hair's breadth away.

"I'm sorry Luka hurt you because of me," I said, breath puffing against his fingertip.

He let his hand drop, carefully not touching me. But he didn't shift away. "I knew you had history with him. Seemed obvious after he showed up at the *yshkiniva*. But I didn't expect to see it played out in front of me."

I winced.

"Did you love him?" he asked after a long pause.

"So much," I said on a shuddering breath. "Or at least, I thought I did. For the first time, someone was looking at me and not my sister."

"Well, now she's got Vitaly running after her, you can have all the boys to yourself."

He chuckled at his own joke, but I didn't laugh. I pressed my palms to my heated cheeks. "I don't want all the boys," I said. "I'd settle for just one."

He cleared his throat, and we avoided each other's eyes. How did I retreat from the dangerous ground we'd wandered onto?

"Luka was the first person to know the truth and not hate me for it," I said. "I thought it was more than that. I thought he loved me, too. Now I know the truth. His family wanted him to recruit me and that was the easiest way to do it."

He gestured to my wrists. My sleeves had sagged, revealing the scars. "He was the one who got you into blood magic."

I dropped my hands and pulled my sleeves down. "You can stop looking for ways to exonerate me. I walked into this with open eyes. I went to Valeria to study. But every time my joints hurt or I got tired, I fell further behind. Blood seemed like the answer, and I wasn't hurting anyone."

"Except yourself."

I nodded. "Watch that first step off the path. It's a long drop. When I met Luka, I thought he was helping me. He showed me how to hide it, kept my secret, and didn't judge me for how far I'd fallen. It wasn't until I—I hurt someone else that I realized he was helping me become a person I hated."

I gripped the shelf again. "He knew. He knew what would happen, and he didn't warn me. He let me hurt her." I hung my head. "So, I hurt him back." I traced a finger down my face in imitation of Luka's scar. "Then I ran."

He shifted, hesitated, then reached out and took my fingers in his.

I jumped and tried to pull away. "Don't. I don't know if O'in cleansed me when They changed my cloak. You'll have to go through the Rites again."

"A small price to pay."

My heart raced as I stared up into his eyes, crinkled at the corners with his smile.

"Don't fool yourself into thinking I'm some sort of hero," I said, voice rough.

"Not a hero.But also not a villain. A person," he said. "You're not just a blood mage. A faceless evil. You had your reasons for every choice you made." He shrugged. "Bad ones, yes, but still reasons."

He twined his fingers with mine, then turned our hands over, exposing the underside of his arm where he'd rolled up his sleeves. "It makes me wonder what his reasons were."

"He never told you?" I said, eyes on the pale lines marching up his skin.

He shook his head. "He kissed me the first time, to keep me from asking. And I wanted to give him what he needed. He told me over and over again, just one more cut and he'd stop. And I believed him. At least for a while."

"What made you stop believing him?"

He winced and his fingers tightened on mine. "Caught him kissing and cutting someone else. Making the same promises."

I squeezed his hand.

"I wanted to hate him. To make him into this terrible monster that lured me in."

"Because that would be easier than realizing he was a thinking, reasoning person who decided to hurt you," I said, piecing together what he'd been getting at earlier.

"Maybe he really did want to stop," he said with a shrug.

"Or maybe he didn't. You can't know," I said.

"No. But I'd rather not hate him anymore. It's...changing me, and not in a good way. Is that...am I allowed to not hate him?"

"Yes. Hate is a sort of control," I said, thinking of Luka. "And he doesn't control you anymore. And it doesn't make you weak. Just because you can forgive someone doesn't mean you have to put yourself in a position to be hurt by them again."

He bent to press his forehead to mine and huffed a laugh. "Thank you," he breathed. "I think I needed to hear that."

We stood there, hands entwined, breath mingling, just being still together, and it was all right. Nothing between us anymore but understanding. A blank slate. The awkwardness gone.

At least until Karina opened the door and said, "Sorry that took so long. Had to dodge a couple of people." Her head tilted and her eyes locked on us in the shadows. "Should I come back later?"

I rolled my eyes as Aleksei reluctantly untangled himself from me.

Karina led us up the tower, right to the pinnacle. Under the rounded dome of the roof stood a wide empty room.

I'd half expected the exiled court to be tucked away under the eaves, but there was nothing except a large pattern set into the wood floor. Blond and mahogany highlights spiraled to the center, and I tilted my head as I realized there was more there than just a pretty design.

"It's a spell-focus," I said.

Aleksei gave me a triumphant grin. "Exactly."

My brow furrowed. "Wait. This is the secret passageway? This is how we get to the exiled court?"

"One of the better-kept secrets of the empire," Karina said. "I've never tried it before. How'd you know about it?" she asked Aleksei.

"One of the nobles gave me the details before he left. He didn't want to stick around to get his valuables out, but he also didn't want to leave them behind. It needs a mage to activate it."

I bit my lip. "Aleksei, I'm a healer."

"This isn't supposed to be complicated," he said. "The spell itself is here already." He pointed to the floor. "All we need to do is trigger the spell."

"And by we, you mean me," I said under my breath. Then I squared my shoulders. "I assume you have the spell words."

"Right here." He handed me a sheet of paper with a couple of lines of crisp, legible handwriting.

I tapped my lip as I studied the spell. I was much better with healing spells than with...whatever this was. But I knew the basics of spell work well enough that I should be able to muddle through.

I sighed, settled myself at the edge of the pattern, and checked Aleksei and Karina.

"Ready?" I said.

He shrugged. "Sure. I'm always up for an adventure."

I knelt and touched the edge of the pattern. As I spoke the words, the wood lit up, glowing with power. Aleksei studied his feet dubiously.

"Does that look—" His words cut off as he disappeared between one moment and the next.

I gasped. "Aleksei?" I stood and stepped over the edge of the spell markings, hand outstretched.

The world moved under my feet and colors blurred around me. I nearly screamed, but I was afraid if opened my mouth, I'd lose my lunch.

Just as abruptly, the world steadied, and I was left standing in a brightly lit room with a line of mountains outside the window.

There were no mountains in view of the Winter Palace,

and I knew these peaks well. I'd traveled across them just a few months ago.

Valeria stretched on the other side of them.

Hundreds of miles in a matter of moments.

I leaned over and retched, heartily regretting the hasty sandwich Eira had made me eat. I'd just cast a spell to transport us across the country with no other preparation than a piece of paper and a deep breath.

"Yeah, that was hard on my stomach, too," Aleksei said from my right.

I shook my head, but couldn't find the words to tell him that it wasn't motion sickness that had unsettled me.

I felt Karina's hand on my back, steadying me.

"You could have warned us," I said.

"I told you, I've never been through the pass-through. I had no idea it was that bad."

"I meant about the distance," I said. I wiped the back of my mouth and straightened, then stepped forward to press my nose against the sun-warmed glass. In Post da Konstantin it would have been frosty. But here, it was bright and clear, and the sun kept the chill air from biting.

"We're at the Summer Palace," I said. "Aren't we?"

Aleksei chewed his lip as he surveyed the view. "We are. I hardly believed it could be true, but that's Elisaveta out there all right."

I swallowed, trying to rid my mouth of the taste of bile. "Then let's get on with it. I imagine we'll have to go back the same way."

I hadn't even known travel across that much space was magically possible. But I'd be the first to admit I wasn't any kind of expert. There were plenty of secrets only taught to students who actually graduated from the University. And who knew how many were hoarded by their creators and kept from common knowledge. Maybe the mages in Valeria hadn't figured anything like this out yet.

Aleksei and I tripped down the stairs of a tower very similar to the one we'd just left. Karina moved silently behind us, exactly two paces behind my right shoulder at all times.

At the base, the stairs opened onto a large hall with windows lining both the north and south walls. I'd expected to find another palace like the Winter Palace, mostly empty except for the bustle of the occasional servant or random noble.

Instead, I found an encampment, far grander than a caravansary, but much less organized. Makeshift beds and tents crafted from fine silks and furs lay directly on the broad flagstones while elegantly carved trunks and embroidered bags were piled haphazardly in between, creating little rooms for the exiled nobles to call home.

Startled gazes met us as we stepped boldly into the room. A hush swept from the stairs to the very end of the hall, leaving a silence broken only by frightened whispers in its wake.

I felt the tension surround me as surely as if a dozen swords had been leveled at my throat, and I knew I was the cause. The color of my cloak had stolen these people's fragile peace.

"What do you want here, *ispor'chennai?*" an older man spat in my direction. He stepped to the front of the crowd as if to keep me from physically tainting everyone in the room.

His eyes narrowed on my face and his lips thinned. "Sorry," he said, though he didn't sound sorry. "*Prevoshkedhova.*"

I recognized him about the same time he recognized me. "Count Yeshevsyn," I said before Karina could lean forward to prompt me. I held up my hands. "I'm not here to hurt you."

I paused, waiting for Aleksei or Karina to step up and say something, but both stood silent and statuesque behind my shoulders. Well, Aleksei did say I was going to have to be the one to convince them.

"I'm not going to give you away to the blood mages that have taken over the court," I said. "And I'm not here to try to win you over to their cause."

Another man pushed to the front, making Count Yeshevsyn stagger. *Otepf* Eriksyn. His tall, pointed hat had a dent in it. "You're the reason our Grand Duchess and her heir are dead. How can we trust you?" he cried, righteous voice ringing from the rafters.

Karina stepped forward enough to draw their eyes. She stood straight and tall. She hadn't put on her *viona krovaya* jacket, leaving only her white shirt. Reminiscent of the *viona semaya.*

Apparently, Count Yeshevsyn noticed the same thing. "Your support means nothing, *viona*. You would follow any murderer as long as the blood of Konstantin flowed in their veins."

My fists clenched, but Karina raised her chin with a steely look.

"I don't follow her because she's Konstantin's many-times-great granddaughter," she said. "I follow her because she's O'in's choice." She reached out to unhook the clasp of my cloak and swing it right side out, then draped it around my shoulders again so it fell in snowy folds. "Because she's *Izavital*."

The count's eyes widened as a gasp spread through the nobles behind him. He faltered, then stepped forward.

I held my place while he reached out, hesitated, then took the white lining between his fingers. The velvet glittered in the sunlight, and I could almost make out patterns shifting through it, too fluid and subtle to catch. At least for me.

Count Yeshevsyn saw something in the patterns though. Something that made his eyes widen and his breath catch. Just like Boris, he stepped back, hands shaking.

"It's true," he said, his voice soft as a whisper, but strong enough to be heard throughout the hall. "*Izavital*." He quavered, then leaned heavily on his cane and lowered himself to one knee. "O'in forgive my doubt."

Another whisper swept through the gathered nobles. Others crowded forward, disbelieving frowns mixed with hopeful smiles. I held my breath while their hands reached and eyes searched. They whispered, their doubts turning to belief as each saw something in my cloak, something that spoke to them. One man growled something low under his breath, then gasped aloud and stumbled back a step after examining me. Another woman with a baby in her arms whispered prayers while tears slipped down her cheeks.

Karina stood protectively over my right shoulder, an anchor among the jostling bodies, her eyes searching each face, each hand that came near me.

I shivered and shuddered under their attention, but as

long as Karina remained, I convinced myself I could stand there.

At last, the rest of the nobles fell back, eyes expectant and waiting. One man still stood, chin raised defiantly.

"*Otepf* Eriksyn," I said. I pulled a fold of my cloak across my body. "What do you see when you look at O'in's gift?"

He glanced at the fabric once, then squeezed his eyes shut. When he opened them, he stared straight at me, refusing to look down again.

"I see a pretender who should have died in the flames long before she dishonored Ballaslav's throne," he said.

I refused to flinch, even though he made it clear he'd throw me on the funeral pyre still alive if given half a chance.

Karina shifted forward a step, drawing her axes with a fluid motion.

I raised my hand to stop her and held *Otepf* Eriksyn's eyes.

A shudder passed through him before he spun and raced away through the makeshift refugee camp.

Count Yeshevsyn remained on his knees looking up at me with eyes as hard as granite and as open as the sky.

"If you are not here to convince us to follow you, then why did you come, *Izavital*?" he said.

They waited breathless for my answer.

"I came because it's not O'in's will that I sit on the Eagle Throne," I said. "And I need your help to ensure I don't."

He raised his chin. "You're planning the coup that will overthrow you," he said.

"I am." Just minutes before, Aleksei had held my hand in

a closet, and I still felt the shock of it in my blood. The human touch I hadn't allowed myself for so long.

I extended my hand to the Count and held my breath. "Will you help me?"

He looked from my hand to my face, then down to the edge of my cloak, where the blood-red underside was still visible. A muscle in his jaw jumped before he lifted his eyes to mine again.

He slid his palm into my hand. "I will, *Izavital*."

CHAPTER THIRTY

Karina, Aleksei, and I returned to the suite anxious to report our success, but when we stepped through the door, we were accosted by a pacing Eira.

"Thank O'in," she said to the ceiling, then raced forward. "Go, go get in the bedroom." She shooed me forward. "I've had word from the *viona* that Volka is on her way to check on you."

"*Da'ermo*," I said under my breath and let her herd me into the other room. The bedroom stood empty except for a full-length mirror and a pile of silks and lace heaped on the bed.

"Where is Mabushka?"

"She's resting in my room," Eira said, stepping quickly to the bed. "Put this on."

The healer in me wanted to ask why she needed more rest. Her fatigue wasn't normal and sent warnings racing through my mind, but Eira pulled the silk and lace from the bed, revealing an elegant gown made from enough fabric to house the entire exiled court in their tent city.

"Hurry," she said, and I pushed the worry to the back of my mind in favor of stripping off my clothes and diving into the opening of the gown.

"Stand here," Eira said, her mouth full of pins as she scooted a small stool in front of the mirror.

I held the gown to my chest and stepped up onto the stool so Eira could lace the back.

"Is this...?" I said, staring into the mirror. The silver gown fell in frothy layers from a cinched waist, little seed pearls and tiny jewels glittering from the seams. The wide neckline, lined with soft, silver fox fur, revealed more of my neck and chest than I was used to. Puffed sleeves covered my arms from shoulder to elbow, leaving my scarred forearms bare.

"Coronation gown," Eira said around the pins. She knelt below me to hem the skirt. "Someone has to make sure it fits for tomorrow. And I didn't want the seamstresses traipsing through here to realize how little time you were spending in your suite."

I opened my mouth to respond, but the door opened with a click, letting Volka stick her traitorous head inside.

She looked me up and down, and I forced away a shiver. My shoulders were just cold, I told myself. I was used to my cloak.

I sucked in a breath. My cloak. I'd thrown it aside hastily, without any care for what color showed.

I glanced over my shoulder to the chair that held my discarded clothes and breathed a sigh of relief. Eira had come along behind me and folded it so only the red showed.

I cast a quick smile at her, but she had her head down, concentrating on making my hem even.

"And how is our future Grand Duchess today?" Volka said in falsely soothing tones.

"Fine," Eira said before I could respond. "Busy, since you threw a coronation at her. And you're interrupting."

I hissed through my teeth at Eira, trying to tell her to be careful, but she didn't look up at me.

"Watch your tone, *mushka*," Volka said with a sweet smile. "There is still much I can take away from you."

"Did you come here just to threaten us?" Eira said. "Fine, consider us threatened."

Volka's eyes narrowed, and I just avoided meeting them in the mirror. I ducked my head and strove to look suitably down cast, since my sister didn't seem capable of play-acting that far.

"Don't forget you still have all your blood. Lovely blood that could power so many spells."

I kicked Eira, who finally glanced up with a glare. Then she sighed. "Yes, *sudinya*," she mumbled.

It didn't sound very convincing to me, but Volka sniffed and slammed the door on her way out.

My shoulders drooped. "Thank you," I said.

"You're welcome," she grumbled. But she didn't stand. She just continued pinning my hem. Eira, who hated sewing and who'd never sat still long enough to sew a straight seam, worked quickly and steadily, pins flashing in and out of the fabric.

She'd spent three months as a seamstress and clearly, she'd learned some things in that time. I bit my lip. I knew that time hadn't been pleasant. I knew what kinds of insults and hardships she'd had to endure because of me.

Apologizing to Eira was harder than apologizing to Aleksei. I'd made all the same mistakes with her, but she was my closest family and the closest thing I'd had to a best friend before I'd met Karina.

"I wanted to say I'm sorry," I said. "For the blood magic. I'm sorry you had to pay for my mistakes."

She finished pinning my skirt with a tug and stood abruptly. "You think that's why I'm angry at you? You think a couple *domy'chist* attendants laughing while they poured freezing water over me made any difference? Reyna, I knew about the blood magic before you healed Evgenia. I knew and I didn't care."

My mouth fell open. "But...how did you...? I never said anything."

"I know. That's the problem. I had to work it all out for myself since you were so reluctant to talk about anything that happened at the University. I only managed to guess when you told me you'd fallen for Luka. You would never have let yourself have feelings for a blood mage if you hadn't already justified it to yourself somehow."

I opened and closed my mouth, trying for a response and failing.

She stepped toward me and deliberately took my hand. "I'm upset you were so miserable that you needed the power. And I'm sad that you had to go through all of that alone." Her lips thinned. "But I'm angry you didn't trust me enough to tell me about it when you got back. Or when Luka threatened Mabushka, or when he ruined all our lives.

You never talk to me, Reyna. You've always been the serious one, and I guess you've always seen me as the thoughtless one. But just once, I wish you could have seen me as your sister."

I blinked. "Seeing you as my sister was the whole problem."

"What?"

I took my hand from hers and pushed my hair back from my face. "I didn't know how to tell you. I didn't want you to hate me. It would have killed me to lose you over that."

"You think I'd hate you just because you messed up? Reyna, I was kind of glad you did. It made you human. Do you know how long I've looked up to you, tried to be just like you, and failed because you've always been so perfect? You think about everything so hard that you never make mistakes."

I swallowed. "I didn't know you felt that way."

"I'll always love you; I just wish you weren't so damn perfect."

I gave her a rueful smile. "Wish granted," I said and gestured to the red folds of my cloak. "Anything else I can do for you?"

She gazed at me seriously. "Talk to me next time?"

"Don't take this the wrong way but I really hope there isn't a next time."

Her mouth twisted. "Yeah, I guess not."

There was a polite tap on the door. "*Izavital*," Boris called. "May I have a moment?"

Eira helped me out of the coronation gown without sticking me with any pins, and I hurried to get dressed again.

"What is it, *viona?*" I asked as I stepped out into the parlor.

Boris stood with his arms crossed, his foot tapping the edge of the carpet. "I don't think I'm going to be able to find *Prevoshkedhova.* Not before your coronation."

I nodded. "If you had more time..."

"Yes. But I cannot search the entire country in a few hours. I do not have enough *viona semaya,* and I do not trust most of the *viona krovaya.*"

"But we don't have any more time," Aleksei said from the sofa.

"No, so we need to do this smarter," Boris said. "We need to talk to someone who knows where she is."

Eira had followed and stood in the doorway to the bedroom. "And you think Volka is just going to tell you..." She trailed off as she realized who he was talking about.

I'd already thought of him. I paced to the sofa and braced my hands against the back. "He won't go for it."

"Do you know for sure?" Aleksei said.

I met his eyes. He wasn't pressuring me either way. He knew what facing Luka again would mean for me. He was just making sure I was honest with myself as well as with them.

I sighed. "No, I don't."

"Don't do this," Karina said, voice rough with displeasure.

"He can help us," I said. "Maybe. Where is he being kept?"

"The Bowels," Boris answered.

"Keep Volka busy while we're gone," I told him, chafing

my hands together. "This is good. I needed to talk to him anyway."

"You don't need anything from that *ublyduk*," Karina spat.

"Except closure."

Her mouth snapped shut, and she shuffled her feet.

She had every reason to want to keep me from him. Her job was to protect me from my enemies and from myself. And I had a history of weakness on both fronts when it came to Luka. I didn't trust myself an inch when it came to the blood mage who'd watched me fall and helped me down along the way.

But we needed the Grand Duchess. More than I needed safety.

Still, I took Karina and Aleksei with me to remind myself what real friendship and attraction looked like. Down we traveled through the depths of the palace, past the laundries and the kitchens, through the basements, where the sewers met the garbage heaps. There was a reason this section of the palace was called the Bowels. Lines of cells lit by uncovered mage lights marched along the passage.

A light sputtered in the damp as I passed. But our prisoner wasn't in one of these cells. He didn't deserve the freedom of bars or a slab of rock for his bed or a bucket for his waste.

Our quarry was tucked in the back behind the normal cells, where an iron-bound door was set into a hole in the ground and padlocked shut. The door and the edges around it crawled with spell symbols. Spells for silence and darkness, spells against escape and manipulation.

Two *viona krovaya* stood to attention when we entered the space. Boris himself had ensured their loyalty and devotion, making sure these two were impervious to bribes and corruption.

They'd been warned we were coming.

"*Viona*," I said.

The one on the left had the grizzled beard of a man who'd been in service for decades. The other was a young woman with a mop of short blonde hair and a carefully serious expression.

"Boris said you wished to interrogate the prisoner, *Prevoshkedhova*," the young woman said.

I winced. "Please don't call me that." Even "*ispor'chennai*" would be better than being reminded that if everything went wrong, I would wear the Eagle Crown before the sun went down tomorrow.

"Open it," I said and gestured to the iron-bound trapdoor. "Now, please."

The young one jumped to obey, touching four points in the spells around the door and whispering to release the *vytl*. With a huff, the grizzled guard knelt and helped haul open the door with a squeal of the hinges.

They stepped back against the walls to let me and my entourage through. Karina arranged herself on one side of the opening, Aleksei on the other.

I stepped forward and knelt at the edge of the opening, my skirts and cloak pooling on the damp, grimy stone.

The dim, guttering light from the mage globes barely reached the bottom of the cramped hole in the ground. Iron lined the stone walls of the oubliette preventing a mage from casting any spells.

My breath caught when a hunched shape moved in the shadows of the squalid prison hole. A pale face flashed as he turned to the light.

I wanted to say something fitting like, "Look how the mighty have fallen," but my throat closed on the nasty words, and I found myself mute for a second while I faced the boy I'd once loved.

"Hello, Luka," I said into the still air.

He seemed to take a deep breath and gather himself. Then he stood shakily to look up at me through the opening. Even standing, his head was still another six feet below me. Too far to jump. Even if he managed to climb the smooth, iron-lined wall, the inside of the door would provide no purchase for scrabbling fingernails.

"Reyna," he breathed. Then he cleared his throat. "Did my mother send you to gloat? To remind me you are her puppet now. Not mine."

My trembling stopped. I had no trouble dealing with this Luka. The danger lay when he started being sweet and understanding. This Luka was all hard edges and cutting angles. This Luka was the truth, and I need only remember this when he smiled and laughed and looked up at me out from under the fringe of his hair. Blood had dried down the side of his face from a wound on his temple and a bruise marred the skin on his left cheek.

"No," I said, voice strong in the darkness. "She doesn't know I'm here. She doesn't know how weak her control is. Over me, and over Ballaslav."

A slow grin spread across his lips, and he tilted his head to give me a sly look out of the corner of his eye. "I see," he said. "Then you came to me on your own. Did you miss me so much?"

My lip curled in disgust even while my heart fluttered against my ribs. Aleksei shifted beside me, drawing Luka's gaze.

His expression soured. "I take it that's a no."

"I'm out of your reach, Luka. If your mother gets her way, I'm hers, not yours. And if she doesn't..." I shrugged. "You can stop pretending you were after me for anything other than my royal blood."

His expression stilled and his eyes went deep and sad. "I wanted you for many things, Reyna," he said. "Your blood was only one of them."

I willed myself to stay strong and was surprised to find it wasn't all that difficult. Yes, it was good to know I wasn't the only one to fall too far into our relationship, but I also knew how dangerous he was for me. And that created a barrier around my heart, paper-thin, but just enough to protect me.

"Will you help me then?" I asked.

He dropped his gaze.

"Luka," I pleaded. "Your mother betrayed you. She made you kill Mikhail and *Prevoshkedova*, then she let you take the fall. That wasn't part of the plan, was it?" I'd seen his face when the *viona semaya* had taken him. I knew he hadn't been expecting this prison for his crimes.

He shook his head. "It's not like that. She sees an opportunity, and she takes it. That's just how she is. It's how she's gotten so powerful."

I waited while he fell silent.

"She saw a way to advance our cause," he said. "And she took it. There's no more to it than that."

"Condemning her own son in the process," I said. "You're facing execution, you know."

When he shook his head again, his hair fell in his eyes. "No. She'll have me out of here the very first hour you sit on your throne."

I regarded him quietly. "And if she decides that letting you die will further her cause? What then? Will she take that opportunity, too?"

He went silent.

"Help me, Luka. Tell me where the real Grand Duchess is. I know she was alive just yesterday."

"I can't," he said. "We've worked too long and lost too much for me to blow it just because I was too weak to play my part."

I blew out my breath. His words felt final. If this was how he felt after several days in the worst prison I could imagine besides the Bastion, there was little I could say or do to convince him.

My fingers clenched hard enough to dig into my palms and I forced myself to relax them. I didn't hate him, I told myself. Like Aleksei, I couldn't let myself hate him anymore, because he didn't control me.

I wove the most basic healing spell I knew, gathering the little *vytl* from the rock and stone around us. The blood on his face had long since dried. I sent it down into the pit—a difficult feat since most healing spells required touch—to spread across the gash on his temple and the bruise on his cheek.

His eyes widened, and he touched his face.

"Why?" he said.

"I'm a healer. I hope I will always choose to heal no matter who it is, or what they've done to me."

I shifted and stood, gathering the folds of my skirt.

"Close it," I told the guards.

"Wait," a desperate voice came from the hole.

I stopped the *viona* with a gesture and stepped to the edge one more time. "Yes?"

His eyes were locked on the corner of my cloak, where a slim strip of white showed.

I waited while his gaze flicked across the fabric.

"I taught you to hurt. To value your own life and safety more than anyone else's. After what happened in Valeria, I thought I'd succeeded."

I shook my head, pieces clicking into place, things he'd said and done that made more sense to me now. Things about myself that I understood better.

"I made one mistake, Luka. One that hurt someone. That doesn't mean I'm like you. In all our time together, you never managed to change the real me." My hands clenched in the white lining of my cloak, taking comfort from its soft feel against my fingers. "Because you don't have the power to change me."

He blinked.

I turned.

"Wait," he said again.

I stopped but didn't face him.

"The Grand Duchess," he said, haltingly. "She's in the Bastion. Held in the obsidian by blood magic."

I closed my eyes and blew out my breath. "Thank you, Luka."

"Don't thank me. You should check on your grandmother. The one who's here."

A shaft of ice raced along my spine, raising the hair along my arms, but I refused to let Luka see my reaction. I gestured to the guards, who finished closing the door, locking it, and setting the spells again.

I jerked my head at Karina and Aleksei. Then I stepped off down the hall to climb toward the light.

Luka's words rang through my head as I climbed the millions of stairs between me and Mabushka. *Check your grandmother. Check your grandmother.*

I raced down the hallway lined with *viona semaya* and burst through the door of Eira's suite. Eira jumped in her chair, papers scattering to the floor around her.

"Reyna, you scared me. What's wrong?"

I didn't stop to answer her, leaving her, Aleksei, and Karina in my wake as I pushed through to the bedroom.

Mabushka lay on the bedspread, turned toward the window. I stepped across to her and sat on the bed, taking her hand in mine.

She rolled her head on the pillow to meet my eyes, and she squeezed my hand. Her hands had once been strong and capable. They'd taught me to weave spells, cut bandages, set bones. Now they could barely grip. She hadn't gotten any better in the time since I'd rescued her from Luka.

Only worse.

"What's wrong?" I asked her. One healer to another.

"I'm dying," she said without prevarication or rancor. She'd been waiting to tell me. Ready all this time, and I'd been too busy rushing around to listen to her. Too busy to check on her.

"What did they do? I can fix it."

She shook her head on the pillow, strands of her iron-gray hair sticking to the linen. "You can't. I've been dying for a long time now, Reyna. Your blood mages only sped it along."

My throat ached so much I thought it would choke me. Quiet footsteps sounded from the door, and Eira joined us on the other side of the bed.

"Why?" My voice sounded thin and strained.

"Even if you managed to rescue me, they didn't want you to have me."

My face crumpled, and I turned away to hide the pain.

"Stop," she said, her voice almost as strong as it used to be. "You did not do this thing to me. Volka did. You will not blame yourself for it."

"Is that an order?" I said, chuckling through my tears.

"Don't interrupt," Mabushka said. "The blood mages didn't start this in me. I've seen it before. Wasting sicknesses that take the old and the weak. The end was coming eventually."

"You've never been weak, Mabushka," Eira said, her voice thick.

My grandmother might not blame Volka, but my gut

churned with fierce heat. The blood mage had stolen what little time I'd had left with her. "Why didn't you tell me?"

"If you'd known they still had their claws in me, you wouldn't have done what you needed to do. You wouldn't have defied them."

"Because they would have killed you," I cried. "They are killing you."

"Exactly." She laid her hand on my cheek, and I clutched it desperately. "I made my choice so you could make yours."

"I can save you."

"Not without blood magic."

"Then I'll use my blood." I threw off the white cloak.

"Don't."

I could have easily shaken off the hand she placed on my arm, but I didn't dare.

"Sometimes healing isn't about saving people," she said. "Sometimes it's about letting them go to the Almighty in peace. There is death in this world. You can't change that no matter how much you want to. Heal who you can, and soothe the ones you can't."

She reached for my sister with her other hand. "Eira."

"Mabushka," Eira said, and her voice stayed steady despite the tears streaming down her face.

"I like that young man," she said as her eyes closed.

Eira choked on a sob. "You want me to forgive him?"

Mabushka's eyes snapped open again. "I want you to do what you want. Your heart and mind belong to you. I just wanted you to know I like him. He makes you smile."

She drew our hands together so she could hug them to her chest. "You both make me so proud."

I bit my lip hard enough to taste blood.

"Just do one thing for me tomorrow," she said as she closed her eyes again.

We leaned forward.

"Kick Volka's ass."

CHAPTER THIRTY-ONE

The day of my coronation dawned bright and clear and my heart burned as strong as the sun on the snow. Today was the day I was going to break Volka's power.

I just didn't know how yet.

Eira adjusted the fur along my collar and the long train trailing behind me and gave me a worried look. She'd managed to pin my cloak to the shoulders of my gown, so the fine line of crimson velvet fell behind me and accented my train.

Mabushka had slipped into a coma sometime in the night. She still breathed, but I had no idea how long she would last. She could pass away even while the blood mages placed the Eagle Crown on my head.

I'd put off so much and now she was gone. There were so many things I would never tell her because I'd thought she would always be there. In her last breath, she'd given me an impossible task. Kick Volka's ass. My lips curved in a smile, appreciating the last of her sense of humor even if I didn't know exactly how I was going to do what she'd asked.

As Eira straightened one last time, I took her hand in mine and held it for just a moment, taking strength from my sister's resilience and lending her mine in return. I gave her fingers a squeeze and then let go to turn to the door. We hadn't said much. There was little else to be said. Things would either go according to plan today...or they wouldn't.

The door opened, and Karina murmured, "It's time."

I stepped through and stopped in shock. Karina waited in the sunlit parlor, dressed in the white uniform of her calling. A gold sash hung across her chest and bits of gold braid glinted from her shoulders and waist. Her white pants tucked into shining black knee boots, and the polished handles of her axes rose over her shoulders from a new leather harness.

I blinked. I'd never seen her dressed as *viona semaya* before. Yes, I'd known that's what she was for days now. But I hadn't seen it.

"I made something for you," I said, my voice coming out a bit rough. I'd spent all night on it. Since I was awake anyway watching Mabushka.

I handed her a simple chain with a teardrop pendant of bright blue. It wasn't exactly Karina's style, but it was the simplest thing in Eira's jewelry box.

"It's a shield spell. Not very fancy since I'm only a healer, but it should keep Volka from dropping you with a stun spell again."

She hesitated, her lips twitching. "I have some actually." She touched the knots of gold braid at her waist. "They're built in in case we ever have to fight mages. I've never gotten to use them before."

"Oh." My fingers tightened on the chain, and I drew it back.

"But I'd like to wear it anyway," she said quickly. "Every little bit helps. And I don't know how long these will last against blood mages."

She took it and slid the chain over her head to tuck down under her collar.

My heart thumped painfully in my chest as I realized Karina was the only one I hadn't apologized to yet. Just because she'd already forgiven me didn't mean she didn't need to hear that I was sorry. She deserved it as much as anyone else—more so—and I hadn't said it yet. I'd pushed her away over and over, rejected everything she'd offered me until she'd given up.

She would still protect me. She'd told me that much, but she'd also said she wouldn't try to get me to accept everything else she offered anymore. And I didn't blame her. She'd chosen to serve a girl who'd hurt her, over and over.

My lip trembled, but I ignored it to open my mouth and actually tell her that I accepted what she offered. I wanted to take it.

But the door slammed open, admitting Baron Ruriksyn and the other courtiers who would escort me to my coronation. With much obsequious shuffling, they herded me out the door. I sought Karina's gaze, but she'd already shifted to stand at my right shoulder while Eira positioned herself at my left. The courtiers strode ahead, solemn and smug as a gaggle of swans among ducks.

At the corner, Volka and Aleksandr slipped in behind us, cutting off my escape route.

I raised my chin and refused to look at them.

Boris had taken a contingent of the *viona semaya* to the Bastion last night to investigate the truth of Luka's words. But the prison had been locked down with blood magic. The blood mages' spells flowed through the obsidian itself, more powerful than any wards created by normal mages. If the Grand Duchess was in there like Luka said, she was out of our reach for now.

We would have to take the palace back first, then worry about prying the blood mages from the Bastion. This was a war, and we had to regain the territory we'd already lost.

That was the plan anyway. I had little to do except wait and watch and hope all of our allies came through.

When we reached the Crown Hall, a pair of footmen threw open the double doors and a set of trumpeters beyond played a fanfare. The courtiers ahead of us stepped forward and spread into the Hall where the rest of the court waited. They sparkled in blues and golds and pinks and greens as the sunlight speared through the high windows, illuminating my path across the gleaming floor between the finely dressed bodies.

The trumpeters blasted another fanfare, but I hesitated. Our allies weren't supposed to move until I was actually in the Crown Hall, but my knees ached and shook and that first step seemed like a mile long.

Volka poked me in the small of my back. I barely felt it through the layers of stiff silk and whalebone, but I knew what she wanted.

I took a shaky breath, raised my chin, and walked down the middle of the Hall as courtiers sunk into bows and curtsies around me. As the last trumpet notes faded from the air, my steps rang in the silence.

At the end of the Hall, a priest dressed in his gold and purple stood beside the pedestal that held the Eagle Crown. This should have been *Otepf* Eriksyn's job, as the High Priest of Ballaslav. But he'd forfeited that right when he'd fled the palace and now I would be crowned by a beardless youth with carrot-colored hair, watery eyes, and knees that knocked worse than mine.

When I reached the end of the aisle, I stepped to the side of the pedestal and turned to face back down the Hall. Karina arranged herself at my left shoulder while Eira knelt to fuss with my train and make sure it lay just right.

As the courtiers rose from their obeisance, I scanned the crowd for familiar faces. I found Aleksei standing under one of the windows, wearing a dark blue coat, trimmed with black fur and a floppy black hat to match. Vitaly stood beside him decked out identically to Karina, in full *viona semaya* panoply. I did not see Corwin anywhere. Or Count Yeshevsyn, and I tried to convince myself that I just might not recognize them amidst all the finery. It did not mean they'd abandoned us.

I held myself frozen in place while the priest squeaked through the litany of loyalty on the other side of the Crown. I clasped my hands in front of myself to keep them from shaking so hard everyone could see.

Just stay upright, I told myself. *Your job right now is to not fall over or collapse. That's it. Shouldn't be hard.*

I realized the Hall had gone quiet, the priest's voice fading into echoes.

He glanced at me, sweat rolling down the side of his face, and I drew in a sharp breath. I was supposed to respond, but I had no idea what he'd just said.

He must have read the panic in my eyes, and he repeated softly. "Do you promise to hold Ballaslav above all else in your heart? Do you swear to serve its people until the day you die?"

A shiver traveled up my spine to lodge in my skull as I said, "I so swear."

"Then in obedience to O'in, I crown you, Reyna Sofya Darya Konstantinadoch."

He jerked his chin at the crown in case I needed prompting, which I guess I did. I unlocked my fingers and reached for the crown even as my eyes raced over the crowd.

Where were they? What had gone wrong? The ceremony wasn't supposed to get this far. I wasn't actually supposed to wear the crown. Karina met my eyes and gave me the world's most unhelpful shrug. Aleksei wasn't even looking at me. He was searching the crowd, too.

With Volka's eyes glittering from her place right below the dais, I took the Eagle Crown in both hands and raised it over my head.

Please, O'in. Please don't make me wear this long.

I brought the crown down to rest on my head.

The crowd cheered, hats and scarves flying into the air as I stood beneath the crown and panicked.

It was a subtle change, the first scream blending into the crowd's joy, a shuffling toward the back of the Hall that turned into a stampede. The crowd of courtiers shifted into a milling mass of bodies trying to escape a threat they couldn't identify.

Certain courtiers turned on their neighbors, jumping on them to subdue them. A group of loyal *viona krovaya* attacked the blood mages gathered in the Hall.

Finally, I saw Count Yeshevsyn wielding a saber as old as he was, striding through the growing chaos calling, "For Yesofya!"

Karina grabbed my arm and hauled me from the crown dais. She pushed me down behind the altar. "Stay there."

"Karina," I started to protest, but she was already gone, drawing her axes as she swept into the fray. I didn't know what I would say anyway. I wasn't a warrior. And I could hardly move in this dress even if I managed to find a weapon.

Another body dove for cover behind the altar, and I yelped before I recognized Anya, her curly hair in wild disarray around her face.

"Are you all right?" I asked.

She met my eyes, and I realized she'd never really looked up at me before. She always kept her gaze down. Her blue eyes were clear of the blood lust ring but wide with fear.

"There's so much blood," she said, her voice shaking. "I want to help. I want to do something, but there's so much blood. What if my spells draw on it? I can't—I can't risk it." She covered her face with her hands and took deep, shuddering breaths.

I knew what she was feeling. That freezing helplessness as you realized that anything you did would only make things worse.

I put my back against the altar and craned around to peek at the battle raging in the Crown Hall. Vitaly, a picture of grace and strength, guarded Karina's back as she fought Aleksandr. Her axes whirled, looking for openings as he shot spell after spell at her. Most didn't hit because of her shield spells, but the few that did, knocked her back until she could regain her footing and her momentum. My heart leaped to my throat as I recognized his spells and the power he'd put behind them. With all the blood in the air, his spells would be bloated with *vytl*, hitting harder and faster than anything a normal mage would call up. The same was true for every blood mage in the Hall. We were evenly matched in numbers with Count yeshevsyn, the loyal *viona*, and Corwin leading a contingent of Valerians, but with the blood mages using more power, the tide was turning.

It didn't look good for us.

I spun back around and clunked my head against the altar. The crown struck with a metallic ting, and I closed my eyes. Even if we somehow managed to overpower them and win back the palace, we'd still face the same thing at the Bastion. The blood mages held it by channeling their extra power through the obsidian itself. If we couldn't beat them here, we'd definitely never beat them there.

So how could we get rid of the blood mages' power entirely? Without it, they would just be normal mages and our numbers would actually mean something.

But a blood mage's power came from blood. And blood was ubiquitous. You couldn't just get rid of it. And blood mages would always choose to use blood unless they chose to fight the addiction.

Anya shivered beside me, her arm brushing mine and raising goosebumps along my skin. She didn't even want to use the blood, but her body left her no choice anymore.

I frowned. That was the real problem. It wasn't the addiction. It was the blood sickness. The corruption in our blood was what allowed us—and forced us—to draw *vytl* from blood. The corruption drew power from blood, not the mage.

If I could get rid of the blood sickness, then the blood mages would be regular mages again.

I gulped. Now I knew why O'in had chosen a healer.

But everyone knew the blood sickness didn't have a cure. The priests all said it was a blood mage's punishment sent directly from O'in. Even blood mages accepted their death from the sickness as inevitable.

But why had he chosen me, a healer, if he didn't want me to heal?

I could only try.

I shifted around and felt something tear in my layers of skirts, but I ignored it.

"Anya," I said, taking her hands and holding them away from her face. "If you could erase the blood sickness and go back to the way you were before you chose blood magic, would you?"

Her eyes scrunched, and she shook her head. Not in denial but because it was such a ridiculous question. But I still had to be sure. "Of course," she said.

I wanted to try it right then, but I had the same problem as Anya. With all the blood in the air, my spells would only draw the wrong *vytl*. And if getting rid of the blood sickness was as easy as a healing spell, someone would have figured it out long before now. I needed something better. Something even more powerful than blood.

"But it's impossible," she said. "There isn't a cure."

My eyes roved, not focusing on anything as I thought furiously. What was the body's natural defense against sickness? Professor Benson's voice asked in my memory.

Fever.

I just needed a really strong fever to burn out the corruption.

Fever. Or fire. Holy fire. Fire cleansed the corruption of blood mages. It cleansed their bodies after they were dead. I could do something similar before they died.

"Anya, I need holy fire. Holy fire to burn away the corruption."

Her brow furrowed like she thought I was crazy, but she didn't pull her hands from mine and her mouth worked like she was thinking. That's what I'd been counting on. Anya was the most religious person I knew, and she hadn't stopped praying after she'd been registered.

"The Hall of Heroes," she said. "It's built like an *yshkiniva* with the Court of Priests in the back. The flame contains O'in's presence. That's the holiest fire I can think of."

I squeezed her fingers. "Of course."

I peeked around the altar again. Karina was flagging, Aleksandr gaining ground against her as the *viona* sagged with exhaustion.

She'd kill me when she found out what I was doing. But not unless she survived Aleksandr.

"If you get a chance, tell Karina where I'm heading," I

told Anya. "Tell her I can't wait or the blood mages will have overpowered everyone."

I lurched for the opening in the map wall behind us.

"Wait," Anya said, raising a hand to stop me. "The Court of Priests, it's just like an *yshkiniva*. If you go into O'in's presence, you won't come out again. Not without someone to pull you out."

I gritted my teeth. "I know." And I lunged upright, took my wide skirts in my hands, and raced for the passage out of the Crown Hall.

CHAPTER THIRTY-TWO

Everyone who was anyone was still in the Crown Hall which meant no one tried to stop me as I raced down the stairs for the Hall of Heroes. I concentrated on running, my knees aching as I went. I didn't think about what I was going to do when I got there. If I did, I might fall, and I didn't know if I'd have the willpower to get back up again.

In the basement of the palace, the kitchens belched clouds of steam into the chilly air. A part of me was a little sad I wouldn't get to taste my own coronation dinner.

I skidded into the columned foyer before the Hall and hit the carved doors running. My left hand closed over an *Izavital's* head as I pushed into the Hall.

My footsteps froze as I registered the rustling and cursing coming from beyond the screen at the end of the empty room. I wasn't alone.

I crept forward and peeked around the screen to find *Otepf* Eriksyn throwing things into a bulging carpetbag. The Court of Priests stretched on this side of the screen almost as long as the rest of the Hall, framed on all sides by carved screens. A column of flame stretched to the ceiling in the direct center of the Court and a little living area furnished with a cot, a table, and a bookcase stood in the far corner. *Otepf* Eriksyn hunched over the table, gathering his things.

"*Otepf,*" I said with a sigh of relief. Maybe I wouldn't have to do this alone after all.

The High Priest stiffened and spun, the bag falling from his hand to spill books and socks and underwear across the floor. "You," he said. "What are you doing in here? You profane this sacred space."

"I hate to tell you this, but I've profaned it once before and nothing bad happened. Or well, nothing worse than this." I reached behind me and spread the edge of my cloak so the white was visible.

"You can't come back here," *Otepf* Eriksyn said. "Only priests are allowed in this Court. Only priests are allowed in O'in's presence."

"That's what I need your help for," I said and ignored his livid glare to step into the Court of Priests. "The only way to beat the blood mages is to heal them. I have to heal the corruption in their blood to break their power."

His mouth dropped open, stretching his jowls until he looked like a surprised dog. "You cannot take away O'in's punishment," he said. "It's O'in's will that your lot die from your sins."

"So, you'll condemn everyone else along with us?" I said, throwing my hands wide. "The blood mages are winning." Karina could be dying as we spoke, and this man stood in my way.

"O'in will provide a way out." He raised his fat chin.

A way out like a secret passageway, I'd bet, so this *ublyduk* could escape and leave all our problems behind him.

I gestured to the flames. "Just tell me how the priests come out again. I know anyone who steps into O'in's presence doesn't come out again."

He scoffed. "You won't survive. O'in will strike you down before you can escape."

I clenched my fists and closed my eyes. This was not helping.

"They chose me for a reason. It doesn't make sense for Them to kill me before I've done what They want." I didn't really want Them to kill me afterward either, but that was a moot point right now.

"O'in will not tolerate your corruption."

"Yes, that's my point," I shouted. "Just get out of here and let me do it. We're running out of time."

"You've already run out of time." The lyrical voice flowed behind me, and I spun to find Volka stepping around the screen.

I gasped and lurched back, narrowly avoiding tripping on the train of my gown. She'd followed me. *Da'ermo*, I hadn't thought to bar the door.

"You cannot enter here, *ispor'chennai*," *Otepf* Eriksyn bellowed.

Volka cut him off with a stun spell that hit his chest and felled him like a fat tree. He hit the tile floor with a thud.

Volka stalked toward me until I ran up against one of the screens surrounding the Court. My fingers curled into the gaps as if she'd rip me away.

"Now," she said. "Let's try this again."

"You'll have to kill me," I said. "I won't sit on the throne, not for you, not for anyone."

"It's too late. You are already crowned. You just need to sign the edict making blood magic legal and then you can die in whatever way you see fit. We'll just put your sister on the throne after you."

The hair along my arms raised. Eira. No, no, no.

She reached for me.

I raised my hands as if to form a spell.

She smiled and cast a counterspell, quicker than I would have managed.

But instead of magic, I thrust the heel of my palm into her nose, just as Karina had taught me months ago. Mages never thought to protect themselves from physical assault.

She staggered back with a cry of pain, and I grabbed the only weapon I had. The heavy bronze crown on my head. I swung the coronet right against her temple, where I knew the bone was thin.

She crumpled without a sound, the imprint of a screaming eagle burned into the side of her face.

I shuddered, standing there for a long moment on shaking legs, wondering if I should bash her again just to be sure.

The crown dropped from my limp fingers, ringing against the tile as it rolled away. I didn't care where.

No one stood between me and the flames now, and I staggered forward a couple of steps.

There was no brazier. No fire-pit or even fuel for the flames. Just a column of fire rising up from the perfectly level tile floor. The hair along my arms raised as I realized it didn't crackle or roar. The flames danced in a perfectly silent room.

With O'in's fire, I could burn out the corruption in every blood mage in Ballaslav, using my blood sickness as the conduit. This was it. This was the reason O'in had chosen a healer. I knew what I had to do.

But healing the blood sickness would do more than just break their power. I couldn't pick and choose. Healing the sickness would break their ties to blood. Their spells would no longer be more powerful. At least for a little while. I had no idea what would happen if a mage tried to use blood after I'd healed them.

But it would also *heal* them. Physically. They would no longer be dying.

How many other blood mages were like me? Living as if they'd burned their last bridge? I had to believe there were others like Anya, who wanted to be free from their mistakes.

But how many more were there like Volka and Luka? People who had hurt innocents.

Luka had kidnapped both my grandmothers. Volka had poisoned Mabushka. They'd killed Mikhail.

If I was honest, standing here in the Court with only O'in watching, I wanted them to die. I wanted them to rot in prison until the blood sickness consumed them.

I knew what to do, but I didn't want to do it. I didn't want to give up my life to save a bunch of people who didn't deserve it at all. With no one to pull me out, I wouldn't come back from this decision.

Maybe, if I knew it wouldn't be my end. I glanced at the door, half-expecting Karina to burst through it, ready to rescue me once again. But Karina was upstairs fighting. I'd spent so many months trying to save myself and everyone else from my mistakes. Alone. I didn't want anyone else to pay for my crimes. And I'd pushed them away over and over again, rejecting what they'd offered. Aleksei, who made me laugh even though I didn't deserve to laugh. Eira, who lent me her fierce strength even when I refused to take it.

Karina, who'd never blamed me.

Now when I knew I needed her, she couldn't come. And when I knew I wanted her forgiveness, she wasn't here to offer it.

"Karina, I'm sorry." She wouldn't hear me. She'd never get to hear me. But I needed to say the words.

I didn't get to apologize to Karina. But if this worked, I'd at least save her life.

I wrapped my arms around my torso and closed my eyes, imagining Karina in her white and gold, wielding justice in each hand as she defended Ballaslav from itself.

And I stepped into the fire.

Light surrounded me, making me blink, and a pleasant spreading heat seeped into my muscles. Now the roar and crackle of flames filled my ears, and I'd never realized just how much that sound made me feel at home. Like I sat in front of the fireplace in Mabushka's cottage listening to Eira putter around and Mabushka hum tunelessly.

I breathed out all the fear and uncertainty and let my shoulders relax. Now I could do what I'd come here to do.

But how? Where did I start?

"What would you like to do?" The voice started as a whisper that grew to fill all the empty spaces inside me until I had no idea if I heard it with my ears or my bones.

"I'm a healer," I said with a little huff. This should be obvious, right? They'd chosen me after all. "I want to heal the blood mages' corruption."

"You will need my fire," it said.

"Yes."

"And my power."

"Er, well, that would be helpful."

The air brightened a shade, and I got the impression someone was hiding a laugh. "Very well."

It began as a sweeping whoosh that carried me through darkness into flesh and blood, bone and tissue, until I saw the creeping, spreading black, taking over lungs, rotting through the blood. And I realized I was looking at the blood sickness from inside.

"This is yours," the voice said.

"My sickness?" I said.

"Yours. You are the healer. So heal."

And fire came to my hands in the form of the most powerful healing spell I'd ever wielded. I burned through the rot, chased the darkness away, singed every last piece of it I could find.

Something pushed and nudged and called until I turned to see what was so important. Stretched out in front of me lay a plain full of little black pools, each one demanding my attention. I floated on wings of light and fire till I found the next clinging darkness. Using my own blood as a template, I cleared the sickness away there, too.

One patient after another. Each one a pool of black. Fire and darkness battling endlessly. There was no way to tell one from another, and from here inside my spell, I didn't want to. All I wanted was to heal, to clean, to burn, as if it was all I'd ever wanted. As if there was no end.

But there had to be an end, eventually. With holy fire between my fingertips, the darkness had to yield finally, and I burned through the last of the sickness that allowed the last blood mage to gorge on unnatural power.

And as I finished, the voice spoke in my ear and said, "Here."

And I saw one more with blood that sang to me. I knew this one. With a corruption and a darkness similar to the blood sickness but not quite the same. The darkness was winning, the last heartbeats carrying the poison into the brain where it would kill. And I knew it was Mabushka.

With the last of the fire, I roared through her blood, carrying away the poison Volka had left and the illness which had tried to kill her in the first place. I was light and fire and magic and there was nothing that would stand in front of me that I could not burn to ash.

CHAPTER THIRTY-THREE

The blood mages around Karina began to falter and sag. Some of them gaped at their hands as if their magic had failed them.

Aleksandr stumbled back a step, shaking his head, giving Karina enough room to breathe for the first time in what felt like forever. But it wouldn't last long. This was a feint or a trick. The lead up to another attack that would level their scrawny forces.

But Aleksandr didn't rally. He sank to his knees and clawed at his sleeves, yanking them high enough to stare at the twin scars on his wrists. "Where is it?" he whispered. "This can't...It can't be gone."

Karina exchanged a look with Vitaly, who shook his head. Over his shoulder, she saw a mass of curls poking up from the altar. She did not see a silver-clad figure beside it. Ice prickled the back of her neck.

Karina strode to Anya, eyes darting behind the altar. "Where is she?"

Anya fell back on her hands, gaze wide and blank. "It's gone. She did it."

Karina's heart beat faster. "Did what?" She reached to grab Anya. "Where is Reyna?"

"She went to heal the blood sickness."

Terror stoked the violence already simmering within her, and she shook the girl. "Where?"

"The Hall of Heroes," Anya said. "The fire."

Karina released Anya, unlocking her fingers very deliberately, and stepped back.

She turned, feet numb enough she could barely feel the floor under her boots, and sought Vitaly's gaze. Aleksei's. Eira's. They all stared back at her, their expressions a blur.

Thoughts and images and fears whirled through her head and heart, too fast to catch hold of. Reyna in the fire. Alone. Out of reach. And Karina stood here at the top of the palace a million miles away.

Another failure, and this one would be her last.

After it all, I stood in the light of the crackling flames of O'in's presence and waited. I had hands and legs and feet and a face once more and it took longer than I expected to settle back into myself and not be surprised when I moved and a body moved with me.

I raised my hands to my cheeks and breathed deep. There was nothing here in the light, except peace and warmth. Nothing to bother me. The worries I'd carried for months, years, seemed dull and distant. The Shaker's breath, which rocked Post da Konstantin, was nothing but an unpleasant memory.

There was no judgment in this air. Only gentle acceptance. I'd expected judgment or disappointment.

Now I knew why people didn't come back from O'in's presence. At least not voluntarily. It wasn't because they died. It was because they didn't want to leave.

At least this would be a pleasant way to spend the rest of my life. I just wished there weren't so many little niggling regrets floating around in the back of my mind. I wished I'd gotten to say goodbye to Eira and Aleksei. And Karina...

"Is this the end?" I asked.

Another feeling like someone was hiding a smile. "Do you think eternity is nothingness?"

I glanced around at the light. It had no distance or nearness. No up or down.

"Do you want to stay?" the voice asked.

"Do I have a choice?"

"There is always a choice."

My lips twisted in a rueful grin. "Is it really a choice if you already know what I'm going to choose?"

Laughter full of pealing bells and thunder surrounded me. "The priests have been debating that one for centuries. Perhaps you can add your experience to the conversation."

I swallowed a gulp. That wasn't what I was expecting. And it seemed to predict my answer. But before I could respond, the light with no borders opened to admit another figure besides mine.

Like an avenging angel, Karina strode through the light, blood splattering her white and gold jacket, a rope tied around her waist. She stared around her at the light with a fierce frown.

"You can't have her yet," she said.

"Karina." My voice broke on her name. Memories of all the things I'd left behind, but mostly the people, came crashing in on me. Eira's scolding voice. Aleksei's quick grin. Mabushka's arms around me. Karina herself, with her axes and her blonde braid. "I didn't think you'd come," I said through tears.

"Stupid," she said, her voice rough. "You know I'll always come."

I nodded and swallowed. "I'm sorry. I'm sorry for all of it...I need you to save me."

She didn't answer. She only closed the distance between us and put her arms around me. I leaned into her strength, my chin fitting over her shoulder. Nothing had ever felt so much like home. Nothing before this.

The light pulsed fierce and bright, and I had to close my eyes or be blinded.

And then the rope around Karina's waist went taut, and we tumbled out of the flames.

We rolled across the floor of the Court of Priests, the tile cold against my bare arms after the warmth. My arms tightened around Karina's waist for a moment, and she returned my embrace before I finally managed to raise my eyes and take in the Court.

Eira and Aleksei dropped the end of the rope when they

saw us roll free of the flames. Vitaly stood over Volka who was bound and gagged on the floor where I'd left her. And *Otepf* Eriksyn spouted curses and threats from his corner. Too bad his stun spell hadn't lasted a little longer.

The others ignored him, and suddenly, I was enveloped by Eira and Aleksei. Even Vitaly left his charge long enough to throw his arms around all of us.

Underneath them all, I tucked my head down into Karina's shoulder and just held on.

CHAPTER THIRTY-FOUR

"It was the strangest thing, *Izavital*," Boris said as he led Karina and me through the Bastion. Here and there, *viona semaya* in their stark uniforms stood over groups of blood mages, some of whom huddled on the floor with their hands over their heads. Some stared blankly at the walls or paced under the watchful eyes of their captors.

"The blood magic flowed through the obsidian just as it had been doing all night, keeping us out. Then one moment it just vanished. Like every spell collapsed and all the magic went out of the prison. We waltzed right in."

We'd left Eira back at the palace with Aleksei and Vitaly to clean up the rest of the blood mages. Most of them were like the ones surrounding us, reacting with variations of shock. Karina had found a new uniform, one which didn't have blood stains spattered across it. I appreciated that detail. The corruption might have been gone from my blood, but I could still feel the craving as an undercurrent.

"We expected some resistance," Boris went on, gesturing

around him. "But most of the blood mages were too shaken to fight back. Do you know what happened to them?" He glanced at me, sharply.

"Their power was broken," I said, simply. "The corruption in their blood was healed so they can't draw power from blood anymore."

He was quiet a moment as we passed down the black, glassy hallways. "They're saying you walked into the fire to save us," he said.

Word traveled fast. It had only been a few hours.

"*Izavital*," he said and stopped in the doorway to the Reckoning chamber.

"You don't have to call me that anymore," I said.

His eyes settled on my bare shoulders. The cold air raised goosebumps along my skin, but it felt very freeing to walk around without the heavy velvet.

"Where is your cloak?"

"I don't have it anymore," I said, looking beyond him into the chamber.

Boris hesitated, then shrugged. "I take it that it didn't leave the fire with you."

If he wanted to assume that, I wouldn't correct him. My relationship with the blasted thing was complicated enough and this seemed like a good time to leave certain things behind.

Several *viona semaya* stood before an opening in the obsidian. The very same cell where Aleksandr had been kept. The Grand Duchess wandered from wall to wall of her tiny cage, staring around her with wide eyes. She bumped into the obsidian, looked up in surprise, bumped into it again, and sat abruptly on the hard ground.

I winced. She looked just like Emil, the blood mage Volka had fed to the creature.

I carried the obsidian flask clutched in my hand. Volka had transferred the Duchess's memories into it, and I'd taken it from her as she lay on the floor of the Hall of Heroes.

I had no idea how it worked, but I could feel the buzz of active spells under my fingertips. And knowing the mage who'd cast those spells, I had some ideas for what to do next.

I knelt on the black floor beside the Duchess, my silver skirts puffing around us. The black sky wheeled over us in the empty space where the ceiling should be.

I held out my hand and Karina stepped up without hesitation and placed her belt knife in my palm. Then, before any of the *viona* could protest, I pricked the Duchess's finger and pressed the flask into her hand, closing her fingers around it.

She rocked gently, her eyes flicking back and forth from my face to the walls to the *viona*.

I held my breath.

Her chest moved with a great, deep sigh like it was the first breath she'd taken after a long nap. She blinked once. Then again, and the muscles in her face twitched as if she called on them to work and found them wanting. I watched as her blue eyes cleared and focused on me.

"Reyna?"

She frowned, then pushed the straggling ends of her iron-gray hair out of her face. Her gaze went from my face to my coronation gown, the silver fox fur ruffling in the freezing air. She took in the black walls around her, the open sky above, and the *viona* standing frozen in the doorway.

"All right. What's happened?"

Nearly a week later, the Grand Duchess made her first public appearance since the blood mages' coup. She may have had her memories and her crown back, but she'd needed time to recover. And mourn.

She stood, resolute and implacable at Mikhail's funeral, her face giving away nothing of her feelings. I stood across from her as the Prince's body was entombed. Grief swamped the sting of guilt in my chest, and I wiped a few tears from my face. I'd liked Mikhail. His honesty, his integrity. I'd liked how he'd managed to welcome me at the same time as upholding his ideals. I wished I'd had more time to get to know my uncle and everything he'd worked for under *Prevoshkedhova*.

Aleksei stopped me later that day outside my suite. He wore a dark, velvety blue coat with silver trim.

"I just wanted to say goodbye. Count Yeshevsyn has contracted us to pick up some grain for him in Elisaveta."

I suppressed the stab of panic. Of course he was leaving. He had a family that would be worried about him. And they'd been stuck in the city while he'd been trapped in the palace. It was time for them to be moving on.

I could tell myself that, but it didn't make it any easier.

"I didn't know if I'd get another chance to see you," he said. "I figured you'd be staying here."

I twisted my hands together. "Eira's still here." She'd been spending a lot of time with the Grand Duchess while I'd been spending most of my time with Mabushka. "I don't really know what's going to happen next if I'm not *Izavital* anymore."

"You're still the heir."

"*Prevoshkedhova* hasn't made a decision yet." I winced. "And there are a lot of angry people."

He jerked back. "What could they possibly have to be angry about. You saved us all."

"But I broke a lot of the Law to do it."

He scoffed.

I held out my hands helplessly. "She has a couple of options now. More than she had before." I hesitated. "I know which one I want her to take."

Silence stretched for a moment. I reached down to check the swelling around my knees. They were hot and achy after spending the morning standing in the snow.

He rubbed the back of his neck and glanced out the window as if calculating how much time he had to put off actually leaving.

I bit my lip. "Say hello to Evgenia and Pyotr for me."

He blew out his breath. "I wish I wasn't going back alone," he said.

I sucked in a small breath.

He smiled like he knew what the words had done to me. I imagined they'd cost him something similar. "There are so many things I want to say or do," he said. "And now I don't know how to say or do any of them. You've had so many titles since I've known you. *Lubonitsva, Izavital.*"

"*Ispor'chennai*," I added without rancor.

"*Prevoshkedhova*." He wiggled his eyebrows.

I opened my mouth once. Then tried again. "Let's just stick with *mushka*. That's the only one that's ever been true."

He took my hand and pressed a kiss to my knuckles. Like Anastasy and Svetanka in their ballad. Then he met my eyes and turned my hand to kiss my palm.

"*Verdey drogoi, mushka.*"

Solid roads, miss.

The next day, Eira and I were summoned to the Regal Court.

Walking through the Little Court now that all the blood mages were gone was an entirely different experience. Word had traveled that I wasn't *Izavital* anymore, or *Prevoshkedhova*, but the courtiers left over after the purge in the Crown Hall still bowed as I passed. There were far fewer of them, of course, but the looks I got bordered on awe rather than revulsion now that I no longer wore the red.

The Grand Duchess sat at the head of the big dark table in the Regal Court. Mabushka sat beside her in the chair reserved for the monarch's counsel. It made my eyes cross to see both my grandmothers in the same room for once. Side by side, no less. Like an army of two, I could well imagine them taking on the world from this spot.

Eira and I arranged ourselves a little ways down the table, while Karina and Vitaly stood at attention against the mirrored walls beside Boris and a couple of other *viona*.

With a jolt, I recognized Anya, in a little chair beside the

Grand Duchess. She looked so different without the red cloak, and I wondered if some people had a hard time recognizing me now, too.

Prevoshkedhova folded her hands in front of her. "I thought you'd like to know Volka, Aleksandr, and their son, Luka, are all serving their time in the Bastion."

I nodded.

She met my eyes deliberately. "Is there anything you'd like to do to modify their sentences?"

My stomach fluttered. Oh. She was asking me?

I tried mirroring her pose, folding my hands as well. "I don't trust myself to make any decisions regarding Luka. I'm not exactly impartial. But he was the one who told us where you were being kept. I'm not sure what would have happened if we hadn't known that."

She pursed her lips, then nodded. "All right. Make a note," she said to Anya, who bent her head to the paper in front of her. "I'd like to have the blood mage, Luka Volksyn, transferred to the prison in Elisaveta. It is designed to hold mages, so we don't need to worry about that, but he will be allowed to serve his sentence a little more comfortably."

Anya made the note then gazed at the Grand Duchess expectantly.

"Now," she said. "I have some good news and I have some bad news. The bad news is that *Otepf* Eriksyn has declared you a heretic of the Law."

Eira gave a little cry and Mabushka harrumphed. I didn't say anything, just kept my fingers clenched.

"Why?" Mabushka asked.

"For a variety of reasons but the one at the top of the list is healing the blood mages."

That hardly counted as heresy since O'in had helped me do it. I bit my lip so I wouldn't smile and stared at my hands. "I did do that."

"Yes, what can I expect from the blood mages now?"

I took a deep breath and met her eyes. "I burned out the blood sickness in all of us," I said. "Blood mages are now no longer corrupt, in and of themselves. The desire for blood is still there." I'd felt that myself. "So there will be plenty who go back to using it, corrupting themselves all over again. But those who want it, have a second chance."

I glanced at Anya, who stared resolutely at the Grand Duchess, her face serene.

"Well, I see why it's considered heresy," she said.

I shrugged.

She glanced at me sharply. "You don't care he's declared you a heretic?"

"I don't recognize his authority to do so," I said, calmly. There was only one being who could say whether I was damned or not. And They hadn't.

"I tend to agree with you. Unfortunately, I can't do anything to prevent him from making a whole lot of noise. He is the High Priest. I have no authority over him. But the good news is that I intend to make sure all of Ballaslav knows what you've done for us. You're also still my heir—"

"No."

She was too disciplined to jump, but her hand stilled on the edge of the table. "No?"

I shook my head slowly. "I wore your crown for a day. I've

also served Ballaslav as *Izavital*. I think I prefer the second one. That, at least, had an end."

She glanced at my shoulders, covered only by my green bodice, and I half expected her to ask about the cloak. She hadn't ever seen it after all. But most everyone seemed content to leave it wherever it was now. Chosen heroes were all well and good in the ballads, but it was awkward seeing one on their way to the privy.

"Are you sure?" she said, finally. "Things are different without the blood mages controlling you."

She was right. Things were different. And I'd spent the last week thinking about those differences. This wasn't about whether I wanted to rule Ballaslav or not. I knew exactly where I fell on that question. It was about whether I should or not. I knew I could. And I would at least try to do a good job.

But like I'd told her, the desire for blood was still there. I had a second chance, and I was going to take it, but that didn't mean I wasn't still dangerous for Ballaslav. People could still use me. They could still use my past mistakes against my country and its people. Ballaslav deserved a clean slate. It deserved a second chance, too.

"I'm sure," was all I said. She'd been ruling this country for longer than I'd been alive. She knew the risks I carried.

"Sometimes we don't get a choice about these things," she said.

"This time we do." I made a point of looking at Eira.

So did the Grand Duchess.

Eira bit her lip. "I didn't want it if you did," she said.

"There's no problem there," I told her. "And I think you'd do a better job than I would. But do you want to?"

"I do, but..." She took a shuddering breath.

"But you have reservations," the Grand Duchess said.

"One," Eira said. "I...I love someone. And I'm afraid that as the Grand Duchess I wouldn't be allowed to love him."

Vitaly's chin snapped up, and he met Eira's eyes in the mirror. Hope and fear flicked across his face.

The Grand Duchess looked between Eira's sad expression and Vitaly's rictus of pain. Then she met Mabushka's eyes. Mabushka winked.

Prevoshkedhova shrugged. I wouldn't have said she even knew how to shrug.

"There's no precedent for it," she said. "But then a lot of things have been happening in the last couple of months that have no precedent. This seems like the least of them."

There was a moment of complete silence while Eira and Vitaly both processed this, looking for rejection and finding acceptance.

Then Eira stood, brushed her hands down the front of her gown, turned, and threw herself at Vitaly.

He caught her with a wordless cry and swung her around so her blue silks and his white uniform flashed in the mirrors. Reflecting back their joy, a thousand times.

CHAPTER THIRTY-FIVE

The Grigorsyn caravan bustled with activity, drivers hitching up their teams, *viona* double-checking weapons and gear, the caravan leads flitting from wagon to wagon, checking the cargo.

I stepped around them all, anonymous in my dark blue cloak, my satchel thrown over my shoulder. I didn't hesitate until I found a tall, slim figure with strawberry blond hair hunched over the back of a wagon, pulling straps taut.

I gulped and locked my hands around the strap of my satchel. This had seemed like a much better idea two minutes ago. Now I wasn't so sure. We'd said things back at the palace, but that had been back when we didn't think we'd see each other again. What if it all changed now that I was standing here?

I cleared my throat. "I heard you might be looking for a healer."

His head shot up and he straightened. "Reyna." Without

a second's hesitation, he caught me up in his arms and lifted me off my feet.

I laughed breathlessly. "That's one way to say hello."

He set me down again but didn't let go of my arms. "I thought—we heard the Grand Duchess had named her new heir."

"She did," I said, smoothing a piece of hair behind my ear. "Eira. Mabushka will stay with her. At least for now while she's learning everything *Prevoshkedhova* can teach her."

He tilted his head. "You don't feel like the Grand Duchess is stealing your family?"

I chuckled. "I know where they all are, so I can find them again. That's a hell of a lot better than last time."

"So...you mean it. You're coming with us?"

I bit my lip. "If you'll have me. I have a promise to keep to a friend. And I...I don't really have a home anymore." Not with *Otepf* Eriksyn stalking the palace halls. "I was hoping this could be mine."

This smile wasn't his normal grin. This one was soft and quiet and full of things I didn't have words for. At least not yet.

"Reyna!"

I stiffened at the familiar voice. I hadn't actually seen Evgenia since the night I'd healed her in the *yshkiniva*.

Aleksei slid his hands down my arms to grip my fingers, then turned me to face his parents. Evgenia caught me up in a fierce hug before I even had time to panic, and Pyotr put his arms around both of us.

I could definitely see where Aleksei got his personality from.

Evgenia pulled away far enough to put her hands on my cheeks. "Reyna, I don't even know where to start. We heard you were the *Izavital* and crowned as the Grand Duchess. Now there are public proclamations out that you're a heretic. But the Grand Duchess says you saved Ballaslav. I don't know what to believe and Aleksei won't stop teasing and saying they're all true."

Aleksei gave us an unapologetic shrug.

I choked on a laugh. "I'll tell you the story, Eva. I promise. Would you mind taking on a healer?"

Eva rolled her eyes. "Would we mind? Will you listen to her? Aleksei, did you make her believe she wasn't welcome?" Eva threw her arm over my shoulder. "You saved my life, *mushka*. You can come with us for the rest of your life if you'd like, as long as you're ready to leave immediately. We've been in Post da Konstantin three months longer than we were supposed to be. It's high time we shook the snow from our boots and got out of here."

"Do you have room for one more *viona*, too?" I said. "I have a feeling Karina will be along shortly."

"Only if your story includes her part in it and what she actually is. Don't think I didn't notice her following you around like some sort of heavily-armed duckling."

I snorted as Evgenia steered me toward the heart's blood wagon standing in the row. A familiar figure leaned against the side.

"And she's proving my point already," Eva muttered before she went to sweep Karina into another hug. The *viona* held herself stiffly but allowed Eva to pat her on the back. She wore nondescript brown pants and the coat she'd worn when we all thought she was simply *viona uchenye*, but somewhere between here and the palace she'd acquired a white stripe around her sleeve. The shield spell I'd given her hung around her neck, glinting against the laces of her shirt.

"Here's the other half of yourself," Eva said, pulling away from Karina and indicating me. "All safe and sound."

"She didn't tell me where she was going," Karina said, casting a mild glare at me. "But I figured I'd find her here."

"That's funny. She told us to expect you." Eva gave us each a pat and started off down the row of wagons. "Get yourselves settled. We leave in a minute and a half. Aleksei, get to your post. I'm not in the business of transporting lazy men."

"Yes, Mamat," Aleksei said. He gave us both a grin, then hopped up to the wagon seat.

I was left staring at Karina, who rubbed the back of her neck and kicked the dirt.

"You...you knew I'd come," she said.

I met her gaze and held it. "Always. Angel, remember?"

"I'm just missing the wings."

I climbed up into the back of the wagon, and she stood at the door, watching as I slung the satchel from my shoulder. I removed my healer's kit and a large red bundle to store under the bunk.

"I thought you left that in the Hall of Heroes," Karina said over my shoulder.

I sighed. "I did. In a way. Being a living hero is uncomfortable." I turned the corner of the cloak over so Karina could see the lining, still pristine white with patterns shifting through the weave.

Her eyes flickered.

"What...what do you see when you look at it?"

Finally, she smiled. "I don't see anything. Only you. Because I've never needed anything else to trust you."

Because I'd always been home for her. The way she was now home for me. "It'll be here if I ever need it again," I said and slid it under the bunk. "But I'd rather everyone forgot about it for now. It'll make it easier to keep my promise to you."

Karina swallowed. "What did you promise?"

"When this was all over, you asked me to live a quiet life and not try to scare you anymore."

"Oh," was all she managed to say.

I hid a smile as I stood and moved toward the door. I could ride on the wagon seat as we moved out. I preferred it to the rocking inside of a wagon. "I can definitely manage the quiet life, now," I said. "Though, I think I might have to try to scare you from time to time. Otherwise you'll lose your edge."

She stepped aside just enough to allow me to jump to the ground. "Thank you," she said, quietly.

"There are a lot of ways I need to work on the friend thing, too," I said, pausing to brush her hand. Whips cracked around us and wagons started creaking. "I figured I'd start there."

Isaiah 1:18

ACKNOWLEDGMENTS

Some books are harder than others. Some are like pulling teeth the whole way through the first draft. Some even refuse to tell you how they end for five whole years. I'm not naming any names here. But there are people in this world who make the process a little bit easier. Thanks go to:

Mom and Dad, for your unwavering support in the face of four creative daughters.

Betsy and Alison, for the *A Matter of Blood* summit and those last final nudges to lock in the awesome.

Arielle, for agonizing alongside Reyna. I know I make you worry, but I like happy endings, too.

Miranda, for listening to my first recording attempts. I'm glad you didn't get tired of my voice.

Lacey, for enthusiastic answers to the question "do you want to read another book?"

Dan Freng, for double-checking my theology. And for

making it through the longest book I've ever written just to be sure I didn't say anything I didn't mean to say.

Fiona McLaren, for copy edits. I promise I read and think about and bemoan every comment and cherish the praise.

Kim Killion, for a brilliant cover on the first attempt. I'm so glad for everything you've done for this series.

Abigail, for telling me your own stories and reminding me that maybe I'm doing this mom thing right.

And Josh, for this life we have together. I wouldn't trade it for dragons or magic or spaceships.

ABOUT THE AUTHOR

 Books have been Kendra's escape for as long as she can remember. She used to hide fantasy novels behind her government textbook in high school, and she wrote most of her first novel during a semester of college algebra.

Kendra writes familiar stories from unfamiliar points of view, highlighting heroes with disabilities. Her own experience with partial paraplegia has shown her you don't have to be able to swing a sword to save the day.

When she's not writing she's reading, and when she's not reading she's playing video games.

She lives in Denver with her very tall husband, their book loving progeny, and a lazy black monster masquerading as a service dog.

Never miss a new release!

Visit Kendra at:
www.kendramerritt.com
to sign up for exclusive excerpts, updates, and book recommendations.

facebook.com/kendramerrittauthor

twitter.com/Kendra_Merritt

instagram.com/kendramerrittauthor

goodreads.com/kendramerritt

Made in the USA
Coppell, TX
11 June 2021

57240767R00270